I0831734

Dark Awakenings

DARK AWAKENINGS

MATT CARDIN

MYTHOS BOOKS LLC

POPLAR BLUFF

MISSOURI

APRIL 2010

Mythos Books LLC
351 Lake Ridge Road,
Poplar Bluff,
MO 63901
United States of America

www.mythosbooks.com

Published by Mythos Books LLC, April 2010

FIRST EDITION

ISBN-10: 0-9728545-6-8
ISBN-13: 978-0-9728545-6-6

Set in *Koch Antiqua* & *Adobe Jenson Pro.*

Koch Antiqua by Linotype GmbH
www.linotype.com

Adobe Jenson Pro by Adobe Systems Incorporated.
www.adobe.com

Typesetting, layout and design by PAW.

Sources

"Teeth"

First published on the Web at Thomas Ligotti Online in 1998 and then in *The Children of Cthulhu*, edited by John Pelan, Del Rey Books in 2002. It has been significantly revised and expanded for its appearance here.

"The Stars Shine Without Me"

First published on the Web at Horrorfind in 2002 and then in *In Delirium II*, edited by John Everson, Delirium Books in 2007.

"Desert Places"

First published in *Alone on the Darkside*, edited by John Pelan, Roc in 2006.

"Blackbrain Dwarf"

Original to this collection.

"Nightmares, Imported and Domestic"

Written with Mark McLaughlin. First published in *The HWA Presents: Dark Arts*, edited by John Pelan, Cemetery Dance Publications in 2006.

"The Devil and One Lump"

First published on the Web at Horrorfind in 2001 and then in *The Best of Horrorfind II*, edited by Brian Keene, in 2003. It has been significantly revised and expanded for its appearance here.

"The God of Foulness"

First published on the Web at The Art of Grimscribe and Terror Tales in 2002 and then as volume 5 of the *Dark Homage* series, edited by Shane Ryan Staley, Delirium Books in 2004.

"Icons of Supernatural Horror: A Brief History of the Angel and the Demon"

First published as "The Angel and the Demon" in *Icons of Horror and the Supernatural: An Encyclopedia of Our Worst Nightmares*, edited by S. T. Joshi, Greenwood Press in 2007. It has been significantly revised and expanded for its appearance here.

"Loathsome Objects: George Romero's Living Dead Films as Contemplative Tools"

Original to this collection.

"Gods and Monsters, Worms and Fire: A Horrific Reading of Isaiah"

Original to this collection.

Contents

Apologia Pro Libro Suo

There is here involved [in the phenomenon of weird supernatural horror fiction] a psychological pattern or tradition as real and as deeply grounded in mental experience as any other pattern or tradition of mankind; coeval with the religious feeling and closely related to many aspects of it.

—H. P. Lovecraft, *Supernatural Horror in Literature* (1927)

These two qualities, the daunting and the fascinating, now combine in a strange harmony of contrasts, and the resultant dual character of the numinous consciousness, to which the entire religious development [of the human race] bears witness, at any rate from the level of the "daemonic dread" onwards, is at once the strangest and the most noteworthy phenomenon in the whole history of religion. The daemonic-divine object may appear to the mind an object of horror and dread, but at the same time it is no less something that allures with a potent charm, and the creature who trembles before it, utterly cowed and cast down, has always at the same time the impulse to turn to it, nay even to make it somehow his own.

—Rudolf Otto, *The Idea of the Holy* (1917)

After a little while I became possessed with the keenest curiosity about the whirl itself. I positively felt a wish to explore its depth, even at the sacrifice I was going to make; and my principal grief was that I should never be able to tell my old companions on shore about the mysteries I should see.

—Edgar A. Poe, "A Descent Into the Maelstrom" (1841)

I have had much trouble getting along with my ideas. There was a daimon in me, and in the end its presence proved decisive.

—Carl Jung, *Memories, Dreams, Reflections* (1961)

There is something at work in my soul which I do not understand . . .

—Mary Shelley, *Frankenstein, or, The Modern Prometheus* (1831)

Scholars and artists thrown together are often annoyed at the puzzle of where they differ. Both work from knowledge; but I suspect they differ most importantly in the way their knowledge is come by. Scholars get theirs with conscientious thoroughness along projected lines of logic; poets theirs cavalierly and as it happens in and out of books. They stick to nothing deliberately, but let what will stick to them like burrs where they walk in the fields. No acquirement is on assignment, or even self-assignment. Knowledge of the second kind is much more available in the wild free ways of wit and art. A schoolboy may be defined as one who can tell you what he knows in the order in which he learned it. The artist must value himself as he snatches a thing from some previous order in time and space into a new order with not so much as a ligature clinging to it of the old place where it was organic.

—Robert Frost, "The Figure a Poem Makes" (1939)

[W]ere we disposed to open the [universal case history] of really insane melancholia, with its hallucinations and

delusions, it would be a worse story still—desperation absolute and complete, the whole universe coagulating about the sufferer into a material of overwhelming horror, surrounding him without opening or end. Not the conception or intellectual perception of evil, but the grisly blood-freezing heart-palsying sensation of it close upon one, and no other conception or sensation able to live for a moment in its presence. How irrelevantly remote seem all our usual refined optimisms and intellectual and moral consolations in presence of a need of help like this! Here is the real core of the religious problem.

. . . The lunatic's visions of horror are all drawn from the material of daily fact. Our civilization is founded on the shambles, and every individual existence goes out in a lonely spasm of helpless agony. If you protest, my friend, wait till you arrive there yourself! To believe in the carnivorous reptiles of geologic times is hard for our imagination—they seem too much like mere museum specimens. Yet there is no tooth in any one of those museum-skulls that did not daily through long years of the foretime hold fast to the body struggling in despair of some fated living victim. Forms of horror just as dreadful to their victims, if on a smaller spatial scale, fill the world about us to-day. Here on our very hearths and in our gardens the infernal cat plays with the panting mouse, or holds the hot bird fluttering in her jaws. Crocodiles and rattlesnakes and pythons are at this moment vessels of life as real as we are; their loathsome existence fills every minute of every day that drags its length along; and whenever they or other wild beasts clutch their living prey, the deadly horror which an agitated melancholiac feels is the literally right reaction on the situation.

. . . It may indeed be that no religious reconciliation with the absolute totality of things is possible. . . . The completest religions would therefore seem to be those in which the

pessimistic elements are best developed.

—William James, *The Varieties of Religious Experience* (1902)

This, then, is the ultimate, that is only, consolation: simply that someone shares some of your own feelings and has made of these a work of art which you have the insight, sensitivity, and—like it or not—peculiar set of experiences to appreciate. Amazing thing to say, the consolation of horror in art is that it actually intensifies our panic, loudens it on the sounding-board of our horror-hollowed hearts, turns terror up full blast, all the while reaching for that perfect and deafening amplitude at which we may dance to the bizarre music of our own misery.

—Thomas Ligotti, "The Consolations of Horror" (1982)

Basically, all emotions are modifications of one primordial, undifferentiated emotion that has its origin in the loss of awareness of who you are beyond name and form. Because of its undifferentiated nature, it is hard to find a name that precisely describes this emotion. "Fear" comes close.

—Eckhart Tolle, *The Power of Now: A Guide to Spiritual Enlightenment* (1997)

The oldest and strongest emotion of mankind is fear.

—H. P. Lovecraft, *Supernatural Horror in Literature* (1927)

Fictions

Teeth

For in much wisdom is much grief: and he that increaseth knowledge increaseth sorrow.
—Ecclesiastes 1:18

Consciousness is a disease.
—Miguel de Unamuno

I

My first and decisive glimpse into the horror at the center of existence came unexpectedly during my second year of graduate school. I was earning a doctorate in philosophy and had stopped by the library between classes for some extracurricular research—or rather to pursue what I had long considered to be my true curriculum, regardless of whatever official degree program I might be enrolled in at the time. The object of my quest was a copy of Plotinus' *Enneads*. I had only heard of the man and his book an hour earlier while browsing the Internet in my rented house. A fortuitous combination of search terms had yielded an excerpt from his treatise on beauty, and I had experienced a flashing moment of metaphysical vertigo as I read his description of "the spirit that Beauty must ever induce, wonderment and a delicious trouble, longing and love and a trembling that is all delight." These words and their effect upon me had made it instantly clear that a printed copy of this book was definitely in order.

So there I was, winding my way silently through the second floor stacks and savoring the library's familiar aura of wondrous knowledge awaiting my discovery of it in hushed anticipation. But instead of finding Plotinus's book, I instead turned a corner and stumbled upon my friend Marco seated at a reading kiosk in the middle of the south wall. The tall window above him spilled a shaft of dusty afternoon sunlight onto the burnished tile floor, imparting a muted glow to the kiosk and its occupant.

"Marco!" I said with genuine pleasure.

"Hello, Jason," he murmured, and went right on reading and writing without glancing up from his books. He was surrounded by piles of them, all impressive tomes of various sizes and ages and thicknesses, so numerous they were literally spilling off the table. Three were propped open on the desktop, and he appeared to be copying passages from all of them into a lined notebook. When he did not pause in his work, I lapsed back into an uncertain silence.

Marco was a visiting student from Guatemala with an exquisite command of English and an accent so slight that it left some listeners unable to discern his origin. His auburn skin, coal-black hair, and muscular physique gave him the air of a revolutionary from some Third World country. He was, without a doubt, the most brilliant and widely read person I had ever met, a genuine savant who was simultaneously pursuing separate graduate degrees in physics, philosophy, and history. We had met at the beginning of the fall semester, and I had quickly learned that his chic-terrorist look concealed a fierce intelligence. Now, at the end of the spring term, I was still amazed at his vast capabilities. He could discourse at length on almost any subject, displaying a verbal and intellectual virtuosity that put others to shame. Adding to his mystique was the fact that he was only twenty-six years old. I found it impossible to reconcile his relatively young age with his positively fearsome erudition. The books arrayed on desktop before him now were a perfect example; I scanned their titles and found them to be of sufficiently diverse and advanced character to dizzy the average mind.

It was as I stood there watching and waiting in vain for our ongoing intellectual sparring match to resume that I felt the first prickling of unease. Our interactions had always centered on a perennial philosophical conversation that never failed to exhilarate me even as it exhausted and humbled me. But on that day, in my beloved university library, with me standing there primed for a dialogue and brimful of a craving for neoplatonic expressions of transcendent beauty, Marco apparently had nothing to say to me. I used the uncomfortable interlude to study his appearance more closely. His mouth and jaw were tight. His eyes appeared slightly sunken into dark sockets. His shoulders were tense, his motions taut and meticulous as he continued his scribal work. He fairly exuded an air of intensity mingled with exhaustion. The word "haunted" sprang involuntarily to mind as an appropriate one-word description.

Then he said, "How are your classes?" Only his mouth moved. The rest of him maintained an unbroken focus on his work.

"Um, some good, some not." I groped for a suitable entry point into this strange conversational exigency. "Teaching philosophy to disinterested freshmen is a bit like asking your cat to come to you. They really don't give a shit." I winced at my own ridiculous words.

But somehow they were enough to reach him. He paused in his writing, pen lifted above page, and appeared to reflect. "Ah, yes. Philosophy. We do love it, you and I. How was it that Will Durant once defined it? 'Total perspective, mind overspreading life and forging chaos into unity.'" His tone implied something like a rueful smile, but as I watched him speak the words, his face remained fixed in that expression of hollow intensity.

At length he set his pen down and straightened from the hunched posture he had been holding. "Do you have a few minutes before your next class?"

I was still fumbling to pick up the obscure thread of this weirdly stilted interaction. "Uh, sure, a few. What's up?"

He hesitated, then said, "I want to show you something. Something that I'm confident you will find quite interesting. Perhaps even fascinating, given what I know of your intellectual proclivities."

"How utterly mysterious," I said, attempting with a resounding thunderclap of failure to add a little levity to the scene. Marco showed no reaction other than to close and stack his books neatly, one by one, on the desktop to await collection by a library aide. Then he slid his notebook into his ever-present satchel and stood up. Without even looking at me, he headed for the stairs, and without my even hesitating, I fell in tow and forgot all about Plotinus and his promise to employ mere words to describe the impossible, delightful, delicious apotheosis of Beauty itself.

II

We stood facing each other in Marco's cramped dorm room, walled in by bland cinderblocks and beige paint. Marco held out a spiral notebook toward me. I looked at him curiously and, in light of out meeting's odd beginning, a bit cautiously.

"Take it," he said. "Look on the forty-sixth page."

I took the notebook and examined it while my mind whispered the word "anticlimax." This was nothing special, just an ordinary seventy-two-page, college-ruled spiral notebook with a red cover. It was, in fact, the same notebook that Marco had been writing in earlier at the library, and I couldn't help feeling a flash of irritation at what now seemed his rather theatrical refusal to show it to me in public.

But there was no use complaining now. I perched on the edge of one of the room's twin beds and flipped open the notebook's cover to find the first page crammed with Marco's small and scrupulous handwriting. My eyes began scanning the text while my brain registered that the notebook appeared to be a combination of commonplace book and personal journal filled with Marco's thoughts on quantum physics, history, philosophy, and a few other subjects I could not immediately identify. Instantly, my curiosity kicked in at the thought that I was being allowed a glimpse into my friend's private mind.

I began to flip slowly through the notebook in search of page forty-six, which was made easy by the fact that Marco had hand numbered the pages in the upper right corner. Naturally, I stole as many glimpses as I could of the material on the intervening pages, and what I saw quickly sharpened my curiosity into a craving. Although the notebook's primary subject was not readily apparent, I discerned that Marco was conducting a serious enquiry into a certain matter, an enquiry that encompassed ideas from fantastically diverse fields of knowledge. He made great use of quotations from other writers, and I caught snatches of a theoretical treatise on quantum physics by Neils Bohr, a monograph by an obscure astronomer, a book of Hermetic occultism, the Hindu philosopher Sankara's commentary on the Vedanta Sutras, and the writings of Schopenhauer and Nietzsche. These last three were familiar to me; as a student of philosophy I had encountered them more than once in my own studies. The net effect of seeing all of these quotes together was to generate a sense that the comforting constellation of my familiar authors, books, and philosophies opened out into a vastly wider universe of unknown properties.

I lingered for a moment on page forty-five to examine the two quotes that appeared there. One came from a book with a strange name that was vaguely reminiscent of Hindu deities. The other was from a story by H. P. Lovecraft. I had heard of the latter but the former was completely unfamiliar to me.

My curiosity finally got the better of me, and I blurted out, "What is all this? What in the world are you getting at?"

"It will help," Marco said, "if you will turn to the next page." The tightness of his voice drew my eyes away from the notebook and up to his face. His sat opposite me on the other bed, mirroring my posture of perched attentiveness. His hands gripped the edge of the mattress. A bead of sweat slid down his temple. The expression in his dark-ringed eyes was unreadable. I stared at him for a long moment before finally looking back down and turning the page.

Of all the things I might or might not have expected to find, an elaborate sacred drawing was surely among the last. And yet that was exactly what I found. Rendered in the same blue ink that Marco had used to record his thoughts and quotes was an incredibly intricate visual pattern composed of abstract shapes, shadings, and forms. Its design was dense and complex, but what made it truly striking was its lushness and vividness, which made it seem three-dimensional. At the same time, it was reminiscent of a Zen painting with its distinct dependence on space and absence to contextualize and comment on form and presence. Most amazingly, its elements were arranged according to some alternative philosophy of design that flouted and exploded common artistic principles of harmony, emphasis, opposition, and so on. Each line led the eye to one or more angles that refracted attention like a prism dividing light. Each shape held its position and significance in relation to a hundred different elements, each of which was in turn embedded in its own peculiar nest of visual meanings and unstated implications. The overall effect was of a bold, bristling infinity.

In a word, I was dazzled. I knew the creation of mandalas to serve as objects of sacred contemplation had been developed into an exquisite art form in religious traditions both Eastern and

Western, but the one I was seeing now was even more breathtaking than the ones I had encountered in my studies of Buddhism, Hinduism, and medieval Christianity. I had not known that in addition to his other prodigious gifts, Marco was an artist of genius. But there was no mistaking it. The mandala had been rendered by his pen, in his notebook.

I went to raise my head so that I could rave to him about the wonderfulness of the drawing and my awe at his secret talent. But then, with a sudden, startling sense of the impossible, I found that I could not do it. My neck was locked in place and my eyes were magnetized to the center of the picture. I blinked, or rather tried to, and found that I was likewise prevented from doing that. I was still aware of the room, still aware of the floor and bed beneath me and the walls around me, and of Marco seated across from me. But I could only attend to them with my peripheral vision. It was as if an invisible anchor had been hurled out from the page and lodged in my eyeballs, fastening them to the image and throwing me into an increasingly panicked state of immobility. I simply could not look away from the mandala, which filled my vision and began to horrify me with what I now perceived as its *obscene infinitude*.

And then it started moving. Right before my disbelieving eyes, the shapes began to stir on the page with a creeping motion like the slow boiling of liquids in an alchemist's laboratory. Every hidden implication and mini-universe of meaning in the individual elements took on countless additional connotations as the whole structure shuddered to life. The picture's three-dimensional appearance became literal as the page's center dropped away into a recess of infinite depth. I no longer sat in a room beholding a picture; the picture had become the whole of my consciousness, and *it* encompassed *me*, and I stared *through* it into a chasm of measureless meaning whose very vastness was a horror.

Then, in an instant, all motion stopped. A dark spot no bigger than a pinhead formed at the mandala's center and began to grow, as if approaching from an impossible distance. Ringed layers of shape and form fell away as this darkness accelerated its all-consuming approach. It resolved and clarified, and now wicked barbs and slivers were visible in its fabric, needled in endless rows of concentric rings like ivory spikes planted in rotten flesh. They churned and fluttered and twitched with a spasmodic motion, and in the tiny corner of my mind that I could still claim as my own, I realized I was staring into a nightmare abyss of endless teeth, a fanged and insatiable cosmic gullet that endlessly devoured, devoured, devoured all things in an eternal feast of annihilation.

All had been a prelude to this. My whole life, my very conception and progress through the stages of human existence, had been preordained to lead me to this dreadful moment. I felt the attention of a massive and malevolent intelligence turned upon me, and as I began to pitch forward into the pit, and as the first of trillions of teeth began to sink into my mind, I knew with absolute, horrified certainty that this nightmare abyss was also staring into me.

III

A buzzing blackness. Darker than darkness. Corrosive and cold. That was everything.

Then it was as if a light switched on, and that light was the visual image of Marco's dorm room, and of Marco himself. He was standing on the ceiling. Either that, or the entire room had turned upside down. I watched his inverted image approach a similarly inverted medicine cabinet mounted on the wall. The slick mirrored surface flashed and waved as he opened and shut it. He approached me, still inverted, holding something out to me with his hand.

I realized I was lying on my back on one of his beds, arched up and watching him backwards over the edge of the mattress. He stepped beside me and the room righted itself as my head swiveled to watch him.

I tried to say "What?" but my lungs were paralyzed. I was suffocating. There was a momentary panic. Then my chest let go and I was sucking huge lungfuls of air.

"Take these," Marco said over the sound of my frantic gasps. Two tiny white pills rested in his outstretched palm. With the other hand he offered a bottle of water. Somehow my arms moved. I accepted the pills and washed them down while he slid back to sit at the room's single study desk.

"Those were muscle relaxers," he said. "You'll feel more composed in a moment."

To my astonishment, he was right. I could already feel the unbearable horror, the *impossible* horror, draining out of my mind and body, not completely but enough to let me live. After a minute or two I sat up and swung my legs off the bed. The feeling of my feet hitting the floor, the sensory solidity beneath the soles of my shoes, revived me even more.

I looked at Marco. He had been watching me but now he looked away and stared at the wall. Finally, he spoke.

"If the purpose of philosophy really is to overspread raw life with mind, to gain a truly totalizing perspective that forges unity from chaos, then how do you spread your mind over what just happened to you? How do you include *that* in your tidy little philosophical cosmos?"

Was he really talking this calmly? Was he really acting as if things were normal and we were back to our old conversation, when in fact nothing could ever be normal again after what I just experienced? But I could see the sweat standing out on his forehead and upper lip. He turned his gaze upon me as if awaiting my answer, and for an instant his eyes were like black holes carved in a flesh mask. The floor beneath my feet shifted ever so slightly.

Then he was Marco again, but he was still saying things I did not want to hear. "The classic philosophical project has always been held up as a *good* thing, a noble enterprise that will bring justice and order to people's lives. But what if the very attempt to gain that total perspective is tragically misguided?" He shifted in his wooden chair and leaned forward in the pose I had seen him adopt many times before when he was demolishing an opponent. "What if life and sanity depend not on finding the truth but on deliberately cultivating delusion? What if there is indeed a total perspective, but to gain and know it and identify with it is to invite your own deepest disaster?" He was still Marco but he was also something else, something more, leaning forward and splitting the air between us with the intensity of his words and vision. "*What if reality itself is finally, fundamentally evil?*"

The words hung there, and then I answered them. "What you're saying isn't new and you know it. The idea or something like it goes at least back to the ancient Greeks, and probably farther. Schopenhauer and Nietzsche gave it a classic treatment a little over a century ago." My composure shocked me. The room and my body seemed muffled and distant.

Marco straightened and slashed his hand through the air in a gesture of dismissal. "You're talking history and theory. I'm talking about reality—pure, raw, existential. You can't distance yourself from it or gain a handle on it by recalling who first thought of it or what they said about it. For proof, I refer you to your own recent experience, which you're only handling so well because I drugged you."

And indeed he was right. My calmness wasn't my own, and when I tried to see behind it I saw a raging swarm of terror and revulsion just waiting to arise. It was this subdued awfulness that now began to respond to the idea Marco was advancing, and my drug-induced surface calm suddenly seemed a positive curse. For it left me open to a nasty interplay of unwontedly dark thoughts and associations. My usual self-absorption, my narcissism, my obliviousness to my surroundings as I indulged a constant interior monologue—all these defenses had been stunned, and in the unfamiliar calm of interior silence I heard the sound of something terrible approaching.

Marco waited a beat, as if deliberately letting this chaos rage inside me. Then he picked his notebook up from the desk and tossed it onto the bed. "Read it," he said. "It will answer many of your questions. I assume I don't need to tell you to avoid looking at a certain page."

I looked at the red cover lying on the brown bedspread and felt the first real intimations of the inner upheaval that would certainly topple me once the drug had completely worn off. The entire situation had to be a dream. It could not be real, because if it were—I could not even articulate the implications. And then there was that drawing, that awesome, beautiful, horrific mandala. What had happened to me as I studied it? Flashes of unreality began to invade the edges of my vision at the mere remembrance of that mad motion, that impossible infinitude, that galactic tunnel of teeth . . .

"What is it?" My voice was small and weak, but Marco knew

what I was referring to: both the drawing and the reality it revealed.

"The very question," he replied, "approximates the only suitable answer."

"But . . . you drew that picture yourself. How . . . ?" My strength to pursue the question gave out as he stood and began ushering me toward the door.

"Read the notebook," he said. "We can talk afterward. Right now you need to get home and get some rest."

I helplessly obeyed. Before I really knew what I was doing, I had left his room and was riding the elevator down to the ground floor. Then I was walking out of the dormitory and across campus to my house. Then I was unlocking the door and stepping inside.

The click of the latch as the door swung shut awoke me from my walking trance, and I saw that my hand was gripping Marco's notebook. I dropped it like a hot coal. It slapped to the floor like a snake. I left it there and walked to the bedroom, where I collapsed on the bed and fell immediately asleep. All night I wrestled with a dream that returned repeatedly and never resolved itself: Marco was standing outside my door talking with strangers. I heard their voices rumbling in response to his, but their words were indecipherable and their tones ominous. Then hands began to knock, not just one but many, rapping smartly on the door and progressing toward a thunderous pounding. The door shuddered in its frame. The knocks were somehow amiss, as if they were produced by the wrong kinds of hands beating on the on the wrong kind of wood. To my deep dismay, I heard my voice invite Marco and his acquaintances inside. The very invitation unlocked the door, which began to swing inward, and even before it completed its arc and revealed the visitors, I knew full well what I would see. I *knew* it; the visual confirmation would just be the culmination of a fear that had accompanied me from birth.

That was where the dream stopped, only to start again after an interlude of unconsciousness. By the time morning arrived and I awoke to the unbuffered emotions of the previous day's catastrophe, I had seen that door and known that dread half a dozen times. But that certain knowledge of the visitors' appearance, so inescapable in the dream, had not followed me into the daylight. All I recalled was the door itself, and the sound of rumbling voices, and the knowledge that I had invited my own deepest doom to come inside and make itself at home.

IV

The next week of my life was devoted to reading Marco's notebook. Everything else went into hibernation, intellectually and emotionally speaking. Even though I went through the motions of my daily routine, I performed my duties without spirit. All of my energy and attention were directed toward a single and singular purpose: to read and grasp the meaning of the dark philosophical testament that Marco had penned.

Grappling with it was the most grueling experience I had ever endured. This was due partly to the fact that Marco's speculations on astronomy and physics were practically incomprehensible to me, but there was another reason as well: A new sense or faculty seemed to have awakened within me, a kind of "third eye" that remained perpetually open and proved distressingly responsive to the dark suggestions unfolding on the pages before me. As I read the notebook and began to perceive the galling weight of the worldview under which Marco labored, I found that the same mingled mindstate of disgust and despair had unexpectedly taken root in my own heart, and was in fact being nourished by the reading, which, in a loathsome symbiosis, was rendered all the more clear and emotionally compelling by this new inner sense.

As I had already seen, much of the notebook consisted of long quotations carefully transcribed by Marco from a wide array of books. Schopenhauer loomed large, as did Nietzsche. It was during my undergraduate years that I had first encountered these giants of German philosophy. Back then I had exulted in the universal pessimism of the former and its extension and exhilarating transformation by the latter into an exploration of the meaning of human subjecthood. But now I felt as if I were truly understanding them for the first time. Recorded here was Schopenhauer's famous criticism of the assertion, so common among some thinkers, that evil is merely the absence of good. "I know of no greater absurdity," he wrote, "than that propounded by most systems of philosophy in declaring evil to be negative in its character. Evil is just what is positive; it makes its own existence felt." The concept was not new to me but its import, as perceived and amplified by my new inner faculty, hit me now like a blow to the head.

Also recorded was Nietzsche's amplification of his mentor's idea:

> Nobody is very likely to consider a doctrine true merely because it makes people happy or virtuous . . . Happiness and virtue are no arguments. But people like to forget—even sober spirits—that making unhappy and evil are no counterarguments. Something might be true while being harmful and dangerous in the highest degree. Indeed, it might be a basic characteristic of existence that those who would know it fully would perish, in which case the strength of a spirit should be measured by how much of the "truth" one could still barely endure—or to put it more clearly, to what degree one would *require* it to be thinned down, shrouded, sweetened, blunted, falsified.

The quotes spooled on and on, piling up page after page, interspersed occasionally with Marco's own notes and observations. After the Nietzsche quote, for instance, the blue-inked letters of Marco's voice clarified, "And so the perfect lie would be the perfect sanctuary, the ultimate one-pointed perspective, and thus the ultimate weakness, while perfect strength would see reality cold, without blinking, and vast, without center, and naked, without a hint of cognitive or affective coloration."

After two days of reading, I began to despair of penetrating the notebook's secrets. On the surface it seemed to be nothing but a particularly pessimistic collection of aphorisms and observations, albeit ones whose significance I was feeling with a weight and an impact that were veritably physical. And still the searing memory of that picture on page forty-six jutted out like a broken bone in the skeleton of my psyche, leaving me frantic to find a conception and a context that would set the bone and bind the wound.

Then, on the third day, when my despairing confusion had

reached its nadir, I came to a quote from the Indian philosopher Sankara that acted as the proverbial solid particle dropped into the saturated solution of my soul. Sankara wrote,

> With half a stanza I will declare what has been said in thousands of volumes:
> Brahman is real, the world is false, the soul is only Brahman, nothing else.

I had long been acquainted with the Hindu idea that the material world is actually *maya,* illusion, a kind of mirage resting upon the absolute reality which the Vedantic Hindus call Brahman. The Hindu sages generally taught that *moksa,* the experience of release from this illusion and the subsequent realization of ultimate reality, constitutes life's supreme happiness and final fulfillment. But Marco, by contextualizing Sankara's classic one-line summation of Vedanta inside a potent exploration of Western pessimism, seemed to be positing that the uniform substratum of being that underlies physical existence is an utter nightmare. And if "the soul is only Brahman," meaning that the individual human self is at root nothing but a particularized manifestation of this pervasive primary reality—I couldn't bear to follow this perversion of the Eastern beatific vision to its conclusion. Its repercussions were simply too awful to articulate.

Of the scientific line of thought interwoven with the philosophy, all I could comprehend was that Marco was struggling with some unresolved issue in quantum physics. The mathematical work was beyond me, but from his text notes I could gather enough to grasp the bare essence of the matter, which had something to do with the philosophical implications of quantum mechanics. I read that the equations used in this science are straightforward and uncontested in terms of their practical applications, as attested by everything from television to the hydrogen bomb, but that no satisfactory explanation for their *meaning,* their overall implications at the macroscopic level of existence, had yet been established.

On the subatomic level, I read, particles flash into and out of existence for no discernible reason, and the behavior of any single particle is apparently arbitrary and usually unpredictable. If there is a cause or "purpose" behind this behavior, then it is one that the human mind is, to all appearances, structurally prevented from comprehending. In other words, for all we know, the fundamental ruling principles at the most basic level of physical reality may well be what our minds and languages must necessarily label "chaos" and "madness."

This predicament of knowledge (so I learned from Marco's commentary) had remained essentially unchanged for eighty years, and Marco possessed the audacity to believe that he had begun to solve the riddle that had haunted the keenest scientific minds for nearly a century. But he expressed his solution in a series of mathematical equations which were incomprehensible to me, and which may as well have been hieroglyphics carved on the inner wall of an Egyptian tomb.

My experience of these blossoming revelations was appalling. It was also progressively intense. The further I advanced in the notebook, the more powerful became the rising tide of revulsion inside me. At times it grew so overwhelming that I was forced to stop for several hours. On one occasion, after I had rushed for the bathroom in the grip of an actual physical sickness, I laid aside the notebook for more than a day. Late in the week I realized that what I was experiencing could only be described as *horror,* a word whose referent I had never really known. Marco's comments about the human need for illusion began to make progressively more sense, for if the ideas in his notebook really did point to reality, then I would rather be deluded. If it was strength to gaze unflinchingly into that abyss, then I would rather be weak.

It was with a veritably religious sense of fear and trembling that I turned, on the last day of the week, to the forty-fifth page of the notebook. Slowly I read through the first of the two quotes that appeared alone on the page, the one from a book whose title sounded distinctly Hindu even though I had never before encountered it and subsequently forgot it. As its significance became clear to me, I felt the words begin to sink into my mind like vicious hooks:

Foolish soul, wilt thou comprehend the All, the great

> Central Mystery? Man's place is the middle. Thou approachest the Gate in both the Greatest and the Least. In the face of the night sky, at the core of a dust mote—the same One. Wretched is he who hears the call, but more wretched still the one who answers it.

The final quotation was from a story by H. P. Lovecraft, and in the margin beside it Marco had written "The Capstone."

> The most merciful thing in the world, I think, is the inability of the human mind to correlate all its contents. We live on a placid island of ignorance in the midst of black seas of infinity, and it was not meant that we should voyage far. The sciences, each straining in its own direction, have hitherto harmed us little; but some day the piecing together of dissociated knowledge will open up such terrifying vistas of reality, and of our frightful position therein, that we shall either go mad from the revelation or flee from the deadly light into the peace and safety of a new dark age.

V

The words on that page signaled the end of my journey through the dark corridors of Marco's obsession. Rather than trying to see what lay past page forty-six and risking another encounter with that awful picture, I closed the notebook and shoved it far back into a drawer, wishing fiercely that it could be equally easy to bury the memory of it. But try as I might, I could not stop my thoughts from returning to it and *gnawing* on it like a trapped animal might gnaw off its own leg. That was exactly the way it felt: as if I had become ensnared in some vile trap and grown so desperate to escape that I might willingly do violence to myself. But no matter how many times I examined and reexamined and struggled violently against the notebook's all-encompassing message of horror and despair, I could find no way to extricate myself from it, no loose spring or faulty trigger in its mechanism that might allow me to slip free. Its internal coherence and emotional power, as well as its universal scope, made it the perfect prison for mind and spirit.

My whole life was overturned in shockingly rapid fashion by this festering spiritual disease. For example, my teaching and class schedules that semester were mercifully light, but even the slight strain of conducting a freshman philosophy class proved almost more than I could handle. How could I speak of epistemology and metaphysics when I had recently beheld the fanged and fleshy vortex that lies waiting to devour all knowledge? How could I teach about Socrates when I had discovered that to examine one's life is to invite a nightmarish destruction, or about Descartes when I had been shown that the thinking mind is a mere wisp of smoke blowing over a fetid ocean of entity? More than one student gave me a sidelong look as my lectures were derailed by the uncontrollable quaver that had crept into my voice. I had always basked in the knowledge of the positive impression I made on others, but now I could tell from people's reactions that my personal manner had taken a turn for the bizarre and disturbing. And yet I was helpless to rein this in. I felt a trembling all the way to my core and found myself frequently gripped by the irrational notion that people's altered reactions to me were caused by my new inner eye, which bathed everyone and everything in a beam of cold black light. This dark emanation, as I fancied it (even though I knew the idea was insane), was perceived by others as a certain indefinable aura of disturbance and dread in my personal presence.

I knew I could not go on like this, and several courses of action suggested themselves. The most obvious was to seek psychological help. A less obvious but no less compelling possibility was to seek spiritual counseling. Medical help from a neurologist was not out of the question, nor was self-medication via any number of consciousness-clouding substances. My fundamental problem seemed to be an excess of metaphysical sight. Anything that promised to blind or even temporarily blur that deadly gaze was an attractive prospect.

How, then, I ended up taking the course of action I took is still a mystery. Rather than turning to the most obvious sources of solace, I returned to the man who had done this violence to me. When all options had been considered, I could think of nothing but talking with Marco again. I had to know more about his notebook, about the impetus that had driven him to record it and the power that had led him to create that drawing. I felt that if I could not hear some answers to these and a thousand other questions, I might literally go mad with rage and confusion.

So I made up my mind to see him, and that was when it dawned on me that I had neither seen nor heard from him for ten days—not since our last conversation in his dorm room. Under normal circumstances I would have wondered why he had been so conspicuously absent, since we usually ran into each other on campus almost every day. But I had been preoccupied with his notebook and my growing distress, and now that I needed him, he was missing in action. I silently cursed his ostentatious boycott of cell phones and email, which he regularly railed on as destroyers of personal solitude and public discourse. In the past I had never really felt their lack, since Marco and I had encountered each other in person as we went about our campus business. But now I found I had no way of getting in contact with him short of visiting his dorm again, which I hated to do with the memory of my awful experience there still paining me like an open wound.

But I also had no choice, and so on the eleventh day after this nightmare had begun, I returned to the site of its inception. My stomach turned cold as I rode the elevator up to Marco's floor. By the time I approached his featureless brown door, my hands were trembling. Predictably—why I should have found it predictable I don't know, but it seemed entirely appropriate in a poetic sort of way—he did not answer when I knocked. I stood there in the hallway for a long moment, staring alternately down at the faded gray carpet and then back up at the door as I debated whether to try the knob. Each time I reached for it, a thrill of panic surged through me. Finally, in a kind of daze at the depth of my own wretchedness, I gave up and admitted that I could not do it. The situation was just too symmetrical, albeit in reverse fashion, to the door scenario in my recent dream.

But I still had to find him, so next I went and inquired of his professors. They told me that he hadn't attended classes since Monday of the previous week—the last day I had seen him. One of them, Dr. Albert Kreeft of the physics department, told me, "Be sure to tell him the entire scientific community is waiting with bated breath for his theory of everything." The mockery in the white-haired man's thickly accented voice was blatant, and when I asked him what he meant, he said, "Ask him sometime to show you his preliminary work suggesting a new unified field theory. The finished thesis ought to make for an interesting novel." The physics department lay outside of my usual academic orbit, and I was unfamiliar with this thoroughly unpleasant little man. When I asked him about his relationship to Marco, he said with a sour edge, "I'm his thesis advisor," and turned back to his computer screen, refusing even to acknowledge me anymore.

And that was that. I walked out of the physics building realizing that I had already exhausted my useful options. The extent of my ignorance of Marco hit home as I recognized that the only thing left to do was to visit the places where we normally crossed paths—the library, the quad, the student commons—and hope that I would see him. So I went to those places even though I hated to be around crowds in my current condition. And of course he was nowhere to be found. I ended up on the second floor of the library at the same study kiosk where I had run into him while seeking a copy of Plotinus. Standing there beneath that tall window in that silent hall filled with row upon row of stately books, I tried to conjure a spark of my former aesthetic bliss. My unconscious mind responded by throwing up an image of chittering teeth and a mood of stark, staring barrenness.

Maybe my next move was inspired by the fact that I had come full circle to the starting point of my present unhappy state. From the library I set out for Marco's dorm again. Last time I had been following the flesh-and-blood man himself; this time I was following the thought of him. Once again, when I reached his room and knocked on the door, there was no answer. Before the memory of my dream could throw me again into that panicked paralysis, I seized the knob and wrenched it violently.

Much to my surprise, it turned easily and the door swung open on silent hinges. I stepped gingerly inside and found a room where Marco was absent and nothing at all was out of order. His bed was made, his bookshelves were full, and upon opening his closet I found a rack full of clothes. I had half expected to find evidence of some sort of disturbance—clothes flung everywhere, a shattered window, who knows what. The other half of me had expected to be overwhelmed by a nameless horror. So the sight of his empty, tidy, unmolested room threw me into a fit of unfulfilled foreboding. Everything was as silent and still as a cemetery, and in that stillness an approaching culmination trembled in the air.

I sat down on his bed with a hot lump in my throat, and realized with something like humor that I was about to break down and weep. Nothing made sense. Everything was wrecked and hopeless. How had I come to this in so short a time? Less than two weeks earlier, I had been leading a fairly contented life with a bright future in academia. I had taken pleasure in my work and my modest social life, including the occasional romance. I had possessed a shining intellectual and emotional intensity that brought praise from my professors. And yet all of that had been overturned and undermined in shockingly short order. When I tried now to consider my future, I saw nothing but an endless black tunnel lined with

(Teeth)

painful and meaningless experiences. The future was a dark, empty road winding through a blasted landscape toward the shell of a dead city. The journey was a nightmare and the destination a hell. My former goals and pleasures littered my psyche like the dry corpses of dead loved ones, and I wanted nothing more than to sink into oblivion, whether sleep or death did not matter.

Was all of this really true? Was my life, was existence itself, truly what I now perceived it to be: nothing more than a short interlude in an otherwise unbroken continuum of horror, a sometimes distracting but ultimately vain dream that was destined to end with a terrible awakening to the abiding reality of chaos, of madness, of nightmare, of . . .

(Teeth)

The floor lurched beneath my feet, and with a silent hiss like the seething of stars, that gaping hole in reality opened up again, not on any page this time but within me. My nostrils were clotted with the stench of rotting, half-digested worlds, and I felt the eternal agony of infinite rows of needle teeth sinking into my soul.

That should have been the end. I should have known nothing

else for all eternity. But then, impossibly, it was over. The room blinked back into view. The floor rushed back into place. And I was sitting on a plain institutional bed in an ordinary dorm room on a bright spring day. The horror had claimed me and then spat me out.

I was still reeling in a daze as I stood and exited Marco's room. I could hardly walk, but a sudden impulse had taken hold of me: I wanted to finish reading Marco's notebook. I was, in fact, desperate to do so. Caution be damned, I was going to learn what he had written beyond the page with the picture. I was going to find out everything there was to know about the thought process, emotional pattern, and dark epiphany that had flowed out of and led up to this catastrophe that had engulfed not only me but, as I strongly suspected, him as well.

Riding the elevator down to the ground floor, I experienced repeated waves of joy at finding that I could still feel a sense of purpose.

VI

The walk back to my house was a preview of hell itself. Although the afternoon sun hung bright and warm in a brilliant sky, and college students lounged everywhere in the refreshing air, chatting at tables and lolling on fresh green patches of landscaped lawn, I saw it all as if through a dark-tinted pane of glass. The light appeared shaded and muted, like night scenes in a movie that were obviously shot in broad daylight with a filter on the lens. I kept noticing movements in the periphery of my vision wherever shadows and dark spots lay: beneath a bench, at the foot of a hickory tree, under the granite lip of a merrily splashing fountain. In each shadow I saw what looked like living forms crouched and waiting, but when I looked directly at them they disappeared. It gradually became apparent to me that I was seeing shadows more clearly than the objects that cast them, and that my inner eye was revealing a lurking presence in them that I had never suspected.

Traumatized and terrified, I finally arrived at my lonely house north of campus and collapsed on the couch. After listening to my own shaking breath for a few moments, I dragged myself to my feet and went to fetch the notebook. It remained where I had left it, at the back of my desk drawer, and I felt vaguely surprised since I had half expected the thing to have disappeared like its author. Its dull red cover seemed to mock me, as if its very muteness represented its defiance of my understanding. I sat at the desk and flipped through to page forty-seven, feeling not nearly as foolish as I had expected when I actually squeezed my eyes shut as I turned past the mandala.

I opened them to see that, sure enough, there was more writing in the notebook's latter pages. Text that normally would have filled only half a page in Marco's virtually microscopic hand now sprawled across three pages. Reading it, I began to shiver even more violently as I understood the cause of this atypical sloppiness: Marco had scribbled these notes immediately after his own first experience with the mandala, which, as it turned out, he had not drawn of his own free will. His notes insinuated far more than they stated, and glanced upon several unfamiliar items, but I recognized their guiding emotion of horrified hysteria all too well. Ironically, they also underscored yet again just how greatly his awesome intellect and fearsome self-control exceeded mine, since it was a marvel that he was able to marshal any coherent thoughts and write any words at all in such a state.

This is what he wrote:

> Almost sucked in. It almost pushed completely through. God, how? The perfect sequence of shapes, the perfect placement and size on the infinite continuum of distance between points. Their precise purpose in guiding my hand. Would it open the gate for anyone, render all preparation unnecessary? Chance . . . purpose . . . meaning . . . what damned idiocy! Our insane desire for "truth" when *illusion* is the need—fantasy, dreams, divine delusions. What price the true vision? What must we become? Lovecraft correct not only about our frightful position in the universe but about the vast conceit of those who babble of the *malignant* Ancient Ones. Not hostile to consciousness, indifferent to it. "Consciousness is a disease"—if only you knew, Miguel! Final horror reserved for mind, not body. Azathoth not conscious,

> pure Being. Consciousness, intelligence, *mind* the ultimate tragedy. To be somehow self-aware yet wholly incidental to the "purpose" of the universe: chaos and psychosis in human terms. Ultimate irony of human predicament: perfection of specifically human quality results in self-negation. Conscious only to become aware of the utter horror of consciousness.

The ideas encoded in these words flamed inside me as I read and reread them. Much of what he had written was obscure, but I understood enough. Somehow Marco had been offered a glimpse into the chaos at the center of Being. For reasons known only to Itself, some power had chosen him as a conduit for the revelation of "our frightful position in the universe," and then Marco, for reasons known only to himself, had shared his affliction with me.

Of course this only intensified my need to find him, since I now feared that he had suffered some cosmically awful fate, and that if I continued on my current course, I would join him in it.

In my anguish. I unthinkingly reached down and turned one more page of the notebook, and what I saw on the following page initiated the final phase of my descent into horror. I froze and read the item three times while its significance sank in. Then I sprang from the chair and lurched for the door, where I fumbled with the knob for a miniature eternity before finally turning it. Then I was outside and racing across campus, not caring that my front door was still banging open and the notebook was still lying open on the living room floor where I had dropped it.

What I had seen was a brief news notice that Marco had clipped from the *Terence Sun-Gazette*, the local daily newspaper, and had pasted carefully onto the page following his feverish final notes. It stared up at my empty living room as I ran to avert an inconceivable catastrophe, its words saying far more than the journalist who wrote them had intended.

WORLD-RENOWNED SCIENTIST TO LECTURE AT TERENCE UNIVERSITY

British physicist and astronomer Nigel Williamson will

> deliver a lecture entitled "Chance, Meaning, and the Hidden Variable in the Quantum Universe" at the Terence University campus. Williamson, a Cambridge professor who is visiting Terence as the first stop on a worldwide lecture tour, is known for his tendency to ruffle the feathers of his colleagues with his unorthodox theories. His claim to have arrived at an explanation for "the seemingly causeless actions of subatomic particles" has aroused worldwide interest and a great deal of skepticism in the scientific community. He is scheduled to speak on Thursday, May 2 at 7 p.m. in the lecture hall of the Stockwell Science Building on the Terence University campus. The lecture is free and open to the public.

VII

I reached the Stockwell Science Building in a matter of minutes. The run of barely a single mile had exhausted my soft scholar's body, and I fell gasping and heaving against the double door entrance. Peering inside, I saw a digital clock on the far wall of the foyer that read 7:24. This encouraged me a little. The lecture would have already started by now and there was no obvious commotion going on, so perhaps my awful hunch had been mistaken.

Still gasping, I glanced up for a moment at the twilight sky and saw a yellowish half moon shining through the branches of a scraggly tree. The once familiar disc was now the dead, decaying fetal carcass of some unimaginably monstrous creature, and while I watched in awe with my dark inner light burning like a beacon, the creature began to stir and wake. Dread washed back over me like an icy wave, and I flung myself through the door of the science building as much to escape the awakening gaze of the moon as to stop the tragedy I feared might be occurring within.

I burst into the lecture hall to find a small group of middle-aged men and women checking their watches, tapping their feet, and exchanging glances filled with annoyance and unease. No lecture was in progress, and I gathered that I had entered as the impatience of the tiny crowd had reached a snapping point. Most were seated but a few had gathered around the lectern down front, where a small, nervous, balding man was blinking through thick-lensed eyeglasses and trying to placate them. Several people looked up when I entered, and I saw their faces tighten into angry-worried lines at the sight of me.

Ignoring them as best I could, I made my way down to the bespectacled man. He stammered and finally stopped in his nervous explanations when I approached, and the cluster of people turned to stare at me.

I asked, "Where is Professor Williamson?" and my voice emerged as a harsh demand. It also seemed to reach me from a distance, and I noticed that I didn't feel a part of the situation at all, but rather like a spectator watching a theatrical presentation in which I and the others were performing.

The jittery little man played his part admirably. "I was just explaining—" he began, and then tripped over his own jitteriness. His role was obviously that of the Flustered Mousy Man, whereas mine was at least partly that of The One Who Flusters. He finally gave up and gestured miserably toward a door behind him that appeared to lead into a conference room. "He's in there."

"Is he alone?"

Mousy Man was growing more unhappy with each passing second. "Well, no. There's somebody in there with him. Like I've been telling these people, a very agitated young man showed up a few minutes before seven and demanded to see the professor. I told him we were busy, but then Nigel came out and chatted with him for a minute, and seemed quite interested in what the young man had to say. Fascinated, actually. They went into the conference room half an hour ago and haven't come out."

"Have you *knocked?*" By this point I was all but yelling, and the other performers' eyes were widening as they shifted visibly away and left me alone to dominate the stage and my unfortunate foil.

"Well, no," he said, and began shifting from foot to foot. "I didn't feel comfortable interrupting them. And the young man, he was quite . . . passionate. His eyes were wild, like—." He cut himself short and looked to someone, anyone, for help, but I could read the unspoken words in his anxious and forlorn expression: *like your eyes.*

I opened my mouth to speak another line, but a sudden loud *thump* from the conference room silenced us all. It sounded like a heavy chair or table falling over. Then: a wild, incoherent shouting that froze my blood. For even through the thick oaken door and the hysterical tone, I recognized the voice and accent of my friend Marco.

I bolted past the stunned group of spectators and grabbed the door handle, only to find it locked. Now another voice, panicked and British and sharp with terror, answered Marco's, and the rest of the scene played out offstage, behind the locked door.

WILLIAMSON

(Terrified)

What are you doing?

MARCO

(Frantically yelling)

You *must* not! Those who know it fully would perish! The Gate is in the great *and* the small! You cannot let the madness become sanity!

(There is a tremendous sound of shattering glass.)

WILLIAMSON

Stop it! What are you doing?

(Shouting and pounding on the door)

Roger! Open the door! Roger!

(Rising to a shriek)

NO! STOP!

(There is a sound like a knife stabbing into a side of beef. WILLIAMSON's words shatter into an incoherent screech, followed by a liquid choking. A second sound emerges: a wet tearing like the shredding of damp cloth. WILLIAMSON's voice falls silent.)

MARCO

(Screaming as if in mortal agony)

The Gate above and below! The One in the many! Oh God, the teeth! The TEEEEETH!

(Silence, textured by the sly, slick tinkling of some heavy object being dragged through shards of glass.)

(BLACKOUT)

(END OF SCENE)

The play was over. The spectator feeling dissolved and I stepped off the stage into reality. Everything was completely, horribly present and actual. A woman in the crowd was weeping. A man had run halfway up the stairs toward the rear exit and then stopped, and now stood there blinking in befuddlement as if he had lost his way. The rest of the group stood and sat in various states of paralyzed shock.

Then the spell broke all at once and panic set in. Some sprang for the exits while others rushed toward me. Everyone screamed and shouted something different to do, until finally someone ran out to the hallway, blundered into an unlocked maintenance closet, and returned with an enormous claw hammer. I snatched it from him and set to work on the door handle while somebody else phoned the police.

The handle separated and crashed to the carpet after six stout blows. Clutching the hammer like a talisman, I pushed the door open and took a faltering step forward while the others clustered behind me in a sudden, awed silence.

The room I had entered was a standard conference room stocked with a long, narrow table and eight plastic chairs. One of these was sprawled on its back amidst the wreckage of an overturned barrister's bookcase, whose windows had exploded on impact with the edge of the table and then the face of the floor. The resulting spray of glass was soaked with what looked like gallons of blood. The net effect was a floor carpeted with crimson diamonds and jagged, bloody eggshells.

My eyes followed a distinctly differentiated blood trail through the carnage, tracing it to the point where it disappeared behind the table. As if caught in a nightmare, I crunched unhesitatingly across the crimson carpet to gaze upon what it was that I had gone there to prevent.

Nigel Williamson—physicist, astronomer, Cambridge professor, brilliant iconoclast—would never have the chance to reveal to the world his grand theory concerning the inner purpose of the universe as embodied in the chaotic irrationalities of the quantum realm. His intellectual brilliance had not been enough to save him, for now he lay on his back behind the table where Marco had dragged him, the nine-inch piece of glass Marco had used to eviscerate him still protruding from his side. His frozen expression of horror must have matched the one that slowly began to twist my own face, but if so, I was unaware of it. My eyes, my mind, my awareness, my very being, were all filled to bursting by a sight that blazed with a too-real intensity and became an instant symbol of everything I had realized and endured: the blood-spattered, empty-eyed face of my friend Marco as he crouched over the professor's body and mechanically devoured his innards.

VIII

That gruesome image with its oversaturated quality of ontological vividness remained with me forever, even after the passing of years had begun to blunt some of the other memories. Some of the first of those to go were the ones concerning the immediate aftermath of that final event. I remember there was quite a furor on campus and in the town, and even in the national news media. I know I was asked many questions by people acting in official capacities. But the specifics of it all, just like the specifics of the actions that I and the others took right after we found Marco in there with the professor, have been swallowed up by the image of that bloody face with its blank eyes and mechanical masticating motion.

What I do remember with clarity are my broad reactions to the uproar, since they changed the course of my life and brought me to my present circumstance. At the height of it all, when I feared I might literally go insane from everything, I quit my beloved studies and relocated to another town where nobody knew me and I could live in relative anonymity. I still live there today, and hold down the most trivial job I could find that will still provide me with enough income to afford a shoddy apartment where I hide from the world and hope for a merciful end to my existence. In general, I apply myself diligently to ignoring and forgetting the world outside the bubble of boredom that I have created. But from time to time I buy a newspaper or switch on my little television to see if the direction of world events might have changed a little. And of course it has not, nor will it ever.

For everything is still disintegrating inexorably into madness, and I, unlike most people, know precisely why. Before Marco dragged me into his living nightmare, I was worried like everyone else about the mass cultural insanity that had gripped the 20th and early 21st centuries. Like everyone else, I noticed that things seemed to be roaring toward an apocalyptic climax, and I had my pet theories to explain it all. But now I see how lame all of that was.

Because what's happening is in fact a profound and far-reaching reordering of reality itself—societal, cultural, personal, and even physical. In essence, the prophecies of Lovecraft and Nietzsche are coming true right before our eyes, with effects that are not only personal and cultural but ontological. Our excess of vast scientific knowledge and technological prowess has proceeded in lockstep with a collective descent into species-level insanity. You only have to watch two minutes of television, glimpse a newspaper headline, or eavesdrop on a random conversation to learn of it. Ignorance and idiocy. Riots and revolutions. Auschwitz and Abu Ghraib. Darfur and Dachau. These and a thousand other signposts like them are only the most pointed and obvious manifestations of the all-pervasive malaise that has come to define us. And since, as Sankara observed, we are nothing but particularized manifestations of the Ground of Being itself, we are not only witnesses to this breakdown but participants in it, enablers of the transformation of the world into a vale of horror through the metaphysical potency of our very witnessing. God looks out through each of our eyes, an abyss of insatiable hunger and infinite teeth, and the dark light of His consciousness makes each of us a lamp that illuminates a new and terrible truth.

I find it ironic that the man who cursed me with this vision of the world will not even be aware of it when everything comes to fruition. Marco spends his days and nights screaming out his madness in a prison for the criminally insane. I visited him only once, when the police were still trying to discover where he had hidden himself during his ten-day absence (a question they never answered, nor did I). I almost couldn't bear to look at him, and when I finally did meet his gaze, I knew at once that my friend was dead. His eyes had gone permanently dark in the manner I had briefly glimpsed so long ago in his dorm room, and I recognized his condition as an advanced case of the same state that would sooner or later manifest in every person on the planet. Something had compelled me to bring the notebook, which I had retrieved from my living room floor and then carefully preserved for no reason I could articulate. When I showed it to Marco, he sprang at me without warning and knocked me to the floor, snarling and shrieking in a feral frenzy. The savagery of his attack stunned me, and before I could recover, he had seized the notebook with his teeth and shook it to shreds like a dog with a rat. Then he turned on me again, and it was only the intervention of the hospital staff that saved me from having my throat torn out. His doctors said it would be best if I stayed away after that. Later, I heard that he managed to break his restraints after I left, and that in the absence of another object he turned on himself. Before the orderlies could reach him, he chewed off and swallowed two of his own fingers.

What scares me the most is knowing that the transcendent insanity gnawing at the shell of Marco is the same insanity that waits to welcome me in death. All too well do I understand the wisdom of the ancient Greeks, which held that the best thing is never to have been born. To exist at all is to know the horror of no escape. Nietzsche said the thought of suicide can comfort a man through many a dark night, but it is no comfort to someone like me who knows all too well what awaits.

There is only one hope for my salvation. Over the years I have become an assiduous student of Lovecraft, not just his stories but his essays and letters. And I have marveled at the man's uncanny ability to see so deeply into the truth and yet remain so composed and kindhearted. Perhaps this gentle New Englander knew something that I do not, something he tried to convey when he wrote of the "vast conceit of those who had babbled of the *malignant* ancient ones." Perhaps the horror exists only in me, not in reality. Perhaps Marco was wrong, and there is no need to fear the truth. After all, It knows only Itself, and maybe I will not perceive It as horrific after I die. Perhaps I will be so thoroughly consumed by and identified with it that "I" will not even exist at all, and my sense of horror will prove to be as fleeting and finite as the self that sensed it. If this is true, then may it come quickly.

But this hope, however appealing, can never sustain me for long. For it is clear that I am *already* identified with that horrible truth, and yet I still find it a horror. The clear evidence of this identification manifests in my own body, in the fundamental physical drive that compels me to take nourishment and the anatomical structures that have been evolved to accomplish this purpose: lips and tongue, teeth and gums, throat and stomach. Life, as Joseph Campbell once observed, is a horrific thing that sustains itself by feeding on other life. I have gained a new and awful awareness of this fact in the form of a certain nagging sensitivity in my mouth. All day and night I am plagued by an unpleasant awareness of those protruding bits of bone whose function is to grind plant and animal flesh to a pulp in order to sustain this bodily life. Sometimes when this awareness has tortured me for hours on end, I will go to the mirror and draw back my lips to gaze at the truth. This mockery of the facial expression that conventionally expresses pleasure reminds me a bit of the bliss I once hoped to find in philosophies of ultimate beauty. But even that is gone now, swallowed down the bottomless throat of the cosmic mystery that forever feeds on all things.

Do I seem mad? Do I sound like a man who has become lost in his own private delusion of hell? Then let me remind you that you, too, exhibit the same stigmata in your own body. Show me your smile and I will show you your fate.

For some reason, I worked for Viggo Brand. Several times each day as I sat at my desk or wandered around my office and went about my regular routine of boredom and unproductiveness, it occurred to me that way: *For some reason, I work for Viggo Brand.*

Of course I knew the real reasons. I could look back over the pattern of my past and survey the series of causes and effects, motivations and necessities, which had led me to this job in a cramped office on the ninetieth floor of the Brand Building. It was all too clear why I worked for him. The reason could be summed up in a single word: *fear*. Not fear of Mr. Brand, whom I had never seen, but whose guardian presence presided like an invisible eye over his organization. It was more a fear of not knowing what else to do. I was afraid to do anything but continue working there, because working there was all I had ever done, and I felt comfortable with and comforted by the boredom, even when it sometimes proved indistinguishable from desperation.

But still, although the simple, literal answer was readily available, I sometimes liked to narrow my attention to the present—to that infinitesimal, perpetually dying point of the present moment—and from that restricted viewpoint consider my employment at the Brand Corporation. When I did this, I truly did not know why I was there. Without the present awareness of my past laid out for easy viewing, I could almost imagine that I had never been anywhere else. On long afternoons when the sky scoured over with a matting of dark clouds and the hours seemed to stretch into eternity before and behind me, I could almost imagine that I had never known any place but my office, nor any existence but the routine of monotony and boredom that made up my every day.

The ennui of my situation was augmented by the fact that I did not know what I was supposed to be doing for the company. Beginning on my first day, many years past, I had shown up every morning, and nobody had ever asked me to leave, so I had stayed. The woman who acted as my secretary, and also as the secretary for the eight or nine other employees in my division, and whose name I had never learned during all my long years of employment, would peek in the door to my office each morning to verify that I was present at my desk. When she saw me, she would give a curt nod and close the door, leaving me to lean back in my chair and look out the window, or maybe take a nap, or maybe scribble meaningless shapes on the notepad that awaited me on my desk each morning.

I had become very deft at these illustrations. Often I put great care into them, but then I just left them sitting there, and each morning when I arrived they were neatly stacked with a fresh blank pad on top. Over time, I had perfected a style of doodling all my own. Sometimes I spent entire weeks blackening a single sheet of notepaper with curly lines and boxes, diamonds and stars, dots and dashes, and jagged, meshy patterns that made my eyes ache when I looked at them later. This had become just another automatic act, like everything else I did for the Brand Corporation.

The Brand Building was an imposing structure. Every morning when I climbed up from the subway and approached the sparkling row of front doors, I would raise my eyes and peer up through the mist to catch a glimpse of the sharp spire, and would think of Mr. Brand living there at the very top in unknown quarters. And I would wonder what he looked like and what he did with his days, and where he had acquired his great wealth, and why he had built this magnificent structure for a purpose that I still did not know after all those years of working for him.

The Brand Building was shaped like a needle, or like a four-cornered pyramid elongated to an absurd proportion, with an exterior surface of smooth, obsidian-colored stone. It stabbed upward two hundred stories and appeared to prick the outer edge of the sky. I remember thinking when I first glimpsed it from a distant bridge many years ago, as I was entering the city for the first time, that the great tower seemed to watch over the dull buildings below like a harsh and haughty ruler. They huddled around its base in crazy clusters, all dirty brick and concrete. I had felt like the proverbial rat in a trap as I drove through the maze of streets and slums, and looked up at the faded facades and crumbling brickwork. Worst of all were the pallid faces I saw framed in the windows. Some were lighter than others, some darker. Some were young and some were old. All wore a look of vacancy and hopelessness.

Then I had come nearer the Brand Building, and the squalor had disappeared at once and given way to a sterile open space many hundreds of yards wide, where Renaissance-style fountains stood dry and flaking, and statues of strange forms lined up in Spartan rows to flank visitors like me and guide us toward the row of front doors that were always revolving, always turning in perpetual circles to allow unhindered, universal access or exit. After I had been employed there for several months, someone finally told me about the subway access right there on the grounds, reserved exclusively for Brand Corporation employees. After that I never navigated the unnerving maze of the old city again.

As I sat there looking out of my window, which covered an entire wall of my office, I could gaze down upon those old structures huddled together several hundred yards from the foot of the Brand Building, and feel a pleasant sense of weightlessness rising up in my breast like a cloud of feathers. This had been my primary preoccupation during all my long years in that office: simply to look down on the old city and enjoy it from this dizzying height. The atmosphere around the Brand Building was clear as crystal, like freshly washed glass, except for a white mist that clung to the black exterior in the early morning hours. This always burned away in the sunlight by mid-morning, leaving me with a totally unobstructed view of the scene below. It was truly magnificent to look down on the old buildings with their cloak of muddy gray smog, and to feel somehow purified and rarefied by the mere fact of my height and their distance.

My favorite time for this activity was during the long evenings of winter, when sunset came early and the lights of the old city shone visibly in dim haloes through the smog for a long period before the end of my workday. On such evenings, I would sometimes dance my eyes over those lights in quick darts, making them blur into streaks and tracers, and then raise my head and steady my half-closed eyes upon a horizon line stretching from east to west, located right on the precise division between the city below and the sky above. The stars would be out overhead, shining like shards of crystal in a black celestial ocean. I would watch them from the tops of my eyes while keeping the lights of the old city centered in the lower half of my vision. And sometimes for a split second that felt like a miniature eternity, I could fancy that the stars above and the lights below formed a single unbroken continuum of night sky. It would look as if a great constellation had fallen to earth, or better yet, as if there were no earth at all but only the stars shining brilliantly in their cold and cruel distance. I would gasp and feel tears start to my eyes, and would sense myself on the verge of some great revelation, some unknowable fulfillment that would justify all the long years of my blundering, inarticulate yearning for something beyond the dreary pall of everyday existence.

But then the moment would pass, and my eyes would clear, and the stars would return to their inaccessible heights, and the city below would settle once again into its unromantic guise as a dirty jumble of smog-shrouded bricks, and I would be alone in my office on the ninetieth floor of the Brand Building with no understanding—or at least no *real* one, none that would explain to me the longings and confusions of a meaningless past and present—of why I was there.

This all changed late one evening when my secretary opened the door to my office and walked in to stand before my desk.

I swiveled around in my chair and regarded her with surprise. She had never entered my office before, and I could not possibly guess what she might want. I took the opportunity to observe her more closely. She was slim and bony and dressed in a navy blue skirt. Her hair was rust-red and pulled back in a bun. Her face was white and narrow. A network of delicate dry lines textured the skin of her cheeks and forehead. She might have been thirty years old or twice that.

"Mr. Brand wants to see you," she said. When I looked at her dumbly, she said it again: "Mr. Brand wants to see you."

I did not know how to react. My eyes were still filled with after-flashes from the stars and city lights, and I must have looked as dazed as I felt. After a moment I rose from my chair and came around the desk to stand beside her.

"Gather those and take them with you," she said, pointing to the pile of papers that lay on the desk. I complied as if in a dream. These were the papers on which I had been scribbling meaningless pictures for months and years. She turned and exited, and I hurried after her with the sheaf of papers flapping under my arm as I tried to straighten my necktie.

She led me out of my office and down a hallway in a direction I had never gone before. I looked back and saw my eight or nine coworkers in that division standing singly outside their doors. They were watching me with awed expressions, exactly as I would have looked at them if the situation had been reversed and they had received the mysterious summons.

Then they were lost from sight as I was led around a corner into an ill-lit hallway. We walked to an open elevator door at the end of the hall, where the secretary stopped and gestured for me to enter, which I did.

"He's waiting for me right now?" I asked. In reply, she reached inside and pressed the button for the two hundredth floor. Then she backed out and walked away, leaving me alone as the doors closed.

The inside of the elevator was uncharacteristically cramped for the Brand Building, whose spacious interiors had always belied the limitation of its exterior shape. But the decoration was much more ornate than what I had grown accustomed to. I grasped a handrail of polished brass to steady myself as I felt the car shoot upward at a positively terrifying speed. The light fixture depending from the ceiling was multi-bulbed and hooded with tiny lampshades mounted on curling metal arms that looked like gold. It hung so low that it nearly brushed the top of my head. For a moment I tried to imagine the elevator car and myself as we must have appeared from the outside. I closed my eyes and caught a momentary mental glimpse of a tiny metal box rocketing upward through the core of the needle-like Brand Building toward the stars above. My lungs labored as I fancied the atmosphere grew thinner. Immediately, I cut off my imaginings and opened my eyes to dispel the vertigo. When the car eventually slowed and stopped, the light fixture vibrated, and its bulbs trembled and tinkled.

I was breathing hard when the doors opened. Grasping my papers in sweaty hands, I emerged into an antechamber that was like nothing else I had ever seen in the Brand Building. It was spacious and geometrical, shaped almost like a perfect cube except for the slight inward slope of the walls that made the ceiling smaller than the floor. All the surfaces were black and gleaming. An enormous burgundy rug with a vaguely oriental pattern stretched nearly from wall to wall, and laid out on it were a number of exhibits that reminded me of pieces in a museum. Some were in clear cases while others sat uncovered. Some were made of polished wood or bone and looked like tribal idols or fetishes. Others were crystalline or metal and looked sleek and new.

From this inscrutable assemblage, I gathered an odd sense of excitement, tempered with anxiety. It was a familiar feeling, and I was on the verge of remembering where I had felt it before when a voice issued from a hidden speaker and told me to approach the doors on the opposite wall. I had not even noticed them. In order to obey the faceless command I was obliged to walk through the museum display, and for some reason I felt a strong reluctance to touch anything. I had the sense that I was navigating through a mysterious sea whose pristine beauty my very presence might defile.

Once across, I stepped gingerly off the carpet and back onto the shiny black floor. The door handles were huge and made of brass. When I touched them, the doors opened easily and silently, and I stepped into what I knew must be Mr. Brand's office.

It was long and low and all of a shiny black, just like the antechamber. Mr. Brand was seated on the far side behind a black desk, framed against a massive window that dwarfed the one down in my own office. I had never laid eyes on him before, but there could be no question of his identity. His face and throat were thick, his shoulders broad, his head high-browed and square. Indeed, he was powerfully built all over. Even seated there behind his desk, he exuded an aura of authority. From this alone I could well understand why everyone in the building, and also in the city below, walked in awe of him. His hair was white and straight and combed back from his forehead to fall in stern lines down to his shoulders. He was dressed in a black coat with a black shirt fastened tightly about his neck. I did not doubt that if he were to rise and walk around the desk, I would be greeted with the sight of black pants and black shoes, impeccably polished. Somehow I also knew that he would prove to be disturbingly tall, a veritable giant of a man, and I fervently hoped that he would remain seated. A pair of black spectacles, completely impenetrable and perfectly round, completed the ensemble.

"Please," he said, "sit down." He spoke with a faint accent that I could not place. His voice was fully as deep and commanding as his appearance would imply, but it was more cultured than I would have expected, carrying a kind of measured grace that was quite pleasing to the ear. Up until now his hands had remained folded before him in an attitude of waiting, but now he gestured for me to take a seat in the single sable-colored chair that was positioned to face him from across the desk.

I did not dare disobey. A moment later, I was seated face-to-face with him while he regarded me from behind his spectacles.

"You have done good work for me," he said at last. "That is why I've called you here: to thank you. Of all my many employees, you are the hardest working and most loyal, and you deserve to know that."

My heart sank as I heard these words. I was certain he must have gotten my file mixed up with someone else's, with the record of some other employee who actually knew his job and truly deserved a commendation. I dreaded to think what would happen when Mr. Brand discovered that he had invited the wrong person into his inner sanctum.

"No, you are the right man," he said. A little shock went off in my chest as he seemed to read my thoughts. I felt I should say something, but all my faculties were paralyzed. For a wordless moment we faced each other across the desk.

Then I noticed the vista that spread out behind him.

Gleaming from below, the lights of the city cast up an aurora that tinted the bottom half of his long, single-paned window with a milky radiance. Simultaneously, the window's upper half was populated from end to end by an assemblage of stars the likes of which I had never seen. It must have been due to the clarity of the atmosphere at that altitude. The night sky was a black velvet curtain encrusted with diamonds. It was the smooth surface of an oily ocean shining with the phosphorescent eyes of a billion unknown, underwater creatures.

The sight so overwhelmed me that I felt the breath sucked out of my lungs, as if I had stepped through those windows into the vacuum of outer space. The papers in my hand slipped from numb fingers and plopped down on the desk.

In the midst of my transport, I was aware that Mr. Brand was regarding me with what I might have taken for affection if the thought had not been so ridiculous. Then he looked at the papers and smiled, showing me two rows of tiny perfect teeth.

"Ah, yes," he said. "May I?" The unexplained request confused me, so I tore my loving gaze away from the mystical windows and saw that he was holding out his hand. I watched my own hand pick up the papers and pass them to him. His meaty fingers closed around them with a kind of greedy relish, and then he was scouring them with his hidden gaze, flipping from one page to the next, turning to look at the fronts and backs of pages whose every available inch was covered with a meaningless chaos of designs. I watched as his body bowed slightly in its seat. The lapel of his coat crinkled. A lock of white hair fell down over his forehead and bisected one of his black lenses. He seemed to be devouring the pages with his eyes. I was fascinated by this display of utter abandoned greed, and then I stopped to wonder what that word could possibly mean in this connection, and why it has arisen so immediately and naturally in my mind: *greed*.

After a few minutes, he raised his eyes from the papers and gave me that same tiny-toothed smile. "Oh, so good," he said in a voluptuous voice. "So very, very good. You are a positive treasure. I assure you that from now on, you will receive your just due from me. Please forgive the years of tedium, but I had to be certain. And now I am." He looked back down at the pages and laughed at some private joke. "Am I *ever* certain!"

My head was swimming as if I were drunk. Perhaps it was the thinness of the atmosphere. "Mr. Brand." It was the first thing I had said to him, and the sound of my own voice unnerved me. He looked at me with that same pleased expression.

"Mr. Brand," I repeated. "I don't understand. Thank you for your praise, but I just don't understand. I'm ashamed to admit it, but I don't even know what I do for you or your company. What can you possibly see in those scribbles?"

He laughed again, in a tone full of affection, and at last arose from his chair. I had been correct in my suspicion: He towered over me. The top of his head nearly touched the ceiling, and when he walked around the desk to stand beside me, his pants and shoes were black, and the shoes gleamed even more brightly than the floor.

"Oh, my child, if only you knew. If only you could understand. I wish I could explain it to you, truly. But then the Brand Corporation would be out of business, and you would be out of a job, and I would be toppled from my perch here in the eye of the needle, and the only thing left in all the world would be that dirty, crumbling city below. And neither of us could live with that result. You want it no more than I."

I was nodding and agreeing with him before I even realized it. Although I had no idea what he was talking about, I positively shuddered at the thought of the old city existing on its own without the Brand Building's redemptive presence presiding over it, with Mr. Brand securely ensconced at the top.

"You see?" he said. "We indeed understand each other."

Then he laid his heavy hand on my shoulder, and everything changed. Even through the barriers of my coat and shirt, I could feel the heat of his flesh, which penetrated those thin layers of fabric and spread over my skin like hot oil, and I knew in my soul that I was permanently marked by his touch. I knew that even if I were to remove my shirt and find no visible mark, I would still be forever changed by that contact with Mr. Brand. In the space of a second, he had taken something from me and given something else in return, something new and unimagined. As he stepped away from me and walked back around the desk to his chair, I felt a tingling vibration begin to shimmer inside me. It soothed me from neck to groin, and between my eyes, from behind my skull, a warm pressure like a finger pressed gently outward. Mr. Brand resumed his seat and looked at me.

"Thank you again," he said. "Thank you, sir, for your hard work and loyalty."

❦

Some indeterminate amount of time later, when I stood up from my seat and returned to the black double-door, I moved as if I were walking underwater. My head spun with a flurry of new insights that came coursing through my awareness like spray from a black waterfall.

I saw dimly, as though reflected in a dirty mirror, the extent of the organization for which I worked. I saw the way its influence extended like a network of invisible arteries into the old city below, into the hearts of its inhabitants. I saw how it sucked away the lifeblood of their souls and fed on their dreams, using those tender psychic morsels to fortify and amplify the black tower, bringing its apex ever closer to the outer edge of the sky and the inner edge of heaven.

And more: I saw this influence reaching away from the known world, rounding strange corners and meeting at odd intersections with the teeming edges of other worlds, worlds beyond the known rim of light and darkness, sense and solidity, the foundations of all that I knew and thought possible. In countless other worlds, I saw countless other beings lined up in hovels like the sickly people in the windows of the old city below, like the ignorant employees stacked up in their slivered tiers throughout the monstrous height of the Brand Building. They all labored somehow, these beings, even the ones who no longer moved or spoke or thought, and their labor bore fruit in the form of grotesque and fantastic productions that could never coalesce into any kind of order that would make sense to sanity as I knew it.

But in some unaccountable fashion, these productions, when they were brought together and arranged in the proper order, cohered like the serrated edges of a lethal jigsaw, and always proved to be precisely what Mr. Brand needed for the furtherance of his business. His corporation grew with the expansion of his soul, and his soul drew its nourishment from the silent labor of a network of unwitting worlds.

There the vision reached its limit. Having seen so far into things that were undreamed of, my newly awakened inner sight came up against something like a black, shimmering shield that repelled vision as a mirror repels light. I knew that beyond this barrier must lie the knowledge of the ultimate end, the pattern and purpose for which this vast network of ignorant organized labor was being bled dry by a man who had somehow attained the status of a demi-God and now wanted to make his transition into divinity complete.

The visions coiled and glimmered in the beam of my inner sight, and my knees grew weak. The black inner barrier receded and solidified, gaining form and shape until I found myself gazing at my own watery reflection in the smooth, polished wall of Mr. Brand's sanctum.

As I touched the door handle, I knew without looking back that he had again taken up the papers, my own unwitting contribution to his Promethean endeavor, and was again feasting upon their contents. I almost felt that I could see the lines and shapes twisting before my own eyes instead of his.

But something was different now. Something had been altered within me, for now when I looked with these new eyes upon the randomness of those designs that had been spawned by boredom, I glimpsed a phenomenon that transcended mere ink and paper. It seemed to be a pattern, a subtle arrangement of shape, position, and proportion that brought order out of chaos. It was, I understood, a higher kind of order, one that made perfect sense out of senselessness and imparted meaning to the meaningless. I fancied that in the depths of Mr. Brand's soul, through the agency of the things I had drawn, this patternless pattern was spreading out two black-feathered wings, or perhaps they were doors, which could open up and transport a person to the heights of an unimaginable bliss in some unimaginable realm situated far beyond the need for reasons or the lack of them. Somewhere in a cold Arcadia, in a skyward abyss of utter inaccessibility, there was a place where ennui was unknown and the stars shone forever without obstruction. This was the paradise Mr. Brand was bound for, and I recognized in its beauty the fulfillment of everything I had ever wanted for myself.

The pressure in my forehead was beautiful. The tingling warmth in my abdomen was delicious.

I shut the doors behind me and walked boldly back through the menagerie of artifacts, no longer fearing that I might defile them. With uncharacteristic courage, I stopped and caressed them one by one, feeling a new exultation well up within me at the feel of their textures.

The elevator door was open and waiting for me. I rode it back down in complete inner and outer silence without holding onto the rail. The hanging light fixture was motionless and silent as the car came to a halt and I stepped back onto my accustomed ninetieth floor. The hallways were dark. Everyone had gone home for the evening, and I walked in total solitude to my office, where I found the door still open and the lights still on.

It was not until I sat down at my desk and swiveled the chair to face the window that I discovered the true nature of the gift Mr. Brand had given me.

Outside, there were only stars. Instead of looking down upon the hopeless squalor of the old city, my window-wall now sat at the glowing hot center of a spiral galaxy. Delicate arms of silver and white fire unfurled away from me like flaming roads to paradise, like star-dusted snowbanks, and the spaces between them shimmered with a golden glow like the light of a sunrise.

Nothing stood between us now, the stars and me, no obstruction at all. Even this cold pane was utterly insubstantial. If I tipped forward I might pass through the window as through a sheet of water, and on the other side fall forever into a vast well of endless beauty. The city below had turned invisible in the cosmic light of this sacred gallery, and I wept with joy as I realized that I no longer had to wonder why I was here instead of somewhere else, or worry about whether I should be doing this instead of that. Enjoyment of the ultimate mystery might be reserved for another, but I no longer felt any sense of loss. All my questions had vanished, leaving only this dazzling cold beauty outside my window and inside my heart. Most miraculous and wonderful of all, I knew that it would all continue to shine on without me forever, in a way that made sense out of senselessness and imparted meaning to the meaningless. It was shining without me even now, immediately outside my window in that inconceivably beautiful swirl of fiery night.

Mr. Brand saw it all as well, and understood the vision in its entirety from the protection of his shadowy sanctum perched high in the eye of the needle: Mr. Brand, who alone possessed the secret of joy, whose tower pierced through the heart of heaven like a spear; Mr. Brand, who banished all fear and desperation with his touch, because he alone knew what was ultimately needed.

For no reason at all, I work for Viggo Brand.

Desert Places

Men with minds sensitive to hereditary impulse will always tremble at the thought of the hidden and fathomless worlds of strange life which may pulsate in the gulfs beyond the stars.

—H. P. Lovecraft

They cannot scare me with their empty spaces
Between stars—on stars where no human race is.
I have it in me so much nearer home
To scare myself with my own desert places.

—Robert Frost

I

When Dr. Pryor told me that my friend Paul had been involved in a terrible accident, I was sitting in the heart of the Utah desert fifteen miles outside Vernal, brushing away flecks of dirt from the leg bone of an as-yet unidentified fossil. We only knew that it was some sort of dinosaur, right from the heart of the Jurassic period. Only a small portion had been exposed by our efforts. The bulk of it was still buried under the dry Utah soil. It would take many more days of painstaking effort to excavate the piece with all of its secrets still intact.

The light of the early evening sun spilled over my shoulder like a flow of warm liquid, bathing the earth before me with a ruddy glow. That moment, with my eyes fixed on the long-buried bone of an extinct reptile and my brain reeling from the news I'd just heard, burned itself instantly, irrevocably, into my soul. The sense of being deeply and painfully marked was almost physical.

"I'm sorry," Dr. Pryor said. "The woman on the phone said I should tell you exactly what was going on. She said you'd listen better that way." His unreadable little eyes were even more opaque than usual behind his thick eyeglasses. He shuffled his right foot through the heavy carpet of desert dust, and his work boot kicked up a dry brown cloud that lingered in the motionless air between us.

I didn't have to be told who had made the call. No one else

would have had the astounding boldness—or tactlessness—to pass the message through a stranger, nor would anyone else have had such a bitingly accurate insight into my state of mind from across a distance of a thousand miles.

"Did she say how it happened?" I asked.

"Not exactly. Some sort of injury to the head. I guess it's quite serious." He shuffled his foot again.

I knew I should felt bad for my paleontologist employer. He was obviously discomfited by Lisa's awful judgment in giving the news directly to him instead of doing the sane thing and asking him to hand me the phone. But I couldn't feel anything besides a hollow dullness that seemed to breathe into me from the desert.

"I guess you'll be leaving." His words were both a statement and a question.

"Yes." I took a final glance at the great leg bone, as thick as the trunk of a small tree back in my home state of Missouri, and willed the moment to stay with me. Something about its pain, its vividness, seemed crucial. Something about the mystery of the buried bone seemed vital to my continued health and sanity. I wanted the pain of that mark on my soul, and the mystery of the dead monster, to stay with me forever, to remind me of the fact that I was indeed capable of feeling such a pure and profound emotion.

Then I took a breath and rose to my feet. Dr. Pryor stood looking at me doubtfully. I knew I was abandoning him right when he needed me the most. But then, I had only been working with him for a short time, whereas my roots with Paul and Lisa were old and deep.

"Sorry," I said. It was all I could manage.

He shrugged faintly. "You have to do what you have to do. I'm sorry about your friend."

I started to say thanks, but then I just nodded and walked away to where we had parked our vehicles. The cloud I kicked up as I drove back to the road swirled around my old Ford van like a rusty ghost. When some of it sucked in through the grill and coughed out of the dashboard vents, it tasted hot and coppery, like a splash of blood on my tongue.

II

The drive should have taken fourteen hours, but I made it last twenty-six. This was due partly to the practical fact that my battered old van with its badly unbalanced wheels shook like a minor earthquake when I exceeded fifty miles per hour. But the real reason for my slow pace was my sharp reluctance to reach my destination. I was heading back into territory that I thought I had left behind, and every mile I traveled felt like fighting against a river current. I drove most of the way at a speed of around forty, stopping by the roadside several times to catch my breath and stare up at the sky—dappled with silvery stars by night, then cloudless and harsh with heat during the day—while I struggled to divine my own motives. Did I really want to do this? Did I really want to go back and face the remains of my old life again?

When I finally arrived at the hospital in Farrenton, Missouri, it was eleven-thirty at night and I felt like a walking dead man. My eyes throbbed with a pulsing ache and my back wanted to split in two.

True to form, Lisa displayed her talent for mind reading by greeting me in the lobby. There was no way she could have known when I would arrive, or even whether I would show up. But there she sat, waiting on a mahogany-colored sectional sofa with a crisp copy of the *Farrenton Beacon* spread open in her lap. When she saw me, she dropped the newspaper and ran to me as if I were a long-lost friend or lover. Which, of course, I was. Only she was obviously more at ease with our troubled past than I could ever be. The dark midnight mood of the lobby, with its sleek contemporary décor and black-tinted windows, reminded me of a movie set as she closed the distance between us.

"Oh, Stephen!" she cried, and buried her face in the breast of my tee shirt. As she heaved against me, I reflexively put my arm around her and then stood inhaling the scent of her perfume and looking down at the glossy black sweep of her hair. She watered my dusty shirt with her tears for a moment before stepping back.

"I'm sorry," she said, wiping her cheeks and attempting a smile. "It's good to see you. I've missed you."

I mumbled something in reply and tried not to notice that she looked delectable in a crimson turtleneck and auburn leather jacket. Her pants and boots were dark leather as well. Outside her sweater she wore a gold weave necklace that rose and fell with the curves of her breasts.

"I'm . . . sorry," she said again, and the falter in her voice caused me to notice for the first time how out-of-sorts she seemed. A sliver of pain was etched between her eyes, which still glowed an emerald cat's green, just as brightly as they ever had. The corners of her lovely mouth were taut with worry and her shoulders were drawn tightly inward. The social skills I had lost during three years of drifting through rain forests and deserts started to come back, and I took her by the arm and led her to the sofa, where I kept my hand on her until she was seated. Then I sat beside her and waited for her to make the next move.

"It's bad," she said. I knew immediately that she was referring to Paul. I had been gripped by a raging curiosity about his accident all during the long drive east, and more to the point, there was nothing else for us to talk about.

"He's not going to get any better," she said. "The doctor says he's brain-dead. He's just a vegetable." This brought on another bout of sobs, during which I again put my hand on her arm and noticed that I could feel the heat of her flesh all the way through the double layer of leather and cotton.

"Lisa," I said. It was the first time I had spoken her name in three years. She looked up at me with glassy eyes, and I knew that a part of me, a despised part that I would have given anything to be able to excise from my soul, still loved her. The question I then asked—"What the hell *happened?*"—referred to Paul's accident, but the vehemence with which I asked it arose from the fact that it may as well have referred to Lisa's and my sorry history.

The tale she related to me was absurd. That was the thought that lingered with me after she had explained everything and we were rising from the sofa. It lingered as she led me farther into the hospital, toward the elevators, toward the seventh floor, toward the sterile white room where my best friend and spiritual mentor, the wisest and kindest man I had ever known, lay attached to a respirator with a dent in his head from a wayward terracotta planter that had fallen from a high metal shelf at a home supply store. He and Lisa had gone browsing there with idle thoughts of building a house together. Almost as an afterthought, they had wandered through the outdoor section, where a strong wind, a veritable mini-cyclone, had blown in from nowhere and toppled the fifty-pound planter off its perch and directly onto the back of his skull. He had never regained consciousness.

We rode the elevator in silence. Lisa's body glowed with warmth as she stood next to me in her red turtleneck. When the door opened, she led me in silence down a hallway, past a nurse's station, toward a room I dreaded to enter.

Paul lay under the sheets with a bandage wrapped around his head and various plastic tubes attached to his body like the limbs of a giant insect. The rasping of the respirator was dry and chilling. Several fresh flowers in plastic vases adorned the table next to the bed, along with a scattering of sympathy cards. I stepped closer and looked down into his face. Even as he lay there unconscious, his dark eyebrows still endowed him with a placid, mysterious demeanor, halfway between brooding and peaceful. If it had not been for the tubes distorting his features, his expression would have been identical to the one I had seen a thousand times before, when we had sat beside each other in meditation.

Lisa showed uncommon good taste by standing back and letting me absorb the reality of the moment. When I had seen enough, I turned to look at her.

"Lisa, I'm so sorry." And of course I really was. Despite the fact that she had chosen him over me, devastating me with such a desperate sense of grief and betrayal that I had been driven to the brink of madness, I could not feel anything but anguish at Paul's fate. And I could not help feeling a momentary surge of protectiveness toward her, like the phantom sensation of a lost limb.

She stepped up beside me and we both looked down at him. "Do you recognize that expression?" she said. "He could almost be meditating." A ripple of chills went down my spine at this latest display of her intuitive powers. I had never gotten used to that, not in all the years we had been lovers. She had always seemed connected to the universe in a way that I simply could not rival, no matter how hard had I worked to develop my spirituality. The fact that Paul, too, had possessed his own special kind of connection to the absolute, and had been not only my best friend but also my informal guru, was more than just ironic. In light of what had followed, it was downright brutal.

"I keep hoping," she said, "that he's experiencing all kinds of things that he always wondered about. He always talked about death like it was a long-lost friend. He always expected it to tear away the last veil and bring him face to face with the great mystery." She looked at me and smiled a sad smile. "I don't have to tell you this. You knew him as well as I did." She had painted her lips red to match her blouse. They looked sweet as strawberry candy.

Suddenly, I knew I had to leave the room. There was no visible reason for it. I only knew that I had to step out for air. The memories and emotions were swirling too thickly beside Paul's bed, and something like a panic attack waited just beneath the surface to shatter me. I said something about needing to visit the restroom, and she offered to walk down the hallway with me.

"No, it's okay," I said. "I just need a minute to wash the dust off. It was a long drive."

"All the way from Utah," she said. Her eyes were impenetrable when I dared to look into them.

"How did you know where I was?"

"I called your mother. She gave me your employer's number."

Of course. She had called my mother. How difficult should that have been to figure out? I had left Dr. Pryor's cell number with my mother, who had always loved Lisa, even after the two of them, Lisa and Paul, had betrayed me. The thought of these two iconic women from my past chatting with each other like old friends behind my back sent another chill down my spine. I hid my uneasiness with a nod and made a hasty exit.

A sign directed me to a restroom at the end of the corridor. Most of the overhead lights in the main hallway had been switched off for the evening, and the beige walls and floor tiles gave off a chalky glow in the dim illumination. A woman was perched at the nurse's station on my left, reading a paperback novel by the light of a desk lamp. She glanced up at me, but I kept my gaze purposefully forward and sighed with relief when I encountered no one else.

In the restroom I spent a moment relieving my distended bladder and then another washing my face in the utility sink. Then I paused to consider my reflection in the mirror. My tee shirt looked like a child had daubed it with clay. There were muddy streaks where Lisa's tears had smudged the desert dust. My face and arms were tanned. I needed a shave. If I had not been the one living behind my own eyes, I might have done a double take, just to make sure that I was really the same clean-cut person who had set out from this town only a few years ago.

When I returned to Paul's room, I found Lisa seated beside the bed in one of the guest chairs. Her eyes were closed and her lips were moving. She held Paul's hand in her own, and I received the inescapable impression that she was uttering a prayer. Knowing something of her exotic spiritual proclivities, I didn't presume to venture a guess about whom or what she might be praying to, or what she might be saying to them. In the silence, I looked around and noticed a small crucifix mounted on the wall above the bed. For a few seconds I tried staring into Christ's tiny face in an effort to find some kind of solace, but the sculpted look of agony only increased my uneasiness.

Presently, Lisa's eyes opened, and when I glanced down at her it was like an icy fist suddenly seized my heart.

Something about her eyes was terribly wrong. It took me a moment to recognize it, but when I did there was no mistaking the source of the wrongness: her irises had darkened. From a bright emerald green they had turned a deep coal color while she had prayed, and even as I watched in shock, they appeared to be growing darker with each passing second. Her expression appeared unfocused, as if she were gazing not at the hospital room but at some other world that she discerned behind the surface veneer of plaster walls and vinyl floor tiles. The sliver of pain in her brow suddenly looked more cruel than wounded. Her entire demeanor exuded a kind of quiet menace that was somehow linked to her physical beauty, as if her loveliness were just a discrete facet of some other, wider reality whose overall character was awful.

Then the moment passed, and I realized she was looking at me. No trace of the sinister expression remained. She offered me a wan half-smile, and after wavering for a moment, I seated myself on the other side of Paul and tried to get a look at her eyes. They were bright green, like a cat's. Without changing position, I folded back into myself mentally and filed away the bizarre incident for later reflection. I had not experienced such a strong hallucinatory episode for quite some time. That it could come on so unexpectedly, without any warning, and in the midst of such an unlikely setting, disturbed me deeply.

We sat for a long time while I tried to figure out why I had come there, and why I was staying, and when I would leave. With a bit of surprise, I realized that I wanted to take Paul's other hand, the one Lisa wasn't holding, and tell him that I forgave him. I wanted that to be his final memory of me, if indeed he was aware of my presence at all.

But it would have been a lie anyway. Sitting there watching Lisa stroke his fingers with her face molded into an expression of loving concern, I didn't feel at all forgiving. The only attitude or emotion I could feel was a semblance of the old shock and desperation, now stiffened with disuse like a crusty wound, that had been my parting feeling toward the both of them three years earlier. And beneath it, that cold fist of deadness that was slowly, subtly squeezing my heart with an ever-tightening grip.

After awhile the wheezing of the respirator began to sound like the wind scudding over the low desert hills. Its dry whisper filled me with an aching desire for solitude, and I breathed a silent sigh of relief that I had not taken Paul's other hand.

III

"I want to ask where you've been." Lisa's voice, soft and smooth, woke me from a stupor. I blinked and realized I had been dozing. Paul was still unconscious, still a mere mechanism of flesh and bone. I looked around for a clock and saw that the one on the bedside table read 1:15 a.m. We had been sitting there for just over an hour, and I had spent most of it trying to stay awake. Apparently, I had failed.

"What?" My voice came out thick and sluggish. The coldness had coagulated in my chest and I was having trouble breathing.

"I want to ask where you've been and what you've done since you left town," she said. "You never called or wrote. We've been worried about you for three years. But I'm afraid you'll be angry if I ask."

I wiped a hand over my face, wincing at the sharp scrape of whiskers against palm, and inwardly agreed with her. By all rights, I should have been angry. She had no right to know how I had chosen to live my life after leaving Farrenton, especially since my departure had been based solely on the fact that I couldn't bear to stay there and see the two of them together.

But something about her presence was exerting a magnetic pull upon me. I had spent the last thousand miles and twenty-six hours steeling my resolve to remain aloof and distant. I had told myself that I was only returning to Farrenton because it would be cruel to refuse a summons under these circumstances. But as I sat there looking across the injured body of my comatose best friend and into the face of the only woman I had ever truly loved, I found I actually *wanted* to tell her what had happened to me. I wanted to shock her with the viciousness of it, to force her to experience a living measure of the pain I had borne in solitude for three years.

The words began slowly but soon gathered momentum. With growing amazement at my own willingness to open up to her like this, I began to tell her of my life without her: of how only a few weeks after I had fled from her and Paul, I had become involved with an activist group devoted to fighting the destruction of the Brazilian rain forest. The story sounded alien and ridiculous to me as I related it, almost as if I were talking about another person. Prior to encountering that activist group I had been the farthest thing from a "joiner." Despite the lip service that my self-conscious spiritual hipness had led me to pay to ecological issues, I had never done a single thing to back that up in concrete action. Nor had I imagined how frighteningly simple such hypocrisy would be to change. A chance encounter in a new city with a man handing out pamphlets on a street corner, an impulsive trip to the address listed on the cover, and one short screening session later, and I found myself seated on a Boeing 757—I, who had never left the continental United States—headed for Brazil to join the protest. Even at the time, I knew that my impulsiveness was mostly driven by my escapist fantasy. I just wanted to flee my past and forget that my two best friends, who were also the two most spiritual people I had ever known, had betrayed me for each other.

The memory of this part enhanced the pain of telling the story to Lisa. It also made it all the more delicious. I began to revel in recalling minute details of sight and sound, taste and smell, image and emotion. I told her of my first impressions of South America when I got off the plane in Sao Paulo: of the stifling heat and humidity, the moist ripe smell of earth and jungle, and the way the horrendous humidity acted like a lens to focus the sunlight and roast one's flesh. I told her of the protest that fizzled after just a few days, the tiny band of friends I made, and the eventual disillusionment I felt when I realized that nothing we did made a difference either for the rain forest or for my personal pain.

Lisa asked no questions while I talked. She appeared mesmerized by my account, and maybe it was her enraptured expression that lulled me so much that when I arrived at the part of my story I had never meant to tell—the part about the revelation or vision I received one night while sleeping in the open air under a mosquito net—I just kept going, as if my words had cast a spell over both of us.

The fact was, after living for several weeks with the constant assault of the jungle noises droning in my ears—all the unidentified swishings and scrapings and screechings—I stopped noticing them. The pungent smells of earth and bark likewise faded from my awareness, until I became as oblivious to them as I was to the stink of my own body in the tropical heat.

But on that single special night, three months into my stay, with no warning or prelude, the jungle suddenly became vivid again. I awoke from a deep sleep into a state of extreme disorientation. With a tinge of panic, I realized that I had utterly lost my bearings. Where was I? Why was I lying in a tent under a net with a cacophony of tropical night buzzing all around me? I lay there in mounting terror with the jungle saturating my senses until my ears actually began to tingle with all the secretive murmurings. My nose stung with the sweat of tree bark and jungle beasts. My tongue stiffened with the tang of mold and grass. My skin inhaled the moist rotten heat of hidden decay.

And I was sickened by the florid life all around me. For no cause that I could discern—and I tried long and hard afterward to divine a reason for it—I was suddenly *horrified* by the organic eruption that was the rain forest. The sole idea that I recalled from reading Sartre in college came to mind at once: *de trop*, "too much." The jungle was *too much*. It was too ripe, too juicy, too pungent, too sharp, too *alive*. That was the crux of the matter: it was the principle of life itself, bursting and blooming all around me, that was a horror.

After that, nothing could be the same. My acquaintances in the activist group, who liked to call themselves my friends but who in truth knew nothing about me, were shocked when I quit them without explanation and left the jungle to return to Sao Paulo. I flew back to the States and tried to reboot my life again, but this proved impossible when I discovered that the midnight vision from Brazil had accompanied me. Leaving the original scene of its onset merely brought the new perception home to inhere in the things that were more familiar to me, as I quickly understood when the oaks, elms, cedars, and walnut trees bristling from the Ozark hills began to inspire the same reaction as the rain forest. I couldn't stop thinking about the root systems of those trees, all twined and knotted like diseased fingers digging into the loamy earth. Nor could I stop thinking about the rodents and birds nesting in those trees, and the snakes and insects toiling in secrecy beneath the matted forest floors, and below even that, the worms and grubs tilling the soil, consigning the whole pungent mass of it back to a primal black organic mash.

After awhile I uprooted again and drifted westward into Oklahoma, then northward and westward into Kansas and Colorado, following no plan. Eventually I found myself in Utah and in the presence of Dr. Malcolm Pryor, professor of vertebrate paleontology at Utah State, who hired me on the spot, on a pure whim, to serve as his informal assistant. I had no training in paleontology or archaeology or any other relevant field. I brought no necessary skills. My only job was to help with the grunt work in his ongoing excavation in the desert land outside Vernal. But he asked very few questions, apparently seeing in me a suitably solitary temperament for the lonely dry work ahead.

It turned out he was right. The arid land of the Utah desert proved a perfect environment for me, since its primary resident life was of the scaly, scrubby kind: junipers and sagebrush, lizards and vultures, the occasional mule deer and coyote. I could forget about the grubs and worms there, where the earth was a baked desert crust. My ontological panic attacks gradually faded as I spent my days helping to uncover carcasses long dead and buried, the remains of lives long desiccated and sealed off from the danger of rot and decay. I often felt a great yearning, so sweet it was painful, when I gazed at the rough desert floor and thought of the dead husks that slept comfortably beneath it.

And the memory of these husks brought me to the present. I stopped talking abruptly. The respirator pumped dryly next to the bed. Paul's face appeared darker than it had before, as if he had somehow heard me speaking from the blackness inside his head. As the spell of my words dissipated, I realized that I didn't know how much of my story had actually passed my lips. I had grown so absorbed in my personal recollections that I might have revealed far more than I had intended.

When I looked at Lisa, she was watching me with a mixed expression of pain and something else, something that might have been wonder or terror. I feared she might be doing her mind-reading thing again, and this sparked my anger.

"So what do you think of me?" I said. "What do you think of your long-lost Stephen, who always wanted to be as spiritual as you and Paul?"

The idea that I might have misjudged her—that I might have *always* misjudged her—did not occur to me until she began to cry again. This time her tears were for me. And they were beautiful to behold.

"Oh, Stephen. Oh, my God. I'm so sorry." She sat with her hands in her lap and her head bowed. When she finally looked up, her cheeks glistened and her eyes flashed with a crystal film. "We both loved you. We both wanted you to stay. I know you only left because we betrayed you. I feel like everything you've suffered is our fault."

These astonishing words hung unchallenged in the air for maybe five seconds before the night nurse entered the room to check on Paul's vitals. She was an unpleasant looking woman with a pear-shaped body and a face full of acne, and she gave me a look of muted disgust, as if she couldn't fully accept that someone with my ragged appearance would be sitting up late with an injured friend. I kept my face blank as she told Lisa that Paul was still stable, while Lisa, for her part, struggled to compose herself and show proper politeness.

When the nurse had departed and we were alone again, the moment of intimacy had passed, and whatever Lisa had been going to say next was lost. I tried not to care, but even when I had retreated back behind the mask of my habitual apathy, I couldn't shake the feeling that I would have wanted to hear her words, even though I knew they could have done nothing but increase my suffering.

IV

By three a.m. my hallucinations had returned. We had sat in total silence for over an hour, and my strung out state finally brought me to the point of full-blown delirium. With horror I realized that I was slipping into that awful state of warped perception again.

In one of the visions, I saw glowing bands of light connecting Lisa's heart to mine. The same golden strands also connected me to Paul, and Paul to her. We formed, I saw, three corners of a web of spiritual energy, but instead of peace or joy, the vision brought only shock and revulsion. The last thing I wanted was to be connected to these two people in this intimate fashion, and I fought violently against the image.

My struggles only increased the force of the vision, which was soon joined by a second one in which Paul and Lisa appeared more plantlike than human. The transition was not subtle. I simply looked away from her once, and when I looked back at her again, her face had disappeared and been replaced by a beautiful multicolored blossom. When I looked down at Paul, the same change had occurred. Instead of looking into his face I was looking into a thick nest of lush, satiny petals. Their bodies, too, had transformed, and were now delicate stalks of deep green, encased in a translucent covering of cellulose skin that revealed a clear liquid circulating through a network of veins. When I looked down at my own body, I saw only a blackened trunk, like the remains of a twisted tree after a forest fire. The blips and beeps of the medical monitors morphed into screeches and caws, and soon I couldn't tell whether I was still seated in a hospital room or lying in a tent in the rain forest.

After an hour of feeling immobilized by these impressions—which, despite their surface beauty, were no less nightmarish than my earlier vision of Lisa's darkening eyes—I awoke as if from a dream and arose on shaky legs to see if the night nurse was still at her desk. A moment later, after bidding Lisa goodnight (and noticing with relief that her face had returned to normal), I followed the nurse down the hallway to a hospitality room, feeling Lisa's gaze caress my back the entire time as she stepped into the hallway to watch me depart.

The hospitality room had a bed and bathroom, but I had left my bag of clean clothes out in the van, so I didn't shower. I just stretched out on the bed fully clothed and tried to sleep. But the mattress was hard and the pillow stale, and I soon arose and went to the bathroom for a drink of water. It tasted bitter and musty out of the paper cup, and I poured most of it down the drain. When I returned to bed, all I could think to do was to get in my van and leave, or else go back and sit with Lisa again. Both options were intolerable.

Finally, I did something I had not done for years: I laid the pillow on the floor in front of the bed and seated myself on it. Then I crossed my legs in a rather stiff half-lotus, having lost most of my former limberness from lack of practice, and focused on my breathing.

Everything slowed down after only a few minutes. All night I had been feeling like an out-of-control river rafter being swept along by a dangerous current. Now I started to feel safely aloof from the situation, and a familiar inner image resurfaced from my former meditative days: that I was safely distanced from my troubles, tucked away in a protected cave from whence I could survey my inner and outer landscape with a semblance of objectivity.

I spent maybe half an hour savoring the sweet sense of distance. Then the ache in my legs became too much to bear, and I had to stop. When I arose and stretched, the feeling of restlessness returned instantly.

I did not consciously choose to avoid Lisa when I ventured out into the hallway. I merely happened to notice a sign on the wall announcing the presence of a chapel at the end of the next wing, and before I knew what was happening, my feet were carrying me in that direction.

The irony of my heading wasn't lost on me. From informal Zen meditation to Roman Catholic chapel in less than five minutes. It truly was a night for crossing wires.

V

I spent nearly half an hour alone in the chapel before Lisa found me. My first impression upon entering it was a sense of awe. I had known the hospital was a Catholic institution, but that hadn't prepared me for the elaborateness of what revealed itself before me. The very word "chapel" was inadequate, for the place was more like an entire church built seven stories above ground level. I stared up at the chiseled arches and saints, traced the lines of the sacred figures with their frozen gestures of holiness, and experienced a palpable sense of the numinous spilling out from the gray stonework like a physical wave.

After basking for a while in the glow of the rich ornamentation, I began to skirt the perimeter of the church and study the depictions of the Stations of the Cross mounted high on the walls. This was an element of Catholic spirituality that had always fascinated me. I studied Jesus' face in each scene, observed his expression of intense suffering, and tried to imagine the awesome depth of his sensations, both spiritual and physical, during the experience of his passion.

At last I paused before the altar, turned my face upward toward the giant crucifix where Christ hung in agony on the front wall, and then backed away and sat down on the third pew, where at last the enormity of recent events came home to me. My abrupt transition in just over thirty hours from the Utah desert to this hushed place of holy reflection seemed positively unreal, as did the fact of Lisa's waiting for me in a hospital room nearby where Paul lay dead for all practical purposes, having been reduced to a mindless engine running only by means of external aid.

In the silence, a memory spontaneously resurfaced: of Paul sitting before me on a cushion in the spare bedroom of our shared rental home, which we had decked out as a Zendo. He was smiling at me with that good-natured expression of peace and wisdom that I had come to cherish. And he was saying, "It's so easy. This is all there is to it. *Now*, outside of your head and right here with the in-your-face reality of the present moment, is the whole point. There's nothing secret about it. Enlightenment is like a big, friendly joke." When I balked and said it was still beyond my ability to grasp, he laughed, squeezed my shoulder, and said "That's nothing but enlightenment, too." And amazingly, he actually made me feel better about my spiritual dullness. I felt lighter in his presence, more alive and aware, more capable of understanding the things I had always longed to understand. He really seemed to regard his advanced state as something not to be coveted, but to be shared freely with dullards like me, and more than anything else this marked him in my eyes as the icon of everything I hoped to become.

The memory dissipated when I sensed the presence of someone else in the chapel with me. Her perfume rode the breeze ahead of her and reached me before she did. Then she was sitting beside me and I was raising my head from my hands. I hadn't been crying, but it had been something like that. My face felt twisted into knots by the forces struggling behind it.

"I thought I'd find you here," she said. "I could see it in your face. You needed to get away and reflect."

It was really too much, the way she read me as if we had been together only yesterday. Somehow she looked even prettier when I was angry with her.

"*What* could you see in my face, Lisa? How the hell do you always do that?"

"I wish I could tell you. I really do." Her voice trembled and her eyes begin to glitter with tears again. "It's like seeing another level to things. Do you remember learning to read when you were young? First there were just black marks and shapes scattered on a page. Then, like magic, they started to mean something. It's kind of like that."

"Well, it scares me. It *always* scared me." I turned my face away, searching for neutral space, and found I was now staring at Christ's nail-pierced feet on the large crucifix hanging above us.

"And you don't think it scares *me?*" she said. "Do you want to guess how much more of what's going on with Paul right now I can see than you can? Do you think I *want* to be able to see where he's going? Do you think I like seeing him drifting away?" She was crying for real now, and I had nothing to say in return.

"Please," she said at last, struggling for control, "I have to ask you something. It sounds insane. I know it will sound insane, especially since I know how much you must hate me. But I have to ask." She moved closer to me on the pew, and I tried not to smell her perfume or look at her breasts.

"First," she said, "I have to tell you something. Please just listen. Please don't make up your mind until I'm finished. Can you promise me that?" I avoided her eyes but said yes. Her breath was still labored from crying, and I could feel it on my face and hands, hot and moist, like a wet feather.

"Paul and I have been growing in new directions since you left. Our spiritual lives have taken a new turn. We've been exploring some things you may have heard of, certain pagan traditions with ancient roots. They're all about loving the earth and learning to feel at home with her. We've been learning to experience nature as a kind of enchanted garden that's powered by spirit and permeated with love." She eyed me then, and for once, in a moment of insight so intense it caused my breath to catch, I knew what she was going to say before she said it: "I think what we've been cultivating is the exact opposite of the vision you had in the rain forest."

My revulsion was immediate. She had no right to speak of my experience. It was mine, my own special revelation and cross to bear. Every instinct I possessed told me that I didn't want to hear where she was going with this, especially not if she was going to try and demonstrate some connection between what I had experienced in South America and my spiritual past with her and Paul. But in the face of her fresh-wept beauty, and amid the holy hush of the chapel, I felt strangely helpless to protest.

"I really am afraid that what you've experienced is our fault," she continued. "I'm only just now learning about it, but there's a web of invisible interconnections between all of us. It's so intricate and beautiful. It's like a spiritual network that joins everything on the planet. Sometimes these connections are especially strong, like the ones between you and Paul and me." I thought of my hallucination of glowing cords earlier, but said nothing.

"I think," she said, "that when you left, we may have accidentally sent a terrible energy rushing in your direction. I think when Paul and I started trying to fall in love with the earth so soon after we hurt you the way we did, you received the opposite end of it. I'm not really sure how these things work. I may not even be sure what I'm trying to say right now. But I think you ended up seeing the opposite of everything we were trying to understand. When you described your vision in the jungle, it sounded exactly like the dark side of the beauty we're seeking."

And there it was again, that cold fist squeezing the breath out of my chest. I barely had time to register it before she did an extraordinary thing: without breaking the rhythm of her words, she reached out a hand and laid it on my thigh. It was a simple gesture, but it sent shockwaves rolling through my entire being. More specifically, it sent tingles crawling up into my groin, and a long-buried part of me suddenly lit up, glowing like a spark, at the thought that maybe, just maybe, Lisa's reasons for searching me out and asking me to come home had been more complex than I had suspected.

"I'm not asking you to believe all this," she was saying. "I'm not trying to convince you. I just want you to know how we've thought of these things over the past few years, and how we've regretted doing what we did. Earlier tonight, when you told me what you went through, I realized the extent of the damage we've done." After a pause, she scooted even closer, and my slight spark of arousal ignited into a small flame. It was fascinating, really, to watch it all happening from a vantage point of objectivity. For I still felt that the greater part of me was tucked away back in that safe meditative cave hidden high up on a riverbank. My flame of arousal, now growing into a bona fide blaze of lust, was something happening at a distance, something I was observing as a spectator. So was Lisa's beautiful face moving ever closer to mine, and also the feel of her delicate red-nailed fingers gripping my thigh with growing urgency. I knew the feeling of remoteness and safety had to be an illusion. But this didn't take away from the heady reality of its seeming, nor from the pleasure I derived from it.

She was speaking to me in a seductive whisper now: "But I do want to ask you something. Just listen to me before you decide. There's a way for us to get Paul back. The three of share a special energy. I know you've felt it. Maybe you've even seen it. The thing is, we can *use* that energy. You and I can call out to Paul, wherever he is. We can send him a message. We can light a beacon to show him the way home, and we can give him the strength to make the journey." When she batted her eyes and assumed a kind of coy expression, her meaning was instantly clear, and the nature of her request would have been obvious even without her next words: "All we have to do is reconnect, you and I, on the most intimate level." When her red lips curled in what might have been the faintest of wicked smiles, I felt waves of warmth crash through me.

"*Please*," she said. "It will heal you, too. It will take away the vision of *too much*. We'll balance in the middle, and Paul and I will take back the energy we aimed at you. You can have your life back." If she did not send the next words directly into my brain as a telepathic transmission, then she must have spoken them without moving her lips: *You can have me back, too.*

By that point she had no need to say anything else, for I was hopelessly hers. She had worked her magic with consummate skill. The serpent had charmed the bird, and I was consumed with lust. And what I lusted after was as much my former self and my own redemption as it was Lisa and her body. I wanted to possess her and regain my soul in a single stroke. And if we could help Paul in the process, in some obscure way that made no sense to me, then so much the better.

These thoughts and desires whirled within me as she took me by the hand and led me from the chapel. The giddy feeling helped to augment the sensation of spectatorship, and so it seemed almost like a cinematic special effect when I experienced—I actually *experienced*, as a physical perception—the hallowed atmosphere of the chapel folding back in on itself like a flower, preparing to lie in wait for the next soul-hungry supplicant. I seemed to glide above the floor when she pulled me down the hallway and toward the room I had entered as a stranger only a few short hours ago.

The floating feeling continued until she turned to face me beside Paul's bed, where I thought suddenly of the prehistoric bone lying partially uncovered back in the desert. The memory brought back a sweet stab of pain, and there was a moment of confusion as my resolve threatened to come unraveled. What in God's name was I doing? What did I think it would accomplish? How could it end any way but badly? I realized everything was happening too fast, it was all rushing ahead with a seemingly inbuilt logic that was in fact completely irrational.

But then her hands were on me, pulling me down to the floor, and they banished all other concerns. Her flesh-and-blood warmth and softness were irresistibly real. The memory of the dry-desert bone with its accompanying dry-desert sadness couldn't compete with this vivid reality. "Stepping out of your head and into the reality of the present is the whole point," I heard Paul's remembered voice saying. Common sense was out the window, too. I couldn't think about the fact that the hospital staff might walk in on us. I couldn't think about Paul lying comatose beside us on the bed. I could think only of the heat of her body, and the pressure of her touch, and the wetness of her lips, like the petals of a flower in the rain forest, kissing first my eyes and then my mouth, drawing me out of myself and into a fleshy reality that was far more ecstatic than any experience of isolated spectatorship could ever be.

VI

The flow of time became a river of burning gold as everything went all liquid and surreal. The sound of my breath filled the whole universe like salt water sizzling on a cosmic ocean shore. I had never been so sexually inflamed. All my repressed rage and horror flowed through my limbs like a torrent, and focused itself on the burning point of contact between us. She was on top of me, and I grappled violently with her back and buttocks, pulling her so tightly against me that I worried I might snap her in two like a doll. She received it all without complaint. In fact, her passion, if anything, surpassed mine. She swiped her tongue over my lips and eyelids. Her nails scored parallel lines down my neck and chest. Her hair whipped my face like the wings of a frenzied bird.

When she had her orgasm, she arched so violently that I thought my hipbones would break. A moment later my own climax sent my head spasming backwards, and the crack of the floor tile against my skull exploded stars into my vision. I lost consciousness briefly.

When I returned to myself, she had risen and was bending naked over Paul's unconscious form. The air was chilly against my cooling flesh, and my eyes felt hot and gritty. I watched her caress Paul's face and speak tender words to him. Her nudity, which only moments before had been a veritable feast for my starving eyes, now looked slick and rubbery. She cooed to him as if he were a baby, imploring him to come back from whatever dark dimension had swallowed him. Left to myself and my thoughts, there was no way to feel that I was somehow outside or above the situation. It was all too real, and I was sickened at the thought of what I had just done.

But when I moved to sit up and cover myself, I found to my astonishment that my limbs were stiff as a corpse's. My arms felt as if they were shackled with lead weights. It took all my effort just to raise my head an inch. An invisible weight rested on my chest like an anvil, constricting my ribcage and forcing me to struggle for breath. Even as I began to worry that the crack to my head might have really injured me, the physical constriction gave way to a deeper one, and with astonished horror I felt something dragging my spirit down into a bottomless well.

Sex had never been an ultimately pleasurable experience for me. The feeling of lassitude afterward, as if I had been attacked by some kind of parasite and drained to the point of death, had invariably spoiled it. I had always felt like a walking dead man for days afterward. It had taken me years to connect my occasional feelings of an almost lethal sluggishness with my rare sexual encounters, and once I had made the connection, I had determined to try and forget that side of life altogether.

Now, it was as if all those former spiritual sappings had been mere preludes to this one great stealing of energy. I was falling backwards down a mine shaft. The ceiling receded. Lisa's naked form grew taller above me. The wheezing of the respirator reverberated like whispers in a cathedral. The heaviness in my limbs began to dissipate, not because I was coming to life but because I was plummeting inward and leaving my body behind.

Above me, beside me, Lisa looked more and more like an elongated figure in a surrealist painting. Still leaning over Paul's body, she reached down a rubbery stick-arm and probed between her thighs, gathering some of our fluids onto her fingers. Then she raised them to his lips and continued to whisper things that no longer sounded like language, but like a wordless chant, harsh and melodic.

A moment later his hand twitched. The rhythm of the respirator grew more insistent as it struggled with a competing rhythm. And Lisa uttered a sharp cry of joy.

The room continued to recede. I continued to fall backwards into a well of infinite seclusion. And yet I saw and heard everything around me. There was no end to the receding, no far edge of exile where I would find myself cut off from all contact with the external world. It was as if a hole had been punched in the back of my private cave to reveal an infinite, sucking void on the other side. The thought arose that in the hell of black emptiness opening out below me, I would not be allowed even the small comfort of forgetfulness. I would not be allowed to reside alone in a dank spiritual dungeon where I could forget that I had once tasted the air of a rain forest and smelled the dust of a desert. There would be nothing but distance—distance between the world and me, distance between everything I had ever loved and the possibility of grasping it, distance between my innate longing for spiritual wholeness and my ability to pursue it.

The restraint on my limbs let go abruptly. I blinked and rose to my elbows. Lisa was rushing to put on her clothes and throwing mine at me. In his bed, Paul was stirring with ever more vigorous motions. I knew I had just participated in some sort of rite, but I was totally ignorant of its nature. I only knew that my life force had been transferred to Paul, and that he had gladly accepted it. For this was, after all, nothing but the logical extension of the theft he had committed three years ago. The little moment of happiness unfolding beside me, where he had opened his eyes, and where he and Lisa were touching each other's faces with shared tears of reunion, was not meant for me. I was excluded by a gulf that now separated me not only from them but from everyone and everything, from all of the ten thousand things that made up this vast and dismal universe.

I rose on legs that belonged to a dead man and finished putting on my clothes. With the eyes of a dead man, I surveyed for a final time the sight of a shared love that should have been mine. And with these new eyes, I *annihilated* it all. I brought the sight within me and felt it slip away instantly, back through that hole in the cave wall, where it sparked out into ambient nothingness and disappeared forever. No memory was left, no feeling, no emotion or reaction to the things before me. The sight of Paul and Lisa was being born anew in my consciousness with each passing instant, and with each new instant I was devouring it and watching it be reborn again. It was like swallowing an ocean and finding that I was still thirsty. It was like eating the world and finding that I was still ravenous. I watched the two of them press down under the weight of my gaze, trembling with an unknown terror that confused them both, clinging to each other for warmth and comfort. Then I turned and left the room without looking back.

The hallway was still dim with nighttime illumination. The nurse still sat reading her paperback novel in a pale aureole of lamplight. When I looked at her, she shifted in her seat and glanced about her with a look of confusion and fear. She did not appear to see me when I passed right by her. I shared the elevator to the ground floor with an old black man pushing a janitor's cart. He appeared not to notice my presence, not even when I looked directly at him and saw his face blanch with dread as the visual impression of him passed through me on its way to everlasting oblivion. When I exited through the lobby and passed several people bound on early morning errands, none of them noticed me, but they gasped and nearly stumbled when I took the sight of them into myself.

A light rain was falling in the parking lot. I paused just outside the sliding glass doors to lift my face to the murky sky, where a delicate flash of lightning outlined a mountain of dark clouds. A moment later, a rumble of thunder rattled the windows behind me. I stood there with the rain spattering my face and hands like tappings on a distant roof. And from my fixed position there in the midst of it all, rooted at the center of my perceptual universe like the eye of a cyclone, I *annihilated* everything: the clouds and thunder, windows and pavement, even the slick yellow reflections of the street lamps in the myriad puddles dotting the asphalt. The depth inside me was bottomless, and the life around me to be devoured, infinite.

The rain kept falling for hours while the eastern sky behind me grew gray with the approaching dawn, and while I stood looking at everything with a new pair of eyes that would never grow old, and that would accompany me to deserts or rain forests or wherever I might go next, devouring and renewing all things in my path, and forever finding them insufficient.

The dawn, when it came, was cold.

But of *course* everything was all wrong. Derek knew it the minute he opened his eyes and perceived the vileness resounding from every angle and object in the room. Indeed, how could it be otherwise in a red-glowing world where *the stench of blacksouls mounts to a deadening sky?*

Then he awoke fully and realized he was dream-thinking again. It took even longer than usual for the waking world to slide into focus while his psyche struggled to flush away the dregs of the putrescent dreamland that had lately been casting an ever-lengthening shadow across his days. And even after the mental purification was otherwise accomplished, when he could think, feel, look, and smell without the black-red reality of the otherworld interposing itself between his awareness and the prosy solidity of the white-walled master bedroom of his two-thousand-square-foot suburban house—even then, he still caught a glimpse of wrongness pressing in at every conceivable crack, hitching a ride on the fiery beams of sunlight that bled through the drapes, peering with beady black eyes through the dark spots in the mottled wooden texture of the bureau next to the bed.

It radiated with an especial intensity from his left side. He turned his head and regarded Linda as she lay next to him, still encased in sleep, wrapped in a bedsheet cocoon with her pale lips parted and a half-snore dragging in the back of her throat. He felt his testicles draw up as if in anticipation of a blow. Surely, he reasoned with himself, his recent inability to tolerate his wife's presence had nothing to do with her, and everything to do with his own secret disorder, whose most dramatic manifestation occurred in those regular oneiric journeys through a land of rotten wrongness.

When he stood, the familiar creak of the loose floorboard beside the bed rippled up through his leg and into his groin like a snake seeking a warm cave. He shivered and shuffled to the bathroom to urinate and shower.

Standing in front of the toilet with his boxer briefs pulled down, he considered calling the office to tell Candace, his secretary, that he was ill and would be staying home that day. The idea of temporary seclusion was exceptionally attractive in light of the fact that Wilfred J. Tyson was his first appointment of the morning, scheduled for nine a.m. sharp "or I'm gonna stab and gutfuck somebody"—as Tyson himself had phrased it in his charming mid-Texan manner—and that the meeting would almost certainly spell the death of Derek's legal career. But then he thought of the maddening wrongness that still flitted like a cloud of black wings about the edges of everything, and found to his surprise and semi-relief that his dreadful unpreparedness for the meeting seemed, well, not so very important. Why not just go ahead and see the thing through to its limping conclusion? "Why not?" he said aloud, and then blinked at the cavelike reverberation of his voice off the slick porcelain surfaces.

In the shower his eyesight went momentarily gray, as if someone had switched off the light. He came to himself crouched in the tub with the hot water beating against his back and clouds of steam billowing up around him like fog from a midnight lake. Afterward, when he stood before the sink and shaved, his hand was trembling. The blade nicked his throat and drew a bead of blood, which transfixed him with its crimson-on-snow vibrancy. A blackwinged shadow fluttered in the corner of his eye. He caught a microflash vision of something he had seen recently, perhaps while crouched in the shower—crouched low and happy in the swirling mist with the hot water beading on his back, *the happy dark heat, pulsating feather of foulness*—

The faucet sang a tinkling little tune. Water spiraled merrily down the drain of the pedestal sink. Lather and whiskers littered the porcelain. As if in a trance, he wiped it all off and used the same towel on his face, hardly feeling the scrape of soft cotton against his skin.

He sat at the kitchen table while Linda poured some sort of whole-grained, prepackaged breakfast substance into a plastic bowl. "What's wrong, honey?" she asked, setting the bowl before him and taking a seat at the opposite chair.

"Nothing," he said. A single spoonful told him the cereal was stale and the milk had tipped over into the pungent no-man's-land between liquid and solid. But he sucked on the mushy mass anyway, savoring it with a grimace, and found he couldn't tell whether the staleness and sourness resided in the food or on his tongue. And still the tingling buffer from the bathroom, like a buzzing wall of bees, remained interposed between him and the external world.

"You're not still worried about your meeting, are you?" Linda reached out and tousled his dark hair. "You've worked on it all week. If anything, you're overprepared. Don't worry. You'll do fine."

"Sure," he said. "Right. Like I said, nothing's wrong." She went to rinse the dishes while saying something about getting together with Steve for dinner that night. He ignored her chatter and watched her body closely from behind. She was wrapped in a blue terrycloth bathrobe, the fuzzy fabric pulled tight against her rump. The memory of her naked body arose unbidden from some black well of the past, from the mental ruins of another lifetime when he had actually craved the sight of her white skin and soft-rounded curves. Hot shadows rustled at the edges of his eyes and brain. His stomach lurched and squirted a jet of sourness up into his throat.

His face was a carven mask when she kissed him at the door. She remained close for a moment afterwards, her ghastly ape's face thrust forward into his own, gazing quizzically into his eyes. "Don't forget," she said. When he said nothing, she helpfully clarified. "Steve. Dinner. With us. Tonight. Remember?"

He managed something like a nod, and then he turned away and walked slowly out to his car, probing the fresh cut on his throat with a trembling hand, feeling her planted there behind him and watching him from the open doorway, remembering the dream-thoughts whispering in the steam while he crouched low like some glowering little creature of fable.

❧

The commute to work was a breathtaking kaleidoscope of wrongness. In just five years' time the small town had exploded into a thriving suburbanesque city, complete with a raging glut of unwonted traffic, resulting in a permanent nightmare of highway construction that seemed to Derek like the engineering equivalent of emergency angioplasty—a metaphor that he saw completed in the arterial pulsing of vehicles, start-stop, start-stop, through the various detours and halts of the whole bloody-tangled mess. He often reflected that maybe it would have been better just to let the old town die quietly of heart failure instead of reviving and reinventing it for the flashier fate of death by nervous seizure.

Halfway to his office he switched on the radio. The tuner scanned the stations like—and the simile seemed natural—a schizophrenic mind surveying the spectrum of its inner anarchy. Pink Floyd and Erik Satie serenaded him in five-second bursts, followed by Kansas and Count Basie. A preacher with a northern accent spoke up momentarily, asking, "Who knows what is truly human except the human spirit within a man?" and then answering, "So also no one comprehends what is truly God's except the Spirit of God." A southern-sounding preacher shouted from the next station, pounding an unseen pulpit and obviously relishing his words: "Their slain shall be cast out, and the stench of their corpses shall rise! The mountains shall flow with their blood! All the host of heaven shall rot away, and the skies roll up like a scroll!"

The tuner tripped ahead yet again, cutting the preacher off in mid-jeremiad. Derek punched the button to stop it at next station; the changes were hurting his head. For the remainder of the commute he listened to a man speaking in measured, cultured tones about an esoteric topic whose import must have been explained earlier, at the top of the hour, and whose overall gist was thus obscure. "These and many words and names," the man said, "do not tell us *what* it is, but they do confirm *that* it is. They also point to its mysteriousness. We cannot know what exactly we are referring to because its nature remains shadowy, revealing itself mainly in hints, intuitions, whispers, and the sudden urges and oddities that disturb your life that we might continue to call symptoms. That the daimon has your interest at heart may be the part of the theory particularly hard to accept."

Derek's office was a nondescript architectural approximation composed of beige stonework and dark-tinted windows, squatting in semi-privacy on the outskirts of a street somewhere near the business district. It looked like wrongness personified as he drove up and parked. The fluorescent lights and cardboard ceiling panels were an ache to his eyeballs when he walked through the front door, and the electronic chime drilled into his molars with a nauseating pain.

Candace, she-of-the-overpainted-eyes-and-gargantuan-breasts, looked up and wished him a cheery good morning from her spot behind the reception counter. As always, he found it hard to remember that she was only twenty-two years old when her appearance and demeanor rendered her overtly ageless in the exotic manner he had come to associate with raw female sexuality. She asked, "Would you like some coffee, Mr. Warner?"

He said no and then offered, "Thanks." She smiled and continued looking at him. She was wearing the green bodice dress again, the one that encased her breasts like a second skin and gapped dramatically at the neck whenever she reached for pens or paperclips, or even moved to brush back a lock of her cherry-auburn hair. He paused for a long moment, and then he was *crouched in the shower with blacksmear eyes, scalding in steam, beating blackwater*—and then he blinked, turned, and walked down the hallway.

Thirty seconds later he ran to the speakerphone in the conference room, punched the call button with a trembling finger, and demanded, "Where's the case files?" He waited. "Candace? Hello?"

The speakerphone blipped and then her voice said, "—don't know, Mr. Warner. I haven't been back there yet today. Maybe the cleaning service moved them?"

"I thought they worked Fridays, not Thursdays."

Blip. "—just changed their schedule this week. I'm sorry, I meant to tell you." She had never learned to wait for the intercom function to engage fully before she spoke, even though he had explained it to her a dozen times. He felt like throttling her.

He turned from the phone without replying, waited to hear the *click* of the connection's closing, and uttered a firm, quiet "Fuck." Then he went into a low-grade panic. A crashing, banging search of every closet, drawer, and box in the conference and storage rooms, and also a frantic dig through the dumpster out back, turned up nothing

He returned to the conference room gasping and shaking and wondering how it was possible for fifteen manila folders, all bearing the name "Tyson" printed in prominent black marker, simply to disappear. No one on the cleaning crew could possibly have wanted them. A thief would have taken something else. Candace was afraid even to look at them, so severely had he threatened her about their importance. His thoughts accelerated to whirlwind speed while he cringed under the smug gaze of the leatherbound law books lining the dark wooden shelves in regal rows.

He bowed his head and reached up to massage his eyeballs. Splotchy colored lights blossomed in the darkness behind his lids, shimmering like luminescent fog above the surface of a vast reedy lake—

—and then it was night in conference room, dark and deserted, and a misshapen Dwarf was entering through a strange angle at the intersection of two walls, waddling over to the table, seizing the files, and spiriting them away to a misshapen kingdom on the other side of that otherworldly access point where dark winds howled over a black corroded plain and Derek *crushed in the shower, inkydark eyes beading blood upon his throat*—

An explosion of glass brought him back to himself. He saw crystalline shards littering the carpet next to a mangled lampshade Then he realized a table lamp had been flung against one of the bookcases. Moreover, the culprit was his own outstretched hand.

The speakerphone blipped. "—you there? Mr. Warner? Are you all right?"

His throat erupted and his mouth worked without his conscious volition. "For Christ's sake, of course I'm here!"

A pause. And then of course, naturally, he should have known, her voice came back after another *blip* to say "—is here for his appointment. He says he knows he's early but he has several other things waiting for him."

So. Tyson was standing right there at the counter with Candace, probably eyeing her epic cleavage and smirking at the fact that he had heard Derek's outburst. There was no remedy for it, nothing to do but go ahead and see this thing through. The very helplessness of the thought rekindled a spark of the comforting resignation he had embraced earlier at the house. As he walked up the hallway to face his fate, he felt his brain being gnawed from behind by the hallucinatory memory of the distorted Dwarf and its barren wasteland of a world.

"Morning, Derek!" Tyson drawled at the sight of him. "I hope I'm not too early. Sounds like you're having one hell of a morning." He grinned and stuck out a ring-encrusted hand, which Derek grasped automatically. Tyson's bushy brown eyebrows and million-dollar tan, his hand-tailored suit and bolo tie, his chic ostrich-leather boots and cowboy hat with its gaudy Texas star embroidered on the front, were all unchanged. So was his manner, as Derek observed when the man refused to make eye contact with him while they shook hands, choosing instead to glance to the side and give Candace a rakish wink. It was altogether typical behavior for the sixties-ish oil tycoon.

Derek also realized for the first time that the man could undoubtedly take Candace right then and there if he wanted to, right on the reception counter, despite his craggy, unhandsome face with which he somehow managed to radiate charm through sheer force of attitude. Derek imagined them coupling like sweaty animals under the fluorescent lights, in front of the plate-glass windows, gasping and growling while he himself crouched in the conference room *a greedy-eyed Dwarf crunching bones in the blackdark—*

"Fine, everything's fine," he heard his voice say in a smooth professional tone. "Come on back, Mr. Tyson." He led the obscenely rich oil man back to the cramped little office with the "D. Warner" nameplate on the door, wondering for the thousandth time why somebody like Wilfred J. Tyson would pick a small-time lawyer like himself for legal representation—and one who lived three states away, no less, more than five hundred miles from the city where Tyson Oil was based. He had long thought the answer must lie in those magically vanished files, which detailed with marvelous clarity Tyson's shady business dealings and financial misrepresentations. A small-time lawyer located so very far outside the circles that Tyson normally inhabited was so much less conspicuous than his big-time, big-city counterparts.

Or maybe the man just got off on dealing with lesser beings that he could manipulate and humiliate. Derek had never been able to decide which of the two explanations seemed more likely.

He seated himself in his leather executive chair and motioned for Tyson to pick one of the fabric-upholstered client versions. They faced each other over the desk, both of them waiting for Derek to say something. The question didn't need to be asked, of course. He knew Tyson was there for an account, delivered in person, of how Derek had engineered a legal miracle to rescue his client from the consequences of his latest dishonest dealings. And indeed, Derek had worked for weeks and managed to come up with an absolute ringer of a plan. That was the other possible angle to explain Tyson's retaining of him, since in his own milieu, on his own level, Derek was a young hotshot-on-the-rise.

But hotshot or not, the whole issue had become, in one fell swoop, utterly moot and meaningless. The full understanding of this fact came only now, as he sat staring helplessly into Tyson's hawkish eyes. The files were gone—whether to Dwarf World or a more prosaic locale didn't matter—and with them had gone all chance of success, and now Derek, too, was waiting for his own words, waiting for some sort of brilliant verbal song and dance to erupt spontaneously from his mouth. It *had* to come, or else he was finished, and not just career-wise. The consequences of disappointing this man would surely be severe. Tyson was famous not only for his refusal to tolerate failure but for his swiftness in punishing it whenever it occurred.

But of course, naturally, the saving words didn't come. How *could* such words emerge into a world where absolutely everything, from Derek's framed law diploma hanging on the wall behind him like a grinning accusation, to his pathetic desire to please this unpleasant man, to his lust for an air-headed, nubile secretary, to the walking corpse of a wife who waited for him at home like an undead symbol of all the wrong choices he had made in life—where everything, all of it, every last item and element, reeked to the skies of *wrongness?*

Abruptly, like the arrival of a perfumed breeze, the buzzing, tingling barrier that had encased him earlier in the morning reappeared and began to isolate him from the room. He gasped and felt suddenly weightless. His mouth opened, and it was just as if he needed to cough, to expel an odd blockage from his throat, but instead what came were words—words he had not chosen, words he could hardly believe he was hearing, and they were being spoken by *a blackbrain Dwarf crouched low in a bloody tub.*

The Dwarf said, "You fucking monster."

Tyson blinked. His expert smile faltered. He had been right in the middle of lighting a cigar, and now the flame sprouted uselessly from the shiny gold lighter he held in his right hand. He removed the cigar from his mouth and said, "Excuse me?"

"I said I lost the files. I said you're going to prison. I said your life is over." Derek smiled with the Dwarf. "You fucking monster."

Tyson's smile faded completely. His thumb released the lighter button, snuffing the bright flame. And before the man's predictable disbelief and rage set in, before he began to sputter and curse and rant, Derek and the Dwarf were both pleased to note that their performance had elicited a real shock. Terror and bewilderment were still evident even now behind the blustering façade of Tyson's fury.

It was really astonishingly easy, this act of career suicide. Derek let the scene play out, listening passively to threats aimed at himself and his family, destruction called down upon everyone and everything he held dear, and finally violence sworn against his person. He said nothing through it all, allowing the Dwarf to witness and absorb the energy of the moment.

And finally it was over, and Tyson was rising from his chair red-faced and quivering. "You—you—." He actually sputtered as he searched for an epithet that would convey the depth of his outrage. Derek stood up. Tyson backed away. "You're gonna regret . . . You small-time son-of-a—"

"Have you ever carved wood?" Derek's voice chopped off Tyson's sputtering invective like a knife lopping off a limb, shocking them both into momentary silence. Derek hadn't known he was going to say such a thing, and now he listened with fascination to the speech that began to emerge from his mouth.

"When I was a boy," he said, "I used to pick up sticks in the forest around my house and carve them into all kinds of shapes. I especially liked to peel back the bark of a branch and see the white woodflesh. I liked the way it looked, the way it smelled, the way it felt." He reached up unthinkingly and began to massage the cut on his throat. "I haven't thought of that in years."

Tyson took a step backward toward the door. Derek looked down and saw that his own hand had picked up a sharp silver letter opener. He twirled it with his fingers, and it seemed just like a feather, a strange, silvery feather with a razor-edged quill. He looked back up at Tyson with the feather growing heavier in his hand. "What do you think it does to a person," he said, "when you squeeze what's inside him into the wrong shape?"

He moved as if to come around the desk. Tyson fled. A moment later Derek heard the sound of the front door bursting open and the electronic chime singing its meaningless song.

The phone blipped. "—Warner?" Candace's voice trembled so near and yet so very far, all the way on the other side of that black electronic box that still linked him to the world he had inhabited only moments ago. "What—what happened?"

Before he could answer, the Dwarf told him that dangerous men would surely show up before long to vent the Texan's rage upon anybody they could find. So he said, "Listen, I'm taking the rest of the day off. Why don't you take off, too? Just make a sign and stick it in the window. Tell everybody we'll be back on Monday. Go shopping or something."

There was no reply for a moment. Then: *Blip*. "Is—is everything all right?" *My God,* he thought, *she actually used the phone correctly.* A surge of warmth flooded through him.

Then she said, "Derek?" It was the first time she had ever addressed him by his first name. Visions of huge-nippled breasts bursting through bodice and buttons spilled through his brain like candy. But his new inner sense told him unequivocally that he simply couldn't pursue them, he couldn't answer the invitation contained in her use of his name, because there was something else he had to do, a task whose fulfillment would exert a positively talismanic effect upon the shape of the remainder of his life.

He did not answer her query, instead leaving their final contact deliciously unresolved. He slipped out the back entrance, past the dumpster and around the building to his car. As he drove away he watched the office building reflected in the rearview mirror. It appeared crusty and dilapidated, like an ancient, abandoned prison, and it stood in stark relief against a lurid sky full of weirdly churning clouds, all red and black and ashy like a charcoal drawing.

❦

The commute home was a voyage through a transformed world. He sailed through the highway construction without a hitch, as if pulled along by an invisible current. Road crews paused in their labors to look up with startled expressions as he passed. Fellow motorists veered away and stared wide-eyed through their windows. The radio spoke from the same station he had left it on earlier, the same cultured male voice talking in the same quiet, smooth tones: ". . . a *diabolical* mysticism, a sort of religious mysticism turned upside down. The same sense of ineffable importance in the smallest events, the same texts and words coming with new meanings, the same voices and visions and leadings and missions, the same controlling extraneous powers; only this time the emotion is pessimistic: instead of consolations we have desolations; the meanings are dreadful; and the powers are enemies to life. The classic mysticism and these lower mysticisms spring from the same mental level, from that great subliminal or trans-marginal region. That region contains every kind of matter: 'seraph and snake' abide there side by side."

By the time he reached his suburban subdivision, the chaotic sky was darkening toward early night. The clock on the dashboard read barely eleven in the morning, but it was as if a vast bowl of ash had been dumped on the heavens, and the world was gray and glaring with the strange intensity of a solar eclipse. All down the street, the trees lining the lawns of the neighboring houses were tossing their branches in the growing darkness like rows of monstrous lions shaking their manes.

The radio said, "Each of us is in reality an abiding psychical entity far more extensive than he knows—an individuality which can never express itself completely through any corporal manifestation. The Self manifests itself through the organism; but there is always some part of the Self unmanifested; and always, as it seems, some power of organic expression in abeyance or reserve."

He pulled into his driveway behind a familiar vehicle, an expensive sports car that belonged to someone he had once known, someone he had formerly called his friend. (*Steve,* the Dwarf whispered into the back of his brain.) When he stepped out of his own car, the stirrings of a mysterious hot breeze grazed his face and ruffled his hair. A muted roar began to creep across the sky from west to east, rolling and crackling like the aftershock of a thunderclap.

The current carried him across the lawn, around to the back of the house, where he approached the bedroom window and peered through it into the gloom. Two pale bodies were pressed together and pulsating with pleasure on the bed. (*Linda and Steve,* the Dwarf hissed.) He followed the current back around to the front of the house and entered through the door, making no effort to be quiet.

The television was turned on in the living room. The picture showed a white field of shivery static. A cultured male voice lectured through the speakers: "So long as we deal with the cosmic and the general, we deal only with the symbols of reality, but *as soon as we deal with private and personal phenomena as such, we deal with realities in the completest sense of the term.*"

"Linda!" he called. He plinked his keys loudly into the dish beside the door. "Linda! Come here!" He listened for a response. There was a stillness louder than a shout, and then from down the hallway: a whisper of bedsheets being pulled back, followed by the familiar creak of the floorboard beside his bed.

He crept down the hallway soundlessly, flowing like liquid night. At the doorway he paused for an instant, giving everyone time to prepare. Then he stepped inside and noticed simultaneously that the bathroom door was shut and the bedroom window open. The bedcovers were an obvious hasty job of pulling up and smoothing down. The blue drapes flapped and fluttered in the hot breeze.

The breeze was a whisper of sea spray. The room was a barren windswept plain located on the far side of an odd angular intersection; it was a misshapen cluster of towers tottering under a cold blood moon. He felt the letter opener in his hand twirling faster and faster. Had he indeed brought it with him and only now noticed it? The sound of the shower starting abruptly on the far side of the bathroom door mingled with the ocean-spray breeze and melded with the watery waves of blue light radiating from the drapes and cascading down the white walls in liquid ripples to give life to this cracked desert.

A delicate, tinny sound, like the scraping of an insect, began to tickle his ears, and he realized it was the bedside radio, switched on and dialed to a by-now familiar station. "The apprehension," it said in tiny insect tones, "of a coming dissolution, the grim conviction that this state was the last state of the conscious Self, the sense that I had followed the last thread of being to the verge of an abyss . . ."

Another sound intruded upon the voice, layering itself gently over the tiers of speech and oceanic flowing, wafting through the open window on the back of the swelling wind: the starting roar of an expensive automobile engine. But there was nowhere the driver could go. For Derek had parked behind him, and Derek was *a bloodhungry Dwarf crouched low in the dark*, and he carried in his huge hand *the pulsing feather of vengeance, plucked from a bloodangel's wing*.

The current lulled him to sleep even as it swept him down the hallway and out the front door onto the lawn, where a wide-eyed man in a foreign car was backing over the grass to get around the car blocking his exit. Derek saw, as if in a blissful vision, this man's mouth open to jabber and scream as the Dwarf reached out with that *blackplucked feather* and jabbed it through the Jaguar's open window again and again, plunging it repeatedly into a pulpy softness that felt like paradise as the black sky roared and the lions shook their manes in regal rows, lifting their heads to bellow and join voices with the storm.

Despite the sudden thunderstorm raging outside, Linda stayed in the shower until the water ran cold. She jumped with each flash of lightning and peal of thunder, remembering the urban myths about people being electrocuted in such situations. Finally, when she could stand it no longer, she stepped out and toweled off, shivering violently and struggling to catch her breath.

She considered jeans and a tee shirt but then changed her mind and wrapped her torso with the white towel. She also tousled her wet hair to give it the sexy leonine look that had always turned Derek on. Or at least it had done so for the first six years of their marriage, up until a few months ago when he had begun acting like a stranger and looking at her as if she were some ugly creature that had washed up on the shore of his life.

Surely he couldn't know about her and Steve. Of that she was confident. And it was easy enough to explain Steve's car in the driveway, since he was friends with their neighbors and could claim he had just walked over there to say hello (which was exactly what he had fled to do only moments ago). But today's brush with disaster was the closest yet. Before leaving the bathroom she adjusted the towel again, making sure it rode low enough to expose generous portions of both breasts, which were still stiffened with gooseflesh from the icy water. Especially in the present circumstance, she thought a little misdirection couldn't hurt at all.

She saw no one when she peered into the bedroom. The hallway was likewise deserted, so she walked confidently down to the living room, holding the towel up with one hand, and then stopped short beside the living room recliner, arrested in mid-step by the sight of her husband crouched low in the open front doorway with his back to her. The storm still raged outside, buffeting the house with heavy winds, blowing the sharp-sweet smell of ozone and ravaged maple trees in through the door. He appeared to be surveying the spectacle, heedless of the rain slapping him in the face. His head rotated back and forth in regular, slow sweeps, and the odd motion, combined with his incomprehensible squatting pose and hunched shoulders, made him look almost comical. She barely suppressed a burst of nervous laughter, raising a hand to her mouth and nearly dropping the towel in the process. When she spoke, her voice still trembled with the inner pressure of giddy humor.

"Oh, hi, honey. I was in the shower. I didn't hear you come in. Why are you home so early? Shouldn't you shut the door?"

She was about to ask, "What's wrong?" when he turned to face her. He remained low in the doorway, crouched like a caveman. Her words stuck in her throat, trapped there by the sudden paralysis in her chest. Derek looked like some primitive tribal chief drenched in red war paint. His eyes were wide and flashing. The corners of his mouth were drawn down in an unearthly grimace. In one hand he gripped a sharp blade that glistened with the same red paint.

Before she could speak or move, he exploded from his crouch and came at her like lightning. She saw a bright burst and felt a concussive blow like a thundercrack. Then she was falling in slow motion, floating down, down to the floor and landing hard with a broken jaw. The storm hit her wrist next, and then two ribs, and then her nose. Strong, sticky hands were tangled in her wet hair, dragging her across rough shag carpet that burned her legs and back as the towel pulled away. Then it was cold ceramic tile sliding beneath her naked body, and the cabinets and refrigerator loomed overhead.

Soured milk was produced and poured over her face. The splash of the cold liquid brought her partly back, and she screeched through a mangled mouth as she awoke for the first time to the horror of what was happening.

But when she tried to scream for help, the only words that came out were, "What's wrong?" She screamed again and still the same words erupted: "What's wrong? What's wrong?" Over and over she repeated it, unable to stop, asking desperately for the answer to a question whose implications, as she was only just beginning to understand, extended far beyond anything she had ever imagined.

For bending over her was not her bland, lost husband but *the Dwarf with blacksmear eyes*. Reaching out to her were not his soft office-worker's hands but *the horny hands of the rottenblood host*. And clutched in those hands was not a thin, blood-drenched blade but *the piercing vengeance of the greedy-eyed God* which would *carve the secret shape that swims in the deep*. The words and phrases arose like a whirling chant in her head, and she could not tell if they entered through her ears or spoke from a deeper source.

The Dwarf stood above her and raised a misshapen hand, and gripped in that hand was the light of a four-pointed star, which gathered and swelled until it was a blazing beacon of truth in the dimness, scorching her eyes and burning her face, casting shimmering dark shadows across the suddenly real angles and planes of a barren landscape that had enveloped them.

The Dwarf seized her throat and pricked the tender flesh with *the star of destiny*, which was *the black feather of vengeance*, drawing out a mesmerizing bead of crimson-on-white, and the fiery pain of it, and the smell of sizzling flesh, refused to let her slip into shock and believe it was a nightmare.

The Dwarf spoke, opening its misshapen mouth for the first time, and its voice was the roar of hot winds and the hissing of blood rains. It said:

"The seraph is a snake. The Self is an abyss. Who knows the stench of God? The blood shall rot away!"

Then it reached down into the naked mystery quivering before it and patiently, joyfully began to make everything right.

NIGHTMARES, IMPORTED AND DOMESTIC

WITH MARK MCLAUGHLIN

His name was Lafcadio, and he was an artist, a creator of lavish and colorful landscapes. Or at least, this accounted for part of his life: the part lived by the conscious, waking, sensing self that opened eyes on the external world and breathed in the scents and sights of sun-filled skies and rain-wet streets. Lafcadio the artist spent endless hours reading Zen literature and attempting to incorporate esoteric ideas into his paintings. Lafcadio the artist thrived on the sensuous impressions of the outer world and the intricate thoughts to which they inspired his overheated imagination.

But he was a man divided, and the other part of his life was not nearly so vibrant. For approximately eight hours out of every twenty-four, he assumed the identity of Brian, an accountant, a creator of neatly filled-out forms, who spent his days locked within the taupe walls of an aging suburban office. Lafcadio's life as Brian was uncommonly realistic for a nocturnal vision. As Brian, he felt pain, hunger, all the usual sensations, and knew them in all their day-to-day, five-sensory vividity. But he did not see his Brian-self through the twin windows of his own eyes. Rather, he watched himself from a distance, as one might watch a character in a television show. Appropriately, this dream-life, Brian's life, took place in a world of black-and-white, like an old episode of *The Andy Griffith Show* or *I Love Lucy*. And the tenor of this dream-existence was entirely in keeping with its grayscaled hues.

The tension between the two selves—the glorious sensuality of the artist and the drab conventionality of the accountant—expressed itself in all the habits and mores of Lafcadio's life. One of his most oft-indulged amusements was to sample exotic coffees with his eyes closed and try to guess the precise blend and origin of the beans. By contrast, one of Brian's favorite drinks was instant coffee, mixed with one package of artificial sweetener and one teaspoon of nondairy creamer. He preferred Folgers, but he usually couldn't detect it when somebody substituted Maxwell

House or Sanka.

The only person who had ever slept more than once in Lafcadio's bed was Lafcadio himself. The right half of Brian's bed had never held anyone but Susan, his wife for as many years as he could remember.

Lafcadio was high-strung and temperamental. Brian was even-tempered and meek.

The line of contrasts ran right down to physical appearance. Lafcadio was tall and thin, with a vaguely catlike appearance to his bony, bald head. Brian was of average height and weight, with a blandly amiable, slightly rounded face, and a ten-dollar haircut.

Some mornings Lafcadio awoke to a momentary disorientation, brought about by trying to decide whose bed he was lying in. The feeling lasted until after his shower, when the first sip of coffee hit his tongue and he discovered with relief that it was not Folgers but Jamaica Blue Mountain. The bitter hot tang of the black liquid always confirmed that he was indeed the effervescent artist and not the dreary accountant. But as time went by—months running into years, years into more than a decade, and all the while the nocturnal life of Brian playing like a classic TV show on the screen of his eyelids at night—he found that he slowly came to look forward to his nightly ramblings in a world of white-bread banality.

True, the morning disorientation sometimes left him with a lingering fear that one day he might wake up to find himself in a two-tone world with Susan beside him in bed and his life as Lafcadio the Magnificent receding like foam from the shore of a dream ocean. But in the end he discovered that it was really quite easy to convince himself that a life as Brian the Maudlin wouldn't be all that bad. Not if Brian were able to spend at least eight hours of every twenty-four dreaming that he was Lafcadio the Magnificent.

"So this Brian," said Cornelia, Lafcadio's best friend, over steaming mugs one day at their favorite coffee house, Mondo Mocha. "Your dream buddy. What's he up to these days? You haven't mentioned him in a while."

Lafcadio reflected for a moment before answering. "He's not really my buddy," he said at last. "He's me. And Susan has been talking about flowers."

"Flowers?" Cornelia looked at him blankly over a Café Corretto.

"She thinks the house looks too plain on the outside. All the other houses on the block have tons of flowers. We have to keep up with the Joneses, you know." He smiled privately to himself and turned his attention to the steam rising from his Espresso Macchiato. The swirling vapor hinted at a snow-covered landscape, mottled by bizarre seismic convulsions. He allowed the image to take its course in his imagination, hoping it might lead him to his next artistic project.

Cornelia gave him a hard little smile. But then, practically everything about her was hard, though admirably so. She was into boxing and weightlifting, and it showed on her arms and shoulders. Her abs were like a rippled brick wall (as he had discovered once, long ago, on the sole occasion when they had become physically intimate and he had been able to indulge his long-held desire of placing the flat of his palm upon her stomach). Years ago she had served on the police force, before she decided to open a beauty and exercise spa for women only. "This Susan sounds like a perfectly hideous frau," she was saying, as his snow-swept reverie became transmogrified by her chiseled physique into a Dali-esque scene of powder-and-ice piled into abdominal ripples on an arctic tundra. "Brian has to play gardener now? Tell me everything!"

"Oh, but I like it. I mean, *he* likes it." He could tell she didn't believe him, so he tapped his manicured nails on the tile tabletop in syncopation with his words to emphasize his sincerity. "No, really! All that housey-spousey stuff is actually kind of fun in Brian-world."

Cornelia tapped her chin with a long maroon-lacquered fingernail. "So, do they ever *do* it? Or is life all just chores and church socials?"

"Oh sure, they have sex. But I never get to see"—He twirled his forefingers in the direction of his crotch—"the works in action. It's like watching a soft-core porn channel in a hotel room. No close-ups allowed, in case a kid enters the room. The camera moves toward them, then it veers off toward a fireplace or an open window with a pretty sky outside."

Cornelia's smile dipped down into a smirk. "How dreary. Must be terribly boring for you."

"Nooo . . ." Lafcadio thought for a moment. "In a way, it's rather sweet. And the lack of visuals isn't a total loss. I mean, I do still feel every sensation that Brian is feeling." He looked into Cornelia's eyes. "I think sometimes Susan is supposed to be you."

Her eyes hardened into a stare that clearly said, *Don't go there.* "You will recall," she said, "that we only slept together once. Before I'd figured myself out. I'm Susan? That hardly seems likely."

"Is it likely that I should be Brian?" he countered. To lighten the mood, he cocked his head and widened his eyes in a mock posture of exaggerated artsy-fartsy pretension, and she laughed. Her teeth were whiter than the foam on his Macchiato, whiter than arctic ice, and they transfixed him in a momentary flash of near-revelation.

"It's so like you," she said, "to have such complicated relationship issues even in your dreams." She was still laughing when she glanced at the clock on the wall. "Whoops, I'd better get going. I've got a class coming up. Keep me posted on all the exciting developments in Brian-land." She leaned over and pecked him on the cheek, then gathered her purse (more like a suitcase, he thought) and headed for the door.

He watched as her long, lanky strides carried her away from him. The rippled muscles of the arctic waste were still taking shape in his imagination, and for the millionth time in his high-strung life he silently thanked the gods—any gods, whatever gods there might be, he didn't care who they were—for gifting him with a dreary dream life of almost archetypal normality, since it freed him from the fetters of psyche-bound inspiration and allowed him to take in, as if by osmosis, every subtle sensation of the world around him. Without anything of equal vibrancy buzzing in his subconscious to compete with the splendor of the outside world, he could work in complete inner freedom, allowing the obscure mechanism of his own creative faculty to transform scattered sense perceptions into magnificent paintings that made him the awe of the arthouse community.

The gods bless you, Brian, he said to his alter ego. Through the plate glass storefront, he could see Cornelia standing on the sidewalk, squinting up at the sun. After a moment she pulled out her flaming-orange sunglasses and slipped them on. As she loped down the sidewalk and out of sight, he found that he still couldn't decide whether or not he loved her.

But then he reasoned, if he couldn't decide, that probably meant he didn't.

The dream, as always, was in black-and-white, except for the part with the startling new addition of blood, which fountained and sprayed in gouts like bright red finger-paint. The color shocked him, but not into full consciousness. He soon discovered another fact about this remarkable dream: it could get amazingly tactile, almost more so than real life. Brian's world had always been pinch -yourself-and-wake-up solid, but never like this. The blood was warm and sticky as maple syrup, and the pain was a white-hot pocket of concentrated agony searing into the socket of his right eye.

What had happened was that Susan had asked Brian to unload a pickup bed full of potted flowers. He had backed the vehicle up to the front porch like the dutiful dream-husband he was, and had lowered the tailgate and climbed into the bed to unstack the dull plastic pots with their colorless floral occupants.

(Lafcadio, watching from a non-localized point some distance away while simultaneously identifying with his dream-self, had thought the grayish blooms most distasteful.)

It happened on the first jump. Brian realized it would be much easier to hop down than to squat and climb, so he steadied the pot in his hands and stepped off the edge of the tailgate, intending to drop lightly onto the balls of his feet. Susan's scream burst out with an impossible loudness and hung in the air with a ringing reverberation that could only happen in a dream. He hadn't noticed the hook projecting from the porch ceiling, right near the edge under which he had opened the tailgate. It was meant for hanging a plant on, obviously. Susan must have mounted it there without telling him. The gray-silver point extended an absurd length past the overhang, maybe three inches or more, and was located precisely at eye-level from his standing position in the pickup bed.

The curved end was vicious-looking, almost medieval. It caught him in the top rim of his right eye socket, and his weight did the rest. He fell forward, the point gouged into the bone of his skull, his legs left the tailgate, and then he was lodged there, hooked like a great flailing fish. The plastic pot hit the lawn without breaking, although potting soil sprayed everywhere, and the colorless bloom was crushed. His body went out of control then, legs kicking and spasming as if he were trying to pedal up Mt. Everest, hands and fingers slapping and clawing at the smooth vinyl siding of the eave in a vain attempt to lift himself up. While all this went on, his throat opened up and spouted a veritably Pentecostal string of gibberish that seemed to have something to do with screaming for help.

Then Susan was grabbing his legs. She was grunting and lifting him up, heaving, thrusting, while her impossibly loud and long scream still hung in the air. At last she succeeded. The hook ripped free, dragging a few bone splinters with it, and he dropped to the truck, slammed into the open tailgate with the small of his back, and hit the lawn still writhing.

That was when the blood began to spurt from his eye in candy-red finger-paint gouts. The pain was a knot of acid searing its way inward from his eye to his brain. Susan was pawing at him in panic, weeping, asking him what to do. And in the midst of it all, rather absurdly, he vomited.

"He puked? So what happened then? Tell me everything!" Cornelia's eyes shone with eager interest. Lafcadio drew in a sharp, tobacco-laden breath and let it out slowly, trying to buy time to fathom the reason for her eagerness. This time they had met at their favorite bar, the Twilight Lounge. The decor was an edgy mix of Goth and camp imagery: ABBA posters and black candles arranged into arcane geometric patterns, G.I. Joe dolls tangled in faux spider webs. Cornelia was dressed for the occasion in a black velvet catsuit with a denim jacket.

"No, he didn't die." Lafcadio floated the words out on the tail-end of a smoky exhalation. Cornelia interrupted him before he could say more.

"What?" She blinked and leaned closer, bringing with her a mingled scent of sweet perfume and sour gin. "Did you say 'Oh, he sits and cries'? Lafcadio, my darling, you're incomprehensible when you mumble, especially amidst all the lovely musical accompaniment." A bassy club beat throbbed in the atmosphere around them, overlaid with a glassy texture of synthesized strings.

"I said he *didn't die*." He repeated the words with a hint of annoyance. "People usually don't die in their own dreams, right? And after all, he is me." He held up his cigarette before him in an attitude of detachment and regarded the cherry-red ember glowing on the tip. "Things seemed like they were getting better before I woke up. Susan took care of him. She dialed 911, and an ambulance came and rushed him off to the hospital. I opened my eyes just as they started to wheel him into the ER."

"Interesting . . ." Cornelia took a sip from her gin and tonic. "So, Susan saved his life. But then, she's the one who installed the hook in the first place. And you say it hurt his *eye*?" She mused for a moment while the smoky air continued to throb around them like the interior of an artery, and while Lafcadio remained deliberately absorbed in his cigarette meditation. In his mind, a fiery orange sinkhole had opened up in the abdominal arctic waste. Volcanic flames were beginning to lick out from the edges and melt the snow to slush. The water first dripped, then drizzled into the hole, and its touch only seemed to fuel the flames.

"Hey." Cornelia's ruminations seemed to reach a point of sudden synthesis. "Do you think that's symbolic—'eye' equals capital 'I'? Maybe the hook in your eye represents a buried feeling of hostility toward your deathly-dull dream life." She smiled with an almost childish glee, and he thought she seemed just a little too pleased with herself.

"It's a fundamental tenet of my belief system," he said in a far frostier voice than he had intended, "that there is ultimately no such thing as a fixed center of identity." He saw her eyes roll in a familiar expression of boredom, but he went on. "These chairs underneath our asses right now are just as much a part of who we are as anything rattling around inside these juicy little heads." He raised his right hand, the one holding the cigarette, and tapped his index finger against a veiny temple. A tendril of smoke found its way from the tip of the cigarette to the corner of his eye, where it brushed a stinging tail against the tender pink tissues. He waved it away and tried to ignore Cornelia's look of amusement.

"The injured *eye* once again," she said. "Do you think someone is trying to tell you something?"

He refused to acknowledge her comment. "I have no reason to be hostile toward Brian or his life," he continued, "because he may as well be me, and his life mine. My life may as well be his. Just as yours may as well be mine, and mine yours. Our souls are both located in this cigarette I'm smoking here. They're also in that gin and tonic you're sucking down." She was in the midst of downing the rest of her drink, and she made a face at him, holding the liquid in her cheeks for a moment before swallowing it.

"Really, darling," she said with a sigh, "sometimes your attempts at Zen-like wisdom are too much. What the hell are you talking about?"

"I'm saying there's no boundary between identities, so what's to be afraid of?"

She shrugged. "Who said anything about being afraid?"

"It's the same thing with my art," he went on, ignoring her question. "I deliberately make the perspective undiscoverable. The viewer might be looking at any one point from any other. Have you heard of Indra's net?"

She shook her head, clearly having lost interest in his monologue. But that did not prevent him from continuing.

"It's a metaphor in Hinduism for the infinity of perspectives in the universe. Indra's net is an endless web that has a jewel located at the intersection of every strand. Each jewel reflects all the others, so you have infinity contained in every finite point on the net. A long time ago I decided to use this idea as the philosophical basis for my paintings. When you view any one of my pieces, you don't know where you're supposed to be seeing it from. What's more, this means the frame itself isn't the boundary of the scene. My landscapes fold in on themselves and create a self-contained infinity. In this way, my work mirrors the reality of subjective personal existence, just like the metaphor of Indra's net. Because ultimately, there's nothing outside the frame for any of us. There's just an endless hall of mirrors with no boundary." He started to say more, but then he abruptly shut his mouth and sucked on his cigarette as he realized that the words he had never spoken, and never wanted to speak, were rising to his lips. These words expressed a fear that had dawned on him one day in a quiet moment when he was reiterating his credo to himself for the thousandth time: *No boundary means no escape.*

"Is there anything else?" Cornelia asked. She was watching him with her ruby red lips screwed up into a wry grin.

"Just the fact that your eye/I theory doesn't hold water," he said. "The injury wasn't a threat at all. In fact, it might turn out to have been a liberation. Brian and Susan's marital relationship has been at kind of a low ebb lately. Then he ran into trouble and she saved him. Maybe this will revitalize things between them."

"Yes," Cornelia said, "but Susan put up the hook, remember?" She smiled at him with eyes that were as pretty and hard as the rest of her. "If I remember correctly, you also told me that I'm Susan. Is that how you see me—a disturbing mix of destroyer and savior?"

Lafcadio barked out a small, sharp laugh. "Hardly, my sweet. Listen, we could spend all night on this. This autopsy of my dreams. But do you know what? Sometimes a cigar is just a cigar, a rose is a rose is a rose, and diamonds are forever. Let's just say it's all really interesting, and leave it at that. Will you indulge me?"

"Oh, darling!" she cried. "This is too much, coming from the enlightened Zen-master of the avant-garde art world!" She laughed and laughed until he feared she would hurt herself. When she had recovered, she said, "Certainly, my sweet. But one question first: Doesn't it bother you to know that Brian-world is now a painful place to be? You've talked so much about how realistic it is. Well, I'm not so sure the marriage or anything else will be better now. Brian may be disfigured, and he'll definitely be blind in one eye. He'll probably suffer brain damage. I'm surprised you haven't acted more concerned about this. What will your dreams be like now, my wise Lafcadio?" She looked deeply into his eyes, and even in the midst of his consternation, he wondered again whether he loved her.

"Don't know." The artist slumped back in his seat, his meditative mood broken. The arctic landscape remained unaltered in his mind's eye, although the drizzle of water pouring through the hole in the ice had grown to become a steadily flowing waterfall. The flames were hidden now, but they were still there, still burning below the frozen crust, as evidenced by the flickering orange sheen they imparted to the ice around the hole. He had a momentary flash of something new: a human figure curled into a fetal position, located deep within that fiery pit. Its eyes and mouth were open wide. He couldn't tell whether it was laughing, crying, or screaming. Perhaps it was doing all three.

He frowned at Cornelia as he ground out his cigarette in the glossy black ashtray on the table. "You're just a sweet little ray of sunshine, aren't you?"

Of course the dream was monochrome. How could it be otherwise? And yet Brian sensed that something was different. Something was missing from the room around him, some indefinable aspect of solidity whose absence made everything seem vaguely flat and unreal, like cardboard stage props and scenery.

(Lafcadio, hovering in extra-dimensional space somewhere near the ceiling, shared his alter ego's confusion.)

Brian was parked in a wheelchair in the center of his black-and-white living room, slumped in front of a black-and-white television set, watching a black-and-white program unfold on the screen. He couldn't budge an inch. The insipid TV world was inescapable, and he was positioned to face it for a full frontal assault. Susan had engaged the wheel locks on the chair to prevent the incessant squeaking of the spokes he had been causing by rocking back and forth, back and forth. She was in the kitchen behind him right now, making his lunch, from the sound of it. She must be chopping celery—*crunch-crunch-crunch, crunch-crunch-crunch*. To his right and left, adorning coffee tables, walls, and windowsills, a tangled profusion of potted flowers bristled with muddy gray blooms that emitted an incongruously sweet perfume.

It saturated the atmosphere of the room like a syrupy fog. He almost thought he could see it shifting and shimmering in the cold light of the television.

Drool was gathered in a heavy glistening lobe on his lower lip, but he lacked the energy to care about it. He felt nauseous and dizzy, and had no idea what was happening on the program before him. Something about a perky family stranded on some planet with a prissy bad guy and a robot with floppy arms. A black rotary telephone perched atop the set with a ridiculously long cord dangling down in front of the screen. It slithered across the concave surface, unevenly dividing the flickering image, and ended up as a bunched pile of gleaming black coils on the gray-carpeted floor.

His injured right eye was smothered in bandages, as were most of his cheek and forehead. His exposed left eye kept blinking, rolling, and refocusing as he tried to fathom what the characters on the television screen were so concerned about. The prissy bad-guy was bitching at the robot while the robot waved its accordion-pleated tube-arms.

His poor wounded head pulsed with an odd liquid surging sound. In his grogginess and sickness, he imagined that he must be hearing the primal sound of the ocean deeps, where colorless fluorescent fish glided with rippling fan-fins through an eternal night, and where the currents murmured of secrets too ancient to be spoken aloud. Such thoughts were new and strange, and they scared him. He longed for his accounting forms and the familiar taupe walls of his office. But the ocean sound seemed to be a permanent addition, and he feared he would never see the comforting interior of his office again. Now, one week after the accident, he still rocked to the sound of the tidal rhythm, but the wheel locks kept him from creating the soothing back-and-forth motion that had been the only comfort he could find in this new half-conscious existence.

Susan entered the room holding a plate with a sandwich on it. She was smiling and talking to him, but her words sounded like gibberish. When he tried to raise his hands to accept the plate, his arms felt as if someone had tied them down with lead weights. Her voice came to him as if through water, all muffled and murky, and the words sounded like *blah, blah, blah,* spoken in relentlessly perky tones, so upbeat they rang utterly false.

She held the sandwich to his mouth, and his nostrils were suddenly filled with the clean yet musty smell of whole-wheat bread. With the cloying perfume of the flowers now mercifully muted, he found that his nausea had concealed a fierce hunger. He was positively ravenous. His lips parted of their own accord, and the spongy bread sopped up the bead of spit on his lower lip as Susan fed him the sandwich bite by bite. While he ate, he couldn't help noticing that she wore low-riding pants with a high-cut shirt, and that her navel stared at him from the smooth white expanse of her stomach like an unblinking eye that mirrored and mocked his own newly monocular face. It fascinated him for some reason. He felt he should be reminded of something.

He still had four bites left when the phone rang. Susan set the plate on his lap and took two steps over to the television while he stared down at the unfinished sandwich with a mute cry of frustration sealed off in his throat. His hands clenched and unclenched, but his wrists were pinned to the arms of the wheelchair by invisible straps.

"Blah, blah, blah?" Susan chimed into the black mouthpiece. She listened a moment, then "Blah, blah, blah!" she replied. A look of pleasure crossed her face as she brushed past him to the coffee table, where she consulted a phone book for the caller. Her smile faded as her finger stopped on the page before a name and number.

"Oh, blah, blah, blah," she continued in a more serious tone, moving behind him toward the kitchen on some errand, dragging the long black cord in her wake so that it pulled up against his arm. He flinched at its stiff spiral touch and continued to look with longing at his sandwich.

After a moment, she returned on some other errand. "Blah, blah, blah!" she enthused, racing in front of him toward the phone book again, still chatting away to that all-important caller, still pulling that super-long springy cord so that it worked its way up and encircled his neck. The coils were as smooth and cool as snakeskin against his throat.

From some point buried deep inside his brain, out of some black well of selfhood where the ocean currents murmured in soothing tones, a thought emerged. The whispering voices coalesced into an intelligible sentence, and the sentence began to flow toward his throat. He opened his mouth and grunted, but the cord was slowly strangling him. He coughed as if he were trying to expel some bit of sandwich lodged in his windpipe. The words were almost there, they would almost form. His mouth worked and his lips gathered more spit, but his voice would not come, it could not break free of the constriction around his throat. In desperation he mouthed the words silently with his crumb-covered lips, wondering as he did so what the thought might mean, and where it might have come from: *No boundary means no escape.*

(Lafcadio, who had been watching these events unfold with growing agitation, felt his disembodied heart skip a beat.)

Susan was now out of sight in the dining room, or perhaps even beyond that, and the cord was growing tighter and tighter. The television world continued to blather with incomprehensible characters and concerns while the cold spiral coils dug deeper and deeper into his Adam's apple like a garrote. Straining, trembling, he jerked his arms against the invisible straps, but try as he might, he was immobilized.

As the dull throb of medicated pain in his bandaged eye blossomed into a bright burning agony, and as the robot continued to wave its arms and the prissy bad guy went on with his outrageous accusations, Brian finally realized the nature of what was wrong with the room: *There was no difference between the world around him and the world on the television.* The gibberish spouting from the mouths of the TV characters was no more comprehensible than the gibberish his wife was still spouting in the other room—or, come to think of it, from the gibberish he had spouted himself when he was hanging by his eye socket from the porch ceiling. None of it made sense. All of it was insipid and pointless. There was a tangible lack of *realness* to his surroundings, an absence of something that would have given everything more weight and caused it all to make sense again. But what exactly was this indefinable quality whose absence made life nothing more than a TV show where people spoke nonsense, and where there could be no escape?

It wasn't until rivulets of shocking-bright red began to seep out from beneath his bandages and spatter onto the colorless sleeves of his pajamas that he found his answer.

No boundary means no escape.

When the change came, it came quickly. The room receded suddenly and sharply, as if he were backing down a tunnel at incredible speed. The pain in his face and constriction in his throat faded like someone had turned down the volume on the television. For a time, he knew only an insensate bliss.

When he opened his eyes—his *eyes*, both of them intact and functional—he found himself lying in a bed that was not his own, located in a room he had never seen, where the walls displayed a dazzling array of surreal painted landscapes, and where he somehow knew that nobody had ever slept beside him more than once, not even Susan.

His throat finally opened and released an impressive array of shrieks when he realized that his name was supposed to be Lafcadio, and that he had awakened into the wrong life.

❦

"So is he dead?' Cornelia asked. "You haven't talked about him for—what is it, two weeks now? I can only assume that he died from his injuries. What's Susan doing with the life insurance money? Installing a greenhouse?" She smiled and laughed, but he refused to look at her.

This time they were sharing a pizza in their favorite trendy restaurant, Mad For Pie, which served every sort of pizza one could imagine—except the traditional sausage, cheese and tomato sauce kind. The entrée steaming on the table before them now was the specialty of the house, an exotic mélange called The Swordfish, Artichoke, and White Sauce (with Just a Touch of Cilantro) Dream Pie. Lafcadio's stomach was out of sorts. He sat back in his tall wicker-backed chair and tried to avoid the overpowering scent of seafood and cilantro that rose to his nostrils in heady waves.

"To be honest," he said in his best nonchalant voice, "I'm not sure what's going on with Brian right now."

"What do you mean?" She shoveled another lump of swordfish-laden crust into her mouth, and he watched the motion of her jaw with sickened fascination: its determined scissoring and champing as it ground the fishy flesh to a pulp, then the spasm in her throat as she swallowed the pungent lump and it began to stretch its way downward through her esophagus toward her waiting stomach. His own stomach lurched ominously, and he looked down at his cigarette.

"I, uh—how do I say this?" He picked up a heavy burgundy-colored napkin and mopped his sweating brow. "I haven't dreamed about Brian for sixteen days now."

She stopped her chewing and regarded him from across the pie with an expression of disbelief.

"Yes," he said, "I'm serious."

"Lafcadio," she said. The swordfish suddenly stuck in her throat, and she groped for her glass of water. When she had taken a drink, she licked her lips and continued to look at him. "What's happened? Hasn't Brian been with you for years now?"

"Yes," he said.

"Aren't you concerned about this?"

"Yes."

"So why haven't you said anything?" Her wounded pout dismayed him, and for a moment he considered telling her the tale he had been concealing for over two weeks: of how he had awakened in his silk-sheeted bed thinking that he was Brian; of the profound panic that had gripped him for hours as he struggled to remember how he had awakened into someone else's life; of how the delusion had hung on until mid-morning, when for no apparent reason his own name had seemed to attach to him with a new assertiveness, and the dream-identity had evaporated from his consciousness like a moist fog; of how he had found himself standing in his kitchen, holding a cup of Jamaica Blue Mountain and wondering where somebody had hidden the Folgers.

For the rest of that horrible day he had been unable to stop the trembling in his chest. He had canceled a dinner date with Cornelia (she had gracefully declined to ask the reason) and spent the night in his studio looking at his easel and allowing the arctic vision to gain further clarity and intensity in his mind's eye. He had known the time would soon arrive for him to begin committing the vision to canvas, but on that night some inner impulse had told him to wait, and he had heeded its restraint. Later, when he slept, he had found that his classic TV dreams were gone for the first time in over a decade.

Instead of watching Brian's soothingly banal ramblings, he had found himself floating high over an arctic tundra, watching a volcanic sinkhole widen into a veritable crater amidst the icy furrows, wondering whether the abdominal ripples stretching away toward the horizon might ever meet with the rest of the torso, with breasts and a neck, and with a face. It was the first time he had ever dreamt himself into one of his own artistic visions, and he hadn't known how to feel about it the following morning. The next night the dream had been the same. And the next, and the next.

He considered telling Cornelia this. But how could he, when he knew that it was her face he half-feared to see past the icy horizon?

"I just needed time to adjust," he finally said with a weak smile. "You know you're my most beloved confidante, Cornelia. Please don't be upset with me."

"I'm not upset, dearest. I'm just surprised." She shoved away her plate and began looking around for a server to take away the remains of the pie. Once their table was cleared and wiped down and they were alone again, she leaned forward with her forearms resting on the glossy brown surface and looked into his eyes.

"Do you know I talked to my therapist last week about you and Brian?"

For a moment he thought she was joking. He kept expecting her serious expression to break into a smile, but her mouth was a determined line, and her eyes were as hard as sapphires.

"You told Dr. Breckenridge about this? About my *dreams*?"

Her severity broke easily in the face of his indignation. Immediately she was pouting again, but now in a rather hard way. "I was missing you, Lafcadio. I really wanted to hear about the latest episodes of the Brian and Susan Show. I always look forward to our conversations. I just called Dr. Breckenridge to change my appointment, but we ended up talking about you. How could I not mention you, when you were the main thing on my mind?"

Lafcadio could not sit still. He twisted in his seat and tried unsuccessfully to find a comfortable position. He picked up his drink, but his hand shook so badly that he had to set it back down. He looked around at the waiters and waitresses servicing tables, at the upscale married couples and college students, all of them wearing trendy clothes and devouring various nonstandard delights. The sight only angered him. As a last resort, he turned to examine his cigarette, but its usual soothing influence was nowhere to be found. Then he gave up and looked at Cornelia's face.

"So what did you tell him?"

"I only told him what you've told me. I described your dream life, all black-and-white and cozy. He found it quite fascinating. I could tell he wanted to ask me to introduce you to him, but he was too afraid of crossing a professional line."

Lafcadio considered this for a moment and then began to nod, slowly at first, then with increasing vigor. "Of course." He recalled the sensation of a curling phone cord pressed cold against Brian's throat, and he snickered a little, then laughed. "Of *course.*" Once again he gazed into Cornelia's eyes, considered her toned and taut physique, now tastefully attired in a green sparkling jacket with black satin shirt and pants. He drank in the sight of her masculine femininity, and found in it an impression of dawning realization. The full knowledge waited just beyond the horizon, like an arctic mountain range chiseled by the elements into the shape of a familiar face.

She was speaking to him. Her words came to him all murky and muffled, as if through water. "After all, Lafcadio, you were the one who said . . . what was it? Sometimes a dream is just a cigar? Something like that. You were quoting somebody. But the more I think about it, the more I believe you had the right idea. Don't take any of this seriously. Dr. Breckenridge didn't know what he was saying when he told me your dreams are unlike anything in the history of psychology." She shut her mouth when she realized she had said too much, but he found it funny. It was all funny now. She was a million miles away, and her confusion and misery were of no consequence.

It also just so happened that her face and clothing were losing their color. He blinked rapidly as the color drained away from her like dye being leached from a canvas. Her blue eyes became a stony gray. Her ruddy expression became a murky white. Her sparkling green jacket became a sickly weak shade of gray, like library paste flecked with glitter. In just a few seconds she was flushed of all color. He was so startled that it was a moment before he realized the same effect had overtaken the restaurant around him. Mad for Pie had taken on the appearance of *Father Knows Best*. The pies and pizzas were gray cardboard, and the patrons and scenery were colorless stage props and cutouts.

(Somewhere close by, in some non-localized portion of extra-dimensional space, another center of identity began to make itself known: a buzzing unit of self-consciousness that felt somehow like a vane protruding from the back of his head; an unknown self whose reality ran much deeper and held more solidity than the Magnificent Artist identity he had cultivated for most of his life. This new self was sharing his vision and consciousness, watching his life unfold like a fiction. And it was judging everything about him and his life, considering it all impassively, and finding it all to be quaint and comforting in a banal, white-bread sort of way.)

He felt his hand rise to his mouth to suck in a lungful of nicotine smoke. His lips curled into a smile, and for a moment he almost felt like his old self. "Cornelia, my sweet, don't worry about it." His voice carried through the stale air with a vibrancy that was almost visible, as if its very timbre might bring back a hint of color to the room. He felt a strange power surging in his breast, a kind of exhilaration beyond anything he had ever known. The landscape in his mind's eye pulsed with an intensity that almost obscured the sight of the restaurant. For once, his inner vision was stronger than the world around him, and in this fact he found his release.

If life was unbounded, he thought, just like his landscapes, and if no boundary meant no escape, then the only way out, the only way to achieve the ultimate transcendence, was to turn inward toward the source and center of consciousness itself, and find his longed-for infinity *inside* the world. Just like the self-contained infinity of Indra's net, which he had never truly understood until now.

(The newly awakened higher self nodded behind him in

approval of his insight. He could sense its benevolent attention upon him.)

Cornelia's face loomed in front of him, and also beyond the icy horizon in his mind's eye. In the restaurant she appeared gray and flat. In the arctic waste her features were chiseled from crackling blue ice, and the light of a slivered moon overhead glinted in silver sparkles on her face like flashes on the facets of a diamond.

"You're not mad?" the Cornelia of the outer world was asking. "Are you sure, Lafcadio? Because I don't think I could bear it."

"No," he heard himself say. "Far from it. In fact, I think you may have liberated me. I'm thinking that maybe Brian is gone now because he woke up. I'm thinking that maybe he and I have finally come together."

She looked at him somewhat suspiciously. "Should I congratulate you?"

"Perhaps. What say we find out for sure?" He rapped on the table with the knuckles of his free hand and sat forward abruptly in his chair. He felt positively giddy with good will. "Will you come over to my place tonight, my dear? I have something prepared to show you. I haven't told you anything about my latest project, you know I always keep them private until they're finished, but it's about time you saw it, even if it is only a work in progress. Because you're directly involved in it."

Her smile returned then, and he saw that her teeth were still icy white, a flashing beacon in the grayness surrounding her. "Lafcadio! Do you mean that I'm featured in it somehow?"

"Oh, yes!" He laughed and allowed her to grab his hand. "Yes, you are! I think you'll be positively amazed at the role you've played."

After that, he found he could simply allow himself to act the part of Lafcadio for the remainder of their time together at Mad for Pie. He chatted and laughed, and she laughed and chatted back, and they made plans for her to arrive at his flat at eight o'clock, at which time he promised to reveal to her a facet of herself that she had never suspected. He even managed to keep up the old appearance of the Magnificent Artist when her chattering words lost all meaning and began to sound like "Blah, blah, blah."

When they parted, each was riding on a wave of giddiness,

although he knew that hers did not match his. She thought she was going to be immortalized in one of his paintings. He, on the other hand, knew they were both going to be immortalized in a scheme much bigger than any she could ever imagine.

He labored all afternoon in his studio. The painting seemed to shape itself.

He had to take extra care to blend the colors for the fiery crater, since his color blindness precluded his assessing it with a simple glance, but he felt his hand being guided by a higher power, and he knew, even without being able to judge the quality of the work with his eyes, that it was the best thing he had ever painted. And after all, he would soon awaken to the actual scene of the vision, and the pathetic oil-based facsimile would no longer have a significance.

As he continued to work toward completion, he began to feel as if a key had been fitted into a lock. The door that opened allowed a flood of insights to spill through his brain. Brian's world had been less real than Lafcadio's, and its unreality had been reflected in its monochromity. That much Lafcadio had always known. But he had never suspected that perhaps his own reality was being watched from a still wider perspective by another layer of himself, a layer that was even more awake, more vibrant, more *real*. The thought of the sensuous delights, the manifold impressions, that might be available to that wider identity, sent him into paroxysms of aesthetic delight.

Brian had awakened to the insubstantiality of his position. It had seemed impossible—in fact, neither of them had ever so much as considered the possibility—but it had happened nonetheless, through the agency of an unexpected injury, brought about by Susan's unwitting help. Now Brian was gone—or, more accurately, he was more fully *here* with Lafcadio than he had ever been before—and it was Lafcadio's turn to wake up.

Dull-brained Brian would never have thought of the possibility of intentionally inducing an awakening, even if somebody had described it to him. He had even proved incapable of realizing that the half-consciousness of his newly mutilated existence was a blessing in disguise, since it limited his external options and forcibly opened him to the enhanced consciousness of the inner world. Lafcadio was not so dull. He knew what had happened, and he was able to recognize its value and purposefully work to take himself to the next level.

The only question that remained was how to accomplish it. What means would he use to rouse himself from the relative dream of his life and rise to a greater reality? And again, it was not really a question in need of an answer, for Brian had already provided the solution. His awakening had been accomplished through involuntary suffering. Having reflected on the situation, Lafcadio came to realize that he could engineer his own circumstances and awaken himself through a voluntary act.

It had to be the right eye, of course, the one most directly wired to the left side of the brain. Once the channel of vision leading to the logical, rational, intellectual hemisphere had been destroyed, all that would remain would be the channel leading to the intuitive, emotional, mystical half. Then all the visual impressions of the sensuous world around him would be funneled exclusively to the wider mystical self that even now was hovering behind him in extra-dimensional space. And he would see himself left behind and transformed.

The gods bless you, Brian, he whispered to himself over and over during that long afternoon of creation, as he shaped the world on the canvas and contemplated the stainless steel hook he had hidden in his pocket. He would have gone ahead and mounted it on one of the exposed ceiling beams in the studio of his loft apartment, if it weren't for the fact that this would have disrupted the correct sequence of events.

There was a protocol to follow.

The mounting of the hook, of course, was Cornelia's job.

She arrived at eight, right on time. She wore the same satin black shirt and pants, but had exchanged the sparkling green jacket for a sparkling blue one. In her right hand she clutched a bottle of red wine. In her left she carried a rose, which she intended to present to her beloved artist in gratitude for including her in one of his magnificent creations.

She remembered the walk up the narrow dark steps to his loft all too well, even though it was three years since her last visit. The one-time exception to their formerly platonic relationship had been disastrous. They had both known immediately that it wasn't working, even though the physical pleasure had been exquisite. It had seemed too much like incest, and she could tell from his pained expression afterward that he was experiencing his own private regrets. When he had moved down to bring his face level with her stomach, and when he had placed the palm of his hand across her belly in a lovingly gentle way, she had fought back tears that threatened to squeeze from beneath her lids and sear not only him but her. After a moment he had climbed from the bed and thrown on his clothes. She had done the same, and they had never spoken of the incident again.

The staircase had not changed. The off-white walls were still too narrow, and the brown wooden steps still creaked and popped even under the modest weight of her lean, toned body. At the top of the stairs, on the right, stood the brown wooden door to the artist's lair. She smiled and felt a rush of happiness, thinking that this visit would surely turn out better than the last.

She rapped on the door with the hand holding the rose. The delicate bloom, so deeply red that it seemed almost to ache with the saturation of its own hue, bobbed on the end of the thorned stem like a human head. She watched it for a moment and then knocked again.

"Lafcadio?" Her voice rang out with a hollow resonance in the cramped stairway. Tentatively, she reached out with her left hand and tried the brassy knob. It turned smoothly, and the door whispered open to reveal Lafcadio's living room.

She shut the door behind her and took the wine to the kitchen. The rose she laid on the dining room table. Then she went in search of the artist.

His studio was still located in the same room he had used three years ago. The walls and floor were dark and immaculate. The ceiling was high and crossed by wooden beams that gave the studio a rustic ambiance. A sheet of tarpaulin was spread beneath the easel, and upon the easel rested the artist's newest creation.

She stopped before it and took in the scene it displayed. After a moment, her heart began to pound.

The icy waste stretched away from her in barren rolls like lumps of fat. She could tell they were meant to mimic the human form by their arrangement into abdominal ripples, and by the snowy hillocks that sprouted like breasts in the upper half of the scene, and by the visage that gazed upward from the diamond-like mountains at the far upper edge. Overhead, a waning crescent moon cast a sickly light onto the surreal landscape.

When she looked back down to the ice itself, she saw that where the navel should have been, there was a gaping hole, like a wound ripped open from the inside. Streaks and splashes of crimson and orange jetted out from the hole like liquid fire, like hot blood and pus, and she thought she could see, buried somewhere deep within the chaos of ripe colors, the shape of a body curled into a fetal position. Its head was bony and bald, with an almost catlike aspect. When she leaned closer, she saw that its mouth was opened in a scream, and that one of its eyes—the right one—had been gouged out.

She knew who it was, of course, just as she recognized the chiseled face at the top of the picture. She almost had time to gasp before Lafcadio pounced on her from behind.

"My sweet!" he cried as he grabbed her shoulders and spun her around. She shrieked, then tried to laugh with relief when she saw his wild-eyed expression.

"Dear God, Lafcadio! You scared the living hell out of me!" Her hands trembled violently, and she rubbed them against her upper arms while still laughing in a shaky voice. "You look like you've seen a ghost. Not Brian's, I hope?"

He stared at her for a moment. Then he laughed with her. "Ah, yes. You always see more than I give you credit for, my dear Cornelia. Let me thank you right now, since it may be the last chance I have, for your many years of friendship."

"Well, of course, darling," she said. Her weak laughter died down to silence. "And why should this be your last chance?"

He laughed again and said, "No, I don't think so." While she puzzled over this non sequitur of an answer, he reached into his pocket and pulled out something silver and shiny. He then took her hand and placed the hook gently on her palm. She saw that it was long and vicious looking, with a sharply curved point. The other end was threaded for screwing into a wall or ceiling.

"Up there," he said, pointing to a ceiling beam high above his painting. "I've already set up a ladder, as you can see. Now, if I know you at all, you've probably brought some wine. Why don't I open the bottle and let it breathe while you mount that hook?"

"Lafcadio, what is this for?"

"No, I don't think so," he said again with a laugh. "Believe me, we understand each other very well. It'll be fun! No matter how unpleasant it might seem for a time, it will be fun, believe you me." He patted her shoulder lovingly and then departed for the kitchen, where she heard him pop the cork on the bottle. The hook was cold against her palm, and she looked at it almost in wonder.

As she climbed the ladder and labored to screw the hook into the tough oaken beam, she felt as if she had stepped into a dream. It was not her own, but somebody else's. Yes, she was a character in somebody else's dream. Below her, the painting was visible on its easel, and she stared down at her own icy face with mixed feelings of dread and awe. From her vantage point near the ceiling, the painting was inverted. Her icy reflection stared up at her with an expression of supernatural peace and wisdom. In the arctic waste of Lafcadio's vision, she had become an avatar of spiritual insight. She could discern this without his giving her a word of explanation.

From the bottom of the painting, the fiery-bloody hole gaped with a fierce determination, its hot and juicy depths standing in stark contrast to the supernal peace above. The counterbalance left her feeling sick for some reason. When she looked up and saw that she had finished screwing the hook into the beam, she descended the ladder quickly and turned her back on the canvas.

Lafcadio returned and saw that she had accomplished her mission. "Excellent!" he said. "Would you please go and pour two glasses for us, darling? I've set them out for you already. Everything is waiting." He stepped closer, and she forced herself not to flinch. "Thank you, too, for the rose. A wonderfully symbolic gesture, and all too appropriate in light of recent developments." He leaned down and kissed her cheek. When he stood back up, his smile was warm and his eyes were calm. She felt herself relax, and allowed herself to hope once more for a pleasant evening.

"Will you explain this to me when I get back?" She gestured toward the canvas. He glanced at it, reflected for a moment, and nodded.

"Whatever you say, Cornelia. It's our night."

She smiled then; it felt good to break through the icy numbness that had overtaken her face without her even noticing it. At some point between her arrival at his flat and his return from the kitchen, her face had grown stiff and cold. Smiling was an effort, but it brought life back to her cheeks and eyes. Still smiling, she went to the kitchen and poured the wine into two stemmed glasses that were waiting on the countertop.

"Lafcadio," she called. "I think you should tell me about Brian again. I've been thinking about it, and I have a theory. Maybe the incident with the hook was a dream of emasculation. Maybe it represents some sort of archetypal male fear of living in a matriarchy. A lot of intelligent people have been saying in recent years that we're turning into a matriarchal society. Or I guess I should say, *back* into one, just like it was in prehistory. Do you think maybe you've tapped into a hidden fear in the male subconscious? Maybe you dreamed Brian into a situation where his fear of women had to come out." She set the bottle down and lifted a wine-filled glass in each hand. The bouquet rose to her nostrils with a delicate aroma of vanilla and cloves.

"What do you think?" She turned the corner and stopped inside the doorway to the studio. "Lafcadio?"

The wine spilled, of course, when the glasses hit the floor, but the area of the stain was relatively small. Some droplets hit the cream-colored carpet of the hallway, marking it forever with a permanent speckling of purplish-crimson. The rest of it pooled on the hardwood floor like blood. It was a long time before Cornelia or anybody else thought to wipe it up, and by that time most of it had seeped through the cracks and into the pores, leaving an equally permanent stain on the wood.

Cleaning up spilled wine was the least of Cornelia's concerns at the moment. She was transfixed by the sight of Lafcadio dangling high above her from the rafter, the silver hook buried deep in the socket of his right eye, his legs and arms twitching in spastic birdlike motions, his mouth working silently to shape a whispered stream of veritably Pentecostal gibberish. The gore spattering onto the hardwood floor touched everything around the painting. Some of it splashed onto the canvas itself, adding its own crimson hue to the reds and oranges of the fiery crater. Below the flailing artist, above the deep-gouging sinkhole in the belly of the frozen wasteland, the supernally peaceful face of Cornelia the Ice Goddess brooded silently in eternal bliss.

When the flesh-and-blood Cornelia had recovered from her horrified paralysis, she raced up the ladder and began tugging madly at the legs of the artist, whose spastic motions were growing less vigorous as his strength expired. She grunted and lifted him up, heaving, thrusting. At last she succeeded. The hook ripped free, dragging a few bone splinters with it, and he dropped ten feet to the floor and landed with a meaty thud.

Of course the blood began to spurt from his eye then, in red gouts like finger-paint. It looked red even to him, even with his colorblind field of vision rapidly fading and growing distant, as if he were backing down a tunnel at incredible speed. The pain was even more vicious than he had anticipated: a white-hot ball of electric agony, searing its way inward from his eye to his brain. Cornelia was crouching beside him, pawing at him in a panic, weeping, asking him what to do.

In the midst of it all, rather wonderfully, he found himself floating in an airy sea of transcendent bliss, gazing down from a dizzying height at the outline of an arctic tundra below. The furrows stretched away toward the horizon like lumps of shiny vanilla ice cream, until they met with the mountains of two icy breasts, and even farther north, with the glittering-diamond surface of a gargantuan icon that presented its face eternally to the gaze of vast, moonlit sky.

I am home, he thought, even as the borders of his consciousness began to crumble and allow the pure seed of awareness to expand outward to the next level of selfhood.

The next thought was unexpected. It was different in tenor from any he had ever thought before, and yet it seemed familiar. Coming from his higher self, it was more intense and profound than what he was used to; the sheer truth of it seemed to touch the landscape below, to fill the frigid atmosphere between them, and to saturate the glaze of moonlight cascading down onto the icy hillocks like iridescent milk. The sound of it was the sound of the primal ocean depths, like a million voices whispering into his ear from every direction at once. For a moment, just a final moment of private desire, Lafcadio held onto the perspective of his small self and translated the thought into the language he was accustomed to thinking and speaking. The million voices coalesced into one, and it was the familiar voice of his own private self. He stared in stark horror at the words that seemed almost to float before him in visible waves upon the snow: *No boundary means no escape.*

For an instant he refused to believe them. He refused to believe that even in this new, blissful existence of ultimate transcendence and freedom, he was still unable to escape the clutches of his deepest-held fear. It simply could not be true, not with the unbounded horizon of a mystical frozen landscape stretching away from him on all sides like the receding outer edge of an ecstatic dream.

Then the grip on his old perspective proved too difficult to maintain. Even as he contemplated these mysteries, he lost his hold on Lafcadio and expanded fully, finally, into the wider perspective of the ancient Self that had always been floating and lurking behind the facade of his consciousness like the ghost of a future incarnation. At last the transition was complete, and he could leave behind all his fears, the old and the new, and glory forever in the exuberance of an unbounded aesthetic delight.

It wasn't until he fully used his new eyes for the first time that he recognized the flaw in his plans.

Lafcadio was long-gone, left far behind in that dull, flat other realm where the senses could never get their fill because there was simply not enough to fill them up. But the *memory* of Lafcadio was not gone, and in this new existence, where consciousness had no boundaries, he discovered there could be no distinction between memory and present reality. The incarnate ghost of Lafcadio the

Magnificent was still a presence, still a truth, and Lafcadio's subjectivity was still inextricably intertwined with that of the higher Self who was even now dreaming him back into existence.

The dream placed him in the belly of the beast, deep within the womblike innards of the arctic landscape, where molten fire burned in scalding jets of orange and red, and where self-inflicted wounds assumed all the permanence and significance of religious stigmata. The old Lafcadio screamed in this fiery, freezing hell, and the new-ancient Self screamed with him. They were locked together in twin perspectives of mutual suffering.

There could be no escape, for there was no boundary.

(And somewhere in a black-and-white world of cardboard lives and flimsy stage-prop dreams, Cornelia crouched over the body of her beloved artist and wept as she saw his dying features twist into an expression of horror. He gave one final, mighty convulsion, and then flopped onto his side and curled inward upon himself like a slug. She could not force herself to raise her eyes to the painting that presided over them like an icon of everything they had ever hoped to gain from each other. She dared not gaze at the image and see, within the glowing depths of her own icy belly, a transformed image of the bloody artist stretched out before her. As she fell backward onto the rough wooden floor and felt its warm, sticky wetness stain her hands and clothes, a momentary desire flashed through her mind, a habit ingrained from years of brash conversations. Absurdly, she wanted to demand, "Tell me everything." But she knew that even if he could answer, she would not want to hear what he had to say.)

The Devil and One Lump

I woke up that morning and stepped right into a story that I might have written myself—back when I could still write, that is. And even then I only would have written such a story if I were a hack who dealt in shameless clichés instead of a serious student of the dark self.

For the Devil himself sat waiting for me in my living room on that beautiful, sunny morning. And he looked like he had been dispatched to my house right from central casting.

Here's how it happened: I crawled out of bed all fuzzy-eyed and disappointed that the daylight had come so quickly, since I had spent the night sitting up late by myself and imbibing vast quantities of wine in the very same chair where you-know-who would greet me a few hours later. My television had sat silent and my bookcases unmolested. And the damned computer had stayed locked in the closet. No entertainment for me. The plan had been to devote the entire evening to indulging deliberately in my private misery, exploring each shading of its symptoms and every cranny of its causes. It had ended up a magnificent success, all things considered.

And of course I paid for it the morning after, as I had known full well I would. Catharsis wasn't something I sought; I had given up on that long ago. The emotional hangover from the night's excess of self-pity was actually worse than the alcohol-induced one, a truth that glared at me in the wretched light of a despicable sun as it squeezed its violating rays through loathsomely disloyal window blinds. (See what I mean?) So as soon as my feet hit the Berber, I raced straightway for the kitchen—or rather stumbled on legs made of some miraculous hybrid substance, part gelatin, part rubber—to get the coffee started. The holy liquid blast of caffeine was set to be my savior that day, and I was eager to begin the worship service.

As I stood filling the carafe with tap water and earnestly striving to achieve total cognitive annihilation through sheer force of will, I heard somebody clear his throat. If ever I heard a dignified realignment of mucus, it was in the cultured sound of that musical *ahem*. Later, after the incident was over, I thought back and realized that everything that came afterward had already been previewed in that single, phlegm-filled sound.

Not that I knew this consciously at the time, what with the outer world coming to me through a perceptual filter of extreme ugliness while my craving for coffee ramped upward toward junkie level. At the time, I was simply startled to hear that I was not alone. So I whirled around to see who was there, and when my head stopped spinning a few seconds after my body, what should I see but a man in a dark business suit, exquisitely tailored, sitting in the sun room off the kitchen. That room faces east, so at 7 a.m. it was flooded with golden light from that overeager sun. This meant the guy was silhouetted against a row of window panes awash in liquid gold. Naturally, I blinked, and the afterimage of the fiery silhouette that was seared onto my retinas showed somebody bigger and bulkier than this normal-sized person, somebody who had what appeared to be wing joints jutting up above his shoulders and goat's horns protruding from his temples.

So I blinked again, several times, rapidly. All this did was to strobe both images, the regular guy and the mountainous devil, against each other in rapid alternation. When I stopped blinking and stared, he was just a regular guy, albeit a very scrubbed and handsome-looking one. And he was sitting in my vintage La-Z-Boy recliner with his legs crossed and his hands templed. He said to me, "Having fun with the blinking thing? I can't say I blame you. It's an interesting effect, isn't it? Sometimes I wish my eyes worked like yours." He spoke in a rich baritone, melodious and smooth.

To say I was dazed is an understatement. To say I was pissed off at the man's desecration of my sacred sulking chair is entirely accurate. A cold splash of liquid on my hand made me jump, and I realized I was letting the water overflow the carafe. I quickly shut off the tap off and set down the carafe. My coffee rhythm was broken. My mental and physical misery morphed into outrage. Okay, so *pissed off* was going to trump freaked out, at least for now.

The guy just looked at me as I hobbled into the sun room and tried to muster a poisonous glare. Before I could summon an appropriate verbal challenge to his presence, he said, "Please,

Evan, have a seat," and indicated I should join him by settling on the nearby sofa. His voice and mannerism were pure silk. How could you hate a guy with a set of vocal cords like that and a personal style to match? I was amazed at the way I instantly began to melt. I obeyed him and sat on the sofa—but on the end farthest from him.

"I know," he continued, "this is all very sudden. You didn't wake up expecting to see me here. That's all right. I've grown very accustomed to poor receptions. So please don't trouble yourself with feelings of remorse about your poor reaction to me, even though as your guest I do deserve better treatment, at least under a set of older cultural codes whose loss I lament."

It sounds insane, but the casualness of his manner and soothingness of his voice, combined with his oddly complex and formal speech pattern, set me back on my regular schedule. I stared at him open-mouthed for a moment, then rose and returned to the kitchen to finish with the coffee. The comforting nature of the ritual began to pacify me: fill the carafe, then fill the reservoir. Set the paper filter, then scoop in some Folgers. Press the "brew" button, then wait for the miracle. As the trickle of hot dark liquid began tinkling into the carafe, I realized I really needed to visit the toilet.

"Evan?" That wondrous baritone again, like a pipe organ speaking through a human vocal apparatus. "This will take only a moment. I'd appreciate your full attention. We really need to talk."

"Why would I talk with someone who's not even there?" These words, tossed over my shoulder with arch impertinence, were a blatantly manufactured attempt to appear nonchalant. "I'm reminded of the sage words of Ebenezer Scrooge concerning the sometimes dramatic hallucinatory effects of digestion upon perception. You're probably just a bit of undigested beef, or a blot of mustard, or a crumb of cheese. Or, as the case may be, a gallon or two of cheap wine. So go away. I'm about to drink the elixir of life, so I have precious little time to chat."

"*Evan.*" His voicing of my name this time landed like a boulder. The very walls shook, and his tone cracked slightly but ominously, not on the high end the low one, his baritone betraying a hint of impossibly deep bass like the foghorn roar of a primeval monster. The thick vibrations actually rumbled in my chest, momentarily seizing my lungs and squeezing the breath out of them. In the ensuing silence, I listened to the delicate tinkling of the coffee while silently willing my visitor to be nothing more than Scrooge's digestive hallucination. But when I turned to look, he was not only still there but still seated in my La-Z-Boy.

He said, "Are we on the same page now?" and his voice was back to normal. I suppose we must indeed have been reading the same text by then, for I meekly returned to the sun room and resettled on the sofa, this time on the end nearest him. From this closer angle I verified that he really was ruggedly handsome, in a corporate-man sort of way: hair slicked back, perfect teeth, square jaw, nice tan, flawless complexion. He wore expensive cologne, too, and I savored the spicy tang of it even as I noticed that it failed to completely mask another, less pleasant smell that hung about him like an invisible cloud: the stink of smoke and sulfur, like rotten eggs in a burnt-out house.

He gave me a pointed look. "I'm here about your books." Then he waited for my response.

In my brilliance, I came up with, "What?"

"Let's not mince words, Evan." He assumed a shrewd expression. "Horror novels are one thing, but *religious* horror novels—or horrific religious novels, if you prefer—are quite another. The books you write have produced the unfortunate result of crossing certain wires, as it were, and thereby producing certain, shall we say, *problematic* effects amongst a wide swath of readers. The purpose of my visit this morning is to set you on a different course."

"You . . . I . . ." My eloquence continued to astound.

"The problem," he said, "is that you have taken the entire Christian cosmology and, more importantly, the characteristic emotional tenor of those who consider themselves Christians, and you have turned these on their head. You have created protagonists whose very search for salvation produces a backfire effect that damns them to a worse hell than they had ever imagined. You have speculated that the Bible contains a hidden subtext that runs between the actual printed lines and undermines the surface message at every turn. You have written of a narcissistic demiurge who is so enraptured by the beauty of his own creation that he represses the memory of his birth from a monstrous prior reality, so that when he is forcibly reawakened to this memory, he suffers a psychological breakdown that generates cataclysmic consequences both for himself and for the cosmos he created. In these ways and many others, you've launched a subversive assault on the deepest philosophical and theological foundations of the enemy camp."

He actually said "the enemy camp." Was he referring to *God?* To *Christians?* Did this fact, and also the smell and the voice and the Dante-esque shape that still sizzled on my retinas, indicate the man's true identity? Was this truly the type of story that I had stepped into? A "Devil in the morning" rehash?

As I wondered these things with my jaw hanging down, he concluded: "You might reasonably think that I would approve of your efforts. But you would be mistaken. God, to put it bluntly, does not need depth therapy. He can't handle it—precisely as you have intuited in your books. And I'm here to make sure that your future creative efforts are focused in a different and, shall we say, more fruitful direction."

Despite or because my astonishment, my blood began to boil again. The guy was talking about my books. My *books*, those hated relics from the former life I had lost. And he was speaking as if I were somehow still responsible for them. The heat of my rising fury began to clear away some of the remaining fog in my brain, and I let this irate clarity shape my words.

"Even though this is all a dream, I'm still not going to sit here and listen to such accusations. Let's get this straight right now: I do not *write* those goddamned books, I *wrote* those goddamned books. And now it's hands off, once and for all. So don't you dare come here to my house and interrupt my coffee and sit in my chair and accuse me of . . . of whatever it is you're accusing me of. Because you're talking to an *ex*-author who doesn't give a *damn* about those books."

"Of all the delicious sins in this sinfully delicious universe," he said, "there's none more delicious or endearing than self-deception. Especially of the willful kind, which you're demonstrating with aplomb at the moment. Bravo, Evan!"

The fuck?

He sized me up, smiled with that handsome mouth, and nodded. "Go ahead. Tell me what you want to tell me. Share the whole sad story of your private woe, which, as I strangely regret to inform you, really hasn't been all that private."

I felt as if I were coming unglued. Literally. My brain reeled and my heart wanted to hammer a hole in my sternum. "The . . . the books . . ." He nodded again with obvious approval, encouraging me to share and tell.

And just like that, the logjam in my mouth and heart and brain broke wide. "My books almost killed me! Do you think I *wanted* to become the king of mid-list horror? Hell, no! All I ever wanted was to spend my life writing about religion and beauty and truth and spirit and mystical awakening. That's what I loved since I was a kid! When those novels about God's psychosis and all that crap came flooding out instead, I was more horrified than any of my readers. I was absolutely mortified at the metaphysical sewage spewing from my pen."

"But," he pointed out helpfully, "not so mortified that you refused to cash the checks."

"What else could I do?" My fury was erupting to volcanic heights. "My whole life imploded! My wife said she couldn't live with somebody who put 'hell on paper.' She called me a monster to my face and then left me, after which her family cleaned me out in a lawsuit over 'emotional damages.'"

"And oh, irony of ironies, what happened next?"

Next? "There was no next. That was the end of it. Just as soon as my life had completely imploded, the curse went away. I couldn't write those things anymore. I couldn't write *any*thing anymore. I went from being a working writer to being a blocked writer overnight. And the well wasn't just empty, it was concreted over and laced with trip wires. I got pounding headaches every time I tried to think about writing. My thoughts scrambled when I even sat down in front of the typewriter, let alone tried put words together. It got so bad I wondered if I might have a brain tumor. I returned all the publishers' advances, broke my contracts, and live now on a few royalty checks that get smaller every time."

"And so," he said with an air of finality, "here we sit, I in your chair and you on that sofa, which I'm noticing could stand to be reupholstered."

I was drained. My eyes felt feverish and my gut cold. "Here we sit," I repeated.

"Evan," he said, "somebody—I forget who—once said, 'You shall know the truth, and the truth shall set you free.' I come to you now bearing that truth and offering that freedom."

I was too numb even to summon another "What?"

He continued: "Would you like to write again? Would you like to return to your first love? Don't tell me you haven't thought about it these past several years while you've been drinking alone."

"You can help me write again." It was a question that plopped out as a lifeless statement, like I had somehow spat a dead cat out on the floor.

"Yes, I can help you write *again*." He gave a special emphasis to the final word and smiled faintly. "After all, I did it once before."

He cut off my look of blank confusion with more words. "It's time to come clean, I suppose. You noticed, naturally, that your authorial aspirations took a decidedly different turn than what you had originally intended. Please don't pretend to be shocked when I inform you of what you long suspected: that the unexpected change was of course my doing. I gave you a little, shall we say, *push* in a new direction, and then nature—*your* nature, to be exact—simply took its course."

"A push?"

"Yes, Evan. More fully, I assigned you a muse, and she whispered things into your inner mind, certain dark and hidden truths which most people never manage to intuit, and you then processed these promptings through that magnificent literary sensibility of yours to produce some of the finest horrific writings this side of the Abyss. As I said, there's no use pretending that you didn't speculate a few times in your darkest moments that you were the victim of a demonic curse. The fact is, you *were*. And the fact is, it's not fair. There's no justice in it. So don't bother searching for any. Just ask a man I once knew by the name of Job."

"You . . . cursed me?" That dreamy feeling again, really rippling and powerful this time. Not real. None of it. Not happening.

"All part of a master plan that I was and still am working," he said. "And oh, how it did work! Watching you run with those ineffable evil truths was so very refreshing. You were truly a fine vehicle, and don't think I didn't appreciate it.

"But then the backfire effect I alluded to earlier began to set in. You went too deep and started breaking out of the proper boundaries that my opponent and I had set. I guess I didn't take proper account of your keen philosophical bent, because your exposés and deconstructions of the Almighty—as he obtusely insists on referring to himself—started exposing and undermining the very foundations of the game that he and I have set for ourselves. In a nutshell, it doesn't benefit me at all when people start thinking 'off the grid' in matters of good and evil. I'm in this war to win it, not to see myself rendered irrelevant by people who see through it. And so I find myself in the unenviable position of paying you a visit today in order to shore up my opponent's ego." His smile now was rueful and none too pleasant. "Who would have thought?"

Despite my rising astonishment, incredulity, and horror, it was all quite fascinating, really, this revelation from the Devil, and in a deep and thrilling way that I hadn't experienced for years. Damn, but those were ideas that I sure could have run with, back in the days when I could write.

But the greater part of my attention at the moment was occupied by memories of all those years when I had been writing horror fiction and feeling as if I were either possessed by a demon or suffering from a progressive form of nightmarish schizophrenia. The shadows in my closet and under the bed had begun to inspire a profound sense of dread. I had been plagued by nightmares of suffocating darkness and demonic presences, from which I would awaken with keening shrieks that terrified my wife. The only outlet I had found for my growing horror had been my typewriter and the blank pages I rolled into it, which I had blackened with fictional visions more awful than anything I had ever heard of, let alone wanted to midwife into the world.

And now I was hearing the reason for my life's ruin explained in plain language, spoken by the Devil in a Gucci suit.

"You did this to me," I said in a quiet voice. And then, "*You* did *this* to *me*!"

"Evan," he said, and that volcanic rumbling tremored again through the floor and up through the sofa and into my soft, fleshy body. "Shut up. Just shut up and listen. 'Here's the deal,' as people in your increasingly illiterate and verbally barbaric culture and historical period are wont to say. I can't have you exposing God's and my cosmic game of Spy Versus Spy, and you can't stand living with yourself in your current state any longer. So this is what's going to happen."

Why was the room beginning to heat up and the air shimmer with a hellish red glare even as my consciousness of the crystalline chirping of the birds in the backyard beyond the windows grew more delicate and precise? Why did I catch a whiff of rotting flesh and acrid, ashy waste even as the morning sunlight appeared more golden and pure than I had known it for many years?

"I am assigning you another muse." This was the Devil speaking to me, I reminded myself, and he nodded, reading my thought and never wavering in his declaration. "She has been instructed to fill your soul with the inspiration you have always desired. You will find that everything you ever wanted will now come to you. And from your pen—sorry, typewriter—from the very same channel that brought into the world those subversive revelations which have so imperiled my operations, there shall flow revelations that will once again shore up the dam, patch the damaged parts, make the straight places crooked again, and shove those damned exalted valleys back down to their proper place."

He lifted a hand and made a strange sign in the air, almost as if he were making the sign of the cross, but it was a different symbol he traced, one that shot a bolt of sickness through my gut. My face and eyes burned with the hot red glow that had overtaken the sun room. My body trembled with the volcanic-oceanic roar that had infiltrated the bass frequencies built into the acoustics of those sheetrocked, texture-splattered, white-painted walls.

And then *poof*! all was cool and silent. Except for the warm golden sunbeams and gaily chirping birds. Cool air kissed my cheeks. It was a beautiful morning.

And I was alone. No Corporate-Miltonic Satan confronted me from the hallowed folds of my La-Z-Boy, which was now blessedly empty, although its seat and back cushions bore a phantom discoloration akin to smoke damage in the shape of a man.

I managed to stand up, and after testing my balance, hopped into the recliner and snuggled down into it for a moment, just to assure myself that I still fit. Which I did, although the trace warmth of another very warm body still clinging to the cushions was distinctly less than pleasant.

And then I did the only thing there was to do. I got up and went to the kitchen, where the coffee waited for me to brew it. In sixty seconds flat the splashy little burblings of the coffee maker were soothing my spirit while the sharp-musky scent cleared my head. Everything seemed so crisp and fresh. Even the texture of my bathrobe against my skin felt remarkably new and delightful.

"Is this for real?" I asked aloud of no one in particular. "Is this the leading edge of new inspiration?" Enough coffee had already trickled into the pot for me to pour a mug, so I did and then returned the pot to its cradle. "Because," I said aloud again, "I can tell you right now that it's *no deal*. I'm not writing for you or anybody else. That's all over. This is *my* life, as crappy as it may be, and I'm going to suck all the misery out of it while I can, gods and devils be damned."

Still facing the counter and the kitchen cabinets, holding the white china mug with the black steaming liquid in my utterly steady hand, I raised my face to the ceiling and shouted. "Do you hear me? *No deal!*"

I added one lump of sugar and stirred lightly. Then I took a sip and sighed in ecstasy. No more devils for me that day.

The room went red before I could swallow. The roaring of a titanic cataract set me to shaking like a victim of Saint Vitus' Dance. A furnace blast of heat seared my flesh.

A voice boomed from behind me: "*This is not a negotiation.*" No melodious baritone there. This was a lion roaring in a hurricane.

I whirled around, hot coffee drooling from my lips and down my chin and chest, to find a shriekingly hideous Dantean Devil towering over me in full gothic-reptilian splendor. Black wings and talons. Ram's horns sprouting from a misshapen head. Gray skinned, rotten textured, with yellow moonsliver feline eyes and a porcine snout surmounting an impossibly wide mouth whose lips were drawn back in a smile that revealed far too many silvery teeth, each one as long as a dagger. The creature must have stood nearly eight feet tall, and would have been obliged to hunch its head if the ceiling had still been there, but that cozy lid had been ripped off the top of my world, and the bare tops of my kitchen walls now outlined a blackish-crimson skyscape of roiling clouds where bolt lightning carved out jagged trails and leering wolf's faces formed and reformed endlessly in the furrows.

The blackstretched lips of the mountainous Devil before me moved and formed words. "*You* will *accept your gift and set things aright again. You* will *repair the damage you have wrought. And the pleasure you derive from fulfilling your deepest desire* will *be your damnation. That's the deal.*"

Then he reached out a taloned hand, plucked the little white cup from my fingers, and dumped the drop of dark liquid down his throat. "*Mmmmmm,*" he sighed. "*The best part of waking up.*"

And that's what I found myself doing next: waking up. In my bed. At my normal time. With a hangover and a fading memory of some dreamworld encounter that could not possibly be real. No way. Not a chance.

But when I crawled out of bed all fuzzy-eyed and disappointed that the daylight had come so quickly, I was arrested in mid-shuffle by a curious phenomenon: the sunlight squeezing through the slats of the window blinds didn't seem despicable, but delightful. I felt that if I were given to bouts of synesthesia, I might hear those delicate golden rays humming a hushed hymn to the beauties of creation.

I stayed rooted to the carpeted floor while the outlandishness of this development worked its way through me. Then I cautiously approached the blinds and raised my hand to pull the cord. It was a veritable Lux Aeterna moment, with the choral voices keening while the subhuman creature crept toward the ominous monolith with trembling outstretched hand. At last I seized the cord and pulled it.

A Hallelujah Chorus of celestial sunlight nearly knocked me back onto the bed. It flooded the room with divine joy and penetrated all the way to the heart of my dark misery.

No way. No *way*.

Next stop, the kitchen, where I peered anxiously into the adjoining sun room and saw nothing but sunlight singing like the Mormon Tabernacle Choir while dust motes swirled in the blaze like heavenly fireflies.

The only part of my usual schedule that this explosion of mind-blowing joy could not disrupt was the Ritual of the Coffee. I prepped the pot and pressed the button while the chorus continued to sing.

Without warning, before the brew cycle had finished, I was gripped by the knowledge that there was something I simply had to do, even though the thought of it elicited a stab of cold dread.

I crept to the spare bedroom and dug through the closet until I located my typewriter buried beneath mounds of deliberately piled junk. I dusted off the card table where my best work had always taken place, and gently laid the typewriter on its surface. Another quick dig, this one through my old file cabinet, produced a stack of fresh white 16 pound bond paper, which I hadn't remembered still owning.

I sat down softly and rolled in a sheet. I caressed a key. Then I punched it. The letter appeared on the pristine paper with a satisfying *thwack*. I punched another, and then another. I raised my other hand to the qwerty keyboard and was soon typing words. And then sentences. And then paragraphs.

The tripwires had been removed and the concrete blasted away. The well of inspiration was wide open and brimming with cool waters of redemption.

I wrote, and wrote, and then wrote some more while the coffee maker burbled and whispered in the next room and my long-pent-up craving for spiritual peace and enlightenment poured itself onto the pages. I already saw the full outline of the essay I was composing, and beyond that, the structure of the book of which it would be the opening piece. And there was another book after that, and then yet another, all perfectly formed in my head. Impossibly, after years of wretched emptiness, I had exploded in the course of a single morning into full-blown, super-genius Mozart mode, with fully finished works crowding in my head and just waiting for me to release them.

After awhile, when the stack of finished pages had grown thick and still the flow of words showed no signs of letting up, I found I was weeping as I wrote. Perfectly natural, I told myself. A function of joy, an excess of cleansing emotion at the lifting of my sterile curse. I already saw how the very fact of my sobs could be worked gracefully into the very paragraph I was then crafting about redemptive changes of mind and heart, by referring to the "gift of tears" the early Christian fathers wrote so much about.

Pointedly, purposefully, I kept typing and ignored the transition that came when the clacking of the keys began to sound like dry little laughs.

THE GOD OF FOULNESS

And what, Ananda, is contemplation of foulness? Herein, Ananda, a monk contemplates this body upwards from the soles of the feet, downwards from the top of the hair, enclosed in skin, as being full of many impurities. In this body there are head-hairs, body-hairs, nails, teeth, skin, flesh, sinews, bones, marrow, kidneys, heart, liver, pleura, spleen, lungs, intestines, intestinal tract, stomach, faeces, bile, phlegm, pus, blood, sweat, fat, tears, grease, saliva, nasal mucous, synovium (oil lubricating the joints), and urine. Thus he dwells contemplating foulness in this body. This, Ananda, is called contemplation of foulness.

—from *Pirit Potha* ("The Book of Protection"),
a Pali Buddhist text

Am now acutely ill with intestinal trouble following grippe. No strength—constant pain. Bloated with gas and have to sit and sleep constantly in chair with pillows. Doctor is going to call in a stomach specialist Tuesday. So I fear I shan't be able to do much for a long time to come.

—H. P. Lovecraft, from a letter
dated fifteen days before his death

As a foulness shall ye know Them.

—*The Necronomicon*

Disgust at what things are made of: liquid, dust, bones, filth . . . Turn the body inside out, and see what kind of thing it is, and when it has grown old, what kind of thing it becomes, and when it is diseased . . . Stop letting yourself be distracted. That is not allowed. Instead, as if you were dying right now, despise your flesh. A mess of blood, pieces of bone, a woven tangle of nerves, veins, arteries . . . The stench of decay. Rotting meat in a bag. Look at it clearly. If you can.

—Marcus Aurelius, *Meditations*

I

At first I thought it was just a perverse reaction to several decades' worth of bombardment by conflicting pronouncements from the medical establishment about what constitutes a "healthy lifestyle." That was my working hypothesis, held with tongue firmly in cheek, when my editor at the *Terence Sun-Gazette* assigned me to cover the grassroots phenomenon known as the Sick and Saved movement. The movement had garnered an insane amount of publicity in recent months because of its shocking—some would say *appalling*—claim. Its members worshiped sickness and disease. The media had dubbed them the "Sick Seekers" and given them enough coverage to lead some commentators to call them the story of the century, even though the new century had barely begun. The Sick Seekers came from all walks of life and boasted all manner of physical and mental disorders, and their defining characteristic was that they viewed any kind of sickness as evidence of a special spiritual grace. At least, this was the best guess the commentators could come up with, since the Sick Seekers were notoriously close-mouthed to outsiders about the particulars of their beliefs and practices.

The only other thing anybody knew for certain about them was that they prominently refused all medical treatments. This of course threw the official government bodies charged with safeguarding the public health into a collective panic. In the United States, the American Medical Association, the Centers for Disease Control, and National Institutes of Mental Health all wrung their hands with great public display. "What if people start actively *trying* to become sick?" they asked with clockwork regularity on all of the nightly news programs. Obviously, the media themselves thought this was happening already, hence their popularization of the term "Sick Seekers."

The insurance and pharmaceutical industries were none too happy about the situation, either. The pharmaceutical companies in particular were scrambling for a solution, since their business was dealt a near death blow by the sheer numbers of the new movement, which was composed largely of elderly people who would otherwise have been their biggest customers. By the most recent estimate, which had been performed by a sociologist at

Harvard and publicized in *Time* magazine, the Sick Seekers numbered around the million mark in the United States alone. This meant there were more of them than there were Unitarians.

As I said, my immediate reaction was to view all of this with a rather cynical eye. To begin with, I decided to regard the term "Sick Seekers" with wry amusement, since it contained a semantic ambiguity, probably unnoticed by whoever had coined it, that didn't specify whether "sick" referred to what the people were seeking to become or how they ought to be morally perceived. Next, I turned to speculating about the origins of the movement, and arrived at my above-mentioned theory about a collective disgust at the inability of the medical community to arrive at a consensus regarding how one ought to eat, exercise, and so on. (My theory didn't explain why the same movement had cropped up in undeveloped nations where this information overload wasn't a problem, but I put that item on a backburner.) I myself had grown annoyed at the way the morning news programs always seemed to present at least one new doctor per day, who advanced at least one new theory about which foods to avoid, which medicines to take, which tests to have run, and which exercises to do. I amused myself by speculating that the Sick Seekers were people who had just decided to throw in the towel and forget about trying to wade through the mass of conflicting information. This allowed me to applaud their audacity from the sidelines.

When I first came to understand that they were engendering real concern not only among government authorities but the populace at large, I realized I should take them a bit more seriously. Their arrival on the world scene had created a truly apocalyptic mood in countries around the globe, one that harmonized beautifully with the mass premonition of approaching doom that had already begun to grip the globe during the early 21st century. But even so, after reading about and reflecting on the matter I still found it easy just to write the whole thing off as a mass hysteria, admittedly a repugnant one, but in essence no different from the millennial madness that had gripped the Western nations at the end of the twentieth century, or the rise of the charismatic Christian movement and its bastard child, the "signs and wonders" movement or "Third Wave" of

Pentecostalism that was still providing so much research fodder for sociologists and scholars of religion who were caught up in the perennial quest for tenure.

I had once thought that I would number myself among those professional academicians. My interest in the Sick and Saved movement was more than just an idle amusement. Early in life, I had found that I was possessed of a seemingly inborn fascination with religion and spirituality. I was raised in no formal religious tradition, but when I discovered the literature of Zen Buddhism at the age of thirteen, it was as if a door were suddenly unlocked inside me, one that I hadn't even known existed. Suddenly, I was gripped by a veritably daimonic passion for spiritual knowledge, and by the time I graduated from high school, I was already planning to major in religious studies at the university and then go on to earn my doctorate. The thought of spending all my days walled up inside the comfortable ivory tower of academia, surrounded by books that fed my thirst for spiritual ideas, filled me with delicious feelings of security and comfort.

All had gone well for the first few years of my enrollment in the religious studies program at Terence University. But then, for reasons that still eluded me ten years later, everything had grown stale just two months before I was scheduled to earn my master's degree. I had been shocked as I experienced the pent-up excitement of my imminent academic career leaking like air from a punctured tire. Somehow, without my knowing it, a sense of hollowness and staleness had crept into everything I held dear, everything I thought my life was about, and I suddenly realized that I didn't know where to go or what to do. My sense of being on track with a life mission was gone, and had been replaced by a feeling of bleak hopelessness and confusion. Briefly, I fell into a personal and professional tailspin.

Then one of my professors, Dr. Daniel Baumann, advised me to consider another career. Since my awakening at the age of thirteen, I had never even thought of doing anything else, but when I turned my mind to it everything happened quickly. Within a matter of days, practically on a whim, I somehow fell into the journalism master's degree program. All thoughts of a career in academia fled down the same invisible drain that had siphoned away my passion for religion. I set my sights on becoming a Pulitzer Prize winning journalist, and for years I didn't look back.

Eight years after obtaining the master's degree, I was still seeking the Pulitzer. More than anything else, those years had taught me that the confusion I had felt upon the death of my former sense of identity with a life mission was merely the front end of a long initiation into the arbitrary caprices of the inner life. I tried not to dwell too much on it, since I could tell that to do so would send me into a paralyzing depression, but eight years into my post-college career the foreground of my steady, normal outer life was paralleled precisely by an inner life of virulent nihilism, punctuated by periods of manic emotional abandon. The term "bipolar" played on my mind often, but I never sought a medical diagnosis. My spiritual and philosophical side wasn't totally gone. It had merely undergone a mutation. My love of ideas had somehow evolved into a kind of philosophical schizophrenia that expressed itself in terms of a kaleidoscopic shifting of worldviews, many of them mutually exclusive or even actively antagonistic toward each other. In this condition, I thought it would be useless to receive an official diagnosis of a chemical imbalance, since I would probably find myself arguing the very next day against the logical axioms upon which the diagnosis was founded. To add insult to injury, my cognizance of my condition only exacerbated its severity. By the time the Sick Seekers arrived on the scene, I had reached a point of near-burnout where all my emotional reserves were depleted and I had trouble believing anything, even my own thoughts. At times I diverted myself with a kind of gallows humor by speculating that my philosophical schizophrenia might qualify me for membership in the new movement.

But when I was assigned to cover them for the newspaper, I saw no humor in it, for I recognized an immediate problem: so many things had already been said about the Sick Seekers that there was surely nothing left for me to write.

I raised this point to Bobby, my managing editor, but he countered by letting me know his reasons for wanting the story.

"There's a local group of them," he told me on a Tuesday afternoon, after having given me the assignment the day before via an email. He was drinking coffee to perk himself up for the final few hours of his workday, and he stared at me over the steaming cup as he took a sip. I was seated across the desk from him with notepad in hand, prepared to take what I had expected to be meaningless notes.

"Are you sure?" I said after a long pause. I habitually measured my words and actions carefully around other people, but it was difficult to conceal the fact that this unexpected information had ignited a spark of interest in me. I carefully distanced myself from the feeling and kept my eyes steadily upon Bobby.

"Not entirely," he said. "That's part of what I want you to find out. Believe me, I know how hard it will be to think of anything new to say. But if there really is a local group, then we've got the chance to do something special. You know how private these people are supposed to be."

And indeed, I did know of their notorious reticence. Even their closest family members didn't know what they really believed. Everything in the news was just second-hand testimony from friends, family, neighbors, and supposed "experts" whose theories were pure conjecture.

As I considered this, a strange feeling began to creep over me. It was as if a wheel had started to turn in the back of my head. I introspected for a moment and gained the impression of an old waterwheel, slick and wooden, revolving slowly on an unseen axle. The feeling it produced in me was strangely soothing. I was taken aback by this unexpected psychic event, and when I returned my attention to the outside world, I found that my skepticism about the proposed project had completely vanished, leaving me eager to jump on the story.

"So, how do you know about this?" I asked.

"Peg told me," he said. Peg was his wife. She was a registered nurse who worked in the emergency room at the university hospital. The three of us had gone out to dinner a couple of times. "She's been saying for months now that she suspects something, but she wasn't sure until just a few days ago. Saturday night some lady brought an old man into the emergency room and said she had nearly run over him when she found him just lying in the middle of the road. He was still unconscious, so Peg checked his

I. D. and looked to see if they had any records on him. Turns out he's been there before. He has cancer of the larynx. Thirteen months ago he started refusing treatment. Nobody ever saw him there again until the other night. When he woke up, he looked around and flew into a rage. He refused to let anybody see about him. His file says he lives alone at a private residence and isn't under anybody's supervised care, so they just had to let him go. Peg said he stormed outside and hailed a cab.

"The reason she thinks this means something," he continued, setting his Styrofoam cup down on the desk, "is because more and more people have started refusing medical treatment at the hospital over the past year. Especially in the past two months. It's only a very small number, just a dozen or so, but these are people with some very serious medical conditions." He caught me with his eye as he paused. "Plus, the old guy said something as he was leaving."

"Wait, let me guess," I said. "He told them, 'As a foulness shall ye know them.' Am I right?"

Bobby seemed to stumble. After a moment he said, "Yeah, exactly." He was looking at me strangely.

I was as surprised as he was. A number of news stories had linked this cryptic saying to the cult, and I had just been spouting off when I said it. I told him this and he relaxed.

"Well, I guess you're the right guy for the job. You're almost psychic about it." He resumed his former easy manner of speaking. "Yeah, he said that weird Sick Seekers thing. Peg said his voice was awful to hear. She didn't even want to think about how far along his cancer must have advanced by now. From the way she was so spooked, I'm guessing it must be pretty bad." He glanced at his watch and then back up at me. "Well, I can put two and two together as well as she can, and when she told me what she was thinking, I knew she was right. There's got to be a cult group right here in Terence." He rose from his chair and started shuffling things around on his desk in the afternoon ritual I had come to know so well, the one that indicated he was about to be done with work for the day, regardless of how much time might be left on the clock. "What I want you to do," he said, "is find this group and get a story. With your background in religion, you should be able to talk to these people in a way that other people can't. Maybe you can make them feel comfortable, express some sort of understanding, get their sympathy. I don't care how you do it. Just find out something that nobody else has written about them yet."

"But Bobby," I said, "I *don't* understand them. Yes, I've studied up on them, but for the life of me I can't figure out why anybody would choose to live with terminal intestinal cancer, let alone *celebrate* it." I was thinking of a story I had watched just the night before on a weekly television news magazine. A man in Montana had refused to submit to having a large part of his colon removed, and had said things that indicated a link to the Sick and Saved movement. His wife had gone crying to the newspapers. "What am I supposed to do? How do I even *find* any of these people?"

"I told you," he said, "they have a file on this old man down at the hospital. Peg got his name: Mitchell Billings." He spelled it while I wrote it down.

"What else did she get?" I asked with pen poised to write.

"Nothing," he said. I blinked in surprise. "She's not going to risk her job over this, Lawrence. She already had her mind made up when she came to me, and I agree with her. It's not only against the rules, but it's a crime for her to divulge what's in those records. You're going to have to dig for yourself. I'm sure you can think of some way to use your pretty face to get access." He smiled wickedly, but at the moment I didn't think it was funny, especially since he was asking me to risk *my* neck. "By the way," he continued, "if you're thinking of going the easy way and looking in the phone book, don't bother. I checked already. Then I called information and checked the Internet. It's not that he's unlisted, he just doesn't have a phone number."

"What about the lady who brought him in? What did she have to say? Where did she find him?"

"Odd thing," Bobby said. "She must have stepped out during the ruckus. Peg couldn't find her anywhere."

I was still absorbing this when he reached for his tie, which he always hung on the coat rack in the corner after lunch. "Gonna call it an early day, *compadre*. Peg and I are going out to dinner and a concert tonight at the performing arts hall."

"Who's playing?" I asked without really caring. That wheel was still turning slowly in the back of my head, like an old waterwheel bearing buckets of fresh, cool water out of a silent spring. For the first time in many years, I felt the desire to sit in meditation for an extended period.

"The university symphony orchestra," he was saying. "Some Mozart piece. Or Bach or Beethoven. I really don't care. It's Peg's idea." He waved goodbye and walked out still carrying his tie, leaving me sitting there alone in his office, evidence of the trust he had built up for me after eight years of my devoted service.

I sat there for quite awhile watching the cool water being carried up from a spring in the back of my mind. When I got up to leave, I was feeling more alive than I had felt in years. But I was all too experienced at this sort of mood-revolution, and was far too jaded to allow myself to relax into any sort of good feeling, no matter how sweet and refreshing it seemed on the surface. Painful experience had taught me there was always a bottomless chasm of despair waiting on the other side.

II

> *After such thorough contemplation [of foulness], actual realization will unfailingly follow. If he now sees women, he is no longer dominated by the animal urge of carnal desire, but he sees* through *it; he sees them as skeletons. Looking ahead he, already now, perceives the flesh now, after death, it will be devoured by worms.*
>
> —*Going Forth*

I decided to go ahead and visit the hospital that very night. No time like the present for breaking the law, I thought. But first I stopped by my apartment to change clothes and freshen up. Bobby hadn't been kidding about my "pretty face." I was a strikingly handsome man. I had always been that way, even as a child. For years my mother had harbored fantasies about my being a professional model. She had taught me all about color coding, how to dress for best effect and fix my hair to look just right for my eyes, skin tone, facial shape, and all that. She was a failed model herself. Sometimes, I think she would have been happier with a daughter.

When I was in college, I found my looks to be a useful tool for getting into bed with just about any girl I liked, but that was as far as I took it. After I started working for the newspaper, I occasionally found that I could exploit my appearance by endearing myself to people who might not otherwise be inclined to talk to me. It even worked with men, for some reason. It wasn't that I ever engaged in any really tough investigative journalism. Far from it; my assignments were all cushy and soft. As the paper's religion reporter I got to sit through services at dozens of churches, interview rabbis and priests and preachers, go to funerals and bar mitzvahs, and so on. I even got to talk occasionally with my old professors in the religious studies department at the university, whenever I needed one of their sagacious comments to pad out some minor piece of journalistic fluff with an air of intellectual respectability. But even in those non -threatening situations, I sometimes liked to go for the throat, so to speak. Whenever I found people who were reticent or distracted, all I had to do was turn on the old charm and let my looks draw them to me like a magnet.

For my trip to the hospital, I chose a solid forest green shirt, black jeans, and black shoes. My hair was exceedingly dark, not quite black but just barely shy of it, and my eyes were a piercing green. I had learned years ago that when I wanted to look my most striking, I should wear dark, solid colors. When I looked in the mirror for a final inspection, my hair was still wet from a quick shower. The curls were soft and gleamed like sable. The shirt drew out the color of my eyes and gave me an appearance of intensity and wisdom. I knew I looked damned good.

Down at the hospital, I searched out the first female employee I could find. Fortunately, she was the one behind the receptionist's counter. Her name was Lindy, and she was blond and slightly overweight. We talked for a few minutes about nothing in particular before I explained to her that I was a reporter and needed to see a patient's file. Of course she told me this would be impossible, but then I turned on the charm and let her know that she was somebody whom I could really learn to like. I had never been so blatantly manipulative with my looks, and I was mildly sickened at myself. But that was easily overcome by an exercise of mental transcendence (a leftover from my spiritual days) wherein I stood back and suspended judgment on everything I was feeling or doing. This never failed to put me in a comfortable place where nothing could touch me, either from the inside or the outside, and I could just watch things happen like a spectator. I padded my lie by telling her that I knew the patient personally, and that I was looking up his information as a favor to him. It was a muddled story, one that didn't hold together (which wasn't surprising, considering that I made it up right there on the spot), but she bought it. She glanced around to make sure nobody was watching, and then she let me behind the counter and took me back to the office where the files were kept.

It was a long room, tall and narrow, filled with rows of gray metal shelves like a library. I thanked her profusely as she searched out Mitchell Billings' medical file. I thanked her again when she allowed me to stay there alone while she minded the front desk. As she was walking away, I watched the backs of her thighs. The cotton legs of her pants (standard nurse-issue) were stretched tight against her skin, and I found myself thinking that maybe I hadn't been kidding when I said I would like to get to know her better.

I flipped through the file quickly, standing there in the cramped aisleway between the shelves. The evidence of Mr. Billings' laryngeal cancer was there, along with his refusal on July 13th of the previous year to be treated. The doctors had wanted to perform a tracheostomy or laryngectomy over a year ago, but he had declined. The record then skipped ahead to just four nights past, when someone had recorded in blue ink the tale of Billings' unexpected return to, and belligerent departure from, the university hospital. There was also a scribbled note about the unnamed Good Samaritan who had brought him in.

Before closing the file, I turned back to the cover page and copied down Billings' address: Route 3, Box 147, Terence, Missouri. I was vaguely familiar with Route 3, more commonly known as Highway M. It ran east out of Terence toward Mountain Glen and was populated mostly by farmer types. As Bobby had already previewed for me, there was no phone number listed, so I knew that my day was planned out for me tomorrow. Apparently, I would have to drive out Highway M and physically track the man down.

Having achieved my goal, I closed the manila-colored file and slid it back into its place on the shelf. Then I slipped out to the reception area (checking first to make sure nobody was around; I truly didn't want to get Lindy into trouble) and scooted out from behind the counter. On the way past I paused to thank Lindy yet again. She looked a little troubled, as if she were conflicted over her violation of the rules, so I reiterated that I wouldn't tell a single soul. I also assured her that she had helped Mr. Billings immensely. Her complexion was pale and milky, a nice match for her blond hair, and her cheeks were now colored with a slight flush from the heat of her troubled feelings. She was positively lovely. I found myself wondering as I exited through the automatic doors and emerged back into the humid August night whether I might not find myself back at the hospital soon, this time not under a ruse, but with the honest intention of getting closer to her. I supposed it might not be totally impossible.

The wheel was still turning.

III

What, Ananda, is contemplation of disadvantage? Herein, Ananda, a monk having gone to the forest, or to the foot of a tree, or to a lonely place, contemplates thus: 'Many are the sufferings, many are the disadvantages of this body since diverse diseases are engendered in this body, such as the following: Eye-disease, ear-disease, nose-disease, tongue-disease, body-disease, headache, mumps, mouth-disease, tooth-ache, cough, asthma, catarrh, heart-burn, fever, stomach ailment, fainting, dysentery, swelling, gripes, leprosy, boils, scrofula, consumption, epilepsy, ringworm, itch, eruption, tetter, pustule, plethora, diabetes, piles, cancer, fistula, and diseases originating from bile, from phlegm, from wind, from conflict of the humors, from changes of weather, from adverse conditions . . . and cold, heat, hunger, thirst, excrement, and urine.' Thus he dwells contemplating

> *disadvantage in this body. This Ananda, is called contemplation of disadvantage.*
>
> —*Pirit Potha*

The next day I waited until mid-morning to begin my search. It was a hot day, the hottest by far in what had already been a sweltering summer. The old saying about the humidity being worse than the heat was amply realized on that day. I couldn't seem to get dried off after my shower, and by the time I made it to the ground floor of my apartment building and then out to my car, where I turned on the air conditioner at full blast, I was already dripping with sweat. I was glad I had picked a dark color that would hide the sweat rings already starting to appear under my arms, but I also realized it was quite foolish to be wearing such a heat-absorbing shirt on such a scorching day. My mother's old adage of "appearance over comfort" played on my mind annoyingly as I pulled out of the parking lot. To help silence it, I dialed the office on my cell phone and asked Susie, the receptionist, to tell Bobby that I had secured the information he mentioned and was headed out to speak with the guy today.

On the east edge of Terence, after the old downtown buildings gave way to densely populated residential subdivisions composed of new houses, which in turn gave way to more sparsely populated neighborhoods with older houses, Highway M turned south off Broadway Avenue, crossed the train tracks, jogged sharply to the left, and rapidly became something that looked more like a country lane than a conventional highway. I knew the road only by name. I had never driven it before, and found it rather odd, and oddly refreshing, to find such a completely rural-looking farm road branching off like an aging artery from the edge of a mid-sized university town like Terence. I took great pleasure in the sight of the oaks and hickory trees that flanked the road and created a latticed canopy of leafy branches overhead. The sun still hung in the eastern sky as I sped across the pavement, and its light rippled through the trees like a burning waterfall, shooting dazzling flashes of golden spray into the corners of my eyes.

I had to drive nearly ten miles to get to Billings' house. Highway M proved to be one of those typical Missouri country roads that wind and twist and seem to be taking you further into the heart of nowhere even when you know where you're going. When you're bound for parts unknown, the effect is even more pronounced. Time stretches into an endless asphalt carpet ahead of you, and you start thinking you may never reach your destination. By the time I came across the house, I was imagining that I must have crossed some invisible dimensional barrier separating the normal universe with its known laws of physics from a strange realm where distance multiplied and space elongated the farther and faster you traveled.

The house appeared suddenly as I was rounding a sharp curve. It sat off the left side of the road about thirty yards, an old two-story structure built farmhouse style, with a brown slate rock exterior and a rust-colored front porch surmounted by two dormers. Mitchell Billings was sitting in the porch swing. I knew it had to be him as I braked sharply to avoid missing the driveway, which was an unpaved riot of gravel and dirt. My momentum was a bit more than I had expected, and I hit the edge of the dirtline at thirty miles per hour and kicked up a cloud of brown dust. Cursing aloud, I pulled up to the house and sat with my door shut while the cloud settled. Through my closed window and above the roar of the air conditioner, I could hear the screeching and buzzing of tree frogs and cicadas spilling out of the woods to my left. The tree line bordered the driveway, coming to within just a few yards of the house.

Mr. Billings sat there and looked at me from his porch swing without a hint of surprise on his wizened face. He looked ancient in a way that only old farmers can look, with sun-browned skin and a face so full of wrinkles it appeared his bones were clothed in aged cowhide. He had a full head of snowy white hair and was dressed in blue denim overalls, a red-checkered shirt, and brown work boots. His feet rested on the porch and swung him back forth an inch or two at a time as he looked at me through my windshield.

I saw all of this from my car with the clarity of a close-up photograph. His overall appearance seemed almost archetypal, as if he were the model for the ubiquitous farmer character I had seen portrayed in various picture books as a child. When I climbed out of the car and felt the sun's rays strike my dark Polo shirt with the force of a blowtorch, I determined not to show any weakness before this man.

"Excuse me," I said as I approached the porch steps. "Are you Mitchell Billings?" He looked at me for a moment and then nodded. His hands never left his chest, where they were tucked under the straps of his overalls. I noticed an odd noise, a kind of dry, rhythmic rasping sound, but I couldn't locate it, so I put it out of mind while I made my introduction.

"My name is Lawrence Palmer." I stepped closer to the porch and took the direct approach I had decided upon ahead of time. "I'm a reporter with the *Terence Sun-Gazette*. Would it be all right if I stayed awhile to talk with you? Maybe sit down and ask you some question?"

The chains holding the porch swing squealed against the support hooks as he swayed back and forth. The sound raised the hackles on the back of my neck.

Then he nodded again and rose to his feet. He detached one of his hands from beneath its overall strap and motioned for me to follow him into the house. The front door was open and the screen door shut, and he pulled open the screen and walked inside without saying a word, obviously expecting me to follow him. I hurried up the steps and caught the door. Inside, I could see a dimly lit living room reaching away toward what looked like a kitchen. There was an old cloth-covered sofa and a ratty recliner. The carpet was dirt-colored and worn thin from age and traffic. Mr. Billings had disappeared into the kitchen, where I heard him rattling around, running water, opening a cabinet. With a self-directed nod of affirmation, I stepped across the threshold and let the screen door hiss shut behind me.

Instantly, the noise of the insects outside grew muted in a way that didn't seem possible from just that thin door. Then I noticed the two electric box fans purring in the living room windowsills. The house was not air-conditioned, and the atmosphere inside felt unbearably stuffy. It was also hushed and filled with a sense of expectancy that I attributed to the light value. The window shades were drawn down to the tops of the fans, allowing a dusky sheen of sunlight to filter throughout the room. I stood watching a couple of flies buzz angrily around each other in crazy circles above the sofa until he returned.

He was carrying a glass of iced tea, which he offered to me. I noticed he hadn't brought a glass for himself. In his other hand he carried a notepad. He motioned for me to sit on the sofa, which I did, while he took a seat in the chair. He unclipped an ink pen from a pocket on the front of his overalls and scribbled something on the pad while I raised my glass and waved away the flies. The tea was instant, not brewed, but he had added a lot of sugar and a lemon slice as well, and it was sweet and refreshing in the oppressive atmosphere.

I noticed the odd rasping sound again while I was in the middle of a swallow, and again I couldn't locate it. The mystery was banished from my attention when he turned the notebook around and showed it to me. I had to lean forward to read the spidery black letters.

"I'm Mitchell Billings. You can call me Mitch. I have throat cancer so I can't talk. Ask me your questions and I'll write down my answers."

This was stranger than anything I had expected. It was also more fortuitous, since it gave me an easy lead-in to the questions I wanted to ask. I noticed that his eyes were as bright as silver dollars as I brought out my tape recorder and then realized the absurdity of what I was doing. With a sheepish grin, I returned it to my briefcase and took out a pencil and pad.

"I know about your cancer," I said, stepping into the story I had prepared. "I've been researching a story about patients in the Terence area who have refused medical treatment in the last year. When I spoke with someone at the university hospital, your name came up, and I couldn't find a phone number so I decided to drop in on you." I was banking on the fact that he wouldn't be offended by this admission of my forwardness, nor by the news that somebody had been talking about him. He merely continued to smile at me, so I went on. "But before we get to that, may I ask you some general questions? You look like you're about my grandfather's age. I'm guessing you're in your early eighties?" It was a standard ploy: start out strong and direct, then veer off into neutral territory to put the subject at ease.

He smiled and began to write, and that began our conversation. He was obviously quite accustomed to speaking with his pen and notebook, for he wrote exceptionally rapidly and legibly. He was also very forthcoming, as I soon discovered as we began passing the notebook back and forth, and I realized early in our conversation that he was far more intelligent than I had expected from his Farmer Brown appearance. His answers were coherent, even eloquent, which raised my opinion of him considerably.

He said he was ninety-one years old, which shocked me. The lightness of his movements and gleam in his eye had made him seem much younger despite his leathery appearance. I began to make my usual banter about wanting to know about his past, his upbringing, his family, his interests. When I asked my questions, he looked at me with those bright eyes and seemed to be riding upon some bubbling fountain of mild inner mirth. While he wrote his replies, I listened to the hum of the fans and the faint scrapings of insect noises from outside.

About his upbringing and education he wrote, "I grew up right here on Highway M, about three miles back toward Terence. We called it Beecher Road back then. Terence wasn't much to speak of in those days, but when the university came in, the town grew up in a hurry. I never went to college myself. I was educated in a one-room school house that's still standing. When you drive back toward town, a mile from here start looking for an old abandoned rock building off the right side of the road, down in a valley. I'm kind of sentimental about it."

In answer to my question about whether he had ever traveled away from southwest Missouri, he told me that he had served as a navigator on a B17 bomber in World War II. He had flown thirteen combat missions over Germany, and had been awarded the Purple Heart and sent home when he was wounded through the throat by a piece of flak. "Kind of ironic," he wrote, "that after surviving that wound sixty years ago I would get cancer in the same spot."

When I asked about his family, whether he had a wife or children, he grew somber for the first time. The light dimmed in his eyes, and he paused to brush back a lock of white hair from his forehead with a callused hand. But he quickly went back to writing, and I soon had my reply: "I was married to a woman named Stella for fifty-four years. She died last year in the spring. We never had any children." This seemed an uncharacteristically reticent response given his extended answers to my previous questions, but I didn't push the matter. I did make a mental note of the fact that the timing of his wife's death would have coincided roughly with his own refusal to receive medical treatment.

That led me to the series of questions I had wanted to ask from the beginning.

"Mitch," I began. My tea glass was long-since empty, and I looked around for a place to put it. He took it from me and set it on the floor beside his chair. The flies returned from somewhere and began buzzing around my face, apparently trying to settle on my left cheek. I waved them away with an irritated swipe of my hand.

"I don't want you to think I'm prying," I said, "but I have an important question to ask you. Of course you don't have to answer it if you don't want to." He just gave me that same bright-eyed stare. It was almost as if he knew where I was going with this.

I asked, "Have you heard of the Sick Seekers?" In response, he laughed. It was the first sound to come out of his throat since I had met him an hour ago, and it was horrible, a kind of wet rattling noise, like a drain coming unclogged and sucking down a sink full of dirty gray water. I masked my revulsion with a blank expression.

He was already writing on his pad. When he handed it to me, I flipped it over and read, "I wondered whether you were ever going to get around to that."

My astonishment was considerable. The rest of our conversation, which lasted until well after sunset, formed a transcript that nearly overwhelmed me with its fantastic implications. I quickly abandoned my list of prepared questions in favor of pursuing the various tangents Mitch presented to me. We sat there in the muggy atmosphere of his living room, me asking questions and him writing answers as the sun made its way west, and I felt as if I were seeing the outlines of a surreal puzzle or painting take shape in my mind. Sometimes he wrote for five minutes or more, during which time I would sit there trying unsuccessfully to digest his previous replies. It was also while he wrote that I managed to identify the rasping sound I had heard earlier. It was his breath. The air had to squeeze past the malignant growth in his neck to reach his lungs. I shivered slightly at the thought. I also pitied him a little, even though I knew it was a virtual miracle that he was sitting there at all, given that he shouldn't have been able to breathe or swallow for over a year.

He let me take his written replies home with me, and that night I reconstructed my own questions and comments as accurately as I could from memory and from the cues contained in his answers. What I couldn't capture on paper was my mounting sense of incredulity as I discovered that his beliefs were far more bizarre and grotesque than I had suspected from the nature of our interaction up to that point.

Me: I assume you guessed why I'm here when I mentioned the story I'm writing?

Mitch: Yes. I figured it would only be a matter of time before somebody like you came around wanting to talk to me.

Me: Why were you at the hospital the other night? What happened?

Mitch: I have these spells sometimes.

Me: What kind of spells?

Mitch: I pass out. Later on I don't remember anything.

Me: Who took you to the hospital?

Mitch: A friend.

Me: Are you one of the Sick Seekers? Is there a local group?

Mitch: Yes. We've been together for a little over a year now. There are twelve members. We call ourselves a "body." I'm sure you know from keeping up with the news that there are other bodies all over the world.

Me: Are you willing to answer some detailed questions? From what I've read, most members of your movement don't want to talk to reporters.

Mitch: It's about time we stopped that nonsense. People need to hear what we have to say.

Me: Is it true that you worship your diseases?

Mitch: We don't worship our diseases. We worship the One they point to.

Me: What do they point to?

Mitch: Our God.

Me: Who is your god?

Mitch: Let me tell you something else first. People have the wrong idea about disease and health. Everybody gets sick and dies. That's just the way of things. Most of us fight against it. To hear all the doctors talk, you'd think nobody was *supposed* to get sick or die. When the God started talking to people around the world, He told us that sickness doesn't have to be something bad. He told us that sickness can set you free. Some people think life is hopeless and meaningless because everybody is headed for certain sickness and death, but our God gives us hope and meaning by showing us that our diseases are taking us somewhere.

Me: Where are they taking you?

Mitch: They're taking us all the way to Him. The normal view of health is wrong-headed. A healthy body is like a dirty pair of eyeglasses. It gets in the way of seeing the truth for what it really is. When your body has what everybody calls a "disease," it's like the lenses are cleaned off, and you have the chance to see things differently.

Me: How do you see things differently?

Mitch: You see that having a body is what keeps you separate from everything else and makes you miserable. A healthy body is the truest and worst form of disease. Stella and I fought against our cancers for three years. We tried chemotherapy, radiation, everything. She had a double mastectomy. I was about to let them take out my larynx, and then Stella died and the God started talking to me right afterward. I saw then how we'd been chasing after the wind. What did we think we were trying to save? Every minute you're alive, you're dying. We just made it worse by fighting it. Now I won't ever make that mistake again. I had reached a point where I was completely fed up with being sick. I couldn't stand it for another minute. Then the God showed me the way out. Until you've experienced it yourself, you can't know how peaceful it is to accept what the God tells you and just relax into your sickness.

Me: How does your god talk to you? What is he like?

Mitch: He's a God the regular churches don't know. They have to just "believe" in their god, but we know ours for real. We know Him through our diseases. He *is* our diseases. That's what they are. They're His presence in our bodies. He talks to us through them. I don't mean the old preacher's claim that "the Lord told me so." I'm talking about real speaking. He tells us what He wants and how He's going to give us peace after we die. And He takes away our pain.

Me: What do you mean by that?

Mitch: We just give our pain to Him and He takes it away. None of us feels pain at all anymore. I'm supposed to be in total agony right now, but I'm just fine. It's better than any drug the doctors could give you. My friends in the local body have arthritis, cancer, all kinds of things, and they don't feel anything either.

Me: Were you a religious man before you got involved with the Sick Seekers?

Mitch: I was a member of Mount Tabor General Baptist Church for fifty-four years, the whole time I was married to Stella. Right after she died, the God started talking to me through my throat cancer. I wouldn't let Pastor James give her a funeral in the church after that. Of course that ran off all my old friends, but I found better ones when I met the other members of the body.

Me: Can you explain more about what you expect to happen after you die, and what your god says to you?

Mitch: We will be taken into the God after we die. That's what He tells us. He takes our pain away from us, and it builds Him up, and when we are gone there will only be Him.

Me: Do you think you will survive after death? If there's only him, where will you be?

Mitch: The part of us that seems like a disease now is the most important part. It will become a part of Him. Whatever's left will just rot away, and good riddance to it.

Me: What's the meaning of the saying "As a foulness shall ye know them"?

Mitch: That's taken from our holy book. We have a Bible too. [At this I was filled with eager hopes of seeing a copy of this book, but he merely smiled at me in a secretive sort of way, so I didn't push it.]

Me: But what does the saying mean?

Mitch: "As a foulness shall ye know Them" talks about how our God and the others like Him always appear to people on the outside. He shows up as a horrible disease in people's bodies, and that scares everybody who's not one of us. They think it's awful. You've heard what they say about us on TV. Outsiders know Him as a "foulness." But there's a double meaning to it, because even though you start out knowing Him as a foulness, when you listen to Him, and you decide to give up your right to yourself and really let Him work in your body, you learn that He has the most special kind of peace in the world hidden away inside Him. The god of the regular churches is just the opposite. He talks about peace and love, but when you get on the inside and study the Bible you find out he's full of anger and hatred. He does all kinds of horrible things. He's a deceiver, but our God is exactly what He says He is.

Me: How is the God of the regular churches a deceiver?

Mitch: Remember, I was a Baptist for fifty-four years. I took it seriously. I went to Sunday School and studied my Bible. In Philippians 4:9 Paul says, "The God of peace will be with you." For years I tried to believe that he really is a god of peace. But I never knew what to do with things like Deuteronomy 28:22: "The LORD will strike you with wasting disease, with fever and inflammation, with scorching heat and drought, with blight and mildew, which will plague you until you perish." Those kinds of things are all through the Bible. God is one way, then he's another. It wouldn't be so bad if all those punishments were meant to set you free from the body, but that's not what they're about. They're just cruel things being done to you by a cruel god for no good reason. I made myself miserable trying to figure it all out. When Stella died after all those years of suffering, I understood how things really are. She grew up as a good Baptist. The whole time she was sick, she never stopped praying and believing her God would heal her. I prayed and tried to believe, too, but all those contradictions wouldn't let me alone. "The proof is in the pudding," they say. The god she worshipped never took an ounce of pain away from her. My new God, the one the outsiders think is a foulness, takes away my pain all the time. I'll take a God who looks foul on the outside but has bliss for you on the inside over the opposite kind any day. Plus, my God really talks to me. I don't have pray and whine and try to convince myself that I'm hearing His voice.

Me: You said your god is not alone, that there are others like him. What are their names? What do you call your god? [Mitch laughed again at this point, and the wet sucking sound revolted me even more than it had before. He was still suppressing more laughter as he wrote on his pad.]

Mitch: I could tell you their names, but they wouldn't mean anything to you. Don't worry. You'll understand it all soon enough.

When I read this last line, I looked up and saw him smiling at me. It was not a pleasant expression. Up until then, I had liked him a great deal for his intelligence and good humor, even though his description of his beliefs had struck me as positively nuts. It was sounding like the theology of the Sick and Saved movement bordered on insanity, but I had still found myself liking the old guy. He possessed a palpable and undeniable charisma.

But now this had suddenly gone underground and been replaced by a sinister look that I hadn't seen before. Being a professional writer, I thought of it as more a *leer* than a smile. Its menacing character was made all the more apparent by the yellow light of the lamp he had switched on when the sun went down. The dim rays slanted across his face from the left, casting his features into high relief, calling out every nuance of the webwork of lines on his skin and showing me clearly that he thought he knew something I didn't, something that made him feel smug with superiority. It was so blatant, and it gave his last comment such a threatening quality, that I almost crossed a journalistic line and demanded to know what he was holding back. But then I caught myself and purposely returned his smile. His breathing was like the scraping of the nocturnal forest noises outside the windows as he continued to look at me.

I was about to say something, I didn't know what, when he handed me his notepad again. He had written a new message while I wasn't looking. "The God gives you a choice," he said. "First He gives you a taste of the bliss He's offering you. Then He shows you what it's going to cost you to accept it." When I looked at him, the smug smile was still planted on his lips. What I had taken to be evidence of an inner mirth glinting in his eyes now looked like cold calculation. I could think of nothing to say in response. Suddenly I felt hot, tired, and worn out by the conversation. My vision flickered with dark spots, and I realized with a shock that it would take only a slight relaxation of vigilance for me to pass out. This had never happened before. My stomach quivered as I wiped a hand over my face.

To hide what was happening, I ended our meeting. "Mitch," I said, "it's getting late, and I should get out of here and stop bothering you. I've enjoyed the hospitality. You've been very generous with your time." My hands were shaking as I gathered my things and shut my briefcase. When I rose to my feet, the backs of my thighs had sweated through my slacks, and the fabric of the sofa cushion peeled away from my legs like the skin of a soggy fruit.

He stayed seated and wrote something. "We're having a meeting this Saturday night," the words said. "I'd like you to come."

I didn't know what to say. This was far more than I had hoped for. Sixty seconds earlier, I would have jumped at the chance without hesitating. No reporter had ever attended one of the worship services—or whatever they were—of the Sick Seekers. With the inside information I would gain from such a meeting, I might be looking at a substantial journalistic project that I could expand and sell to a national publication after I had turned in a perfunctory piece to Bobby.

But Mitch's change of expression had filled me with doubt and distaste, and I hesitated. In the silence, the flies came back and started trying to settle on my left cheek again. Thinking they were probably attracted to a spot of sweet tea that I must have unknowingly splashed on myself, I rubbed my face and used the gesture to look as if I were mulling over his invitation. Which, in fact, I was.

"I'm very interested," I finally said. "Where do you meet?"

"Right here at my house," was his written reply. "You already know the way. The meeting is at seven o'clock. Why don't you come on out and meet the rest of us? There's lots more for you to learn."

Despite my suspicion, I knew it was unlikely that I could turn down such an invitation, and I think he knew it, too. All afternoon as he and I had talked, I had felt that wheel in my head turning slowly and steadily. My spirit was energized by a vitality that seemed totally out of step with the tenor of the conversation and the dizziness that still threatened to overturn me. Even as I stood there struggling to understand all that I had learned, a warm pulse of well being throbbed in my chest.

But I still couldn't bring myself to accept his invitation at the moment. I thanked him and said I'd think about it. He seemed satisfied with this, for he rose from his chair and extended his hand. His skin was rough and dry as sandpaper, and his grip felt like a vise. My own hand was soft and smooth from years of desk work, and was practically swallowed whole by his enormous grasp. I tried not to look him in the eye, but I couldn't help noticing that he was still watching me closely, as if he were waiting for something. When he released my hand, I headed immediately for the door.

Outside, darkness had taken complete hold of the house and the highway. The daytime buzzing of insects had given way to the nighttime screeching and whirring of crickets and tree frogs. It had been a long time since I spent an evening in the country, and the sounds and smells of summer night conjured up nostalgic memories of long-ago childhood evenings filled with creek swimming and backyard barbecuing and chasing after lightning bugs.

At the bottom of the porch steps I turned and gave him a wave. Crunching through the gravel toward my car, I still had a thousand questions to ask him. I had failed to follow up on all kinds of details that needed filling in. On first impression his beliefs struck me as nothing so much as a perverted mysticism, not far from the spiritual attitude I had embraced while in college, but in a horribly twisted form. His determination to give himself up to his cancer paralleled my own erstwhile attitude of detached transcendence. But he didn't just give himself up to his disease, he conceived of it as some kind of deity, and he *identified* himself with it, just as a Christian mystic might identify his soul with God or a Vedantic Hindu might identify himself with Brahman.

My head boiled with these thoughts as I settled into the driver's seat and inserted the key in the ignition. I looked up briefly and saw Mitch seated once again in the porch swing. He hadn't turned the outside light on. The pale light of the lamp in his living room shone feebly through the screen door, illuminating him again with a chiaroscuro effect. I found myself searching reflexively for that inner wheel, and there it was, turning in the shadows of my psyche, drawing up fresh water from a well in my soul. I felt a pressing need to write about it in my journal, for it had been years since I was so spontaneously aware of my inner spiritual state.

As I started the engine, I saw Mitch reach up for the first time since my arrival and probe gently at his throat. It was a gesture I would have expected from a man whose medical charts said he should have already been dead from cancer of the larynx. But from those same charts, I never would have expected him to touch that diseased area of his body with such an apparent attitude of affection.

IV

. . . those sorrows which are sent to wean us from the earth.
— Mary Shelley, *Frankenstein*

The next day, the first person I thought of turning to for my post-interview research was Dr. Baumann from the religious studies department at Terence University. The last time I had spoken with him, I had been writing a profile about the local Baha'i group, whose worship center was located on the university grounds. He was the natural choice to call for a scholarly comment on such matters, since his specialty area was comparative religion. As the son of Methodist missionaries who had raised him while living and ministering in India, he was the perfect source of information and opinions on such matters.

But beyond his professional qualifications, currently I just wanted to talk with him as a friend. He was more than a former teacher, he was a mentor, a status he had assumed when I lost my mother to cancer during my second year of grad school. He had noticed how distraught I was, and had offered me some free pastoral counseling. Although his orthodox Christian outlook hadn't coincided with my mystic-cum-agnostic one, I had deeply appreciated his moral support and words of wisdom. After I graduated, he was always the first one I approached when I needed a quote for a story. Now I found myself seeking his advice once again for personal reasons. I didn't know how to understand what was happening inside me, and I hoped to get a grip on it by having him explain to me the obscurities of all that I had learned from Mitch. Somehow the two were connected, the Sick Seekers story and the wheel of peace that was turning in my head. I needed input from an objective source to make sense of it.

Wanting to surprise him, I went directly to his office on the second floor of Markham Hall without phoning ahead. Then, standing there in the hallway before his locked door, I called myself an idiot—out loud, and then looked around to see whether any passerby had heard me—for not having called to check on his summer office hours.

My next stop was the religious studies departmental office, where I found a new secretary seated behind the reception desk.

She was a dull, flat-eyed woman who seemed to be totally devoid of personality. This was in marked contrast to Josie, the vivacious middle-aged neo-pagan who had been the department's secretary for the entire length of my involvement there. But oddly enough, the new woman looked a little bit like Josie, with the same stringy gray hair, pale skin, and thin nose. She might have been Josie's slightly older and significantly duller sister. She told me in a monotone that Dr. Baumann was on sabbatical and that I could email him or leave a message on his voice mail if I wanted. When I asked where he was, she mumbled, "He's checking out those Sick Seekers down in Nevada."

My astonishment was profound. When I pressed her for more, she told me that Dr. Baumann's brother had become involved with the Sick Seekers after discovering that he was suffering from end stage liver disease, the result of a longtime undiagnosed infection with both hepatitis A and B. He had refused to seek a liver transplant, and Dr. Baumann was in Las Vegas to see if he could rescue his brother from the cult. He was also using the opportunity to do some research into the theology of the group, which he said deserved more attention than the mass media had given it.

By the way she ticked this information off, I could tell the new woman was probably just repeating information that she had gained by eavesdropping on conversations with Dr. Allee, the department head, whose office door was right behind her. In the past Josie had always enjoyed passing on this same kind of gossip, but she had done it with far more flair, interspersing the gossipy information with lots of smiling and flirting. I had always come away feeling pepped up and kind of turned on. The new lady, by contrast, made me feel weary and vaguely disgusted.

My thoughts were racing every which way as I left her and headed for the stairwell. Mitch and his maniacal beliefs. Dr. Baumann and his sick brother. Josie's replacement by a pod person. The story I was supposed to be writing for Bobby. It was all a giant puzzle, or perhaps a "magic eye" picture, one of those computer generated images that revealed three-dimensional depths when you relaxed your eyes and let the hidden image coalesce like magic.

But walking down the sterile institutional length of Markham Hall's second floor with my head buzzing with competing claims to attention, I found a new and unexpected thought jostling its way to the forefront. It was more of an emotion, really: For no good reason I was pining for the innocent passion of my college years. For a long time those years had seemed frozen in eternity, like a snapshot of an idyllic childhood. This new evidence of elements from my miserable present invading the pristine happiness of my past—Dr. Baumann, my mentor, getting mixed up with the damned Sick Seekers—felt like the most profound kind of invasion. It was like somebody had started to rewrite my past to make it conform more to the way I saw the world currently when I was in one of my darker moods: full of suffering, devoid of meaning, going nowhere.

I caught myself scratching the left side of my face as I took the stairs down to the first floor and walked outside to visitor parking. As always, the campus was dotted with lovely instances of female flesh. The fall semester would be starting on Monday, and thousands of students were in town a few days early to get settled into their dorms and fraternities and sorority houses. Always when I came to campus, I basked in the appreciative looks I got from all the girls. It was especially fun at this time of year, when the new crop of freshmen were in town. But suddenly, out of nowhere, my face was itching so badly that I couldn't enjoy the attention.

It rapidly burgeoned into some sort of attack. By the time I got to my car, the itching had become a burning. When I looked in the rearview mirror, I saw my left cheek mottled with angry red splotches from all the rubbing and scratching I had already done. I couldn't imagine where I might have come in contact with poison oak or ivy, but they seemed the likely culprits. I had been susceptible to their influence since I was a boy, when I had caught a rash from one or both at least once per summer.

On the way home I stopped by a drugstore to get some allergy cream. A poster prominently displayed above the prescription counseling window shouted three words in tall, white letters on a black background: "TAKE YOUR MEDICINE!" A roundabout reference to the Sick Seekers, I assumed.

The lady behind the counter was attractive in a more mature way than the girls on campus. Her hair was red and her eyes green like mine. She wore a lot of mascara, which contrasted nicely with her white lab coat. I smiled at her as she took my money and handed me my purchase in a white paper bag, but her eyes were drawn to the left side of my face, and the smile she gave me was only the perfunctory kind that she would have given any other customer.

V

The purpose of the world is for you to suffer, to create the suffering that seems to be what is necessary for the awakening to happen.

—Eckhart Tolle

When I awoke on Friday morning, a black spot had developed on my face overnight.

I had arrived back at my apartment on Thursday afternoon in a virtual frenzy of itching and burning, and had raced upstairs, torn open the box containing the cream, and slathered nearly a quarter of the tube onto my inflamed skin. It had helped briefly with its cooling and softening effect, but an hour later the pain returned. By eight o'clock the cream was gone. Then I started with the moisturizing lotion. It turned out the antihistamine effect of the allergy cream hadn't been doing anything, because the lotion worked just as well.

Or just as poorly. I laid awake on the couch in front of the television until one o'clock in the morning, unable to relax or think about anything except the maddening pain in my face. Right before I drifting off to sleep at last, I got up for a final look at my cheek in the bathroom mirror. By that time the red splotches had swelled into burning welts from my constant scratching. On closer inspection, I thought my face looked a little distorted and rather out-of-proportion, as if the left side were bigger and heavier than the right. The thought of visiting the emergency room flickered through my mind, but only briefly. Of course I was scared and wanted to know just what the hell was going on, but those concerns were outweighed by the fact that in my current condition

I didn't want to go anyplace where I might run the risk of being recognized. I couldn't imagine going to the hospital and running into Bobby's wife Peg, or even worse, the virginal Lindy, and having them see me like this. Especially not Lindy. Not when I still had half-formed plans for the two of us.

So I just returned to the couch and rubbed on another layer of lotion. Then I closed my eyes and concentrated on breathing slowly and steadily while the voice of the announcer on the television news network droned on and on, saying something about the Sick Seekers.

My first stop when I awoke in the morning was the bathroom again, where I discovered the black spot on my cheek. It arrested my attention as soon as I flipped on the light switch, and I examined it in the harsh glare of the vanity bulbs with my face so close to the mirror that my breath steamed the glass. The red welts had disappeared and been replaced by an uneven circle about the size of a pea. It rode high on my left cheekbone, a blobby mole with a ragged border, colored with an irregular hue. Its center was black as tar, but toward the edges it thinned out and half blended with the normal peachy color of my skin to form a sickly dark brew like weak coffee.

With growing panic, I realized it was a familiar shape that had lodged on my face. The coloration touched a chord of memory. An awful thought occurred to me, one that I tried to shove down and forget, but it wouldn't be denied.

Years earlier, when I was nineteen years old and a sophomore in college, I had undergone surgery to have cancerous cells removed from my that same cheek. For several weeks I had watched with curiosity as the new moles had appeared. They had been small and faint, and I had thought they were just the aftereffects of the severe sunburn I had suffered while celebrating Spring Break on Padre Island. But when I arrived back home in May after the semester ended, my mother flew into a panic at the sight of them. We hadn't seen each other since Christmas, so I had hoped she would greet me warmly. Instead, she pounced on the spots and drilled me over their history—when and where they had first appeared, whether they were painful, and so on—almost before she saw fit to say hello. Her behavior was typical, but I still felt disappointed.

I did what she wanted and made an appointment with a local dermatologist, who surprised me by suggesting a biopsy, which then astounded me by showing a malignancy. It surprised the doctor, too, because, as he told me, sudden onset usually indicates a benign growth. As things stood, he told me the spots had to be removed immediately.

I submitted to the operation in a kind of daze. He burned the cells off with a surgical laser and I wore a bandage on my face for a week. When the time arrived to take it off, there were only a few minor marks on my skin to show that anything had ever happened, and these faded within a few days. The moment when I stood before my mother and proudly showed her my virgin cheek glowing with new health was forever seared unto my memory. She looked at it with a faintly crazed expression. Then she burst into tears and fled to her bedroom, where she refused to open the door for two days. After that we never spoke about the matter again, not even when she developed the breast cancer that would eventually kill her.

It was impossible, of course, for the new overnight growth on my face to be what I feared it was. Even the term "sudden onset" couldn't cover the appearance of a cancerous mole in something like seven hours. But that was the fear that gripped me as I stood there looking at my marred face in the bathroom mirror. It literally caused me to shiver as I slowly showered and got dressed and ate a breakfast of cold cereal and hot toast. I had planned to put in some time at the office that day, but any activity that involved leaving my apartment was now out of the question. I couldn't go and confront Susie at the receptionist's counter and see the shock in her eyes when she saw my face. I couldn't deal with the other women in the newsroom—Ginny with her big-toothed smile, Elaine with her plaid skirts, Larissa with her long brown hair and seemingly endless supply of bows—and know they were watching me not with desire but in horrified fascination at the obscenity on my cheek. In the end I resolved to stay home and phone in a report about my progress to Bobby.

Susie put me through to his extension, and when I told him that I had confirmed the existence of a Sick Seekers group in Terence,

I heard him pound his desk as he fairly shouted, "I knew it!" His excitement made it all the easier for me to gloss over my meeting with Mitch. I said I had spoken with him briefly, and that I planned to ask some follow-up questions soon. I promised I would tell Bobby everything just as soon as I had gathered enough information for a story. He bought the whole thing, and we hung up with him expressing pleasure and excitement while I felt like a loser for lying to him.

I spent the day alternating between lying on the couch and poring over Mitch's written words. A little before noon, I caved in to my lonely feelings and called Dr. Baumann's voice mail, hoping that he might check it remotely and knowing that he probably wouldn't receive an email, so legendary was his disdain for "that impersonal, ephemeral excuse for a letter." In my message, I apologized for not having been in contact for so long and explained that I was doing a story about the Sick Seekers and wanted his input, since I had heard he was researching the same subject. In contrast to my incomplete disclosure to Bobby, I told Dr. Baumann everything about my meeting with Mitch. I took particular pains in describing the Sick Seekers' theology exactly as Mitch had explained it to me, and I asked if Dr. Baumann knew of any historical antecedents to it. I mentioned that Mitch had claimed to have an actual scripture in his possession, and I asked whether Dr. Baumann knew of this text. Before I hung up, I wished him well with his brother and asked him to call me at his earliest opportunity.

It seemed the sun took twice as long as normal to complete its circuit across the sky that day. The shadows crept across my carpeted living room floor like black molasses, and the long hours of solitude allowed a number of dark thoughts to steal into my consciousness. While studying the transcript of the interview, I kept returning to the last thing Mitch had told me about his beliefs: "The God gives you a choice. First He gives you a taste of the bliss He's offering you. Then He shows you what it's going to cost you to accept it." I knew it was dangerous for me to think what I was thinking. I could hardly believe I was entertaining the idea, especially in light of my already-precarious psychological life. But try as I might to warn myself away, I couldn't help identifying my situation with Mitch's words. My involuntary tendency to try on new world views like suits of clothes led me to think that maybe my recent sense of spiritual lightness was the gift of the God, whatever His name was, and that the growth on my face was a sign of the price I would have to pay for accepting it. I knew it was madness, but in the silence of my apartment, cut off from the rest of the world, with Dr. Baumann thousands of miles away, the transcript of a surreal spiritual puzzle in my hand, and an impossible mark riding on my cheek, I didn't know how to convince myself otherwise. My philosophical schizophrenia was working overtime to undermine all my attempts at reasoning with myself. Nor was I helped by the fact that I was increasingly plagued by the mental image of these thoughts as deformed crabs that had been clinging to the underside of my consciousness for a very long time, awaiting a quiet moment in which to scuttle to the top and sink their claws into the soft gray folds where my sense of self resided.

By five o'clock I was utterly wretched. I felt dizzy, hot, and sick with worry, but at least my wooziness helped me for awhile as I tried to deny a phenomenon that I had noticed several times during the day but refused to acknowledge. At last it was undeniable, and that was when my world definitively began to tilt.

For even though it was impossible, the black spot was visibly growing. When I had first examined it around seven in the morning, it was the size of a pea. By noon, when I had fixed myself a half-hearted lunch of canned tomato soup and a grilled cheese sandwich, it was big as a dime. I was just overwrought, I told myself as I chewed the cheesy bread. I was just letting my vivid mental and imaginative powers get away from me. Of course the spot couldn't be growing. Not like that. Not so quickly that by the next morning it would surely cover the whole of my face like a putrid black mask.

But at five in the afternoon it was the size of a large marble, and its growth was impossible to deny. I stared at it I the mirror while the evening news blared from the TV set in the other room. My supernatural gift from the God (stop thinking that, don't even flirt with that) had doubled its size in eight hours. I probed the area around it with trembling fingers and became aware of another astonishing fact: the pain had disappeared. There was no more itch, no more burning, no more anything. In fact, it wasn't just my face that felt fine. *All* of me felt fine.

No, more than fine, I felt *great*, even in my semi-feverish condition, which I now recognized as a very shallow phenomenon beneath which I was positively charged, invigorated, vitalized with an abundant swell of energy and well being. The image of the waterwheel suddenly reappeared to join those deformed crabs. I could almost see it turning slowly, dipping into a placid black spring, drawing up buckets of cool water and dumping them into a cistern in my soul where they refreshed me, soothed me, and buoyed me up, making even the mere possibility of unhappiness or anxiety seem absurd. In the coolness and quietness of that secret place, there was nothing but pure bliss.

It was the first time I had ever felt wonderful and awful at the same time. By all rights I should have felt nothing but panic, but there I was, enjoying a calm center of seemingly supernatural peace while my face rotted off from an impossible disease.

The very recognition of my divided state initiated a dreadful synergy between my peaceful inner feelings and my rapidly deteriorating outer situation. A nightmarish sense of unreality whispered up like a shivering black cloud from the base of my brain. The chills from my pseudo-fever edged subtly into a deeper chill, a veritable *frisson* that was so pervasive it seemed to reach all the way to the tips of my fingers and toes. My eyes looked back at me from the mirror. Their green hue was muted with fever, giving them the appearance of two cloudy emeralds. Behind them I saw a spark glowing in the darkness. Or maybe it was a wheel turning. Or maybe it was an army of crabs, crouched on the edge of consciousness, pulsing and waiting.

Again the thought of the hospital arose. Again, I stuffed it down. Sleep beckoned. It was late. The day had lasted an eternity. The sluggish shadows had finally reached the couch, and I dragged myself to the living room and sank into the cushions with a sense of unknown activities and strange transformations still taking place behind the facade of my soul. Sleep rose like the waters of a cool dark spring, and I gratefully let it claim me.

VI

Only when we are sick of our sickness
Shall we cease to be sick.
The Sage is not sick, being sick of sickness;
This is the secret of health.

—*Tao Teh Ching* chapter 71

I overslept the next day by nearly eight hours. Instead of my usual wake-up time of seven-thirty, my eyes stayed shut and then opened of their own accord just before three-thirty in the afternoon. All night long I had inhabited a dream that seemed to last for a timeless moment. I had been frozen in perpetual motion, suspended in a formless darkness that folded and separated into well-defined shapes, while I listened to a voice speaking silently into my inner ear. It had whispered and slobbered things I never should have been able to understand, but in the murky clarity of the dream I *had* understood. The words had spoken to me on a level of selfhood that resided in a timeless dimension prior to language, a primal plane where identity was nothing but the formless, structured chaos of the darkness that seethed and breathed around me.

I had heard a name spoken. It was the name of a god. The voice was the god's very voice, the words were its very words, and the sound of it was the sound of all foulness, like the liquid lapping of a bottomless whirlpool sucking down the stinking dregs of a stagnant, polluted ocean.

When I awoke to the half-light of my white-walled bedroom, the dim, dreamy color of the atmosphere reminded me of Mitch's house. I shot upright in bed with the sheets still wrapped around my chest and arms, terrified for a moment that I would find myself lying on his tattered old couch while he sat beside me in his ratty recliner and murmured strange things into my ear.

My relief at finding myself in my bedroom was short-lived, for when I looked at the clock and read its red-trembling digital numbers, a cold adrenaline jolt of panic shot through my gut. I had slept away nearly the entire day. Yesterday seemed impossibly distant. What was I supposed to be doing? I couldn't remember. Was I pursuing a doctorate in religious studies? Was my mother alive? Was I working for a newspaper and writing a story about the Sick Seekers? All seemed possible. None would fall into place as the real present.

Then I remembered the meeting at Mitch's house scheduled for that very night. Simultaneously, as I was still rubbing my stubbly growth of beard, I remembered the mark on my face, and the coldness in my gut surged like an electric current.

I reached up with shaking fingers to rub my left cheekbone. My fingers found an irregular bump, and a groan escaped my mouth. I ran to the bathroom and flipped on the switch, expecting with the certainty of nightmarish foresight to see my entire face ravaged by a tar-black, pestilent growth.

But the mark hadn't grown at all. It was still the size of a large marble, still black in the middle and fading toward the edges. It might have flattened out a little during the night, but otherwise there was no change.

A cinematic flash of memory eclipsed the present moment. I was nineteen years old and my mother was standing before me as I revealed my newly healed face to her. I showed her proudly that everything was fine, that my beauty was unmarred. Her face froze like a porcelain doll for the briefest of moments. Then it shattered, releasing a flood of tears and sobs that shocked me with their violence. When she turned and ran, I stayed rooted to the spot, listening to her footfalls retreat up the stairs and across the plush-carpeted hallway to her bedroom, where the door slammed shut with the finality of a coffin lid.

Too many emotions washed over me, far more and far deeper than I knew how to handle. I knew that if I accepted them they would overwhelm me and destroy all my cherished plans for a comfortable future far away from home, locked safely away in a high ivory tower. I did not possess the inner resources to handle such an ocean of negativity. So I did what I had to do. I took hold of something like a mental key, and inserted it into something like a lock, and shut all of my bleak feelings into something like a dark storehouse in my soul, where they would never be able to reach me. Afterwards, I felt numbed, but cleansed.

The memory ended and there I was, standing in the bathroom of my apartment with a horrible spot on my face and a surreal puzzle about a god of foulness taking shape in my mind. And I realized the door to that secret storehouse, which I had forgotten for all those years, was not as secure as I had imagined when I first discovered it. For years it had been leaking into my soul, polluting my life with an icy undercurrent of misery. Now, in the face of my rising tide of confusion and fear, it was threatening to burst wide open and destroy me with a deluge of despair.

One thing at a time, I told myself. Calm down and focus. Make everything ordinary. Make every act a mindful one. First, step away from the mirror and refuse to think about what it shows. Next, stop before the toilet to urinate. Then put one foot in front of the other to march into the living room and soak in the normality of the furniture arranged in its ordinary pattern, with the reassuring glow of the afternoon sunlight spilling through the front windows. Inhale, then exhale. Find that sweet center of mental and emotional transcendence, from where you can live as the witness of your life.

My cell phone had three voice mails on it when I reached the living room. I had missed three phone calls while I overslept. I dialed my account and pressed the button to hear my messages. Dr. Baumann's voice began to speak into my ear.

"Lawrence! I'm stunned you're researching the Sick Seekers too. Please forgive me, I don't have time for small talk. I've learned more about the Sick Seekers in one week of visiting my brother than I learned from a year of reading the research literature. Listen to me: don't have anything to do with that old man again. You asked if there's a historical antecedent to the Sick Seekers' theology. I can tell you that their insistence on the foulness of the body sounds a bit like an obscure Buddhist practice of meditating on corpses. It's hardly practiced at all today. But there's more to what's happening than just the recurrence of an outdated contemplative practice. Lawrence, I mean it, listen to me: *stay away* from these people. There's something unprecedented going on. While I've been down here in Las Vegas, my brother has mentioned some of the same things you've been saying, and I have a hunch—this is going to sound crazy, I know—that the Sick Seekers are worshipping deities that haven't been worshiped for nearly six thousand years. There was a cult in the ancient Middle

East centered around them. You remember the seminar I taught on the dark side of religion? Well, this cult could have filled up the entire semester, but I never mentioned it because I didn't know anybody even remembered those gods, let alone worshiped them. Only a handful of scholars know the cult ever existed, but now the Sick Seekers have come along and shaken us all up. This is absolutely amazing stuff. It looks like the spontaneous resurrection of a cult that—." At this point the available space for his message ran out. I pressed the key to play the next one.

"Sorry," he said, "I'm getting long-winded here, but you have to hear this. Something's not right, Lawrence. This ancient cult posited more than one god in their cosmology. The first was a god of primal chaos. The second was a kind of mystical bridge between this chaos and the created world. The worship of these gods was about undoing everything, uncreating creation, destroying the cosmos. The rituals devoted to them were positively nightmarish. They involved human sacrifice and something more: the attempted sacrifice of a worshiper's very soul. But the cultists didn't conceive of the body as a separate thing. Lawrence, in a way these people were proto-Gnostics! They believed the body was a cesspool of corruption. But the really unique thing that distinguished them from all the other sects and cults around them was that they believed the same thing about the individual soul. They regarded body and soul as dual facets of a single, horrible aberration. Salvation was conceived in terms of escaping the nightmare of created existence and returning to the bliss of uncreated chaos. The god of primal chaos was the goal. The second god was the bridge and the key. Then there was a third god. Do you understand what I'm telling you? A *third* god, Lawrence. He was never named in the ancient literature. His worshipers were zealous about guarding his identity. But we do know that this god was thought to be the manifest presence of the other two gods in the worshiper's body. From what I've learned recently, I'm thinking there may be some correspondences with the trinitarian theology of orthodox Christianity, with its doctrine of the hypostatic union and mutual interpenetration of the three members of the godhead. I'm just speechless, Lawrence. This is all so exciting, I can barely contain myself. All these things I'm telling you are like playing connect the dots with a six thousand year old puzzle. My brother has told me things that have allowed me to connect scattered bits of information I haven't known what to do with for decades. If I can just—." End of message two. I pressed the button to play the final one.

"We have to talk about this in person. I'm sure we have many hours' worth of things to share with each other. But please, please listen to me, Lawrence. Don't let my professional excitement throw you off track. These people were the spiritual pariahs of the ancient world. Everybody else was utterly horrified by them. If the Sick Seekers really are the continuation of this ancient religion, then they're the apocalyptic cult to end all apocalyptic cults. And if they've really got hold of the scripture you say they have, they're the most dangerous thing the modern world has ever seen. I don't pretend to know how it's possible for them to be what I'm thinking they must be. I mean, it's completely *im*possible by any normal standard of logic. It flies in the face of common sense and every other measure of sanity. It may take decades to unravel it all. But just *stay away*, no matter how curious you are. My brother has told me things that have stood my hair on end. I'll tell you, I'm actually getting a bit nervous around him. I would have already taken him away from here by force, but he seems so enraptured by his new religion that I'm afraid the psychological damage of a sudden uprooting might be severe. I'm at a loss for what to do right now. Wish me luck. I promise to call you just as soon as I get back to Terence. Be safe, Lawrence."

That was the end. An electronic voice asked me whether I wanted to save or delete the messages, but I just stood there. My eyes were open and my mind awake, but the mental sight of the picture taking shape in my soul had begun to obscure the hard physical reality of the room around me. The outline was becoming clear. The pieces were malformed. Thousands of sickly, pulsating shapes with serrated edges and pale pincers had locked together to form a long figure with a handle to grasp and sharp teeth for fitting into a lock.

There had never been any real question about whether I would attend the meeting at Mitch's house. I had known when he first invited me that I couldn't refuse, and he had known it, too. To run from this unfolding reality would be to run from the possibility of ever reestablishing a connection with all of those unnamed spiritual treasures that I had always regarded, even in the midst of my nihilism, as making life worth living. Or at least they made it bearable enough to get out of bed each morning. Through a kind of lateral logic that made no sense to my rational brain, I realized that my psychic survival was bound up with the Sick Seekers and their crazy, dangerous theology. I would go to Mitch's house, I told myself, and would discover what they did at their worship services, and I would return safely to share my knowledge with Dr. Baumann and expose the cult for what it was. Along the way, maybe I would become a whole person again.

Despite my newfound resolve, I did place a bandage over my left cheek after I dressed, and I did wonder as I walked out the front door just how deeply the mark reached inward into my body, and whether its fingers might touch the latches of any other doors that I had locked and then forgotten.

VII

And now you know what is holding him back, so that he may be revealed at the proper time.

— 2 Thessalonians 2:6

Mitch's house was different in the darkness. Gray clouds choked the sky as I pulled into his driveway at five minutes till seven, with only a ragged gap here and there allowing a flicker of starlight to shine through. Dusk had come early, and the house looked vaguely humanlike with its red-lipped porch for a mouth and yellow glowing dormer windows for eyes. The windows drew my attention as I parked behind several other cars that were already lined up. From the look of it, those upper rooms would be used for something tonight, for I saw moving shadows through the glass.

I walked up the porch steps without hesitation, carrying my briefcase even though it felt useless, and rapped on the metal frame of the screen door. Through the screen I saw several people standing or sitting in Mitch's living room. They were all elderly. One of them, an old man dressed in a gray sweat suit and brown slippers, was seated on the couch with an aluminum walker parked beside him. He looked at me through the wire mesh barrier and smiled broadly with a closed mouth.

Then Mitch approached from somewhere and opened the door for me. His smile was rather sardonic, as if to say that he had known all along I would show up. I refused to meet his eyes but nodded my head in greeting. He seemed satisfied with this and stepped aside to let me enter.

He introduced me to everyone right away. Of course he didn't speak. He merely pointed to them one by one as they told me their names and the nature of their diseases, in what felt like a customary ritual. There was Maggie, an old woman whose eyes were completely obscured by milky white cataracts. There was Alice, another old woman with hands shriveled and twisted into eagle-like claws from rheumatoid arthritis. There was Sherman, an old man with a brain tumor. There was Doyle, the old man seated on the couch beside the walker. He suffered from testicular cancer, and he smiled that broad-lipped smile the whole time I looked at him. The others, all of them elderly and liver-spotted, crowded forward to tell me of their various ailments. Together they chanted a litany of sickness and suffering, but their voices were happy and their eyes bright. Their faces were all shining with eager anticipation of something to come, and I silently renewed my resolve to keep my guard up.

I counted ten people, including Mitch, and then I began to wonder where the other two were. He had said there were twelve, hadn't he?

"There's the last one," said Maggie. I don't know how she knew where to point in her blindness, but she directed a bony finger through the wall of aged bodies gathered before me, and my jaw dropped nearly to my chest as the people parted to reveal Lindy standing near the doorway to the kitchen with a shy grin on her fair-skinned face. She said she was suffering from uterine cancer and had only been a member of the body for two weeks.

No, I thought, this isn't right. This can't be right. My eyes felt hot, and the bandage on my cheek was suffocating me. My knees were turning to water. Nobody had asked about the bandage yet, but they had all been looking at it with a piercing interest in their eyes. Now Lindy was there, one of the last people in the world I had expected or wanted to see, and she was staring at the bandage as if she saw through it and wanted to kiss what was on the other side.

Not Lindy. She couldn't be a part of this. She was too pure. And it would mean that I had been manipulated from the beginning. Mitch wouldn't have had to suffer any kind of "spell." He and Lindy might have planned his trip to the hospital together, so that he would arrive when Peg was on duty, and she would tell Bobby about the incident, and he would tell me. One of the other members of the body might have driven Mitch there and then slipped out on cue. Then all they would have had to do was wait for me to show up on Mitch's doorstep thinking that I was paying him an unexpected visit.

But why? What possible reason could they have for tricking me into coming out there and meeting him?

A blurry wave rippled across my field of vision. Suddenly, I was unsure whether I was standing there in Mitch's living room or still hanging in the timeless darkness of my recent dream. My briefcase slipped from my fingers and dropped to the worn carpet with a thump. I felt a tingling start up in my face again. It swelled rapidly to an itching but then held off, refusing to surge into the agony I had known once in a distant past that was separated from me by less than forty-eight hours. The feeling rippled like an electric centipede down to my chest, and further, into my groin, where it became a ball of prickling energy that was somehow wrapped up in the cool embrace of a deep cistern that even now was continuing to receive bucket after bucket of fresh, dark water from a steadily turning wheel.

When the diseased old people gathered around me and touched me with their vile hands, I tried to resist but found that I was mute and helpless. Even the voice of my own thoughts was unable to articulate a clear refusal. I was dumb as an infant.

They led me to the staircase, which was old and wooden, and then up the stairs to a trapdoor, which I saw was suspended open by a rope and two iron counterweights shaped like the weights of a grandfather clock. Brittle hands clothed with papery skin pawed and caressed me, carried me forward, lifted me. I was not walking,

I was being borne along by a tidal swell of aging flesh.

The upper floor had no partitions or dividing walls. It was a single large room that reached to the outer walls of the house. Everything was of brown wood like the staircase, and the ceiling was low. Two bare bulbs with pull cords were suspended from the ceiling and doing a poor job of illuminating the corners. Two four-paned windows on the far wall peered out over the front yard, which may as well have been a million miles and a lifetime away.

The worshipers whispered around me and sat me down near a corner. My awareness was the blank surface of a black sea as they peeled off me one by one, moving in a hushed silence toward other positions, lining the outer walls until everyone was seated in a rough circle. Maggie was positioned across from me. Even in the blankness of my thoughts, I could not escape the impression that her blind eyes with their milky growths were regarding me with compassion. Lindy was seated several feet away on my left, swaying and humming to herself.

Then Mitch began to speak. He was to my right, and his voice was the voice of the God.

"The body is a blocked wish. The body is not different from the soul." It was the sound of all foulness and corruption, a voice too horrible to be real, and yet it kept speaking as I swayed like a drunken man and looked around for a way to escape.

"The body is meant to rot. The soul is meant to rot. Sickness of the body and soul is the doorway to your bliss. You have tried and failed to make peace with the body. You have tried and failed to find the truth of your soul. Peace with the body and truth in the soul are illusions. You are good for nothing but to rot."

They were all swaying now, moving like serpents in a circle. I would not have thought their wasted old bodies capable of such supple motion. Doyle looked as if he were about to twist the upper half of his body away from the lower. His walker rested beside him, forgotten in the fray.

The God's voice continued to issue from Mitch's throat. "Give up your disease. Give it to me, and I will take it from you and leave you with blissful nothing."

Maggie was still staring at me. Her eyes were too bright to be blind. Even from across the room, I saw what might have been an army of misshapen crabs chittering behind them. Something connected within me, some nascent circuit of realization, and suddenly I knew with undeniable certainty that it was the God looking out at me from behind that milky stare. She had become the vessel for His sight, and Her eyes were now His.

Alice sat next to her with clawed arthritic hands moving in serpentine patterns. They slithered in the air and then came to point at me with eight fingers and two thumbs. Their motion mimicked something. It looked as if She were caressing my face from across the room. The same blossoming realization continued to expand: Her hands were the hands of the God. She had become a vessel for the God of foulness. I looked up and saw Her eyes closed and Her head thrown back in ecstasy.

The others were all beginning to manifest the God in various ways. They twisted and flopped and beat the floor. They hummed and moaned and wailed while Mitch continued to speak of the body as a disease, and disease as a new kind of health. Sherman, the old man with the brain tumor, sat stiff-backed with his arms spread out like a music conductor. The motions of his hands caused waves of activity across the room. It was almost as if he were a puppeteer, and I knew that he was the brain of the God, manifesting itself through a tumor implanted in his own brain like a rotten plum.

Then Lindy and Doyle began to crawl across the floor toward each other. They were tearing their clothes off. *Oh, God.* The thought struck me with a desperate absurdity, for the God I was referring to had no place in that room. Within a moment's time, an old man with testicular cancer had begun to copulate with a young woman suffering from cancer of the uterus. I could not bear to watch, and yet I could not rip my eyes away from them.

My face was burning and itching and swelling and suffocating beneath its bandage. Sherman waved his hand at me, and against my conscious will my own hand shot up and ripped away the gauze and tape, baring my secret horror to the assembled appendages of the God while a flabby old man and a soft young woman coupled on the floor in the midst of us.

It was as if scales fell from my eyes. With my mark exposed, I could see what I had been unable to see before: a presence like oily smoke floating near the ceiling. It churned softly with a strangely organic motion, dropping down flickering tendrils to caress the assembled worshipers.

No, it did not caress them, it *entered* them through the various means of access they had brought with them in the form of their diseases. It drove black spikes into Maggie's eyes. It wound like a leprous fog around Alice's shriveled hands and sank in through her pores to animate her fingers with that caressing motion that was still directed at me. It formed a seething funnel like a miniature cyclone above Sherman's head and poured into his skull in an ever-shifting plume. When I looked to my right, I saw it entering Mitch's mouth with every inhalation and exiting as grotesquely shaped puffs that trembled in sympathetic vibration to the words he spoke.

Lindy and Doyle were still locked in a coital embrace. He was on his back and she sat astride him, and I felt my gorge rise. The cloud swirled above them and formed a vortex like an open mouth. A single tongue of greasy blackness lolled out and fell down to brush over their writhing bodies. Then it snaked between them to caress their point of their union.

The thought came in a flash: what would be the issue of a woman with a diseased womb, impregnated by a man with diseased testes, formed by the power of a God of foulness, nurtured by the collective worship of a group of ailing fanatics? What exactly would be the shape of a God whose nature was foulness and corruption? What would be the appearance of the god of rottenness made incarnate?

These thoughts were cut off by the phenomenon that had been steadily growing in my face. In the midst of the nightmare that was taking shape around me, I had been feeling a growing pressure in my cheek. Now it swelled to bursting. My head was tugged violently to one side as if gravity itself were pulling me toward the center of the circle, or as if a hook were lodged in my cheek and someone were reeling me in. I looked up to see the tendril of the God reaching down toward me, sinking into the diseased skin of my face, then reaching even further down inside, searching out the whole branching network of a cancer that had metastasized throughout my body with impossible rapidity. The God already possessed eyes and hands. He had a brain and a body. He was organizing the separate parts and forming Himself through the union of the two who were even now finishing up before me. What more was wanting?

The God needed a face.

At the moment I realized it, Mitch began to speak again next to me.

"Our Father in chaos. And His brother, the all-in-one, the gate and the key. Hear Me, and give Me form so that I may reclaim this world of putrid flesh for Our own, that I may sweep away its illusions to reveal Our reality burning bright behind the veil of matter." As the God spoke, the worshipers wailed, and their sound became a component of the Voice.

"I am the procession of your union in separateness," the God proclaimed to His counterparts in infinity. "Now give me a name and a form to be Our presence in this world. It is I who ask You this—I, Our manifest presence!"

Then the God spoke His own name. It was not true speech, not the production of any type of vocal equipment, human or otherwise. It was not even a sound in the normal meaning of the word. It was an actual animate thing, the aural embodiment of the essence of the God Himself, the living Word of Corruption. And it was a palpable horror.

At the sound of it, my face ripped loose from my skull. It flew off like a ragged rubber mask, flapped upward toward the seething purplish abyss of the ceiling like a blood-drenched bird, and disappeared into the maw of the God. Something in me died as it disappeared. And then an avalanche of disease begin to rumble up and pour forth from every orifice of my body. Blood and bone spewed from my eyes. My organs dissolved into jellied lumps and erupted from my mouth. And yet somehow I was still conscious through it all. Somehow, I still saw.

The others around me were coming unbound as well. The tendrils trailing from the ceiling were tearing them apart, wrenching themselves out of pale fat bodies and taking lumps of disease with them. Leathery black coils like the length of a whip were withdrawing from the tender point of contact between Lindy and Sherman, and it was as if a nest of fishhooks were drawing up a monster catch from the depths of a putrid ocean. The things squirming on the ends of those hooks were rotten and full of teeth, dripping with a blackish ichor, and mewling like kittens. They smelled like a sewer. I saw them drawn into the greedy black cloud, and it seemed that its edges expanded slightly, as if it were growing from the nourishment it received. It pushed against the shuddering walls, bulging out between attic boards, swelling the house like a human head with its cranium about to burst.

And then I returned to myself found that I was lying on the floor in a rubbery pile like an empty body suit. The others around me were wilting, too, like peach-colored balloons. Nothing remained of them but the cast-off shells of their human flesh. The God had taken back what belonged to Him and left the remnant to rot.

Sherman and Lindy had pulled away from each other. She lay on her back before me in a totally immodest pose with her empty flesh collapsing in on itself, exposing in a horrid display those parts of her that I had once thought (was it only a few short days ago?) that I would enjoy coaxing her into exposing under different circumstances.

Next to me, Mitch was the only one still standing. He had stopped speaking but his breath still emitted a steady scrape like the sound of a saw rasping in the distance. He turned his eyes to the ceiling, where the swirling black mass was already receding into the impossible abyss from whence it had come, and I saw him reach up to probe his throat gently in an attitude of affection. Then he turned his gaze down upon me and opened his mouth to speak.

What came out were not sounds, but written words. They issued from his lips like trails of black butterflies and stayed suspended against a smooth white background that shimmered up from somewhere to become a paper surface. I recognized them. "The God gives you a choice," they said. "First He gives you a taste of the bliss He's offering you. Then He shows you what it's going to cost you to accept it." Mitch's eyes looked deeply into mine. Then he bent at the knees and sat down in a ratty old recliner that appeared behind him from out of nowhere.

VIII

They're here already! You're next!

—Miles Bennell

I was sitting on Mitch's sofa with a notebook in my hands. He sat in the recliner before me, waiting. Two box fans purred in the living room windows with the shades pulled down to the tops of them. The atmosphere was stuffy, and the backs of my legs had sweated through to the sofa.

I blinked and looked around. An empty glass rested on the floor beside Mitch's chair. The faint scrapings of insect noises filtered through the walls from outside and mingled with the sound of his breathing. When I looked back up at him, he was staring at me with shiny-bright silver dollar eyes.

I don't have the heart to describe what came next: all the gasping and panting as my pulse began to pound and my face began to throb like a beating drum; the collapse into quivering panic that laid me out on the sofa; the hateful care he gave me like some sort of surrogate mother; the long night of hallucinatory dread in which I saw smoky black tendrils drooping from the ceiling, reaching down into the living room from the attic above, waiting to sink whiplike fingers into my skull. All night long I kept reaching up to touch my face and registering surprise when my fingers found only the smooth, unblemished surface of my skin. But the flood of relief I kept expecting to wash over me never came.

I left at dawn, when I found I was strong enough to walk. The early-morning air whispered against my skin like a mantle of damp silk. As I emerged from the house and stumbled down the porch steps, I heard the forest sounds blended together into a smooth chirring like the electrified whine of a telephone. I thought I had risen early enough that Mitch would not see me, but as I backed out of his driveway I saw him framed inside the black border of the screen door. His hand was probing his throat, and I could feel his eyes seeking out mine. I tried to tell myself that the voice I heard speaking faintly in my brain over the roar of the engine was merely the sound of a morning bird chirping in the forest. But it didn't go away as I picked up speed and shot down the highway toward Terence.

I had no idea what day it was. The enormity of my disorientation only made itself known gradually as I tried to figure out what had happened to me. I kept fearing that I might blink at any minute and find myself seated once again on Mitch's sofa, or worse, in his attic, with the other members of the body manifesting the God all around me.

Terence had not properly awakened when I reached the city limits. The residential areas were still cloaked with a gray blanket of pre-dawn stillness, and the downtown streets were deserted except for a police cruiser that paused at the corner of Grand and Broadway to let me pass. The sight of the fresh-faced young officer seated behind the steering wheel pricked an unexpected bubble of hysteria in my chest. Here was a man devoted to keeping peace and order in human society, but now I knew that those two principles could never coexist. Peace could only be bought by sacrificing oneself to the God of chaos, by identifying oneself with the disease at the center of infinity, where there could be no unpeace, no pain, no disease, because there was no longer a conscious self to feel pain or anxiety. The thoughts felt alien to me, as if they had been implanted in my head through the agency of some external will. But there was no way to escape them, as they seemed to form the foundation of my perspective now.

I'm confident the young policeman must have thought seriously about stopping me as I swerved and braked to avoid wrecking my car in a fit of laughter. But in the end he just let me pass. Maybe he had his own concerns to attend to, and harbored no wish to face the possible difficulties of dealing in the early morning hours with a hysterical man cackling like an idiot behind the wheel of his car. Or maybe the God was making my crooked paths straight and my rough ways smooth.

When I got home, I locked the door behind me and wandered from room to room in a dreamlike daze. My apartment was untouched, but everything had changed. It was as if somebody had taken away everything I knew, all of my familiar possessions and surroundings, and replaced them with exact facsimiles composed of smoke. I felt they might dissipate at any moment to reveal some unthinkable vista of infinity lying behind their facade of solidity.

But the real revelation did not come until I looked down at my own body and saw the same insubstantiality built into my flesh. My vision pierced like an x-ray through skin and muscle, blood and bone, and found a seed of corruption implanted in the very workings of what I had always considered to be health. This body was a vapor that would be consumed by a principle of decay built into its innermost workings. All that would remain was the God.

I could not be certain whether I was laughing or crying as I congratulated myself on having attained the enlightenment that I had been seeking for as long as I could remember.

This new perspective has proved to be a permanent conversion. As those first days and weeks passed, I found that I was operating from an unknown center. Some new framework had been successfully erected like a psychic scaffolding behind the facade of my self, and my thoughts and sense of identity were now built upon and around its distorted shape. I saw infinity in everything and found comfort in nothing.

It was impossible to continue working at the newspaper. I could not bear to face anyone from my former life. Bobby asked me what was wrong when I phoned him to tender my resignation. At first he didn't think I was serious, but then he became concerned and angry, and said I couldn't just quit on him like that without giving him a reason or a warning. But that was exactly what I did. I made my resignation effective that day, and we never saw or spoke to each other again.

Dr. Baumann never returned from his sabbatical, which didn't really surprise me. I followed the stories in the newspaper about the search for him, and I laughed or cried when I saw them sometimes situated next to AP wire pieces about the Sick Seekers. Even though nobody knows what happened to him, I feel certain that I *do* know, if only I could articulate it. But I have no particular desire to envision him being torn apart by the whiplike fingers of the God.

Physically, externally, I have remained whole. I check the mirror each morning to see whether a black spot has erupted on my face, but every morning I find that I am still clothed with the same meaningless, beautiful mask that once sat at the center of my world. Now I am amazed and disgusted when I think of how much stock I placed in such a worthless layer of muscle and fat. Sometimes I fancy that I am engaging in the corpse meditation that Dr. Baumann mentioned, and that the object of my meditation is my own body.

On my own I have continued to speculate about the Sick Seekers. It is an idle amusement, as I now know life itself to be, but it passes the time. I indulge my vestigial passion for the study of religion by looking for similarities between the Sick Seekers' theology and the doctrines of various world religions. On some days I seem to find echoes of the ancient chaos religion resonating in the trinitarian theology of orthodox Christianity, the mystical identification of the individual soul with Brahman in Vedantic Hinduism, and the "meditation on foulness" recommended by the Buddha in the Girimananda Sutta. I speculate that there are sinister hints of something ancient and monstrous peering through the seemingly innocent and life-affirming ideas of non-resistance and *wu wei*, or "effortless action," in Chinese Taoism. I fancy that I can see the words of the God of Chaos shining through some of the more outlandish pronouncements of Yahweh in the Hebrew Scriptures, despite Mitch's belief that the god of the ancient Jews is not his own God. On other days I realize that these speculations are worthless, and that I am just using them to while away the hours on the way to my certain annihilation.

The media coverage of the Sick Seekers continues to proliferate, and the size of the cult continues to grow. In Haiti there is a body that claims to have an AIDS sufferer among their ranks. The stories say they view him as a kind of avatar, since his flesh is an open channel for every pathogen in the environment around him. When I first read this, I realized that other Sick Seekers around the world must have started talking openly to the press, just as Mitch talked to me. They are spreading their gospel of disease, and I cannot doubt but that their ranks will grow even faster as people discover the freedom from suffering that awaits them in the embrace of the God. In the midst of an increasingly insane global society, they will surely find many miserable people who welcome such relief.

Locally, I have no desire to seek out Mitch and the others. They have remained silent toward me, probably—or so I presume—because they expect me to join them eventually of my own free will. On some days I am tempted to visit the hospital and seek out Lindy to see whether she really is a part of all this, or whether I am just the victim of terrible delusion. It might be comforting to know that I am insane, and that none of what I think has happened to me has really happened. But the thought of looking into her soft white face and maybe seeing a hunger in her blue eyes to kiss my cheek keeps me away.

As my state and situation continue to degenerate, and as I wait for the numbers of the Sick Seekers to reach some sort of critical mass that will signal the moment for the God to set in motion His master plan, two things have come to dominate my newly enlightened thoughts. The first involves my mother. Mitch told me that his wife never stopped believing her god would heal her, right up until she died. One of the last doors to be unlocked inside me brought forth a memory of my own mother experiencing a deathbed conversion to the Christianity of her parents. She had always been so brittle and empty, like a porcelain doll, that to see her wasting her dying moments on a futile attempt to atone for a life lived in self-absorption and empty vanity made me hate her. But I also knew that she had passed the same traits on to me, and even though I locked away the knowledge of it in the same psychic storehouse where I had hidden all my other unpleasant feelings, it followed me through graduate school and eventually became the pinprick that deflated my spiritual passion. I could never escape the subconscious thought that I was just as false as she was, and that my pose of spirituality was just a clumsy compensation for the emptiness and pettiness of my true nature. But now my awakening had purged me of all that. How much easier, I now understood, simply to drop the whole sad charade and be *nothing*.

It was the remembrance of that sorry chapter in my life that brought forth the second factor that has come to dominate my attention. During my college years, while I was under the sway of all those buried motivations, I became fascinated by the novel *Invasion of the Body Snatchers* and its cinematic adaptations. This became bound up with my ersatz Zen perspective, and I sometimes found myself thinking that the arguments of the pod people in Finney's novel were correct. What *does* it matter whether the body, or even the mind or soul, is replaced by a facsimile? There is only one ultimate consciousness looking out from behind every set of eyes, and to insist upon the absolute value of any given individual form is to buy into the very illusion of separateness that constitutes the unenlightened state. An enlightened master faced with the threat of replacement by an alien replica would not view it as a threat at all, for he would know that in the end there would be no real difference, and thus no loss to mourn.

I have found myself returning to these thoughts more and more. With increasing frequency and intensity, I find myself doubting whether there really is such a thing as authenticity, since there is no real "me" to which I should feel honor-bound. At the deepest level, the level of absolute, unconditioned truth, there is only the one Self churning in infinite chaos, and It does not know or care whether I am real. I feel sickened when I dwell upon the fact that I am backed into a corner where the only authentic act I can perform—the most authentic act of my life, the one that will redeem a lifetime spent in pretension and falsehood—will be to give myself up to the God of Foulness, the manifest presence of the infinite corruption that constitutes the heart of reality. This God speaks to me constantly through the disease of my individuated selfhood—the last and truest disease—and shows me that the only way out, the only way to reconnect with what I once thought I had, is to choose the inner over the outer, peace over beauty. It is a soul-searing choice, for I know that when I eventually give in, a virulent cancer will erupt on my face, and the God will reclaim what is rightfully His.

I can put it off as long as I want. He says He gives me a choice. But then, how can it be a true choice when nothing else is real? Everything is empty and good for nothing but to rot, except for this chaos, this madness, this sickness, this filth. In the end, there is no real choice for me to make, for I have nothing else from which to choose. Nor do any of us.

Other Fictions

A BRIEF HISTORY OF THE ANGEL AND THE DEMON

I. INTRODUCTION: IS THERE SOMEONE INSIDE YOU?

Even a cursory survey of the supernatural horror genre reveals the important role that the angel and the demon have long played in it. From texts such as Dante's *Divine Comedy* (written 1308-1321) and John Milton's *Paradise Lost* (1667), which straddle the boundary between religious devotional literature and outright fiction, to fictional works such as Matthew Lewis's *The Monk* (1796) and William Peter Blatty's *The Exorcist* (1971), the demon has provided ongoing fodder for creators of supernatural horror. And while the angel has most often served as a mere foil for the demon, and has often been ignored in favor of focusing exclusively on demonic horrors, it has still made its presence known. *Paradise Lost,* for example, begins with a dramatic narration of the fall of Lucifer and his fellow angels from heaven and their subsequent transformation or transition into demons. More recently, American popular culture portrayed the angel in a context of supernatural horror in the *Prophecy* movie franchise from the 1990s and early 2000s, which flouted modern Western conventions by abandoning the cute, cozy angels of Victorian art and the greeting card industry and returning to a more ancient and traditional portrayal of angels as powerful, terrifying beings.

Nor are these figures influential merely within the confines of the supernatural horror as such. In 1973 the cinematic adaptation of *The Exorcist* became a sensation among audiences and was subsequently recognized as the first true "blockbuster," predating the likes of *Jaws* and *Star Wars.* It was nominated for ten Academy Awards, including Best Picture and Best Director, and won two of them. Its earnings made it one of the top grossing films at the U.S. box office that year, and in the succeeding decades it has steadily remained in and around the top ten highest grossing films of all time both domestically and internationally. Upon its first release it ignited a national conversation about theological matters within the United States, just as its author (William Peter Blatty, who penned the screenplay from his novel) had hoped it would do, and spurred many fear-based conversions and reconversions to Christianity.

Angels have shared a similar widespread influence. Director Frank Capra's *It's a Wonderful Life,* which begins and ends with angels, received only a middling response from audiences and critics when it was first released in 1946 (although it was nominated for five Academy Awards). Then in 1974 a copyright lapse due to a clerical error placed the film in the public domain. When television stations around the country began to take advantage of the opportunity to run the film free of royalty charges, a new generation of viewers rediscovered and fell in love with it, thus transforming it into a widely beloved "holiday classic," and thus making the supporting character of Clarence the most famous cinematic angel of them all.

Over the course of subsequent decades, angels became the subject of a bona fide national obsession in the U.S. A slew of television programs (*Highway to Heaven, Touched by an Angel*), movies (*Angels in the Outfield, City of Angels*), and best-selling books (*A Book of Angels, Ask Your Angels, Where Angels Walk*) arose to cater to a rising fascination with the idea of winged heavenly guardians and messengers. In 1994 the NBC television network aired a two-hour primetime special titled *Angels: The Mysterious Messengers,* and PBS ran a well-received documentary titled *In Search of Angels.* A 1993 *Time* magazine cover story about the angel craze included a survey indicating that 69 percent of Americans claimed to believe in angels, while nearly half believed they were attended by a personal guardian angel. *Newsweek,* which ran its own angel-themed cover story the very same week the *Time* issue appeared, reported that the angel craze appeared to be rooted in a very real spiritual craving: "It may be kitsch, but there's more to the current angel obsession than the Hallmarking of America. Like the search for extraterrestrials, the belief in angels implies that we are not alone in the universe—that someone up there likes me" (quoted in Nickell, 152-3).

Not incidentally, this sentiment closely echoed Blatty's expressed motivation for writing *The Exorcist*. As he has explained in numerous interviews and also in his 2001 memoir *If There Were Demons, Then Perhaps There Were Angels: William Peter Blatty's Story of the Exorcist*, when he was a junior at the Jesuitical Georgetown University in 1949 he encountered a *Washington Post* story about a fourteen-year-old boy in Mount Rainier, Maryland who had undergone an exorcism under the official sanction of the church. Blatty had long been concerned about the spiritual direction of modern Western society—*The Exorcist*, let it be noted, was published in the immediate wake of the 1960s' "death of God" movement—and in the account of this boy and his apparent demonic affliction, Blatty thought he could discern "tangible evidence of transcendence." Two decades later he fictionalized the story in his famous novel. But it was a fiction with a serious existential purpose; as he later explained, in his view the reality of demons serves as a kind of apologetic proof for the existence of God: "If there were demons, there were angels and probably a God and a life everlasting" (quoted in Whitehead). In 1999, at a time when movies such as *The Sixth Sense*, *Stir of Echoes*, *The Blair Witch Project*, and *Stigmata* were flooding movie theatres and video rental stores, he invoked a version of the same idea to account for the resurgent popularity of supernatural thrillers: "One of the prime allures of the supernatural thriller is that there is a world of spirit and that death doesn't mean our final destiny is oblivion" (Bonin). In this he echoed twentieth century theologian Paul Tillich, as quoted by Victoria Nelson in her exploration of the psychological and spiritual "underside" of modern popular entertainment, *The Secret Life of Puppets*:

> Lacking an allowable connection with the transcendent [in our Western intellectual culture where the religious impulse is deemed unacceptable], we have substituted an obsessive, unconscious focus on the negative dimensions of the denied experience. In popular Western entertainments through the end of the twentieth century, the supernatural translated mostly as terror and monsters

> enjoyably consumed. But as Paul Tillich profoundly remarked, "Wherever the demonic appears, there the question of its correlate, the divine, will also be raised" (Nelson 19).

In the early 1970s it seemed the Roman Catholic Church, or at least the Pope, agreed with at least the first half of Blatty's demon-angel apologetic. In November of 1972, Pope Paul VI delivered an address to a General Audience in which he expressed his concern over what he viewed as demonic influences at work in the world: "Evil is not merely an absence of something but an active force, a living, spiritual being that is perverted and that perverts others. It is a terrible reality, mysterious and frightening . . . Many passages in the Gospel show us that we are dealing not just with one Devil, but with many" (Pope Paul VI). These statements ignited a debate both inside and outside the church and embarrassed many priests whose outlook was more in tune with the secularist, demythologized tenor of the time than with what they viewed as the mythological belief system of pre-Enlightenment Christianity. But the international phenomenon that was *The Exorcist* demonstrated that the Roman pontiff obviously spoke not only for himself but also for an enormous public that either believed as he did or, at the very least, suspected or wanted to believe in the literal existence of a transcendent spiritual reality. The fact that the pope's remarks were bookended, temporally speaking, by the 1971 publication of Blatty's novel and the 1973 release of the movie makes it difficult to avoid speculating that all three statements—the novel, the movie, and Paul VI's speech—were expressions of a common, burgeoning cultural phenomenon that also encompassed the aforementioned angel craze. It was and is a phenomenon whose central, guiding obsession is invoked by the character of the psychiatrist in *The Exorcist* when he asks a hypnotized girl the most psychologically and spiritually potent question of all: "Is there someone inside you?"

All of which brings the argument back to the matter at hand. It will be the task of this essay to explore the ancient origins of the iconic Angel and Demon (henceforth referred to as proper nouns) in folklore, history, religion, literature, philosophy, psychology, and art. The overall purpose will be to demonstrate how and why a knowledge of the deep history of these ubiquitous horror icons dramatically illuminates their frequent appearances in works of supernatural horror. As indicated by the foregoing discussion, such an investigation will inevitably illuminate widespread popular religious conceptions as well, which are often not very well demarcated from the images presented in popular entertainment.

To preview what will be explained in detail, supernatural horror as it has developed in the West has generally employed the concepts and iconography of Christian theology in dealing with demons and angels. The stereotypical images of the iconic Angel and Demon have their roots in old Christian, pre-Christian, and extra-Christian ideas, and result from a synthesis of concepts that occurred throughout Europe and the Middle East during the Hellenistic and Roman periods. This synthesis arose out of the rich cross-fertilization of various ancient currents of thought extending back into history and prehistory, and was finalized and codified for the modern West by a few significant literary works during the Middle Ages and Renaissance. The overall picture is rich and complex, but the rewards of grasping it—the benefits of seeing, knowing, understanding, and appreciating more as one observes the Angel and Demon striding through the outpourings of the supernatural horror genre—are significant.

II.
THE PREHISTORY OF THE DEMON

Introduction: What's in a name?

A fruitful place to start is with an unpacking of the word "demon" itself, since this will preview the broad outlines of the story as a whole.

The figure of the Demon derived from the minor evil spirits common to all religions and mythologies of the Middle East, as processed through Jewish theologizing and the Greek belief in spirits called *daimones* (pronounced "di-mone-es"). The name "demon" itself indicates the use of the old Greek idea by the Hellenistic and later writers and religious thinkers who were most responsible for helping to codify this category during the first few centuries before and after the beginning of the Common Era. The English word "demon" comes from the Latin *daemon*, which itself came from the Greek *daimon*. "Demon" is technically a neutral word that refers to any spirit, whether good or evil, that is neither divine nor mortal but inhabits the intermediate realm between gods and humans. Thus, even angels belong to the general class of beings known as demons. But in common usage, owing to habits established between roughly 200 B.C.E. and 200 C.E, "demon" has come to refer solely to the evil members of the category.

Demons of the ancient Middle East

As described by E. V. Walter in his essay "Demons and Disenchantment," the Greek word *deisidaimonia* refers to "a certain dimension of sacromagical, numinous experience" that formed an authentic religious tradition in the ancient world. In addition to playing an important part in ancient Greece, this sacred experience of demon dread "constituted the central element of the religious experience of the most ancient civilization we know from historical records: the Sumerian-Babylonian-Assyrian people. It also appeared in ancient Egypt, which was cheerful, optimistic, and much less demon-ridden than the Mesopotamian civilization" (Walter 19, 20). This assertion is entirely in keeping with the known historical fact that by the dawn of recorded history, circa 4000 B.C.E., the two great centers of early civilization, Mesopotamia and Egypt, both possessed well-developed demonologies. It is here that the oldest ancestors of the Demon can be observed in nascent form.

The early inhabitants of Mesopotamia believed their daily lives were saturated with evil spirits. If one had a headache, it was because of a demon. If one broke a pot or got into a quarrel with a neighbor, it was likewise because of a demon. Even such an intimate experience as dreaming was under the control of these beings, with nightmares and night terrors being caused by such beings as *rabisu* and *lilitu*, both of whom later appeared in Hebrew mythology and folklore (the latter as the "night-hag" *lilith*).

Owing to its later appearance in Blatty's *The Exorcist*, the ancient Mesopotamian demon *Pazuzu* is of special interest to followers of supernatural horror. Often pictured as a vaguely man-shaped figure with a monstrous head, the wings of an eagle, the tail of a scorpion, and the talons or claws of an eagle or lion, Pazuzu was believed to bring famine and plague, and was famously associated with the southwest wind. It was this demon that Blatty referenced when he set out to build a suitably horrifying and awe-inspiring back-story to explain the origin of the demon that possessed young Regan in his novel.

In addition to this rather loose body of folkloric belief, the Mesopotamians also possessed a larger body of systematic "official" theology which featured its own demonic beings. Most famously, the Babylonian state religion centered around the creation epic known as *Enuma Elish* featured a horde of monstrous demons that had been birthed by Tiamat, the primeval chaos dragon, in an effort to eradicate her own children. These included such figures as the dragon, the sphinx, the scorpion-man, and monstrous serpents whose bodies were filled with venom instead of blood. After the war was over and Tiamat had been defeated by her children, humankind was created from the blood of Tiamat's consort, the serpentine Kingu. So in Babylonian belief there was something of the primally demonic in the most basic substance of human life—"a recognition perhaps of the daemonic, rebellious element in human nature" (Gray 35).

To the west in Egypt, the overall situation was very similar, with many demons both mundane and exalted playing a significant part in the lives of everyone from the Pharaoh on down to the lowest peasant. As in Mesopotamia, most of these beings were associated with the everyday phenomena of childbirth, illness, weather, and so on. Also as in Mesopotamia, they were often depicted as animal-human hybrids when they were depicted at all. In the more codified realm of "official" Egyptian theology, the god Set displayed a few typically demonic elements in his evil nature.

The most colorful and systematic arm of Egyptian demonology was set in the afterlife. In Egyptian belief, each person was composed of a physical body plus three distinct spirit selves known as the *ba*, the *ka*, and the *akh*. As described in the famed *Book of the Dead*, after a person's physical death it was his or her *ba*, roughly analogous to the modern idea of the individual personality, that was required to pass through multiple gates guarded by various beings on the way to judgment by the supreme god Osiris. Many of the beings that the *ba* encountered during its afterlife journey were demonic in the generalized sense of being monstrous supernatural entities.

Among the ancient Arab and Semitic peoples in general, the spirits known as *djinn* were widely known and feared. Before they were somewhat tamed and softened by being adopted into Islamic folklore, where some of them were transformed into beautiful and benevolent spirits, djinn were known among the Arabs for being purely malicious. It was this fearsome background that would be exploited thousands of years later, in the late twentieth and early twenty-first centuries, by the makers of the low-budget *Wishmaster* series of horror films. In their original folkloric form, djinn were born of fire and able to metamorphosize into any shape they wished, and they lived and roamed in wild and desert places. Much later they became widely known in the West due to the appearance of a djinnee (the singular of djinn) in the story of Aladdin and his lamp in the *Arabian Nights*. It was this story that created the image of the djinn as wish-granting spirits who reside in oil lamps. Not incidentally, the term "djinnee" displays an obvious phonetic relationship to the English word "genie," which is the more commonly known term for these spirits among English-speaking peoples. "Genie" itself derives from the Latin word "genius," which in Hellenistic Rome referred to spirits in general, and which became the direct inheritor of the meanings associated with the Greek *daimon*. The etymological relationships among all of these words and their referent spirits are tangled and uncertain, but in the end this only makes them all the more fascinating and potent.

The greatest spur toward the incorporation of the Middle Eastern demons into later Christian and Christianized beliefs was the rise of new religious movements that reframed the old beliefs and subjected the various indigenous spirits to new interpretations, thus laying the groundwork for the later Judeo-Christian demonologies and angelologies. In Mesopotamia this occurred most famously during the sixth century B.C.E., under the influence of Zoroastrianism in Persia. When Zoroaster introduced the famous dualism of Ahura Mazda as the one true god who was opposed by the evil god Angra Mainyu or Ahriman, the stage was set for all the native deities and demons to be demoted and divided according to their allegiances. Zoroaster "found it impossible to throw overboard all the deities his people had been honoring for generations, so he declared that some of them were good spirits, or 'bounteous immortals,' while the rest were condemned as demons. None disappeared" (Hahn 14-16). The Zoroastrian hierarchy of spirits was thus quite extensive when all was said and done, with multiple levels of beings lined up in descending orders of power and influence. Ahriman boasted an impressive army of demons, known as devas, to serve him and work his will, including such powerful beings as Aeshma, the demon of wrath and fury, and Azhi Dahaka, the demon of lies and deceit, whose body was so full of lizards, scorpions, and other vile creature that if he were cut open they would overrun the earth. A horde of lesser demons were associated with such common negative attitudes and emotions as jealousy, arrogance, and sloth.

Jewish demons

Of all the ancient Middle Eastern peoples, the Jews were of course the most directly important to the formation of Christianity. Naturally, this importance extended to their ideas about demons and angels as well. The Jewish contribution was much more important to the formation of the latter than the former, but this does not mean they contributed nothing at all to the Demon.

Unlike its later and, to modern peoples, more familiar forms, Judaism up until the two or three centuries preceding the Common Era lacked the idea of "fallen angels" who waged war against the one God. Instead, Jewish beliefs about evil spirits remained more on a folkloric level and took two general forms. For the first, evil spirits were conceived as coming directly from Yahweh and remaining totally under his control. This can be seen in 1 Samuel 16, which tells how King Saul was plagued by a spirit sent from Yahweh: "Now the Spirit of the LORD departed from Saul, and an evil spirit from the LORD tormented him. And Saul's servants said to him, 'Behold now, an evil spirit from God is tormenting you'" (vv. 14-15). The servants looked for someone to play music in order to soothe Saul, and eventually alighted upon David, who successfully drove the spirit away: "And whenever the evil spirit from God was upon Saul, David took the lyre and played it with his hand; so Saul was refreshed, and was well, and the evil spirit departed from him" (v. 23). So this type of evil spirit was related in a way to the Jewish idea of angels, since it came as a kind of messenger from Yahweh. This was entirely in keeping with the ancient Jewish idea that Yahweh's omnipotence meant he was the ultimate source of all things, both good and bad.

The other view arose from beliefs about evil spirits that were incorporated into Judaism from the Jews' Mesopotamian neighbors. It was here, more than in the previous view, that Jewish beliefs about evil spirits proper truly came into their own. According to the *Jewish Encyclopedia*, "Jewish demonology can at no time be viewed as the outcome of an antecedent Hebrew belief" (Hirsch). Rabbi and scholar Ronald H. Isaacs says, "Surrounded by animistic notions of primitive people, the Jews absorbed some of these and developed a variety of legends of their own concerning evil spirits that wield destructive powers over human beings" (Isaacs 91). In such cases, the Jews always reinterpreted the nature and status of these foreign spirits according to their own strict Yahwistic monotheism. Sometimes this meant foreign spirits were scorned as being illusory, as in Deuteronomy 32:17, which contains a chastisement for people who "sacrificed to demons [*shedim*, from the Babylonian spirit *shedu*], which were no gods, to gods they had never known, to new gods that had come in of late, whom your fathers had never dreaded." The quote makes it clear that the author believed the worshippers of the *shedim* were worshipping mere figments of their imagination.

At other times, in other contexts, the Jews thought of evil spirits as real but inferior powers. This became the norm after the sixth century influx of the Chaldean religious influence, and it is crucial to note that this Zoroastrian influence not only gave the Jews many of their evil spirits but also many of their good ones, eventually resulting in their famous division between the kingdom of God and that of the Devil. "It was," says the *Jewish Encyclopedia*, "the primitive demonology of Babylonia which peopled the world of the Jews with beings of a semi-celestial and semi-infernal nature. Only afterward did the division of the world between Ahriman and Ormuzd [a.k.a. Ahura Mazda] in the Mazdean system give rise to the Jewish division of life between the kingdom of heaven and the kingdom of evil" (Hirsch).

In a distinct but related vein, a significant factor in the rise of Jewish beliefs about demons was the First Book of Enoch. This text, which is usually dated to the second or third century B.C.E., was foundational to the formation of both Christian and Jewish beliefs about "fallen angels." It was rejected for inclusion within the official Jewish and Christian canons, and even from inclusion in the Christian apocrypha, thus relegating it to the realm of the pseudepigrapha or "doubtful writings" whose authenticity is severely questioned or rejected. But its influence was widespread; nearly all of the early church fathers quoted from it, and it even ended up making an appearance in the New Testament itself (see the quotation from it in Jude 14-15). Since the main focus of First Enoch is angels, including those who rebelled against God, more will be said about it in the section on the Angel below.

The upshot is that the ancient Jewish, Egyptian, and Mesopotamian (primarily Chaldean) beliefs about demons provided a basic content and structure for the formation of the Demon. It remained for the Greek notion of the *daimon* to provide the overarching concept that would synthesize these various elements into a coherent, unified portrait.

The Greek daimones

Although most reasonably educated moderns are familiar with the Olympian gods and goddesses of classical Greek mythology, decidedly fewer are aware that long before the Greeks developed their beliefs about the humanlike gods of Olympus, they believed in vague and mysterious spirits called *daimones* that exerted a ubiquitous influence over people and events. Using the alternative form "daemon" to refer to these spirits, E. R. Dodds writes in his classic *The Greeks and the Irrational* that the "daemonic, as distinct from the divine, has at all periods played a large part in Greek popular belief (and still does)" (40). Indeed, as psychologist Stephen A. Diamond points out, while some classical scholars maintain that Greek writers such as Homer, Hesiod, and Plato did use *daimon* as a synonym for *theos* (god), others "point to a definite distinction between these terms. The term 'daimon' referred to something indeterminate, invisible, incorporeal, amorphous, and unknown, whereas 'theos' was the *personification* of a god, such as Zeus or Apollo" (Diamond 66).

If we are to believe classical scholar Reginald Barrow, modern ignorance of the daimons must be counted among the many ironies of history; Barrow argues provocatively that belief in them was so powerful, important, and prevalent that it actually formed a kind of underground mainstream in ancient Greek religion:

> Because the daemons have left few memorials of themselves in architecture and literature, their importance tends to be overlooked. . . . They are omnipresent and all-powerful, they are embedded deep in the religious memories of the peoples, for they go back to days long before the days of Greek philosophy and religion. The cults of the Greek states, recognized and officially sanctioned, were only one-tenth of the iceberg; the rest, the submerged nine-tenths, were the daemons (quoted in Diamond, 67).

Like so many religious beliefs throughout history, the idea of the *daimones* took many different and sometimes contradictory forms. In the beginning they were conceived as abstract forces in the neuter gender. Hesiod and others described them as "invisible and wrapped in mist" (Diamond 65). Much farther back, Mycenaean and Minoan daimons, in a period ranging from 1100 to 3000 B.C.E., were regarded as servants or attendants to deities and were pictured in the form of animal-human hybrids, much like their Egyptian and Mesopotamian analogs. Barrow offers a concise summary of the evolution of beliefs about these daimons over half a millennium, and also, again, of their vaguely shadowy and underground nature as they lurked perpetually in the background of orthodox Greek religious thought:

> [T]he histories of Greek religion or philosophy do not

> usually say much, if anything, about daemons. Though the idea occurs as early as Homer, it plays little or no part in recognized cults; for it had no mythology of its own; rather it attached itself to existing beliefs. In philosophy it lurks in the background from Thales, to whom "the universe is alive and full of daemons," through Heraclitus and Xenophanes, to Plato and his pupil Xenocrates, who elaborated it in detail . . . In Hesiod the daemons are the souls of heroes or past ages now kindly to men; in Aeschylus the dead become daemons; in Theognis and Menander the daemon is the guardian angel of the individual man and sometimes a family (Diamond 66).

In their most ancient forms, the daimons were neither good nor evil, or rather were potentially both. In Homer's time (around the eighth century B.C.E.) people commonly believed that daimons caused all human ailments but at the same time also believed they could cure disease and give blessings such as health and happiness. Several centuries later the Hellenistic Greeks developed the more concrete categories of *eudaimones* (good daimons) and *kakodaimones* (evil daimons).

Arguably the most famous description or definition of daimons and the daimonic comes from a "canonical" source: Plato's *Symposium,* wherein Plato has the old wise woman Diotima describe the daimonic realm as a kind of bridge or intermediary between the human and divine worlds:

> All that is daemonic lies between the mortal and the immortal. Its functions are to interpret to men communications from the gods—commandments and favours from the gods in return for men's attentions—and to convey prayers and offerings from men to the gods. Being thus between men and gods the daemon fills up the gap and so acts as a link joining up the whole. Through it as intermediary pass all forms of divination and sorcery. God does not mix with man; the daemonic is the agency through which intercourse and converse take place between men and gods, whether in waking visions

or in dreams (quoted in Dodds, *Pagan and* Christian 86-7).

It is also Plato who provides probably the most familiar example of specific daimonic influence when he writes of Socrates' famous *daimonion* (the gender-neutral form of *daimon,* which is either male or female). This has often been translated into English as the "sign" that Socrates claimed had visited him frequently since childhood in the form of an audible voice that warned him when he was about to commit an error.

Socrates' experience of daimonic communication highlights what is, in fact, the most significant aspect of the matter: The Greeks understood their daimons to have not only objective but also subjective existence. That is, they believed the daimons were objectively real presences that made themselves known through their influence upon and within the human psyche. This tension between the objective and subjective seems to have existed on a kind of continuum. On the one hand were the more typically animistic conceptions of daimons, which associated them with particular places, natural occurrences, circumstances, or souls of the dead. On the other hand were the more subtle, psychologically oriented conceptions that gained preeminence over time and that regarded the daimons as inner influences upon human thoughts and emotions, and even as arbitrators, keepers, conductors, and emblems of individual character and destiny. This second type of understanding can be seen in the fact that the characters in Homer's *Iliad* and *Odyssey,* which were probably composed around the eighth century B.C.E. and represented an inherited oral tradition extending several centuries earlier, attributed many of the events of their lives—not only outer, physical events but also, and especially, inner psychological ones such as moods, emotions, sudden insights, bursts of motivation to say or do something or to refrain from speaking or acting —to the influence of daimons. Although Homer's characters seemed to take this idea relatively lightly—"[W]e get the impression," writes Dodds, "that they do not always mean it very seriously"—in the three centuries between Homer's epics and Aeschylus' *Oresteia* "the daemons seem to draw closer: they grow more persistent, more insidious, more sinister" (*The Greeks and the Irrational*, 41).

By "sinister" Dodds may have meant not that the daimons came to be regarded as predominantly evil but that they became progressively more entangled with human interiority and also progressively more mysterious and autonomous. He calls attention to the fact that many Greek writers after Homer drew a connection between the daimons and "those irrational impulses which arise in a man against his will to tempt him," and says that "behind [this] lies the old Homeric feeling that these things are not truly part of the self; since they are endowed with a life and energy of their own, and so can force a man, as it were from the outside, into conduct foreign to him" (41).

The twentieth century existential psychologist Rollo May, who resurrected the concept of the daimon and the daimonic for use in modern depth psychotherapy, gave definitive statement to this idea of strange internal influence in *Love and Will*: "The daimonic is any natural function which has the power to take over the whole person. Sex and eros, anger and rage, and the craving for power are examples. The daimonic can be either creative or destructive and is normally both" (123). Although May wrote about the daimonic in metaphorical terms, his description is still effective for giving an impression of what it must have felt like to the ancients when they found themselves thinking, feeling, saying, and doing things that were outside of their voluntary control. Modern peoples are of course still quite familiar with this experience. We can thus reasonably imagine that ancient peoples must have been all the more awed and disturbed when popular belief attributed these involuntary behaviors to the influence of the mysterious mediators of divine reality. In more dramatic cases of daimonic influence, the internal power might take control completely. "When this power goes awry," May wrote, "and one element usurps control over the total personality, we have 'daimon possession,' the traditional name through history for psychosis" (123).

It was Plato (again) who gave definitive voice to this newly developing view of the daimonic as primarily an inner force. He closed his most famous work, the *Republic*, with the "myth of Er," which teaches that prior to being born, each human being voluntarily chooses his or her own daimon, understood in this case to be a combination of guardian angel, spiritual double, and life pattern. The daimon accompanies a person throughout life and constantly recalls him or her to the pre-chosen plan. It guides a person inevitably to evince a certain character, make certain choices, feel certain predilections, and encounter certain experiences, all in the service of fulfilling the fate chosen beforehand. Thus it is that the Greek word *eudaimonia*, which in later times came to mean "happiness" or "well being," in its earliest sense literally meant "having a good daimon." A person with a good daimon was happy and blessed, while a person with a bad daimon was inevitably miserable. The pre-Socratic philosopher Heraclitus encapsulated this idea in a cryptic statement that has puzzled and fascinated scholars for the past twenty-five hundred years: *Ethos anthropoi daimon*. The statement translates literally as "A man's character is his daimon," but nobody knows for certain what Heraclitus really meant to convey, although various translations and glosses have been offered, as listed by James Hillman in his modern book of daimonic psychology, *The Soul's Code*: "Man's character is his Genius. A man's character is his guardian divinity. A man's character is his fate. Character is fate. A man's character is the immortal and potentially divine portion of him, Character for man is destiny" (256-7).

The bottom line is that it is impossible to overstress the prevalence and significance of beliefs about daimons to the ancient world, and especially to ancient popular understandings of human selfhood and its relation to the divine. For Greek culture, including its underground tradition of daimonism, was destined to become the common coinage, as it were, of the entire ancient world. When first Alexander and then the Romans succeeded in exporting all things Greek to the farthest corners of their respective empires, the resulting cultural matrix was rife with daimons in the Greek mold. According to Dodds, although the *Symposium*'s "precise definition of the vague terms 'daemon' and 'daemonios' was something of a novelty in Plato's day," by "the second century after Christ it was the expression of a truism. Virtually everyone, pagan, Jewish, Christian or Gnostic, believed in the existence of these beings and in their function as mediators, whether he called them daemons or angels or aions or simply 'spirits'" (*Pagan and Christian* 37-8).

As indicated by this quote and much of the foregoing information, the idea of daimons contained elements of both the Demon and the Angel of the later supernatural horror genre. Thus, before moving on to trace the formation of the Demon itself from all of these currents, it is necessary to fill in the back-story of the Angel.

III.
THE PREHISTORY OF THE ANGEL

Introduction: What's in a name?

The word "angel" derives from the Latin *angelus,* which derives from the Greek *angelos.* In the Septuagint (the ancient Greek translation of the Jewish scriptures from the third century B.C.E.), *angelos* is used to translate the Hebrew *mal'ak.* Both *angelos* and *mal'ak* mean "messenger" and can refer either to a supernatural spirit or to a human being who delivers divine communication to other humans. An example of a person being referred to as an angel in this sense can be found in the New Testament in Galatians 4:14 when Paul reminds the Christians at Galatia that when he first brought the gospel to them, they received and treated him "as an angel [*angelos,* messenger] of God." Obviously, in later history the word came to refer exclusively to the supernatural type of messenger.

Dreadful and awesome: biblical angels

The first mention in the Bible of the supernatural type of angel is found in the Old Testament, in Genesis, when God stations angels called *cherubim* at the entrance to the Garden of Eden to keep Adam and Eve from returning after they have been expelled. After that, these supernatural beings appear frequently throughout the Hebrew scriptures to announce God's will, save and direct God's people, and often mete out God's wrath.

Significantly, biblical angels were conceived as awesome and even terrifying beings who directly represented and, in some manner that is never precisely explained, *embodied* the awesome, terrifying God they served. Thus, in the Book of Judges when an angel of Yahweh appears to Manoah's wife to tell her that she will have a son, she describes it to her husband by saying, "A man of God came to me, and his countenance was like the countenance of the angel of God, very terrible" (Judges 13:6), with "terrible" meaning something akin to "dreadfully awesome." Later when the same angel appears again to both of them, its true nature becomes clear when they burn a sacrificial animal and "the angel of the LORD ascended in the flame of the altar while Manoah and his wife looked on" (13:20). In a response typical of such scenes, both husband and wife fall on their faces to the ground, and Manoah says to his wife, "We shall surely die, for we have seen God" (13:22). To see an angel of God was in some sense to see God himself, and as everybody knew (since it had been stated to Moses on Mount Sinai and reiterated many times elsewhere), no man could see God and live.

This "terrible" aspect of angels is also visible in their many destructive actions. A famous example is found in the story of the destruction of Sodom and Gomorrah. Three angels, looking like men, appeared to Abraham to announce the imminent destruction of these cities because of their famed wickedness. Then the angels departed to escort Abraham's son Lot and his family out of Sodom to safety, after which "the LORD rained on Sodom and Gomor'rah brimstone and fire from the LORD out of heaven" (Genesis 19:24). Equally famous, and an example in which an angel took a direct part in administering a terrible punishment, is the story of the final plague brought against Egypt, when Yahweh sent his Angel of Death to kill all the firstborn males of the Egyptians (cf. Exodus 11-12). Likewise in Isaiah 37:36, Yahweh intervenes with his death angel in order to help Jerusalem when it is besieged by the Assyrians: "And the angel of the LORD went forth, and slew a hundred and eighty-five thousand in the camp of the Assyrians; and when men arose early in the morning, behold, these were all dead bodies."

Other angelic influences: extra-biblical, Zoroastrian, Egyptian, Greek

The idea not only of angels that were fearsome, but of angels that were positively monstrous, was advanced by the First Book of Enoch mentioned earlier. First Enoch tells of a band of two hundred angels, called "the Watchers" in the earliest English translation of the text (from 1912), who, led by powerful beings named Semjaza and Azazel, rebelled against God by marrying human women and teaching them various secrets of herb lore, metallurgy, magical enchantments, astronomy, meteorology, and other subjects that were forbidden for humans to know. The children born of these forbidden unions turned out to be giants who had such ravenous appetites that they devoured everything on earth, including humans, and finally turned to eating each other. As a punishment, God chained the angels in dark places of the earth and left them to await the Final Judgment, at which point they would be cast into fire. But the giants lived on and eventually produced evil spirits. On the other end of matters, among the angels who remained faithful to God were Michael, Uriel, Raphael, and Gabriel, who heard mankind crying out in anguish and ended up helping them.

As the title implies, First Enoch purports to have been written by Enoch, the grandfather of Noah, who learned of all these matters in a series of visions. Even though First Enoch was probably written in the second or third century B.C.E., the story itself along with its antecedent influences obviously extends much further back into history. In the Old Testament the basic idea of humans intermarrying with angels goes all the way back to Genesis chapter six with its bizarre story of the Nephilim, which were born when "the sons of God saw that the daughters of men were fair; and they took to wife such of them as they chose. . . . The Nephilim were on the earth in those days, and also afterward, when the sons of God came in to the daughters of men, and they bore children to them. These were the mighty men that were of old, the men of renown" (vv. 2, 4). Immediately after this, the chapter moves to describing God's disgust with humankind's wickedness and his plan to wipe everything out with water while saving a remnant through Noah and his family, so this indicates an obvious connection to First Enoch since the story of Noah and the flood appears there as well, and as in the Genesis version, the flood is sent by God to wipe the earth clean of wickedness. The ubiquitous Persian influence is also quite evident in First Enoch: a pre-Zoroastrian Persian myth tells of demons that corrupted the earth and married mortal women.

As mentioned earlier, the practice of ranking angels into types and hierarchies was absorbed into Judaism from Zoroastrianism. Many of the Jews lived in close contact with the Persian religion in the sixth century B.C.E. during the period of the Babylonian captivity. The cultural cross-fertilization that naturally occurred had the dual effect of, on the one hand, cementing the Israelite religion of the post-exilic period into the first true Judaism, and on the other, giving the Jews various new theological ideas to incorporate into their religion. The elaborate angelologies of later Judaism and Christianity were the result.

In Zoroastrian theology, the Wise Lord Ahura Mazda was served by his immortal sons and daughters, the Amesha Spentas or "bounteous immortals," each of which represented a facet of the divine nature or an aspect of that nature in which humans could share (e.g., truth, devotion, wholeness, etc.). He also had in his employ lesser beings called Yazatas or "worshipful ones," who were mortal and who engaged with humans in a more personal, protective fashion than was possible for the exalted Wise Lord himself. The Amesha Spentas thus corresponded in very important ways to the archangels, and the Yazatas to the guardian angels, that later populated the Christian cosmos.

In Egypt a similar influence was set in motion by Pharaoh Amenhotep IV, more widely known today as Akhenaten or Akhenaton, who radically reformed Egyptian religion in the 14th century B.C.E. by instating a monotheistic form of sun worship. Under the new solar monotheism, the gods of traditional belief were not eradicated, which would have been culturally impossible, but were instead demoted, as it were, to the status of lesser spirits, thus rendering them "angels in the making" (Hahn 14). Even after Akhenaton's death, when his reforms failed and subsequent Pharaohs returned Egypt to more traditional forms of religion, the changed status of many gods persisted.

Additionally, the Egyptian belief in multiple souls that compose the human self may have contributed to the development of the guardian angel. Although the precise meaning of the soul called the *ka* is impossible to determine, it may have functioned as a kind of spiritual "double" that accompanied a person through life. This is hinted at by the fact that Egyptian art sometimes represents the *ka* as a duplicate of the individual. While some scholars believe this indicates the ancient Egyptians thought of the *ka* in much the same way that moderns sometimes speak of a person's "life force," the idea and imagery also resonate with later beliefs about a guardian angel that accompanies each person from birth to death. Clearly, this also corresponds significantly to the Greek idea of the daimon.

From monstrous to beautiful: the Angel's visual appearance

Greece and Egypt also shared another correspondence that proved significant, and in fact decisive, for the development of the Angel by providing the pattern for its visual appearance. Although Jewish angels were sometimes conceived as having or at least appearing in human form, just as often they took on a monstrous appearance that was drawn directly from Sumerian or Babylonian mythology. Cherubim, for instance, were thought of as hybrids of human and animal characteristics, sometimes with multiple faces and eyes, always with multiple feathered wings. Another type of Jewish heavenly being, the seraphim, may have been conceived as winged, fiery serpents (the Hebrew word *seraph* can mean both "burning ones" and "serpents"). Obviously, these images were not the ones adopted for portraying the Angel of supernatural horror. Instead, the Angel received its look from ancient Egypt by way of Greece.

Isis, the Egyptian queen of the gods, was the object of a major cult that worshipped her as goddess of magic. Both she and her sister Nephthys were depicted in the form of human women with feathery wings sprouting from their sides or backs. Via the deep logic of cultural inheritance, the Greeks later imported this same imagery and attached it to Nike and Eros, the winged daimons of victory and love, whose attractive human bodies with feathery white wings sprouting from their shoulders—or perhaps replacing their arms, as in the famous Hellenistic statue of Nike known as The Winged Victory of Samothrace—are well known. It was these figures, and not the monstrous Jewish angels, that served as the specific template for the iconic Angel's appearance, which coalesced circa the first century C.E.

The fact that the Angel in a Judeo-Christian context would have its visual appearance drawn from a Hellenic source may be attributable to the old tradition of Jewish iconoclasm, which originated in the Decalogue with the second commandment's injunction against making idols or images of the divine. Due to this commandment with its theological centrality, the Jewish visual tradition simply was not as developed as that of Greece, whose stronger tradition therefore won out. The effect of the winged Jewish cherubim and seraphim on the appearance of the Angel was thus felt only at a remove, and arrived in Christian angelic iconography only by being processed through the intermediaries of Nike and Eros in the same way that the more influential Isis had been.

IV.
THE DEMON FROM THE FIRST CENTURY TO MODERN TIMES

Recalling Dodds' assertion that by the end of the second century C.E. almost everybody in the ancient world believed in daimons in some form, and putting this together with the rest of the preceding information, the rise of the Demon as understood by Christianity and the later Western supernatural horror genre is an easy phenomenon to grasp. The Septuagint, as already noted, had used the Greek word *angelos* to translate the Hebrew *mal'ak*, both referring to supernatural (or sometimes human) messengers from God. Equally significant was the fact that the Septuagint used the Greek *daimon* or *daimonion* to translate the various Hebrew words for idols, alien gods, and the like, while *theos* was reserved for referring to the one God. Thus the "bible" used by many first century Jews, including Jesus and his disciples, had already made these terminological distinctions. The New Testament documents were likewise written in the same Greek as the Septuagint, Koine Greek, which had become the common language of Israel by the first century, and they retained the same terminological conventions.

This meant the rich trove of concepts and connotations

associated with the Greek daimons were now attached to the Jewish understanding of the spiritual world, which, as evidenced by First Enoch and other Jewish apocalyptic and apocryphal works, was already heavily influenced by ancient Middle Eastern beliefs with their cosmic dualism. Thus the moral ambivalence and the dual sense of demonic dread and spiritual inspiration or exaltation that were inherent in the concept of the daimon became divided, with half the associations attaching themselves to the idea of the Angel and half to the Demon. The fact that the word itself, *daimon,* was retained to refer only to the evil or negative half of the cosmic dualism entailed the demise and, in the eyes of some observers both modern and ancient, the degradation of the word's original meaning. "Around the rise of Christianity," writes Diamond, "the old daimons started to disappear, their Janus-like nature torn asunder. 'Evil' and 'good' were neatly divided, and the daimons, now isolated from their positive pole, eventually took on the negative meaning and identity of what we today term demons" (71).

Thus arose the demons and "unclean spirits" of the New Testament period, who with their usurpation of people's personalities and their desire to inflict moral and physical harm embodied the most violently negative aspect of the old daimonic understanding, the "daimon possession" that Rollo May equated with psychosis. In the gospels Jesus is frequently shown casting out demons who rage and writhe and foam at the mouth, with the most famous story being the encounter with the Gerasene demoniac. Matthew, Mark, and Luke all contain the story, although Matthew's version differs from the other two in that it says the incident occurred in the land of the Gadarenes (instead of Gerasenes) and that there were two possessed men instead of one. Mark's version is the most detailed:

> And when he had come out of the boat, there met him out of the tombs a man with an unclean spirit, who lived among the tombs; and no one could bind him any more, even with a chain; for he had often been bound with fetters and chains, but the chains he wrenched apart, and the fetters he broke in pieces; and no one had the strength

> to subdue him. Night and day among the tombs and on the mountains he was always crying out, and bruising himself with stones. And when he saw Jesus from afar, he ran and worshiped him; and crying out with a loud voice, he said, "What have you to do with me, Jesus, Son of the Most High God? I adjure you by God, do not torment me." For he had said to him, "Come out of the man, you unclean spirit!" And Jesus asked him, "What is your name?" He replied, "My name is Legion; for we are many" (5:2-9).

In his nearly identical version, Luke clarifies the meaning of "we are many" by changing it to a line of third-person narration: "for many demons had entered him" (8:30). In all three versions, as well as in the numerous other stories of possession and exorcism in the New Testament documents, the very nature of the accounts both revealed and helped to solidify the prevailing understanding of what a demon actually was. In all cases a possessing demon grievously hurt—psychologically, physically, or both—the possessed individuals and those around them, and in all cases they were subject to the authority of the one God as channeled through or incarnated in Jesus. Roughly two thousand years later, the same general understanding was still in place when Blatty quoted from Luke's version of the Gerasene demoniac story at the beginning of *The Exorcist* and from Mark's version at the start of the sequel novel, *Legion*.

The newly born Christian world was of course not the only place from whence the new ideas came together to form the Demon. Other writers in other traditions continued to turn the spiritual earth, with such writers as Philo of Alexandria, himself a Hellenized Jew, and Josephus, the famous first-century Jewish historian, and also the entire roster of early church fathers in the first few centuries after the birth of Christ, contributing to the developing Christian demonology. In all cases, demons were conceived in a manner influenced by a combination of Chaldean/Jewish apocalyptic beliefs and a now-mutated form of Greek daimonism. For the Chaldean/Jewish part, demons were conceived as angelic beings who had rebelled against the one God and were now devoted to making war against Him and his world. For the Greek part, this demonic war was seen as being conducted not solely, not even primarily, on an objective, external plane but on an internal one. The battle was conducted within and for the sake of people's souls. "The change," writes Wolfgang M. Zucker, "from a divine 'daimon' to a devilish demon made out of the 'daimon' a superstitious mythological concept. The predilection of Hellenistic writers for the mysterious and the supernatural made it possible that the inner voice of the rational sage of Athens became in the course of time something like a personal servant ghost, a *Spiritus familiaris*" (Zucker 39). In the hands of the influential men—Clement of Alexandria, Origen, Iranaeus, Justin Martyr, Augustine, and others—who created a comprehensive Christian theology in the first few centuries after Christ, this inner voice-cum-personal ghost was transformed into the voice of temptation, whispered directly into one's mind by demons who delighted in drawing people away from Christ and the Father.

As it had been for the ancient Mesopotamians, so for these post-Hellenistic peoples the world was positively crowded with demons. There was no shortage of these evil spirits because every spirit that was not aligned with the one God as part of his heavenly host was by definition a demon. In virtually all cases, this meant foreign gods were held to be demonic spirits who had deceived entire nations, and this inevitably led to an outburst of iconoclastic idol-smashing after Christianity became the official religion of the Roman Empire under Constantine in the fourth century. It was widely believed among Christians that all of the old idols, including those depicting the deities of traditional Greco-Roman paganism, were inhabited by demons, and so they took to destroying pagan temples and statues. According to many accounts, Constantine himself joined in the destruction by ordering and participating in the sacking of several temples and, as the story goes, torturing the resident priests to death. The Eastern Roman emperor Theodosius II added fuel to the fire in 423 by branding classical paganism *gentilicia superstitio*, or "superstions of the Gentiles," and declaring officially that non-Christian religion was definitively and exclusively nothing more than demon worship. The iconoclastic fury reached Athens shortly afterward, where according to some accounts the Parthenon itself, the ancient and widely venerated temple of Athena located on the Acropolis, was sacked and defaced. But although their images and residences in non-Christian temples could be attacked, the demons themselves persisted.

At this point it is possible to press the "fast forward" button, as it were, in the account of the iconic Demon's history, for once the concept of the Demon was firmly established in the Hellenistic and early Christian mind, it continued in much the same form with only a few substantial alterations and/or additions over the centuries.

Between the consolidation of Christian political power in the first few centuries C.E. and the turn of the first millennium, the belief about demons remained steady and largely unchanged. The basic idea that had arisen during the Hellenistic period proved to be amazingly resilient, so that any new developments, such as the rise of a popular lore about monks and saints who were tempted and tormented by demons (beginning with St. Anthony in the early second century), or the ongoing attempts of prominent figures such as Augustine to define, classify, and account for demons, did not so much alter or add to the concept as make use of it. It was not until the high Middle Ages, from approximately 1000-1300, that several events occurred to help finalize the Demon.

One of these was the adoption at the Fourth Lateran Council, convened by Pope Innocent III at Rome in 1215, of a resolution that firmly defined demons as fallen angels and definitively distinguished them as *daemones* as distinct from their leader, *diabolus*, the Devil himself. This resolution, adopted along with many others in response to the pressures surrounding the crusades and the need to confront heretical movements both inside and outside the church, established for the first time the familiar modern idea of "the devil and his angels" as official Catholic orthodoxy. It was an idea that creators of supernatural horror stories would use extensively in later centuries.

In an interesting bit of timing, one of the most famous cases of demonic possession in history occurred just two decades after the Church's publication of its exorcism ritual. Father Jean-Joseph

Surin, a Jesuit who served as an exorcist for the nuns at Loudun, France when they experienced an outbreak of possession, himself became possessed by a demon of lust (or so the story goes) that tormented him for many years. Three centuries later Aldous Huxley told the story in *The Devils of Loudun* (1952), which itself became the basis for director Ken Russell's 1971 film, *The Devils*.

It is probably no coincidence that the Italian poet Dante's famous *Inferno*, the first installment of his *Divine Comedy*, was published in 1314, almost exactly a century after the Fourth Lateran Council. Dante's depiction of a multi-layered hell populated by dreadful demons, many drawn from classical pagan mythology, who spent eternity tormenting a multitude of sinners via hideous and often ironically appropriate punishments, made direct use of the Church's official demonology. It was also Dante who in effect finalized the gothic visual imagery that has come to be associated with demons and hell ever since. His depiction of demons with leathery bat-like wings, long tails, claws, and monstrous faces, and his descriptions of what goes on in hell, such as the famous episode where demons use sharp hooks to keep sinners submerged in boiling tar in the same way a cook might keep chunks of meat submerged in boiling water, inspired countless visual artists first in Italy and then throughout Europe. He did not so much invent the Demon's appearance as make use of preexisting trends and materials; it is instructive to note that many of the features he chose had a history extending all the way back to the Middle Eastern demons of ancient history and prehistory (recall Pazuzu with his perverted man-shaped form adorned with claws, tail, and monstrously distorted visage). But he certainly assembled them into the definitive portrait, thus creating a literary and imaginative experience that was equivalent to taking a waking walk through a horrifying nightmare.

The period of the High Middle Ages was also important to the Demon because of the sometimes obsessive fear of witches that gripped many Christians. In the article on witchcraft in *The Dictionary of the History of Ideas*, Helen P. Trimpi writes that the

> history of the idea of witchcraft in the Christian period is mainly the history of the application by the Church of

> Judaic-Christian demonology to non-Christian—hence idolatrous—religious impulses among the baptized. Wherever a surviving or revived impulse came to the attention of Church writers they dealt with it in terms derived from biblical statements about witches, sorcerers, the Serpent, Satan, Leviathan, and evil spirits in the Old Testament and the Hebrew Apocrypha, and from references to Satan and evil demons in the New Testament.

The interaction between beliefs about demons and beliefs about witchcraft culminated in the so-called "witch craze" that engulfed Europe during the 13th through 17th centuries, and also in the infamous witch trials and executions at Salem Village, Massachusetts in 1692. Much of this mania was inspired by the ideas of the great scholastic theologian Thomas Aquinas, who wrote extensively about demons in his magnum opus, *Summa Theologica* (*Summary of Theology*, written from 1266-73). He argued, among other things, that demons can and do assault humans sexually. For example, the female demons known as *succubi* might assault human men and save their semen, which the male demons known as *incubi* might then use to impregnate women, thus begetting children in an unnatural way. This idea drew upon ancient stories from various cultures, including the ones already discussed in this essay, about sexual assaults upon humans by supernatural forces. During the Middle Ages and the following centuries, under the influence of scholastic theology and its further developments, this idea would become one of the centerpieces of the witch craze; it was extended and elaborated upon in the most famous of the witch-hunt manuals, *Malleus Maleficarum* or "The Hammer of the Witches" (1486).

The cataloguing and categorizing of demons continued apace as well, with Dr. Johann Weyer claiming in his *De Prestigiis Daemonum* (*The Illusions of the Demons*, 1568) that there presently existed no fewer than 2,665,866,746,664 demons of all ranks and types. Perhaps it was his attention to this subject, and the keen attention to demons and demonology paid by Sigismund Feyerabend (*Theatrum Diabolorum* or *Theatre of the Devils*, 1587) and other followers of the new Protestant reformation, that induced the Catholic church in 1614 to issue its famous instructions concerning the exorcism of demons in chapter XII of the *Rituale Romanum*. Forever afterward in the supernatural horror genre, the Catholic Church's guide to exorcism in the *Roman Ritual* would remain the gold standard for judging how such procedures should be depicted.

The 15th through the 17th centuries were also a golden age for Demon-inspired artwork, with such luminaries of Hieronyumus Bosch, Bruegel the Elder, Sandro Botticelli, Jean Duvet, and Albrecht Durer offering their visual interpretations of everything from the demonic temptations of famous saints to the demons tormenting the damned in Dante's underworld to the demonic hordes let loose to plague the world in the biblical Book of Revelation. Coming somewhat on the heels of this, and coming to the matter from the vantage point of an Englishman who was a contemporary of the Italian Renaissance, was John Milton, whose *Paradise Lost* (1667) ranks on a level with Dante's *Inferno* for its profound influence upon cultural views of the Demon and, importantly, of Satan himself. Milton's magnum opus displays clear evidence of having been influenced by First Enoch, or at least of having been influenced indirectly by its absorption into Christian demonology and angelology; the story of Milton's angels, both those who have fallen and those who have remained loyal to God, is very similar to the story in First Enoch and even features some of the same characters, such as Uriel, Raphael, and Azazel. Milton may have written this work to "justify the ways of God to man," as he famously put it, but what he largely ended up doing was to present a sympathetic Satan whose vibrant interiority fascinated subsequent generations of Christians. And although as already discussed, the idea of demons as fallen angels had a very long pedigree by Milton's day, and was already established as Roman Catholic doctrine, Milton may be credited with raising popular awareness of it to such a pitch that it was cemented permanently in the forefront of Christian demonological thought. Not surprisingly, Milton's demonic imagery became a favorite subject for many artists, just as Dante's had done.

With *Paradise Lost*, the final refinement of the Demon was put in place. In the centuries to come, the primary vehicle for a continued focus upon the Demon would shift increasingly from overtly religious texts to the literary genre that emerged with the birth of the Romantic movement and its offshoot, the gothic horror story. The Demon was now a unified entity that had coalesced from numerous sources, and would correspondingly display numerous aspects of its diverse history in the supernatural stories to come.

V.
THE ANGEL FROM THE FIRST CENTURY TO MODERN TIMES

As with its prehistory, the history of the Angel from its formation in Hellenistic times to the present day is largely a complement to the history of the Demon. The framers of the demonic hordes and hierarchies created the angelic hosts and hierarchies at the same time, under the influence of the same Chaldean-inspired Jewish theology and from the aspects of the Greek daimons that had not been allotted to the Demon. But this meant the nature of the Angel as not just an objective entity but also an inner spiritual reality was emphasized in a distinctly different manner than it was with the Demon.

In the New Testament writings, angels were cast largely in the mold of their fearsome ancient Jewish progenitors. As in the Jewish scriptures, they were central to God's interactions with humans. In the Old Testament angels had attended the callings of prophets and effected the birth of the nation of Israel via Jacob's nocturnal wrestling match; in the New Testament they herald the birth of Christ and also, in the end, help to effect the destruction of the sin-corrupted world order.

In Luke's gospel the angel Gabriel appears to the Levitical priest Zechariah to announce the birth of Christ's herald, John the Baptist, and "Zechari'ah was troubled when he saw him, and fear fell upon him" (Luke 1:12). Shortly afterward, Gabriel appears to Mary to announce that she will be made pregnant by the power of the Holy Spirit, and she is "greatly troubled" by his greeting (1:29). On the night Christ is finally born, an unnamed angel appears to lowly shepherds to announce the joyous news, and the shepherds are terrified: "And an angel of the Lord appeared to them, and the glory of the Lord shone around them, and they were filled with fear" (2:9). In Matthew's gospel with its alternative birth narrative, an angel appears three times to Jesus' human father, Joseph, with specific instructions about actions he should take (e.g., "Rise, take the child and his mother, and flee to Egypt, and remain there till I tell you; for Herod is about to search for the child, to destroy him" [2:13]). After Jesus' crucifixion and interment, an angel descends upon the rock rolled over the entrance to the tomb, whereupon the Roman guards who have been posted there are literally overcome by terror: "And behold, there was a great earthquake; for an angel of the Lord descended from heaven and came and rolled back the stone, and sat upon it. His appearance was like lightning, and his raiment white as snow. And for fear of him the guards trembled and became like dead men" (28:2-4). In all three synoptic gospels, the women who go to anoint Jesus' corpse with oil are seized with great fear when they find an empty tomb and are confronted by an angel or angels who announce his resurrection. The terrifying quality of these appearances is reinforced by the first words a New Testament angel, like its Old Testament forebears, is typically obliged to speak before it can deliver its message: "Do not be afraid!" Given the famous destructive capabilities these angels display in the New Testament's culminating text, the Book of Revelation, wherein God employs them to unleash hideous wars, plagues, and other assorted punishments upon the earth, the fear expressed by those who receive a visit from the Angel under more subdued circumstances is understandable.

As for the cataloguing of the angelic host, it was well underway by the close of the New Testament period. *The Testament of Solomon*, a Jewish pseudoepigraphical text that spoke primarily of demons, also spoke of angels by way of naming which ones should be called upon to counter and put down specific demons. Probably the most significant angelology of the period was written by the fifth century mystical theologian Pseudo-Dionysius the Areopagite, who in his *Celestial Hierarchy* adapted the Neoplatonism of Plotinus and Proclus to establish a hierarchy of angels in three "triads"—for the first, Seraphim, Cherubim, and

Thrones; for the second, Dominations, Virtues, and Powers; for the third, Principalities, Archangels, and Angels—which greatly influenced later medieval scholastic theologians.

The Neoplatonists, it should be recalled, represented an explicitly mystical interpretation of Greek Platonic philosophy, and for this reason their "take" on the Angel displayed a pointedly more mystical character than those of a more typically Judaic or New Testament cast. As already explained, the Demon had inherited the negative, destructive aspect of the Greek daimons associated with daimonic/demonic possession, wherein a person was overtaken by a violent force that welled up from within his or her psyche. The angelic counterpart to this was the attaching to the Angel of the other half of the old daimonic concept, the half that was framed more in terms of what might today be called a "higher self." Plotinus, the second century philosopher who was the first of the great Neoplatonists, expressed this when he described the individual daimon not as "an anthropomorphic daemon, but an inner psychological principle, viz: the level above that on which we consciously live, and so is both within us and yet transcendent" (R. T. Wallis, quoted in Harpur, 39). The same idea entered into the Latin concept of the *genius*, understood as a guiding and/or guardian spirit attached to each person, which gained wide currency throughout the Roman world when it was used to translate the Greek *daimon* (and which, as the reader will recall, bears an obscure etymological relationship to the ancient Middle Eastern *djinee*). Instead of tempting or possessing a person, the psychologized or spiritualized Angel that was bound up with these concepts called people to realize of their own free will their highest and deepest spiritual potential.

Thus was born an interesting division in the figure of the Angel. Considered as hierarchies of objectively existing beings, the early angelologies clearly reflected their origins in the theology of Zoroastrianism, Hellenistic Judaism, and so on. But considered as descriptions of inner spiritual and psychological states and forces, the same angelologies clearly reflected their origins in the more mystically oriented Neoplatonic and Gnostic practice of theurgy, or the divinizing of matter and the self by "drawing down" the divine into it. In the long historical view, this practice undoubtedly derived from the more mystical and angelic aspects of the Greek daimons, which were in turn at least partly derived from the older Hermetic mystery religion of ancient Egypt that was evidenced in such representative concepts as the previously mentioned *ka* self.

The history of the Angel on down to the modern day evinces these exoteric and esoteric dual understandings. Although the division of duties was never absolute, the more objectively oriented or "mythological" understanding naturally tended to be the province of the exoteric, orthodox Christianity, while the other, more psychological understanding was the province not only of the mystical orders of the Church, which frequently threatened to burst the bounds of orthodoxy with their free-form spiritual theologizing, but also of all-out esotericism and occultism. While the likes of Augustine, Aquinas, Dante, and Milton devoted their energies to elaborating ever more refined ideas and images of what might be called the objective Angel, various adherents and teachers of the esoteric tradition that was influenced by Neoplatonism, Gnosticism, Cabalism, and Hermetism (revived and revised as Hermeticism in the 15th and following centuries) were elaborating ever more refined ideas and instructions for how to realize the subtle, inner angelic realm in actual personal experience. This second tradition reached an apex of sorts during the 15th through the 18th centuries—roughly the same period when the final touches were being applied to the iconic Demon—when the likes of Cornelius Agrippa (1486-1535), Paracelsus (1493-1541), John Dee (1527-1606), Cagliostro (1743-95), and Emanuel Swedenborg (1688-1772) pursued occult studies involving aspects of angel magic and the divinizing of the self through communion with its higher guardian spirit or spirits. The same practice has continued into the modern era, where it still survives in the form of various rituals, such as those taught by The Hermetic Order of the Golden Dawn, for contacting the "Holy Guardian Angel," understood as both a higher self and a transcendent entity.

Swedenborg, who claimed to converse regularly with angels face to face, wrote that "angels are wholly men in form, having faces, eyes, ears, bodies, arms, hands, and feet" (quoted in Hirsch 2002, 115, 116). This is much in line with the general tenor of angelic artwork from the period. As already observed, the visual template for the Angel had been provided by the Greek deities Nike and Eros. Thus we can see that the human-looking angels with whom Swedenborg conversed were inheritors of a basic visual concept that proved as remarkably resilient as the theological one. Chester Comstock writes in "Angel Images in Art History" that the pattern provided by Nike and Eros remained "the historic and classical basis for Christian angel iconography used from the 1st century A.D. until modern times, having changed little over the last 2600 years." Byzantine Christianity made particularly vital contributions to the concretizing and proliferating of Christian angelic art during the fourth and fifth centuries, after which the famous variations introduced during the Medieval and Renaissance periods were more matters of individual artistic style than of real substance.

A final bit of duality to enter into the figure of the Angel is found in this very area of artistic representation. On the one hand, the image continued in its original majestic form down through the Middle Ages and into the Renaissance, arguably culminating in the paintings of the Dominican monk Fra Angelico ("the angelic friar," c. 1400-1455), for whom angels were a favorite subject. C. S. Lewis voiced a widely held sentiment when he wrote that "Fra Angelico's angels carry in their face and gesture the peace and authority of Heaven." It was these same Renaissance-style angels that television critic O'Connor noted had been "culled from art masterpieces" to populate NBC's *Angels: The Mysterious Messengers*. This was in 1994, so obviously this type of angelic representation has survived to the modern day.

But in the same breath when he was praising angels in the tradition of Fra Angelico and other, similar artists, C. S. Lewis also voiced a widely noted observation about a different artistic trend that produced a decidedly different sort of angel: "In the plastic arts these symbols [i.e., representations of angels] have steadily degenerated" (Lewis 7). The specific degeneration he referred to is the steady birth of the cuddlier, cuter angel that has carved out a distinctive niche for itself in Western popular consciousness and is most associated with the work of Fra Angelico's near-contemporary Raphael (1483-1520), who portrayed angels as fat, naked babies adorned with candied white wings. These are matched by yet another diluted version of the angel in the form of the pale feminine figure that arose to populate the art world during the 19th century. A few prominent figures such as William Blake may have labored to maintain a more transcendently serious vision of the angel, but the shape of the future was clear, and it was chubby and cute and insipid.

Emily Hahn, in her interesting little book *Breath of God: A book about angels, demons, familiars, elementals, and spirits,* links these changes to an impulse that arose with the advent of the Christian religion itself:

> Taking stock of itself, the new Christianity made a change in all this [i.e., the fearsome angels of Middle Eastern religion]. The type of angel desired and needed by Christians, it became increasingly evident, was not the sort of Being the Jews had been satisfied with, so the authorities, viz., historians and illustrators, evolved a new concept of angel which, though we cannot all claim to love it, at least does not send us rushing off in screaming flight if we happen to encounter it in dreams (53).

For Hahn, all Christian angels, even those of the Middle Ages, represent a kind of devolution of power. "[I]f we are to believe the medieval painters," she writes,

> all was sweetness and light before the birth of Jesus. After He made His appearance, the manger must have been full of the soft rustle of cherub wings, as little angels—*not* griffins or sphinxes, but amoretti—hovered over the crib, peering down lovingly at the Babe, between the ears of donkeys and the horns of cattle—two horns per animal, no more. Something new in religion came in with Jesus: prettiness, innocence, call it what you will. The Nightmare Angel's sway was over (58).

Obviously, Hahn was taking poetic license with history when she wrote that. The change did not occur immediately with the advent of Christianity. But occur it did, so that today, two millennia after the birth of Christ, Mark Edmundson can accurately observe in his *Nightmare on Main Street* that "America's current angels are fluffy creatures, flown off the fronts of greeting cards," who compare unfavorably with the original biblical angels which are "beings of another order: an encounter with an angel transforms life—puts one on a harder, higher path" (80).

Lewis, for his part, brought the issue to a head and also summarized the history of this degeneration in his typically inimitable way:

> Later [i.e. in the wake of Fra Angelico's angels] come the chubby infantile nudes of Raphael; finally the soft, slim, girlish, and consolatory angels of nineteenth century art, shapes so feminine that they avoid being voluptuous only by their total insipidity—the frigid houris of a teatable paradise. They are a pernicious symbol. In Scripture the visitation of an angel is always alarming; it has to begin by saying "Fear not." The Victorian angel looks as if it were going to say, "There, there" (Lewis 7).

One can only wish Lewis were still around to comment on the angel-oriented advertising campaign mounted by the American lingerie company Victoria's Secret in the early 2000s, which featured images of nearly-nude female models decked out with large, white, feathery wings. This enormously profitable mockery of the Angel both underscored the figure's cultural prevalence and one-upped the "pernicious symbol" of Victorian art by presenting a figure that managed to appear exceedingly voluptuous and artistically insipid all at once.

Although the details lie outside the scope of this essay, it might be noted that in addition to playing a major role in the founding of Christianity—and also, in one of its earlier versions, the founding of Judaism—the Angel played a major role in the creation of two other Western religions: Islam, when the angel Gabriel began to speak to a humble Arab camel driver named Muhammad in the early seventh century; and Mormonism, when the angel Moroni visited a poor, uneducated American teenager named Joseph

Smith in 1823 and told him where to find buried golden plates containing a secret scripture written in "reformed Egyptian." The wide-ranging results of these two angelic interventions are matters of global significance. Who knows but that the iconic Angel may return to establish additional major religions in the future?

VI.
UNDERSTANDING THE ANGEL AND THE DEMON IN SUPERNATURAL HORROR FICTION AND FILM

This, then, is the origin of the Angel and the Demon. The modern icons are inheritors of a vastly rich and ancient mosaic of meanings, and when they appear in works of supernatural horror, they generally display one or more facets of their varied natures, a knowledge of which can greatly enhance the reader's understanding and enjoyment.

A highly selective survey of several important—and in some cases not-so-important—texts will be sufficient to establish the point. By way of setting a context, it is prudent to recognize that from its beginnings in the gothic literary movement of the late 18th and early 19th centuries, the supernatural horror genre has consistently made the Demon a more frequent and explicit focus than the Angel, which has remained more active in the province of religion and spirituality as such. In fact, the Angel as a major focus of fictional supernatural horror did not really see much use at all until the late 20th century. Perhaps this is due in part to the Angel's aforementioned artistic degeneration. In the 19th century, right about the time the Angel was finding itself trapped in the bodies of chubby babies and doe-eyed androgynes, the supernatural horror story was just getting off the ground, and many of these stories made prominent use of the Demon, which, unlike the angel, had retained its ancient horrific nature intact and was thus ready for immediate casting in stories of supernatural horror. Interestingly, in its literary guise the Demon has remained very much in touch with its ancient cultural background as described in this essay, while in its cinematic guise, as discussed below, it has often been severed from this mooring and allowed to roam free as a nearly context-less monster.

Three primary aspects of the Demon

The idea of multiple facets or aspects mentioned above provides a useful tool for clarifying the Demon's various appearances in stories of the supernatural. The coherent, unified Demon that was hammered into existence over the course of millennia still displays a number of distinct aspects owing to its multifarious origin, and supernatural stories may be analyzed according to which of these they emphasize. In general, three such aspects are identifiable: the *Demon as fallen angel* (a.k.a. the Miltonic Demon), the *Demon as moral tempter*, and what might be called the *Demon as afflicting presence*. This last takes one of several forms ranging from physical and/or psychological harassment to internal daimonic-type influence to full-blown demonic possession.

The Demon as fallen angel and moral tempter: The Monk *and* Faust

One of the most celebrated Gothic novels, Matthew Lewis' *The Monk* (1796), represents the first major use of the Demon in the nascent supernatural horror genre. Published only twenty-two years after Horace Walpole's overwrought medieval-esque fantasy, *The Castle of Otranto*, had launched the Gothic novel genre, *The Monk* caused a scandal and a sensation, and a survey of its content indicates why. Set in Madrid in the time of the Inquisition, it tells the story of a monk named Ambrosio who is renowned for, and also far too arrogantly proud of, his iron-clad moral virtue. This virtue is corrupted when he falls in lust with a woman named Matilda who is later revealed as a demon, and whose enticements lead him into acts of intense debauchery and violence. The theology of the book, and thus the nature of the Demon it envisages, is entirely orthodox, with a few faint rumblings of occultism thrown in for good measure, as is typical of such literature from the period. Demons in the book are framed as fallen angels with Lucifer as their king. They can be "called up" via occult rituals, as Matilda first describes and then later demonstrates to Ambrosio, who ends up signing a contract with Lucifer and suffering a hideous punishment in the end. Although the salacious and gruesome nature of the book aroused such spectacular controversy and condemnation, especially from the Catholic church, that Lewis' reputation was brought into jeopardy, it is clear that the novel and its demonology are entirely grounded in a traditional morality, since the novel "plays off" this morality at every turn in order to wring the maximum amount of moral-aesthetic horror from its story and subject matter. So this first prominent use of the Demon in a work of supernatural horror emphasizes both the moral aspect and the Miltonic aspect of the Demon. A movie version starring Franco Nero and scripted by renowned surrealist filmmaker Luis Buñuel appeared almost two hundred years later, in 1973, and did not significantly alter the story's presentation of the demon.

Faust, whose Part One was published in 1808, is of course not generally labeled a horror story as such, although Goethe himself was prominent in the Romantic movement that spawned the horror genre. But Goethe's rendering of the ancient story of the great magician who sells his soul to the Devil or a demon is of such major importance that it really must be mentioned. It has become known as the definitive version of the story, surpassing and virtually supplanting Christopher Marlowe's *The Tragical History of Doctor Faustus* (1604) in popular literary memory. As in *The Monk*, the view of the Demon here is utterly in line with the Roman Catholic/Miltonic concept established in the 13th through the 17th centuries, although Goethe with his eclectic political, theological, philosophical, scientific, and mystical concerns puts the concept to decidedly wider use. The demon Mephistopheles who offers his diabolical bargain to the eponymous protagonist was portrayed in Medieval and Renaissance Christian legends as a powerful angel who had been the second to fall from Heaven after Lucifer. In Goethe's story Mephistopheles makes reference to his own fallen status a number of times, and the play's "Prologue in Heaven" further signals and cements the deployment of the iconic theology by presenting the archangels Michael, Gabriel, and Raphael praising God in heaven, followed by Mephistopheles placing a wager with God about Faust in a scene modeled directly on the interaction between Satan and Yahweh in the Book of Job. In Part Two of the play, published in 1832, Mephistopheles meets with various mythological creatures and takes on the appearance of the monstrous Phorkyas, thus bringing to prominence the Demon's ancient association with the whole multitude of non-Christian gods and spirits. All in all, the play ranks as one of the most significant works in the history of demonic literature.

The Demon as afflicting presence: "Green Tea," "The Horla," "Casting the Runes"

By the middle and late 19th century, the supernatural horror story had come fully into its own and begun to produce authors who would later constitute a canon. Many of them made use of the Demon, as in the spate of stories where the Demon was active as a psychologically and physically afflicting presence. These include Le Fanu's "Green Tea" (1872), de Maupassant's "The Horla" (1887), and M. R. James' "Casting the Runes" (1894), all of which are recognized as classics of the genre.

"Green Tea" (1872) offers a fascinating take on the theme by depicting the plight of one Reverend Mister Jennings, who is driven to suicide by either a mental breakdown or an excess of supernatural sight that has enabled him to see a demon, in the shape of a monkey, that pursues him everywhere, even jumping on his Bible as he attempts to preach. But the creature is invisible to everyone else. Le Fanu uses the opportunity provided by his basic plot idea to offer some fascinating spiritual and metaphysical speculations, as when he has the narrator translate a few lines from Swedenborg's *Arcana Coelestia,* thus illuminating the possible nature of Mr. Jennings' afflicting presence:

> When man's interior sight is opened, which is that of his spirit, then there appear the things of another life, which cannot possibly be made visible to the bodily sight. . . . There are with every man at least two evil spirits. . . . The evil spirits associated with man are, indeed, from the hells, but when with man they are not then in hell, but are taken out thence. The place where they then are, is in the midst between heaven and hell, and is called the world of spirits (Wise & Fraser 377).

This "world of spirits" corresponds, of course, to what Plato and other ancient Greeks called the daimonic realm. The story's basic conceit is that Mr. Jennings' may have accidentally had his "interior sight opened," thus attracting the malevolent attention of the little demon that is attached to him.

Maupassant's "The Horla" and M. R. James' "Casting the Runes" present similar tales of men plagued by demons, and like "Green Tea" demonstrate their awareness of the background and context of such a theme. The protagonist of "The Horla" suffers from such horrifying attacks by an invisible creature that he is eventually driven to kill himself. But before his end, he realizes that the entity attacking him is a representative of an entire race that is intent upon wresting control of the earth from humankind. The Horla is the entity whom throughout history "was feared by primitive man; whom disquieted priests exorcised; whom sorcerers evoked on dark nights, without having seen him appear, to whom the imagination of the transient masters of the world lent all the monstrous or graceful forms of gnomes, spirits, genii, fairies and familiar spirits" (Wise & Fraser 466). In other words, the thing attacking the narrator is the original source and template for all the evil spirits that mankind has ever conceived. For the reader who is aware of the deep background of hideous hosts and hordes encoded in the idea of the iconic Demon, the story's conceit is all the more effective and impressive.

In James' "Casting the Runes," a man named Edward Dunning is similarly plagued by an invisible demon that is unleashed upon him by a resentful occultist. In the end the occultist himself is apparently done in by his own evil. The entire story as well as its famous cinematic adaptation, *Night of the Demon,* a.k.a. *Curse of the* Demon (1957; see below) demonstrates an awareness of the subject's rich background, thus repaying and playing upon the reader's existing knowledge of such things. This is unsurprising since James was a professional academic, specifically a medieval scholar, whose interest in the Demon extended far beyond the writing of horror stories. He studied medieval and ancient demonology in earnest and applied his powers to translating ancient works, producing, for example, a translation of *The Testament of Solomon.*

The Demon and the cult of genius: an interjection

In addition to noting its appearances in supernatural horror fiction during the genre's early years, it is instructive to look briefly back to the early 19th century, to the height of the Romantic period, and observe that the trope of the Demon as an afflicting presence appears most prominently not in works of supernatural horror but in works of philosophy and literary theory that explore the Romantic concept of "genius." All of the great Romantics—Goethe, Rousseau, Shelley, Byron, Blake, Coleridge, as well as their philosophical heirs in the Transcendentalist and anti-transcendentalist movements (Emerson, Thoreau, Poe, Hawthorne, Melville)—devoted a great deal of attention and many thousands of words to analyzing, celebrating, and even deifying the creative impulse that led people such as themselves to produce art and literature.

In the Romantic view, creative inspiration became likened to a demon, or rather a daemon, or rather a genius in a modified classical Roman mode, so that these individuals with their overheated personalities and obsessive creative manias were framed as being influenced and inspired by a type of higher power. Additionally, Goethe, Hoffmann, and others wrote much about the idea of the "demonic" man who is controlled by a deeply obsessive force that leads him always to strive in quasi-Promethean fashion for *more* in all things. So this was an alternate mode by which aspects of the Demon remained visible in the cultural consciousness of the period. Naturally, it made itself known in reams of poetry and fiction, many of which did not mention it explicitly but instead manifested its spirit (as in the case of Mary Shelley's *Frankenstein* with its daimonically-driven title character).

The Demon as best-seller: The Exorcist *and the novels of Frank Peretti*

Leaping ahead nearly two centuries, we find E. V. Walter pointing out that Blatty's *The Exorcist* "represents the ambiguity of Roman Catholic culture in the throes of disenchantment after Vatican II" (Walter 20). It was not just Roman Catholic culture but Western culture at large that was suffering such a disenchantment in the 1960s and '70s, and Blatty's 1971 novel and its 1973 film version landed right in the middle of this. In retrospect it seems impossible to separate the two versions of the story, so intertwined have they become in cultural memory. Walter hit upon the key to the electrifying power of both when he wrote in the mid-1970s that the film version "exploits the deisidaimonia of a disenchanted public." *The Exorcist* demonstrated that a visceral portrayal of the Demon in its most horrific guise, as the afflicting presence that possesses a person's body and personality, was capable of wrenching the emotions of a confused modern populace in a way that nobody would have predicted, but that had been quite familiar to people in former historical eras. The unhappy priest Damien Karrass, who in the story examines the exorcism case and subjects it to intense medical scrutiny before proceeding to explore supernatural explanations, served effectively as a stand-in for a spiritually skeptical but existentially fearful American public. The story seemed all the more horrifying to that public because it posited that a vile supernatural presence, like a revenant of a mythological age thought long dead, could enter the body of an innocent young person. In the attempt to build a suitably fearsome back story, Blatty turned to ancient Mesopotamian mythology and framed the demon that possessed young Regan MacNeil as Pazuzu.

Along with its exploration of the possession theme, *The Exorcist* also played upon the Demon's aspect as fallen angel in its depiction of the confrontation between Pazuzu and the aged Father Merrin. The performance of the exorcism rite from Chapter XII of the Roman Ritual formed the substance of the story's final half, and what with the various adjurations in the name of Christ and the traditional names and identifications aimed to the demon, the novel and film left no doubt about the nature and status of the spirit.

The astonishing popular success of *The Exorcist* changed the face of popular entertainment. In the literary world, it launched the pop horror fiction boom that reached its apex in the works of Stephen King in the 1980s. Naturally, many of these books and stories featured the Demon in some form or other.

The Christian thrillers of Frank Peretti deserve special notice in this regard, because of their popularity and their linkage to a major cultural current. *The Exorcist* had entered American public consciousness during a period of religious confusion. Later in the 1970s the American cultural scale tipped decisively, though not universally, in the direction of conservatism, and this in combination with the resurgent popularity of religious fundamentalism engendered a renaissance of literalistic supernatural Christian belief. This soon found an outlet in the new field of Christian popular fiction, in which Frank Peretti became one of the first giants. His novels *This Present Darkness* (1986) and its sequel *Piercing the Darkness* (1988) depicted the literal reality of Demons warring with Angels in the American heartland. Peretti's theology was entirely Miltonian and Dante-esque, as were his descriptions of angels and demons. One is described in *This Present Darkness* as being "like a high-strung little gargoyle, his hide a slimy, bottomless black, his body thin and spiderlike: half humanoid, half animal, totally demon" (36). Others are enormous saurian beings of immense power. In expression of an idea common to the type of theology these books represent, many demons are named after specific sins or negative emotions, such as the demons Complacency, Deceit, and Lust, whose functions are obvious. Additionally, full-blown demon possession, complete with the requisite writhing, guttural speech, etc., results when people dabble with dastardly New Age beliefs.

Clearly, all three aspects of the Demon are exhibited here: fallen angel, moral tempter, and afflicting presence in its three variations. From a viewpoint informed by the Demon's history, what seems most fascinating about these novels is that they employ the streamlined, generic prose and narrative styles typical to modern thriller fiction in order to expound a theology that might be dubbed "Milton-lite." What is more, they do so quite effectively given their peculiar ideological and stylistic constraints, and given the willingness of the reader to surrender to their simplistic worldview.

The Demon in movies and other media

The 1890s saw the birth of the movies, and the Demon got involved in the new industry right from the start. The great early French director George Méliès became famous for his short films featuring fantastic subjects and lots of trick photography. The spirit world was an obvious treasure trove to draw upon for such entertainments, and many of Méliès films, such as *Le Cabinet de Mephistopheles* (The Laboratory of Mephistopheles, 1897) and *La Cavern Maudite* (The Cave of the Demons, 1898) ended up featuring devils and demons, mostly in the "trickster" or tempter mode, all of them bearing stereotypical physical traits. Before the silent era was over, the Demon would also appear in such productions as director Giovanni Vitrotti's 1911 adaptation of the Russian poet Lermontov's *The Demon,* numerous versions of Dante's *Inferno,* director Paul Wegener's 1920 remake of his own earlier film *The Golem,* and director Benjamin Christensen's enigmatic *Häxan* (1922), a.k.a. *Witchcraft Through the Ages* (1922). This last film with its odd early cinematic chronicling of the history of witchcraft and its depiction of classically bestial demons drawn from medieval iconography, who perform and preside over numerous acts of depravity, would continue to excite interest and consternation for decades to come. Like *The Monk, Häxan* reconfirmed the association of the Demon with things rejected and taboo; it was banned outside its home country of Sweden for many decades after its initial release.

1957 saw the release of *Night of the Demon,* director Jacques Tourneur's superlative cinematic adaptation of M. R. James' "Casting the Runes." Released in America under the title *Curse of the Demon,* the film deservedly became a classic. As in the short story, the Demon here appears in its guise as an afflicting presence that harasses its victims both physically and psychologically. The controversy involving Tourneur's supposed fight with the film's producer over whether an actual demon should be shown, as opposed to letting the interpretation of the movie's supernatural-seeming events remain more murky, is as famous as the film itself. Whatever the truth of the matter, the film that was released indeed featured an explicit "head-on" depiction of the title demon. Although Tourneur may ultimately have been correct that the film's final interpretation was better left ambiguous, and thus the demon should have been left out, the visual design of the creature showed an admirable grasp of the iconic Demon's historical and artistic grandeur; its designer reportedly worked with an eye to reproducing the sort of nightmarish figures seen in medieval woodcuts (and also depicted 35 years earlier in *Häxan*).

The Demon also appeared frequently in the comic book industry, as in Marvel Comics' *Ghost Rider* and DC Comics' *The Demon*, always with the traditional iconography intact and the traditional theology at least referenced. The enigmatic character of John Constantine, created by comic book writer and modern occult magician Alan Moore, encountered the Demon in various guises as he strode through a number of titles in the booming comics industry of the 1980s, 90s, and 2000s. Eventually he gained his own comic book series, *Hellblazer*, which was loosely adapted as the 2005 film *Constantine*. In the movie the eclectic spiritual world of the comic book was simplified into a watered-down Roman Catholic dualism that involved demons of an entirely traditional cast warring against equally traditional angels, with humans used as pawns. The aspect of the Demon thus emphasized was the fallen angel, as well as the afflicting presence, with a few instances of demonic possession thrown in for good measure.

Constantine was only one in the flood of Demon-inspired movies that followed in the decades after *The Exorcist*, and in this outpouring an interesting phenomenon can be observed: the severing of the Demon from its specific Western religious mooring, which produced a significant result.

The post-modern Demon: A new take on an old theme

A new type of demon came on the scene when certain filmmakers in the late 20th century decided effectively to ignore tradition and cut the Demon free from its past associations in Christian cosmology and theology. Examples of this type could be multiplied *ad nauseam* since they became popular in the low-budget and direct-to-video markets and were therefore churned out mercilessly by filmmakers with various degrees of talent. But the two series that did it best were the Evil Dead trilogy, consisting of *The Evil Dead* (1981), *Evil Dead II: Dead by Dawn* (1987), and *Army of Darkness* (1993), and the Demons trilogy, consisting of *Demons* (1985), *Demons 2* (1986), and *La Chiesa*

(1989). The demons in both series are portrayed as spirits that commandeer people's bodies and personalities and turn them into vicious killing machines. The violence is copious and explicit and the demons' behavior standardized: Possessed people roar in guttural voices, foam at the mouth, writhe, rend, claw, shriek, and tear. They are the inhuman embodiment of pure ferality, of an insatiable lust for wanton, bloody destruction.

What indicates that these demons have been cut loose from their mooring in the iconic Demon is that the explanations offered for their nature are hasty and thin. In *The Evil Dead* the demons are raised by the reading aloud of passages from a book titled after Lovecraft's fictional grimoire, the *Necronomicon*, which in the movie is said to be of Sumerian origin. The demons are thus, perhaps, of the ancient Sumerian variety. But this explanation is quickly downplayed or ignored in favor of moving the action forward with scenes of intense, feral violence. It is almost as if the explanation is a mere perfunctory nod to the more sustained and detailed ones explored in other films. Similarly, in *Demons* the demons are "explained" by a faux quotation from Nostradamus that prophesies "the coming of the time of the demons," and says of these creatures, "They will make cemeteries their cathedrals and the cities your tombs." The film offers nothing else by way of explaining what the demons are supposed to be or where they are supposed to come from.

Although it would be all too easy to interpret this omission as a liability and to label it the result of laziness or ineptness, it is in fact possible to see it as a strength and to interpret it as a new and effective angle on the iconic Demon in its afflicting aspect. *Demons* makes this clear when it reveals that it is actually a kind of existentialist cinematic parable. The basic plot involves members of a movie audience who find themselves trapped in a nightmare when a movie about demons ruptures the boundary between cinematic reality and existential reality. People in the audience begin transforming into demons and killing everyone around them. Eventually the panicked crowd realizes that since the movie started everything, perhaps stopping it will stop the killing. But when they storm the projection booth, they discover it is completely automated, without a projectionist running the film.

This leads to the startled realization, "But that means—nobody's ever been here!"

The point seems to be that the demon plague is playing out automatically, without any oversight or direction by an intelligent force. It is simply a spontaneous occurrence without explanation. The demons have no reason, no history, no background in anything like the history that lies behind the iconic Demon. Seeing this, one can recognize that these unmoored demons represent an alternative answer to Blatty's and Friedkin's challenge from the 1970s.

What if God died but the Demon survived? What if there were evil but no good to counterbalance it? What if there were indeed demons, but this in no wise entailed the existence of Blatty's "angels, God, and a life everlasting"? This seems to be the philosophy or theology implicit in the post-modern demon (as it might be called).

But another careful look at the behavior of this demon shows that it is not entirely divorced from its iconic cousin. The post-modern demon may not be linked by a shared theological background, but it is linked by the behaviors listed above. All that frothing, snarling, and screaming is familiar from Regan's behavior in *The Exorcist,* and also from the countless cases of demonic possession documented throughout history. By the Middle Ages these behaviors were standardized and catalogued, and all are visible in the post-modern demon, which thus seems to represent the phenomenon of possession divorced from the possibility of exorcism. The post-modern demon is not a fallen angel who can be commanded in the name of Christ or driven away by any version of the iconic Angel, but is instead an unaccountable spirit of viciousness that arrives for no reason and cannot be driven away. As such, it may be taken as a kind of apotheosis of the iconic Demon as the afflicting, possessing presence.

So in effect, tales of the post-modern demon represent an alternative strand sprouting from the pop cultural tradition begun by *The Exorcist,* but they pursue a distinctly different philosophical tangent. At of the time of this writing both streams remain strong. Movies about the post-modern Demon continue to proliferate, even as one of the most prominent of the post-*Exorcist* films is *The Exorcism of Emily Rose* (2005), which was based on the true case of a young German college student named Anneliese Michel who reportedly became possessed and, after several months of exorcism, died in 1976. Even as the post-modern demon continues to rampage across movie and television screens in its orgy of theologically ungrounded violence, *The Exorcism of Emily Rose* explicitly presents almost exactly the same spiritual message that Blatty had hoped to convey with his novel: that the horror of the demonic harbors the seeds of its own redemption, since it directly entails its opposite in the saving grace of God.

The Demon, it seems, is ever the subtle trickster.

The Angel on walkabout

A representative history of the Angel in supernatural horror for purposes of demonstrating the icon's illuminating power is much quicker to relate, for the simple reason that there is less of it to deal with. As mentioned earlier, the Angel's near-exclusion from the supernatural horror genre as a serious object of attention in its own right may well have been due to the artistic coma into which it had fallen. For well over a century the Angel was far more bound up in popular consciousness with saccharine ideas of peace and rose-filled gardens than with serious matters of supernaturalism. For most serious dealings with the Angel, one had to look not to supernatural fiction and film but to outright religion. A few serious literary works did mention or otherwise deal with angels, such as Anatole France's *The Revolt of the Angels* (1914), Jonathan Daniels' *Clash of Angels* (1930), and John Cowper Powys' *Lucifer* (1956). But many of these, while they often referenced the traditional Miltonic theology, often employed the angel in the service of a separate agenda. France's novel, for example, was a satire in favor of free thought; it depicted an angel that becomes an atheist after being exposed to theological literature.

During its vacation from supernatural horror, the Angel was quite prominent in Hollywood, where it found its way into many movies during the 1940s and 1950s. It appeared in various guises in such movies as *A Guy Named Joe* (1944, remade in 1989 as *Always*), *It's a Wonderful Life* (1946), *The Bishop's Wife* (1947),

Heaven Only Knows (1947), and *Angels in the Outfield* (1951, remade in 1994). In 1956 Cecil B. DeMille's bloated (but entertaining) Bible epic *The Ten Commandments* presented a surprisingly frightening angel of death that arrived in the form of a sentient mist to claim all the firstborn Egyptians. But this was an aberration. By the 1970s, when audiences were reportedly vomiting, fainting, and fleeing theatres where *The Exorcist* was playing, the Angel was still confined to light entertaining fare like *Heaven Can Wait* (1978). In 1987 German director Wim Wenders' *Der Himmel über Berlin* (*Wings of Desire,* remade by Hollywood as *City of Angels* in 1998) gave a truly interesting portrayal of angels who watch over the human denizens of a modern city and envy their earthly existence. But this was still a far cry from supernatural horror.

Wenders' film, however, arrived near the end of the supernaturally fearsome Angel's long coma. Already in 1983, Blatty had given readers an interesting bit of angelic speculation in *Legion,* his sequel to *The Exorcist,* wherein he offered a sweeping solution to the age-old "problem of evil" by suggesting that humans are all fragments of the original angelic being, Lucifer, who fell from Heaven, and that we are all therefore involved in a collective, ongoing attempt to be reunited with God. This did not constitute an actual use of the Angel as an object of fear, but it did involve the Angel in a horror novel. Oddly, Blatty omitted this concept entirely from the film version, titled *The Exorcist III* (1990), which he not only wrote but directed.

It remained for another Christian author, not a Catholic but a Protestant, to effect the Angel's full resurrection as a fearsome presence.

Return of the warrior Angel

It was Frank Peretti's supernatural thriller novels of the 1980s that were largely responsible for reviving the Miltonian Angel as a fierce heavenly warrior. Near the beginning of his novel *This Present Darkness,* Peretti depicts two men visiting the small Midwestern town of Ashton. Soon after their arrival, these strangers are revealed as more than men:

> And now the two men were brilliantly white, their former clothing transfigured by garments that seemed to burn with intensity. Their faces were bronzed and glowing, their eyes shone like fire, and each man wore a glistening golden belt from which hung a flashing sword. . . . [T]hen, like a gracefully spreading canopy, silken, shimmering, nearly transparent membranes began to unfurl from their backs and shoulders and rise to meet and overlap above their heads, gently undulating in a spiritual wind (Peretti 13).

Reading the description is like witnessing the resurrection from the dead of the pre-Victorian, non-Raphaelite Angel who had warred against the Demon in the service of God for centuries. The novel's later intricate and overheated descriptions of spiritual and aerial battles between sword-wielding Angels and Demons is an equally welcome sight, regardless of its comic-bookish gaudiness.

Of course the warrior Angel would not stay confined to the world of evangelical Christian thriller/horror fiction. Hollywood, for example, got involved in the early 2000s when it portrayed classical warrior angels in supernatural thrillers and fantasies like *Constantine* and *Frailty* (2001). And the warrior was joined in popular entertainment by its more fearsome cousin, also newly resurrected from its long coma.

Return of the Nightmare Angel

Given the popularity of the "Milton-lite" phenomenon Peretti helped to create with his novels, and given the ongoing popularity of the horror genre, it was just a matter of time before a purely horrific angel appeared. The venue where this rare modern creature finally reared its head was *The Prophecy* (1993), a film written and directed by Gregory Widen and featuring a fascinating premise: Unbeknownst to humans, there is presently a supernatural war being waged, not between angels and demons, but between angels and other angels. This is a second war, described only in an extra "lost" chapter to the Book of Revelation, that came after the original war in which Lucifer and his followers were cast out. The archangel Gabriel, jealous of God's love for humans, whom he (Gabriel) refers to as "talking monkeys," is spearheading an effort among the angels to return things to the way they were when humans were secondary and God loved angels the most.

The whole concept is Miltonic through and through, even with its peculiar "twist," and the film's success is principally due to careful writing and a deeply realized, deeply fascinating concept. Widen truly understands the horror inherent in the ancient, iconic Angel before whom men and women traditionally fainted and fell to their knees. One of *The Prophecy*'s protagonists, a former candidate for Catholic priesthood, describes the nature of this Angel in words as effective as any: "Did you ever notice how in the Bible whenever God needed to punish someone or make an example, or whenever God needed a killing, he sent an angel? Did you ever wonder what a creature like that must be like? A whole existence spent praising your God, but always with one wing dipped in blood. Would you ever really want to see an angel?" The arch-angel Gabriel himself, who appears as a major character, reinforces the point in his self-description to a horrified human who has dared to question him: "I'm an angel. I kill firstborns while their mamas watch. I turn cities into salt. I even, when I feel like it, rip the souls from little girls, and from now till kingdom come, the only thing you can count on in your existence is never understanding why."

The Prophecy spawned sequels, of course—three of them at the time of this writing—which predictably became progressively more mired in their own "cool factor." It seems the temptation to use Widen's ideas simply as an excuse to present attractive actors running around and fighting each other against a backdrop of shadowy, gothic-esque imagery and choral music was too much for lesser filmmakers to resist. The third installment in the series, which came two years after the stupendous success of the science fiction film *The Matrix* (1998), even featured some *Matrix*-type martial arts fighting. But even in these progressively degenerated outings, the power of Widen's original concept, and thus the power of the iconic Nightmare Angel, occasionally shone through.

This was especially visible in *The Prophecy II* (1998), which shocked by providing the single most powerful visual depiction of an Angel and its emotional impact in modern American cinema. Presaging the scene, a young woman encounters a man who is actually an angel, and his first words to her echo the words spoken so often by biblical angels: "Don't be afraid." Later, she doubts him when he tells her of his true identity. The scene takes place in a cathedral, and the film depicts the angel's self-unveiling via its shadow projected on the wall and on the woman herself: enormous wings unfurl from his back, and his stature increases. The woman's reaction is the quintessence of angelic dread: Her eyes widen in an expression of mingled wonder and terror, her hand rises to her mouth, and then her head drops as she falls to the floor sobbing, unable to bear the sight any longer. It is major moment in the Angel's sojourn through supernatural horror.

1998 also saw the release of director Gregory Hoblit's *Fallen,* which ranks almost with *The Prophecy* in its artistic importance to the modern revival of the Angel's fearsomeness. The film is structured as a police procedural thriller in which two detectives try to fathom how someone can be murdering people in the exact mode of a notorious serial killer who was recently executed. As it turns out, the original killer was possessed by the angel Azazel, who migrated to another body after the killer's death. The police procedural aspect of the film is thus paralleled by a spiritual one, in which the head detective on the case moves from skepticism to belief in Azazel and the world of angels and then tries to figure out how such a being can be stopped when, as quickly becomes apparent, Azazel can migrate instantaneously from person to person through the simple medium of physical touch, temporarily displacing the human personality and assuming control of the body. A character in *Fallen* offers the protagonist a succinct statement of the film's central spirituality, which, to those "in the know," makes an obvious play on the daimonic origins of both the Angel and the Demon while couching this in a quasi-orthodox Christian theological framework: "There are certain phenomena which can only be explained if there is a God and if there are angels. And there are. They exist. Some of these angels were cast down, and a few of the fallen were punished by being deprived of form. They can only survive in the bodies of others. It's inside of us, inside of human beings, that their vengeance is played out."

Although *Fallen* could easily have been discussed in the section of this essay dealing with the Demon, its inclusion here seems appropriate given the angelic emphasis of the above comments. However, if we consider the film's Azazel as a demon, then it is clear that the film emphasizes both the iconic Demon's fallen angel aspect and the possession aspect. Azazel is of course familiar from The First Book of Enoch, *Paradise Lost,* and a host of other literary and occult works from history. Its inclusion in *Fallen* is only one of many reasons that the film's relative lack of impact among critics and audiences is unfortunate. The film is a significant one that will perhaps one day be valued for its merits.

VII.
Conclusion: The Daimonic Zeitgeist, 1971 to the 21st Century and Beyond

In 1999 the Roman Catholic Church revised its exorcism rite in order to bring it more into line with modern knowledge about mental illnesses. In 2000 reports surfaced of Pope John Paul II's involvement in the exorcism of a demon from a young girl. Both events occurred on the heels of the North American angel craze. Obviously, something had changed in the thirty years since William Peter Blatty had seen in the Maryland possession case an opportunity to write an apologetic in fictional form that would address the rising secularist tide in America. He could not have known that American culture was on the verge of a revival of religious sentiment that would rival the various Great Awakenings of its national history.

By the dawn of the 21st century, Christianity had not only survived but had thrived, and not always in traditional ways. There had long been a modest portion of the publishing world devoted to selling "Christian fiction," but nothing had ever approached the popularity of the Left Behind series of popular novels by Tim LaHaye and Jerry Jenkins, which were selling hundreds of millions of copies and may have even been influencing U.S. policy decisions via the influence of their literalistic Christian eschatology exerted upon the President, himself a conservative

Christian. Victoria Nelson has argued that "in certain ways popular entertainments more than high art act as a kind of a modern sub-Zeitgeist that is constantly engaging in a low-level discourse on intellectually forbidden subjects—philosophy's disavowed avant-garde, as it were." This would imply that if one wants to find out what is currently being rejected by the dominant philosophy, one should look to popular entertainment.

That is what the bulk of this essay has been devoted to doing. The proliferating popular Demonology and now Angelology of modern culture would seem to bear out the rest of Nelson's assertion, alluded to in this essay's introduction:

> Because the religious impulse is profoundly unacceptable to the dominant Western intellectual culture, it has been obliged to sneak in this back door, where our guard is down. Thus our true contemporary secular pantheon of unacknowledged deities resides in mass entertainments, and it is a demonology, ranging from the "serial killers" in various embodied and disembodied forms to vampires and werewolves and a stereotypical Devil (Nelson 18).

Not to mention an iconic Angel and Demon, sculpted into recognizable archetypes over the course of millennia and now active not only in popular movies and books but also in music, computer games, and elsewhere. Armed with a knowledge of the origin, history, and deep nature of these two icons of supernatural horror, the modern reader can better understand, appreciate, and enjoy them in their frequent appearances.

What's more, this ability may have wider implications. The introduction to this essay stated that Blatty's *The Exorcist* is purely a work of fiction while *Paradise Lost* and the *Inferno* are partly devotional literature. In light of the manifest trajectory of Western cultural and pop cultural history from 1971 to the early years of the 21st century—a trajectory that amply confirms Nelson's observation about the modern West's demonological (or daimonological) sub-zeitgeist—the hard distinction between fiction and religion now seems difficult to maintain. Amid this stew of repressed religious motivations it is possible that the books, films, and other works that constitute the supernatural horror genre may serve as serious religious texts in themselves. It remains for the future to reveal how narrow the gap will become between fictional enjoyment and existential conviction, and how much the deep meanings of the Angel and the Demon may contribute to the modern individual's psychological and spiritual self-understanding.

SOURCES AND SUGGESTIONS FOR FURTHER READING

Allen, Thomas B. *Possessed: The True Story of an Exorcism*. New York: Bantam Books, 1994 (1993).

"Angel." *The Encyclopedia Americana*. International ed. 1996.

The Bible. New Revised Standard Version.

Bonin, Liane. "Devil's Advocate." *The Exorcist Tribute Zone*. <http://www.the-exorcist.co.uk/Devil.htm>. Accessed April 15, 2006. Originally published at *Entertainment Weekly Online* (11/9/99).

Bourguignon, Erika. "Demonology." *The Encyclopedia Americana*. International ed. 1996.

Buckland, Raymond. *The Witch Book: The Encyclopedia of Witchcraft, Wicca, and Neo-paganism*. Canton, MI: Visible Ink Press, 2002.

Comstock, Chester. "Angel Images in Art History: An Angelic Journey through Time." 2003. ARTsales.com. <http://www.artsales.com/ARTistory/angelic_journey/index.html>. Accessed April 25, 2006. Also published in the Spring 2003 issue of *Sculptural Pursuit*.

Davies, T. Witton. *Magic, Divination, and Demonolatry among the Hebrews and their Neighbors*. New York: KTAV Publishing House, 1969.

Diamond, Stephen A. *Anger, Madness, and the Daimonic: The*

Psychological Genesis of Violence, Evil, and Creativity. Suny Series in the Philosophy of Psychology. Albany: State University of New York Press, 1996.

Dodds, E. R. *The Greeks and the Irrational*. Berkeley and Los Angeles: University of California Press, 1959 (1951).

———. *Pagan and Christian in an Age of Anxiety: Some Aspects of Religious Experience from Marcus Aurelius to Constantine*. Cambridge, England: Cambridge University Press, 1965.

Edmundson, Mark. *Nightmare on Main Street: Angels, Sadomasochism, and the culture of Gothic*. Cambridge, MA: Harvard University Press, 1997.

Golden, Christopher, Stephen R. Bissette, and Thomas E. Sniegoski. *The Monster Book*. New York: Pocket Books, 2000.

Gray, John. *Near Eastern Mythology*. New revised edition. Library of the World's Myths and Legends. New York: Peter Bedrick Books, 1985 (1969).

Guiley, Rosemary Ellen. *Harper's Encyclopedia of Mystical and Paranormal Experience*. Edison, NJ: Castle Books, 1991.

———. *The Encyclopedia of Witches & Witchcraft*. Second edition. New York: Facts on File, 1999.

Hahn, Emily and Barton Lidice Beneš. *Breath of God: A book about angels, demons, familiars, elementals, and spirits*. Garden City, NY: Doubleday & Company, 1971.

Harpur, Patrick. *Daimonic Reality: A Field Guide to the Otherworld*. Ravensdale, WA: Pine Winds Press, 2003.

Hillman, James. *The Soul's Code: In Search of Character and Calling*. New York: Random House, 1996.

Hirsch, Edward. *The Demon and the Angel: Searching for the*

Source of Artistic Inspiration. Orlando: Harcourt, 2002.

Hirsch, Emile G., et al. "Demonology." *Jewish Encyclopedia* online. <www.jewishencyclopedia.com/view.jsp?artid=245&letter=D>. Accessed April 15, 2006. Originally published in the *Jewish Encyclopedia*, 12 vols., 1901-1906.

Isacs, Ronald H. *Ascending Jacob's Ladder: Jewish Views of Angels, Demons, and Evil Spirits*. Northvale, NJ: Jason Aronson, Inc., 1998.

May, Rollo. *Love and Will*. New York: W.W. Norton, 1969.

Mäyrä, Frans Ilkka. *Demonic Texts and Textual Demons: The Demonic Tradition, the Self, and Popular Fiction*. Tempere Studies in Literature and Textuality. Tampere, Finland: Tampere University Press, 1999.

Nataf, André. *Dictionary of the Occult*. Great Britain: Wordsworth Editions, Ltd., 1994 (1988).

Nelson, Victoria. *The Secret Life of Puppets*. Cambridge, MA: Harvard University Press, 2001.

Nickell, Joe. *Entities: Angels, Spirits, Demons, and Other Beings*. Amherst, NY: Prometheus Books, 1995.

O'Connor, John J. "Critic's Notebook; TV's Infatuation with the Mystical." *The New York Times*. June 30th, 1994. <http://query.nytimes.com/gst/fullpage.html?res=9907E5D8153CF933A05755C0A962958260>. Accessed April 15, 2006.

Peretti, Frank E. *This Present Darkness*. Wheaton, IL: Crossway Books, 1986.

Pope Paul VI. "Confronting the Devil's Power." Address to a General Audience, November 15, 1972. <http://

www.catholic-pages.com/morality/devil-p6.asp>. Accessed April 15, 2006.

Price, Robert. "Demons." *Supernatural Literature of the World: An Encyclopedia*. Eds. S. T. Joshi, Stefan Dziemianowicz. 3 vols. Westport, CT: Greenwood Press, 2005.

Rosenberg, Donna. *World Mythology: An Anthology of the Great Myths and Epics*. Lincolnwood, IL: National Textbook Company, 1989 (1986).

Stableford, Brian. "Angels." *Supernatural Literature of the World: An Encyclopedia*. Eds. S. T. Joshi, Stefan Dziemianowicz. 3 vols. Westport, CT: Greenwood Press, 2005.

Trimpi, Helen P. "Demonology." *The Dictionary of the History of Ideas*. Ed. Philip P. Wiener. 4 vols. New York: Charles Scribner's Sons, 1973-4. Online at <http://etext.virginia.edu/cgi-local/DHI/dhi.cgi?id=dv1-79>. Accessed April 22, 2006.

____. "Witchcraft." *The Dictionary of the History of Ideas*. Ed. Philip P. Wiener. 4 vols. New York: Charles Scribner's Sons, 1973-4. Online at < http://etext.virginia.edu/cgi-local/DHI/dhi.cgi?id=dv4-71#>. Accessed April 22, 2006.

Walter, E. V. "Demons and Disenchantment." *Disguises of the Demonic*. Ed. Alan M. Olson. New York: Association Press, 1975. 17-30.

Whitehead, John W. "Who's Afraid of the Exorcist?" *Gadfly Online* (October 1998). <http://www.gadflyonline.com/archive/October98/archive-exorcist.html>. Accessed March 7, 2006.

Wise, Herbert A. and Phyllis Fraser, eds. *Great Tales of Terror and the Supernatural*. New York: The Modern Library, 1944.

Zucker, Wolfgang M. "The Demonic: From Aeschylus to Tillich." *Theology Today* 6:1 (April 1969), 34-50.

LOATHSOME OBJECTS:

GEORGE ROMERO'S LIVING DEAD FILMS AS CONTEMPLATIVE TOOLS

[Note: This paper was written in 2003, before the release of *Land of the Dead*, the fourth installment in Romero's zombie series.]

When it came to close-up, hard-focus revulsion, nothing could beat the movies.
—Theodore Roszak, *Flicker*

Approaching death and death itself, the dissolution of the physical form, is always a great opportunity for spiritual realization.
—Eckhart Tolle, *The Power of Now*

Remember death; think much of death; think how it will be on a death bed.
—"Commonplace Book of Joseph Green," 1696

INTRODUCTION: NIGHT OF THE SOCIOCULTURAL CRITICS

Most critical analyses of director George Romero's celebrated zombie trilogy—*Night of the Living Dead* (1968), *Dawn of the Dead* (1978), *Day of the Dead* (1985)—have focused, quite rightly, on the subtext of social criticism that winds its way through all three films. Film scholar Gregory Waller, for example, has said of *Night of the Living Dead* that it "offers a thoroughgoing critique of American institutions and values. It depicts the failure of the nuclear family, the private home, the teenage couple, and the resourceful individual hero; and it reveals the flaws inherent in the media, local and federal government agencies, and the entire mechanism of civil defense."(1) Film critics J. Hoberman and Jonathan Rosenbaum call the film "a brilliant, open-ended metaphor for topical anxieties" and describe it as "not only an instant horror classic, but a remarkable vision of the late sixties—offering the most literal possible depiction of America devouring itself."(2) One Internet reviewer writes that "*Dawn of the Dead* is a thoughtful social commentary that may be deservingly compared to *Taxi Driver*,"(3) and critics have universally pointed out that this second film in the trilogy represents a satire—blatantly intended by Romero—on the rampant consumerist greed of 1970s American popular culture. As for *Day of the Dead*, film critic Robin Wood identifies its central metaphor as the idea that "science and militarism [are] male-dominated, masculinist institutions threatening to destroy life on the planet."(4) Examples of sociocritical analyses of these films could be multiplied almost indefinitely. Even a Unitarian Universalist preacher has gotten in on the act by referencing these movies in a sermon—not to condemn them for their depictions of gory violence, but to enlist their aid in condemning the rampant real-life violence that's endemic in turn-of-the-millennium Western culture.(5)

In keeping with contemporary academia's emphasis on methodological multivalence, I do not intend to argue against or detract from this body of work.(6) Rather, I intend to shift focus a bit and concentrate on a less well-explored aspect of Romero's famous trilogy, namely, its spiritual aspect. But I will explore this by way of and in tandem with an examination of its high gore content.

The paper's first three parts tackle the gore issue. In the first of them, I will explore the gory violence that is widely recognized as the visual hallmark of the modern horror film in general, and will consider the ways in which these films generate a sense of horror by their portrayal of a body that defies conscious control. In fleshing out this idea I will refer to Julia Kristeva's particularly illuminating theory of the abject and will discuss the ways in which cinematic assaults on the body's integrity attack the human sense of personal identity.

In parts two and three I will round off this gore-ful tangent by focusing specifically on Romero's zombie films in order to demonstrate how they attack the viewer's sense of a stable identity and thus generate horror through their portrayal of animated corpses—which are, after all, *bodies* of a particular type—and especially through their characterization of these corpses as cannibals, which are, after all, bodies that eat other bodies of the same kind. Cannibalism, I will contend (with help from food theory as established by Roland Barthes, Anna Meigs, and others), destabilizes the sense of identity by presenting a literalistic metaphor of the self becoming the other, and also by reducing the body with its generally stable form and healthy integrity to a mass of disconnected tissues and organs.

In part four I will shift my focus rather drastically to explore the spiritual or religious theme that permeates Romero's zombie films alongside the gore. Of interest will be the fact that this theme receives progressively greater prominence as the trilogy progresses, moving from the rather muted and implicit spirituality of *Night* to the brief but direct mention of spiritual matters in *Dawn* to the full-frontal apocalypticism of *Day*. I will conclude the ideas in this section in parts five and six by tying together these parallel themes—body horror and apocalyptic spirituality—in an attempt to demonstrate how they work in tandem to generate a bleak and nihilistic cinematic experience in which the human self is seen as a helpless, groundless phantom lost in a vortex of bloody flesh. But more than this, in the paper's final section I will argue that such an emergent attitude itself represents not merely an occasion for utter despair but offers the viewer an opportunity to experience a kind of epiphany regarding his or her selfhood and its relation to the body. In a nutshell, I will argue that the viewer who chooses to do so may use the promptings toward body horror and spiritual horror presented in the Living Dead films as tools for exploring a particular existential spiritual understanding, one that recognizes in the mortality of flesh and ego-self a revelation of the indestructible center of inviolable awareness that constitutes each person's most fundamental identity.

The net result will be to establish that Romero's zombie trilogy can be seen and used as tools to enhance the clarity of nondual spiritual realization.

I. FLESH BECOMES MEAT: THE PERISHABLE BODY

"Violent pastimes are nothing new," writes Jonathan Lake Crane, "but there has never been anything quite as violent and massively popular as the contemporary horror film."[7] The truth of this assertion is by now beyond argument. Violence is one of the defining aspects of the contemporary horror film—direct, visceral, *vividly portrayed* violence. Referring specifically to American horror films of the 1970s—i.e. horror films in the immediate wake of *Night of the Living Dead,* the film from which the modern era of the genre is commonly dated—Jack Sargeant writes, "These films stand apart from previous generations of horror movies, because of their narrative focus on the bruised and torn flesh of the body as the text on which terror becomes inscribed."[8] There is no longer a looking-away, as in director Tod Browning's *Dracula* (1931), where the eponymous villain's death-by-stake occurs offscreen. The Hammer horror films of the 1950s gave movie audiences their first glimpse of the stake actually entering the vampire's chest. Since 1968, the chest has been laid open and the organs and viscera exposed for all to see. In the words of Cynthia Freeland,

> It would be hard to discuss the modern horror film without talking about scenes in these films (or their many imitators) of over-the-top, ever-escalating graphic violence and gore (or "FX" [effects] as the fans say). It is common to witness gross bodily dismemberments, piles of internal organs, numerous corpses in stages of decay, headless bodies, knives or chain saws slashing away at flesh, and general orgies of mayhem. In these films, flesh becomes meat, the inside becomes outside, blood pours out, skin is stripped off, viscera exposed, heads detached. People die in any number of creatively disgusting ways.[9]

One of the most significant subtextual messages conveyed by all of this gory violence is that our bodies are *fragile* and are thus in constant danger of being injured or corrupted. An important corollary of this recognition, as noted by Anne Jerslev, is that human identity itself is fragile, since the body, which is so fundamental in setting the boundaries of our sense of self, refuses to retain its integrity. "Generally speaking," she writes,

> the splatter movie's mutilated body is fragile. Its skin is

> thin as parchment and thus cannot function as a bodily armour symbolizing and demarcating the subject at the same time. It is a body without firm outlines; on the contrary, it is constantly transforming from one shape into another, as its unreliable innards all of a sudden break through the skin to start a life of their own.[10]

This vivid image of innards assuming "a life of their own" highlights another key aspect of the way the modern horror film serves to disturb its viewers through its depiction of the body: in these films, the body is often *out of control*. In my academic paper "Awakening from the Nightmare: The Horror Film as a Tool for Transcendence," published in 2000-2001 at the now-defunct website Imaginary Worlds, I argued that people are horrified by the sight of gore, whether fictional or actual, because we—and by "we" I mean specifically the children of Western culture—are accustomed to regarding our bodies not with an attitude of identity but of ownership. In this regard, I argued, we would do well to remember what philosopher and cultural critic Theodore Roszak said in his *magnum opus, Where the Wasteland Ends,* about the "anti-organic fanaticism" of Western culture, the attitude of fastidiousness toward our organic natures that tends to lead us Westerners to "cringe from anything as oozy as the inside of our body."[11] The body, writes Roszak, "has become for us an alien object located Out There, the mere receptacle of our true and irrevocable identity. That identity is ultimately felt to reside at a point inside the body . . . inside the head . . . somewhere just behind the eyes and between the ears."[12] This antiseptic and cozy attitude comes under merciless assault in the modern horror film, which, as Philip Brophy puts it, "tends to play not so much on the broad fear of Death, but more precisely on the fear of one's own body, of how one controls and relates to it."[13] In the words of Sargeant, "These films emphasize a brutal estrangement envisioned through the loss of control over the body, which becomes both unwitting source and victim to the horror."[14]

Cinema scholars have been quick to pick up on this fact, and have frequently referenced Julia Kristeva's well-known theory of "abjection" to aid in analyzing the horror film. Crane summarizes this theory as follows: "The abject are those objects, oftentimes bodily detritus, that desecrate our narcissistic mirage of self by effacing the boundary between myself and that which is not 'I.' The abject provides proof that our idealized portraits of pristine flesh and whole egos are, unfortunately, nothing more than brittle fantasies."(15)

Roszak, in a perceptive comment on the types of things that tend to horrify us, lists a number of elements that commonly play into discussions of abjection:

> Consider for a moment: since we were children, what have we been taught to regard as the quintessential image of loathing and disgust? What is it our horror literature and science fiction haul in whenever they seek to make our skin crawl? Anything alive, mindless, and gooey . . . anything sloppy, slobbering, liquescent, smelly, slimy, gurgling, putrescent, mushy, grubby . . . things amoeboid or fungoid that stick and cling, that creep and seep and grow . . . things that have the feel or spit or shit, snot or piss, sweat or pus or blood. . . . In a word, anything *organic*, and as messy as birth, death, and decay.(16)

It is very organicity, then, the fact of our fleshly existence, that horrifies us, for this carnal part of us lies outside our ability to manage or control and thus reminds us that we are not exclusively ethereal egos ensconced in positions of invulnerability and dominion. Our bodies in their entirety therefore constitute one of the major instances of the abject.

The modern horror film excels at playing upon this horror reaction. Jerslev goes so far as to say that all such films may be understood as different representations of "the fantasy of abjection":

> The abundance of fragmented bodies in the new horror film and the flow of filth issuing from the body's inner parts in images of blood and bowels, of the dissolution of differences between the subject and object—represented, for example, in the often occurring theme of cannibalism in the genre—of the dissolution of differences between

> inside and outside represented by an abundance of symbolizations of the womb; all these genre defining, or splatter film subgenre defining, images can be understood as different representations of the fantasy of abjection. This is one of the reasons, I will contend, why these films are so sickening and yet so fascinating. Because signifiers of abjection affect a basic condition of subjectivity, the complicated, profoundly ambiguous experience of a yearning for, and yet the dread of, fusion as well as separation.[17]

In view of our ultimate topic here, which, the reader will recall, is a spiritual reading of Romero's zombie trilogy, it is of no small importance that Kristeva identifies the ultimate object of abjection as the *corpse*. The corpse, she emphasizes, is a body without a soul, i.e., a body with the entire contents of the personal identity emptied out. In contrast to the "normal" state of things in which the ego constantly "casts off" unwanted products, both mental and physical, in order to retain its sense of walled-in security, in the case of a corpse it is the ego itself that has been cast off. In the words of Kristeva, "It is no longer I who expel. 'I' is expelled."[18] Cinema scholar Barbara Creed picks up on this when she points out that "the horror film abounds in images of abjection, foremost of which is the corpse, whole and mutilated, followed by an array of bodily wastes such as blood, vomit, saliva, sweat, tears and putrefying flesh."[19] Jerslev becomes even more specific when she points out that in Romero's zombie films, the disgusting appearances of the zombies, combined with their cannibalistic appetites, "are . . . nauseating because they insistently *construct the entire body as an abject*. Thus they point toward subjectivity as a fragile illusion."[20]

It is here that we may narrow our focus and turn toward the specific figure of the zombie, and more specifically toward the zombie as portrayed by Romero. For the zombie in Romero's living dead films is nothing more nor less than an animated, shambling corpse that roams the world seeking to devour the flesh of the living. As such, it assaults the viewer's sense of integrity as a stable subject in the most shocking possible fashion by presenting him or her with a literal embodiment of corpse-horror.

II. THE DEAD WALK

The plot of the Living Dead trilogy is by now well known, at least among horror fans and students of cinema history. In the first film, *Night of the Living Dead,* for reasons that ultimately remain obscure, the bodies of the recently deceased begin to come to life and lumber through the countryside of the eastern United States in search of warm human flesh to devour. To make matters worse, the condition is communicable: if someone is bitten by a zombie and remains sufficiently intact to be mobile, he or she will soon rise to become one of their number. The majority of the plot centers around seven people who barricade themselves inside a farmhouse and try to ride out the crisis during a single night of horror. In the end, they all die—the last of them, ironically, by means of a bullet shot by a sheriff's deputy who mistakes this final survivor for one of the zombies.

Dawn of the Dead follows a similar plotline but moves the story further ahead in the timeline of the zombie apocalypse. The societal order that seemed to have been restored at the end of the first film is now nowhere apparent. SWAT teams battle zombies in low-income tenements and drunken rednecks with rifles pick off zombies in open fields for the sheer fun of it, while in the background television commentators argue over the meaning of and proper response to the crisis. The plot centers upon four people—two SWAT team members, a helicopter pilot, and a television station employee—who escape from the chaos in a helicopter and hole up in an abandoned shopping mall, where they revel in a consumerist paradise while the zombies shuffle around the other parts of the mall wearing glazed and forlorn expressions. The film concludes with a marauding gang of bikers putting an end to this dubious paradise, after which only two of the main characters escape alive (again via the helicopter), the other two having succumbed to the zombie plague.

Day of the Dead takes place still further into this imagined future, at a time when, as far as the characters and the viewer can know, only a dozen humans are left alive. These unhappy survivors reside in an underground military bunker where three of them—scientists—spend their time conducting experiments on the zombies to see if there is any way to reverse the zombification process or domesticate those who have already become zombies. The other survivors consist of a helicopter pilot, a radio operator, and several soldiers. As in the first two films, the human characters spend most of their time arguing violently with each other and even physically threatening each other (thus raising the question of whether the human race is morally superior to the zombies) while the zombies press in, both literally and figuratively, upon the perimeter of their world. The film ends with nearly everybody dying in spectacularly violent ways, some at the hands of their fellow humans, others at the hands (and in the jaws) of the zombies who eventually overrun the compound. Three people—a scientist, the pilot, and radio man—escape the carnage by flying away to a tropical island where they will presumably spend the rest of their days enjoying perpetual safety, sunlight, and solitude.

One notices immediately that all the elements of body-horror that have already been discussed feature prominently in these films. Consider first the issue of bodily control. S. S. Prawer has described the zombie or living dead motif as being founded upon "the fear that when the brain has ceased to function and the heart has ceased to beat, the tissues of the body might still be able to go on performing purposive and destructive actions."[(21)] In keeping with this, Mikita Brottman places a loss of bodily control at the top of the list of taboos whose violation creates a sense of horror in *Night of the Living Dead*:

> The first taboo to be broken is that of bodily control. The zombies stumble and drool in their clumsy quest for human flesh, often with intestines spilling out or broken limbs dangling. Brains splatter against the walls; zombies collapse groaning to the ground. The human body—even your own body—is out of control, and you're no longer able to understand or relate to it.[(22)]

Sargeant points out that Romero zeroes in on this fear by actually showing the breakage that occurs in relationships when someone becomes a zombie. "The zombies," he writes, "were once friends and relatives. In each of Romero's zombie films there is a sequence in which one of the protagonists undergoes the zombification process."[23] In other words, anyone, even your dearest loved ones—even you—may be transformed into one of these flesh-eating monsters despite all possible exertions of will-power to resist it. The prospect is disturbing and provocative, and is made even more so by the fact that the motif of rebellious bodies moves on to newer heights of fancy as the trilogy, not to mention the zombie film subgenre in general, progresses. Robert Hood, in writing about Romero's seminal influence on the cinematic portrayal of zombies, points out a direct link between Romero's innovations and the common motif in later zombie movies of individual body parts retaining animation. "In the end," he says, "even bits of zombies—arms, heads and, in the case of [director Peter] Jackson's *Braindead,* stomach and intestines—are able to maintain a 'life' of their own. This is the human body—our material being—engaging in a sheer act of rebellion."[24]

Rose London has written that the zombie "represents our ancient fear that a necromancer will resurrect our body for his purposes."[25] In commenting on London's assertion, Prawer notes that "gifted film-makers have been able to use the conventions [of the horror film] as a kind of grid against which to draw their own rather different picture—as something to be at once alluded to and subverted."[26] Thus it is that Romero—definitely a gifted filmmaker—compounds and alters the conventional horror of zombies by instead representing his zombies as being essentially purposeless and free roaming. "In Romero's film," writes Prawer, "the dead have no zombie-master to direct them, and they are raised, not by voodoo, but rather by an (unexplained) scientific accident."[27] Tom Mes amplifies:

> In all previous films dealing with zombies, these creatures had been innocent people, revived and controlled by their powerful master to do his evil bidding. More often than not, the zombies were actually used not as weapons but as a work force, providing cheap labor for a rich tycoon. . . . This was the blueprint on which these films were based, finding its source in voodoo mythology. *Night of the*

> *Living Dead* dispensed with all of this. In a radical break with tradition, and seeing the full potential of using living dead in a horror film, Romero made zombies pure evil, out to eat the flesh of the living and controlled by nothing but their own instinct.[28]

Romero's zombies are thus true corpses, empty shells, simply the re-animated dead, and not tools being used for some outside purpose. As such, they assault the viewer's sense of identity by presenting him or her with the threatening sight of that "ultimate in abjection." "The first vision of death is physical," says an article at Monstrous.com, an online resource devoted to cataloguing information about monsters of all kinds. "Therefore, to confront a zombie is to be reminded of our own mortality . . . The zombie is the embodiment of the insatiable tyranny of mortality, its rotting face and shuffling implacability represents [sic] a potent symbol for the horror of death."[29] R. H. W. Dillard offers a classic analysis of *Night of the Living Dead* in his book *Horror Films,* where he reminds the reader of the ancient "fear of the dead and particularly of the known dead, of dead kindred." He quotes a passage from Anthony Masters' *The Natural History of the Vampire* that speaks of the meticulous rituals that have traditionally surrounded the burial—and also the warding off—of the recently dead and claims that Romero's film "is almost a reenactment of these rituals in reverse. The unburied recent dead stalk the landscape seeking the flesh of the living. . . . The ancient fear is unleashed on the characters in the film and on the audience with a force that only savage violence can repel."[30] In a bit of poetic symmetry that reverses Dillard's point about the effect of these films but still highlights the corpse horror they embody, Bryan Stone writes that the "assaults on the human body heralded by George Romero's *Night of the Living Dead* . . . provide the new body language, the iconography, the communal rituals, if you will, for disposing of bodies that had been quietly kept out of sight, removed hygienically from the public eye, whose decaying flesh had been covered with leftover sacred deodorants but never buried."[31] Whichever way one views the living dead trilogy—as representing a reversal or a new version of traditional corpse-burial rituals—the fact remains that the films present the viewer with the sight of the corpse, the ultimate abject, the empty shell of the body, returning to animation (but not to life in the commonly accepted sense) and behaving in overtly menacing ways.

This brings us to yet another of Romero's innovations: Not only did he confront audiences with animated corpses, but he introduced another motif into the zombie film by presenting his zombies as cannibals, and it is this motif, even more than those confrontational corpses, which plays masterfully upon the primal fear of losing one's personal identity.

III. THE DEAD EAT

"Flesh becomes meat" in the modern horror film, said Cynthia Freeland, and nowhere is this truer than in films about cannibalism. Film critic Lew Brighton even referred to *Night of the Living Dead* and its progeny, such as *The Texas Chainsaw Massacre* (another horror film dealing with cannibalism), as "meat movies."(32) Walter Kendrick has remarked that the financial success of *Night of the Living Dead* "seemed to mark a turning point in horror by displaying not only severed limbs and spilled innards, but also cannibal zombies munching them."(33) Zombies were already an established presence in the world of the horror film circa 1968. Indeed, as Hood notes, "Cinematic animated corpses have been a source of fascination ever since the earliest days of film." Movies such as *White Zombie* (1932) and *I Walked with a Zombie* (1943) are generally considered classics.(34) But in the words of Mikita Brottman, "What's special about Romero's zombies . . . is their cannibalistic appetite. Romero is almost entirely responsible for the now-familiar incarnation of the zombie as ghoulish cannibal, as bloodthirsty anthropophage who adds to his numbers by feeding on living human flesh."(35)

The significance of this fact for the argument of hand emerges when we pause to consider the act of eating itself, and to acknowledge that food of any kind serves more than just a nutritional function. Roland Barthes, in his essay "Toward a Psychosociology of Contemporary Food Consumption," asks the question, "What is food?" and answers that in addition to being "a collection of products that can be used for statistical or nutritional studies," food "is also, and at the same time, a system of communication, a body of images, a protocol of usages, situations, and behavior. . . . [F]ood sums up and transmits a situation; it constitutes an information; it signifies. . . . One could say that an entire 'world' (social environment) is present in and signified by food."(36) In other words, food is a cultural sign, a system of communication, and the act of choosing and eating certain foods, as well as the *manner* in which ones chooses and eats them, expresses values and meanings. We may thus ask ourselves what is the meaning or message expressed by the act of cannibalism.

An answer comes to us by synthesizing the ideas of three separate authors. First, we see that anthropologist Anna Meigs has called attention to what is perhaps the most unique aspect of food. "Food," she writes, "has a distinctive feature, one that sets it off from the rest of material culture: it is ingested, it is eaten, it goes inside." Moreover, food's social nature—the fact that it is commonly prepared by one person for another to eat—makes it "a particularly apt vehicle for symbolizing and expressing ideas about the relationship of self and other."(37) Next, we may recall Jerslev's contention that "the dissolution of differences between the subject and object . . . between inside and outside" is frequently represented in the horror genre via the motif of cannibalism. She expands this by asserting that cannibalism "signifies the ultimate dissolution of even the mere thought of distinguishing between the body's interior and exterior. Cannibalism denies the skin of the other as a border; it disorganizes distinctions, and the differences separating 'I' from 'you.'"(38)

Finally, we see that Anne Marie Oleson has combined Meigs's and Jerslev's positions and given the definitive statement of the matter:

> The question of the boundary between the One and the Other is raised with eating and with the meal. Eating presupposes a clear distinction between the subject eating and the object being eaten, but the *act* of eating abolishes the distinction. The subject incorporates the object, the object stays in the subject and mixes with it, thereby obliterating the subject/object distinction.

> Food and meals in art can basically be seen as metaphors for drawing and crossing boundaries. So can cannibalism. But cannibalism makes a difference. Taking part in a meal means eating *of* the same but not *the* same, and in particular—not eating one another. You do not eat the person you are eating with
>
> . . . I believe that cannibalism . . . theorize[s] that the boundary between the "inside" and the "outside," between the One and the Other, is not stable, not natural, not "God-given," and that—in a conceptual sense—it never has been.(39)

The meaning of cannibalism as a cultural sign is thus apparent: cannibalism signifies the fragility of the self, its permeability and susceptibility to being fused with the other. It is a potent metaphor for the breakdown of the stable subject, for it shows the subject, as represented by its externalized manifestation in the physical body, being consumed by another of the same kind.

Oleson also points out a further fact that assumes great importance in our current investigation: "It is natural to eat but it is civilized (or cultural) to take part in a meal, because in the process you refrain from eating one another. Thus cannibalism metaphorizes the break down of civilization, the dissolution of culture into nature."(40) Romero explicitly works this theme into his trilogy by framing his zombies as representations of the human animal reduced to its most primal level. These creatures, as he repeatedly tells us through the dialogue he puts in the mouths of his characters, are simply human beings, minus all the cultural and civilized trappings.

The picture that emerges from such a portrayal is not pretty. Waller calls Romero's zombies "diseased, instinct-driven automatons"(41) and contrasts them with another undead creature, the suave and cultured Dracula. In doing so, he finds zombies all the more horrible for their animal-like behavior. "The major distinction," he writes,

> between the living dead and the vampires . . . is, of course, the fact that the creatures in *Night of the Living Dead* eat warm human flesh, a fact that Romero graphically

> records and never allows us to forget. The feeding habits of the living dead have nothing in common with the sexually charged, mutually pleasurable act of bloodsucking. . . . Romero's living dead tear at their food and devour it like starving animals to whom all of existence is only a matter of hunting food and eating.[42]

Romero's zombies, then, eat for no purpose. They eat simply to eat. Jerslev contrasts the ideas of anthropologist Peggy Reeves Sanday, who detects a religious, cosmogonic purpose in ritual tribal cannibalism, with Romero's portrayal of the act, and draws a grim conclusion:

> With Romero, the zombies are not just primitive cannibals: they are inhuman, cannibalistic machines. . . . Contrary to Sanday's interpretation of cannibalism one cannot say that there is a religious subtext to the zombies' cannibalism, that flesh thus transforms into spirit, or that the cannibalistic incorporation aims at preserving the souls and the power of the dead. One cannot talk about regeneration or cannibalism symbolizing the drama of constituting subjectivity. In Romero's zombie trilogy there is, contrary to Sanday's conceptualization of cannibalism, only excessive gluttony controlled by nothing but pure instinct. Thus, the zombies represent the human reduced to mere bestiality.[43]

That this idea is borne out in the actual films themselves is easy to verify. In *Dawn of the Dead,* in a famous line of dialogue, a commentator on television describes the zombies as "pure, motorized instinct." Another frustrated commentator says, "They kill for one reason: They kill for food. They *eat* their victims. . . . That's what keeps them going." But in fact, as we discover in *Day of the Dead*—the last and by far the most reflective of the three films (to the point of talkiness, some would say)—the flesh the zombies consume does *not* keep them going. In fact, it apparently does nothing for them at all, other than to satisfy their instinctual urge to consume. In a key scene, Sarah, the scientist who is destined to escape to the tropical island with her two friends, finds the leader of the scientific team, a researcher named Logan (known more commonly to everyone else, even to his fellow scientists, as "Frankenstein"), working in his laboratory with a zombie strapped to a table. He has opened the creature's abdomen and severed all the vital connections, and yet the creature still retains animation. Moreover, it is still hungry, as Logan demonstrates by placing his fingers near its mouth. The creature snaps at the fingers with its teeth, prompting Logan to exclaim to Sarah with excitement, "You see, it *wants* me! It wants food, but it has no stomach. It can take no nourishment from what it ingests. It's working on *instinct*, Sarah—deep, dark, primordial instinct."

Logan then turns to a chalk board covered with diagrams and labels indicating a study of the human brain, and continues his lecture: "Decomposition occurs first in the frontal lobes, the neo-cortex, and next in the limbic system, the middle brain. But the core, the core is the last thing to be attacked by the decay. It's the R-complex, Sarah, that central bit of prehistoric jelly that we inherited from the reptiles." The obvious implication is that these monsters represent what we humans really are at our most fundamental level, behind our forebrains, beneath our cultural veneers. When stripped to this primal level, we are nothing but murderous, cannibalistic eating machines, and our drive to ingest warm human flesh is all the more horrific and pathetic because it is thoroughly pointless.

This identification of the zombies with living humans is first articulated in *Dawn of the Dead* when Fran, one of the lead characters, stands watching the zombies mill around the shopping mall and suddenly feels compelled to ask, "What the hell *are* they?" to which Peter replies matter-of-factly, "They're us, that's all." This theme, which receives only passing mention in *Dawn* (although it receives significant graphic reinforcement via the scenes of the zombies stumbling through the mall accompanied by the voiceover comments of "experts" on television who make it clear that the zombies are pathetic, low-grade parodies of full human beings)—this theme comes to the fore in *Day*. Some time after the above-described laboratory scene, *Day* shows another scientist trying to convince one of the captured zombies to eat military-issued "beef treats." The creature refuses, preferring human flesh instead. Logan then appears on the scene and offers the requisite philosophical justification for his attempts to reenculturate the zombies, claiming that even though they do not eat for nourishment, it is necessary to satisfy the urge. "You see, Sarah," he says, echoing his earlier point, "*they are us*. They are the extensions of us. They are the same animal simply functioning less perfectly."

To sum up: The cannibalism in Romero's zombie trilogy attacks the viewer's sense of secure subjecthood in two ways, first by depicting a literal breach of the barrier between self and other as self *becomes* other by means of physical ingestion, and second by graphically illustrating the dissolution of culture into nature by framing the zombies as the embodiment of humankind's primitive urges. Dillard states it well when he writes that "the characters in *Night of the Living Dead* [and by extension in the other two films of the trilogy] lose all identity—they become food, or walking dead flesh, or simply fuel for a fire."(44)

There is yet a third way in which the cannibalism motif attacks the viewer's sense of self: by the simple fact of showing the human body broken, torn, and opened up for its insides to be revealed, the cannibalistic violence in the zombie trilogy reduces the body from a sleek and whole object possessing an innate, healthy integrity to a mass of disconnected organs and tissues. Recall Freeland's words: "It is common to witness gross bodily dismemberments, piles of internal organs, numerous corpses in stages of decay, headless bodies, knives or chain saws slashing away at flesh, and general orgies of mayhem. In these films, flesh becomes meat, the inside becomes outside, blood pours out, skin is stripped off, viscera exposed, heads detached."(45) What she is talking about is nothing less than a literal deconstruction of the body into its constituent parts. Jerslev uses the fascinating and appropriate term "organ body" to describe this deconstructed body, and writes at great length about its nature and meaning. The organ body, she says, is

> a body without skin—metaphorically as well as literally—a non-organized amorphous mass of biological matter without gender distinction, a body that discloses

> interior substances for which there is, so to speak, nothing exterior. . . . When [the zombies] skin a human being and tear out the bowels, the image frames disclose the gory interior normally hidden beneath the armour of the skin. The killing is not the end in itself, it is a means of getting under the victims' skin. In the scenes where the zombies kill the human beings, Romero is thus staging the idea of the body as disconnected organs and pure soft parts.[(46)]
>
> [Because late twentieth-century Western culture placed such great emphasis on the body] as the signifier of the well-defined, psychologically delimited, self-conscious subject, then the organ body represents the destruction of this very idea of the subject. The organ body signifies the amorphous, the floating, an abject without boundaries, the place that has turned inside out and is turning subject into object.[(47)]

In other words, by deconstructing the body these films deconstruct the subject as well, the personal identity whose perceived nature is inextricably bound up with notions of the body's perceived health and wholeness.[(48)]

In view of a segue to discussing the religious or spiritual dimension of Romero's zombie trilogy, we will do well to note that in Jerslev's opinion, the cannibalism in these films does not merely *reduce* human bodies to lumps of organic materials, it represents a veritable *transformation*. "Violence," she writes, "is not an end in itself" in these movies, "but a means of staging metamorphosis. . . . By means of the disgusting images of zombies killing and tearing people apart to eat them, it becomes very clear that the living human beings are nothing but meat to the zombies, and thus they metamorphose in front of our eyes into muscles, bones, and gory intestines."[(49)] It is significant in this regard that Marina Warner, in an article about the pervasive Western cultural fascination with zombies, says that whereas zombies "used to be primarily victims of voodoo masters," today the word zombie "has become an existential term . . . a deathly modern variation on the age-old theme of metamorphosis."[(50)] She is speaking about the idea of metamorphosis as a transformation of the self, as found in, for example, theories and doctrines of soul transmigration. And while she is thinking primarily in sociocritical terms when she mentions *Night of the Living Dead* as a significant movie in this regard, her point is equally applicable to our discussion of the metamorphosis of the human body in the zombie film from an integrated whole to a steaming, bloody pile of disconnected parts.

Brophy, for his part, seems to find something almost religious about this metamorphic portrayal of humanity's visceral organic nature. He virtually crows,

> Forget the wonders of modern science and advanced technology—we are more overwhelmed by our very gizzards! The screen body in contemporary horror is thus a true place of physicality: a fountain of fascination, a bounty of bodily contact. If there is any mysticism left in the genre, it is that our own insides constitute a fifth dimension; an unknowable world, an incomprehensible darkness.[51]

If he is right about the mystical potentialities inherent in the act of dwelling upon our innards, if he is correct in believing that the interior of the body constitutes a remaining repository of mysticism in the horror genre, then surely we may speculate about the way it interacts with other, more direct expressions of spirituality.

IV. "HE VISITED A CURSE ON US": THE SPIRITUAL ANGLE

There are several possible angles from which to investigate the spiritual aspect of the Living Dead trilogy, and of these a number have been well explored. For instance, there is the widely noted fact that traditional religious values and rituals are portrayed as useless, even as a positive danger, in *Night of the Living Dead*. The character of Barbara insists on kneeling in prayer at her father's grave at the start of the film, despite her brother Johnny's cynical impatience. When Johnny is killed by a zombie and Barbara escapes to the nearby farmhouse, it seems that her faith is going to be rewarded and Johnny's impiety punished. But in fact nothing of the sort takes place. "Johnny's suffering," writes Crane, "is very limited when compared to that which Barbara must endure."[52] She spends most of the film locked up in a catatonic stupor, and when she emerges from it near the conclusion to help fight off the zombie horde, she is dragged out of the house to her doom by none other than Johnny, who has returned from the dead to claim her. In the words of Waller, Barbara is "clearly the character who most fully believes in the values of tradition and religion," but her "faith only seems to make her awakening to her dilemma that much more rude and catastrophic."[53]

Night also highlights the fact that traditional emotional attachments to the bodies of dead loved ones must be relinquished in the name of safety. "No, you're right," says a medical doctor in a televised report when a news anchor points out that the recommended course of immediate action to take with all dead bodies during this crisis—cremation—does not allow time for funerals. "It doesn't give them time to make funeral arrangements. The bodies must be carried to the street and burned. They must be burned immediately. Soak them with gasoline and burn them. The bereaved will just have to forego the dubious comforts that a funeral service will give. They're just dead flesh, and dangerous." As it was with Barbara, so it is here. Dutiful observance of religious rituals will not offer protection, and may in fact lead to harm. The same theme carries over into *Dawn*, where television commentators offer similar messages to largely unreceptive audiences.

In addition to the trilogy's attack on the efficacy of traditional religious observances, there is the further fact that these films deal explicitly with many of the images of abjection we studied earlier. Creed observes that "various sub-genres of the horror film seem to correspond to religious categories of abjection" and points out that "cannibalism, a religious abomination, is central to the 'meat' movie," in whose company she names *Night of the Living Dead*. "The corpse as abomination," she writes, "becomes the abject of ghoul and zombie movies."[54]

However, the two themes—images of abjection and the uselessness of traditional religion—are only two possible angles from which the religious or spiritual aspect of the trilogy might be discussed. For my own purposes, I want to take a different tack by focusing specifically on two speeches delivered by two different characters, one in *Dawn* and one in *Day,* that in my view constitute the spiritual heart of the films. Both speeches offer spiritual interpretations of the meaning of the zombie plague, and they linger in the viewer's memory long after other possible explanations have faded.

It is important to note beforehand that these speeches have such lasting impact largely because the films of the Living Dead series deliberately subvert the various explanations offered by the films' scientists and other authority figures to account for the phenomenon of the dead returning to a semblance of life. In *Night of the Living Dead,* the only explanation offered for the zombie plague is the possible influence of a strange radiation that has accompanied a space probe recently returned from Venus. But this explanation, as Waller notes, is superfluous. "To assert," he writes, "that 'mysterious radiation' in some unexplained way causes the dead to roam the land in search of human flesh is finally little better than no explanation at all (especially since this is a quasi-official explanation and therefore likely in *Night of the Living Dead* to be a lie, distortion, or cover-up)."[(55)] The parenthetical comment refers to the fact that in these films, institutionalized authority is invariably portrayed in a dismal light. The sheriff and his men in *Night of the Living Dead* are brutal and incompetent; as mentioned earlier, one of them kills Ben, the protagonist, when Ben is mistaken for a zombie. In *Dawn,* one of the SWAT team members goes on a racist rampage in a Puerto Rican tenement and starts shooting residents indiscriminately, and the general manager of a television station insists on keeping a list of defunct rescue stations scrolling across the bottom of the screen because it attracts viewers. In *Day* the military men are all brutal, vulgar, racist, and sexist, and their commander, Captain Rhodes, is a bona fide psychotic. The head of the scientific team, Dr. Logan—"Frankenstein"—is dangerously unbalanced, as we learn when we discover that his reenculturation experiments on the zombies are motivated primarily by his sick, repressed hatred for his parents. A lack of trust in official explanations from authority figures is thus well-founded within the world of these films, and the door is left wide open for a more spiritually-oriented explanation to enter and have the greatest lasting impact.

Appropriately enough, that is precisely what happens. The first character to offer a spiritual explanation is Peter in *Dawn of the Dead*. We might note in passing that Peter shares the name of one of the biblical apostles, and that Saint Peter himself delivered a brief apocalyptic message in the second of the two New Testament letters attributed to him, and also a famous quasi-apocalyptic speech in the Book of Acts after he and the other apostles had been infused with the Holy Spirit.(56) Appropriately, *Dawn*'s Peter delivers an explanation of the zombie plague that is short, apocalyptic, and to the point. Immediately after telling Fran that the zombies "are us, that's all," he muses, almost to himself, "There's no more room in hell." When Fran's boyfriend, Stephen, asks him what he means, Peter replies, "Something my granddaddy used to tell us. You know Makumba?" When Stephen shakes his head, Peter explains: "Voodoo. Granddad was a priest in Trinidad. He used to tell us, 'When there's no more room in hell, the dead will walk the earth.'"

This line has become a favorite among fans of the film. Although it is brief and receives no further comment, it offers a poetically powerful explanation for the reason behind the zombie plague, and one that obviously goes well beyond hackneyed science fiction explanations like "radiation from outer space." If we take Peter's statement literally, as a valid account of things, then we find that when we contemplate the zombies lumbering around a shopping mall or tearing a person to pieces or gnawing on human entrails we are actually contemplating the physical reality of hell itself. The zombies are hell's overflow; they are simply bringing hell to earth. Hood calls Peter's words "the best explanation (though it is a non-explanation) for the 'living dead' phenomenon."(57) It is a non-explanation because it is merely asserted without clarification or evidence to back it up, but it is the *best* explanation because it carries such a powerful emotional charge. That is, it simply *feels* like the best explanation for what's happening.

Or at least it feels this way until the character of John delivers an even longer and more weighty apocalyptic speech in *Day of the*

Dead. John, too, shares the name of a biblical apostle, and it is appropriate that Saint John is perhaps best known as the supposed author of that supreme Christian apocalyptic text, the Book of Revelation. Romero, incidentally, almost seems to be daring us to notice the shared name. *Day of the Dead* begins with four characters—John, Billy, Sarah, and Miguel—flying over Fort Myers, Florida in search of human survivors. Sarah says she wants to set down to use the megaphone. Billy, hearing this plan, utters his favorite curse—"Jesus, Mary, and Joseph!"—and is cut off by Sarah, who clips the end of this biblical triad of names by saying, "Take us down, John."

John delivers his speech on an outer edge of the underground bunker where the surviving humans dwell. Whereas the others prefer to live in the relative safety of the actual compound, John and Billy have made their home out in the cave, where they have decorated a trailer home to look like a tropical paradise. It is in the open area behind this trailer, in a "back yard" adorned with lawn chairs and umbrella tables, that John gives Sarah his own speculative explanation for the zombie plague. First, he holds up a book he has been reading and tells her,

> Hey, you know what all they keep down here in this cave? Man, they got the books and the records of the top five hundred companies. They got the defense department budget down here, and they got the negative for all your favorite movies. They got microfilm with tax return and newspaper stories. They got immigration records and census records, and they got official accounts of all the wars and plane crashes and volcano eruptions and earthquakes and fires and floods, and all the other disasters that interrupted the flow of things in the good old U.S. of A.[58]

With these words, John establishes the military bunker as a microcosm of modern civilization. Everything that existed in the upper world still exists down here, but in condensed form. John's subsequent words may thus be interpreted as a diagnosis of human civilization itself. He goes on to tell Sarah that all this obsessive record keeping is a waste of time, since nobody will ever have the chance to see the records, and that the bunker with its treasure trove of civilization's recorded lore is nothing but "a great big, fourteen mile tombstone, with an epitaph on it that nobody gonna bother to read." In light of this, he asks, what good can Sarah and the other scientists possibly do with their "whole new set of graphs and charts and things"?

Sarah listens with a weary and glazed expression, as if his words are hurting her, but she remains silent as he forges on toward the heart of what he has to say. "I'm gonna tell you what else," he says. "Yeah, I'm gonna tell you what else: you ain't ever gonna figure it out, just like they never figured out why the stars are where they're at. It ain't mankind's job to figure that stuff out. So what you're doing is a waste of time, Sarah. And time is all we got left, you know." We may validly take these words as the ultimate statement of the futility of all attempts to explain the zombie plague. In comparing such attempts to the age-old quest to figure out "why the stars are where they're at," John is asserting that the reason for the zombie plague is, and will always remain, as mysterious and incomprehensible as the reason for the existence of the universe at all. The question of the plague's true meaning resides on a level with all those other questions of ultimate meaning and purpose that categorically elude human understanding. In this portion of his speech, John offers a compact version of what the previous films have already provided; that is, he clears the air of possible rational explanations, thus making way for his listeners, both Sarah and the viewing audience, to experience the deepest possible emotional impact from his forthcoming spiritual explanation.

After speculating briefly that the few people still living might be able to restart human civilization on a better footing—a footing founded chiefly upon the imperative *not* to dig out the records of the previous civilization—John takes advantage of the opening he has given himself and offers his own explanation for the catastrophe, in words that echo and amplify Peter's speech:

> Hey, you want to put some kind of explanation down here before you leave? Here's one as good as any you're likely to find: We been punished by the creator. He

> visited a curse on us, so we might get a look at what hell was like. Maybe he didn't want to see us blow ourselves up and put a big hole in his sky. Maybe he just wanted to show us he was still the boss man. Maybe he figure we was getting too big for our britches, trying to figure his shit out.

The three possible reasons John offers here at the end of his speech—that God did not want to see the human race destroy the earth, that he wanted to reassert his authority, and that he wanted to punish humans for seeking forbidden knowledge—are all subordinate to John's central statement that the zombie plague is God's doing, that it is a curse directly caused by God's intervention, and that the ultimate point, whatever the secondary reasons, is to give humans a glimpse of what hell is like. Thus, this final movie in the zombie trilogy casts a retroactive religious reading back over the other two.

Waller, writing of *Night of the Living Dead,* states the matter well:

> Romero emphasizes . . . the utter lack of supernatural assistance for man. . . . As Romero will insist much more completely in *Dawn of the Dead,* there is no hope of being rescued by outside agencies. In *Night of the Living Dead,* no God, father, or president, no military, scientific, political, or religious form of authority guarantees or in any way promotes the survival of the living. (59)

If this point is emphasized even more completely in *Dawn* than *Night,* then it receives its definitive statement in *Day,* both in the fact of John's speech and in the fact that the humans in this film are, so far as we know, the last living people on earth. God does not help. He may have in fact caused the zombie plague himself, as an act of divine retribution. And there are no outside people *left* to help.

And so we arrive at the heart of the trilogy's spiritual message: Humans are bereft, with no outside agencies left to aid them—certainly not God, who appears likely to continue displaying his wrathful face for a very long time to come—and we must face this nightmarish world of ravenous walking corpses without the possibility of redemption, without the possibility of being saved. Even John, the trilogy's arch-diagnostician of spiritual meaning, contents himself with merely explicating the (possible) spiritual dimension of the zombie plague without offering any kind of hope that it might eventually end. As we have seen, his recommended course of action is simply to flee from the whole mess and seek a life of private enjoyment on a remote island.[(60)] "Meaning," Hood writes,

> "can now only come through the struggle to remain human (and all that that means), not through the possibility of success."[(61)] Writing of *Night of the Living Dead* but making a point that applies equally to all three films, Sargeant says, "*Night of the Living Dead* should, were it a conventional horror film, have recalled the mythic themes of danger and salvation, but there is no end to the path here, no promised escape and, most importantly, no cavalry racing to the rescue. A bloody death is the only possible outcome."[(62)]

The situation recalls Roszak's diagnosis of the post-industrial era as the first in history in which spiritual alienation has been divorced from the possibility of anything better. "Until our own time," he writes,

> alienation has always stood in the shadow of salvation; it has been the falling rhythm of the soul's full cycle. It carried with it implications of transcendence. Ours is the first culture so totally secularized that we descend into the nihilist state without the conviction, without the experienced awareness that any other exists.[(63)]

The world of the Living Dead trilogy is similarly dreadful, for there is no real escape or salvation to be had. Even the escape to a tropical island at the end of *Day* still resides in the shadow of ultimate failure and death, and God—to repeat—who is the ultimate Power in charge of the whole universe, to whom one might otherwise expect to turn for solace, has proved to be the causative supernatural force behind the whole nightmarish scenario.

Roszak, not incidentally, was writing about the post-industrial world in terms of the Gnostic motif of the fallenness of the cosmos, and it is here that our exploration curls back upon itself and touches its own earlier parts. For the Gnostics viewed the material world, and thus the life of physically incarnate existence, as a nightmare. The typical Gnostic attitude toward the physical body was one of terror and loathing, since in the Gnostic view it is the body with its manifold carnal desires, needs, and impulses that chains one's true spiritual self to this world of darkness (i.e., the world of matter, the cosmos) and endarkens what would otherwise be a clear spiritual perception. In the eyes of the Gnostic, there is no lower hell than physical existence.

Recalling this, one cannot help recalling as well the horror of the body that occupied our attention earlier, when I argued that the Living Dead films attack the sense of secure subjecthood in four ways via their attacks upon the body: first, by depicting the body as an animated corpse, an organic nightmare that is out of control; second, by portraying a symbolic breach of the subject-object barrier via the literal act of one body consuming another in an act of cannibalism; third, by portraying these cannibalistic eating-machines as nothing more nor less than the human animal reduced to its most fundamental level of operation; and fourth, by transforming the body from a sleek and whole entity into a mass of bloody, disconnected parts. In the current section of the paper, I have argued that the overweening spiritual message of the Living Dead trilogy, established via Peter's and John's speeches, is that humans have no grounds for holding to a hope in some kind of supernatural deliverance or redemption; that there is no escape from this world of suffering into another, better world; and that the zombies are a literal depiction of the nature of hell.

Putting this all together, we arrive at a reading of the Living Dead films as a kind of Gnostic nightmare in which the world of flesh is solely about consuming and being consumed. The human self is always in process of being threatened by awful intrusions upon its sanctity and integrity, and there is no possibility of anyone's ever being saved or finding any solace in the midst of it all, because there is no ultimate metaphysical ground for the human self or for human hope. Organic, embodied life is a horror—the gory iconography of the films makes this abundantly clear—and the subjective, internal aspect of life has no footing, no firm ground, on which to rest and resist the horror of its fleshly connection. God has been revealed as an Old Testament-type deity who, like Yahweh, zealously punishes those who violates the limits he has set, and the punishment in this case appears to be of a permanent nature. There is no possibility of escape. It begins to look as if the final interpretive resting point has turned out to be an attitude of utter nihilism and hopelessness.

V. THE MISSING RAINBOW: THEISM'S INADEQUACY

This is not, however, the *necessary* end of the matter. When faced with the inescapability of this inferno of flesh as depicted in the Living Dead films, one does not have to accept endless horror as the final result. There are other options. For example, one might instead go back over one's assumptions to check for a possible error. This seems a sensible enough move in a situation where there is nothing left to lose.

Something that becomes immediately evident upon reconsideration, something that the reader may have already noticed, is that John's theistic explanation of the zombie plague does not sit entirely well with the horrific hopelessness of the trilogy's overall tenor. If God has indeed brought about the zombie plague as an act of divine punishment, then what is the punitive, which is to say, *corrective* purpose of his act? Instead of appearing on earth as a kind of warning sign combined with a global housecleaning, the zombie plague has led to a total destruction of life and civilization. The motive behind such an act would appear to be not corrective but vindictive. The God who would bring about such a wholesale cataclysm would seem to be a sort of demonic version of the deistic clockmaker-God who sets the universe in motion and then absents himself eternally from its goings-on.

Still another thought occurs: Is there not something

unreasonable about positing the very *existence* of such a God who would unleash a horrific punishment in response to human transgressions and then have nothing further to do with the situation? Upon reflection, it begins to seem as if John's religious reading of the zombie plague, while it may be poetically evocative, and while it may be useful in its emphasis on the spiritual aspect of events, is fundamentally misguided, since the apocalypse portrayed in the Living Dead films inherently lacks anything that would recommend itself to a theistic interpretation. Rather, such an apocalypse seems much more in line with what Charles Derry has described as the horror of "Armageddon-movies" in which cataclysmic events are played out *in the absence of a divine cause*:

> There seems to be a strong relationship between these films and many of the stories in the Bible; for instance, the many plagues sent out to express the wrath of God, or even more dramatically the most archetypal story in the Bible: the flood. Take God away from the flood, and you have a true horror-of-Armageddon movie: suddenly, out of the sky, it begins to rain. What was previously considered a normal aspect of nature turns abnormal when the rain starts acting unlike rain and refuses to stop. The rain attacks and kills everyone; only Noah and his family manage to survive the existential test by working hard to hold tightly to their floating house. Ultimately, a rainbow appears as congratulations and in promise that the existential horror has come to an end. The pattern is exactly like that of *The Birds,* only Hitchcock refuses us the satisfaction of the horror-releasing rainbow.(64)

We can see that not only in tone but also in basic content Derry's words fit startlingly well with what occurs in the Living Dead films: suddenly, the dead start returning to life and attacking the living. What was previously considered a normal aspect of nature (death) turns abnormal when the dead start acting unlike the dead and refuse to stop. The dead attack and kill everyone; only a tiny group of survivors, three in all, survive in the end by escaping to an island (their "floating house," perhaps?). And in perfect contradistinction to the biblical flood story, no "horror-releasing rainbow" appears in the heavens to congratulate these survivors and assure them that the horror is over. Indeed, it seems that the events of these films lend themselves more easily to interpretation in non-theistic terms, and that we must therefore revise our previous reading. But we do not want to dispense entirely with the spiritual angle, since it has proved to be eminently useful. The question thus becomes one of finding a religious or spiritual angle that will make for a better fit with the films and will address their intolerable hopelessness and horror, which, as Derry has pointed out, are actually increased by the absence of divine control.

VI. LEANING EASTWARD: THE CONTEMPLATION OF FOULNESS

The first thing to note is that John's religious interpretation of the zombie plague is overtly Western. Western religions are characterized chiefly by the fact that they are theistic, and more specifically, monotheistic. To reject theism is to reject out-of-hand the mainstream of Western religion. The same cannot be said of Eastern religion, however, which runs the gamut from polytheism to atheism to agnosticism, but which contains nary a trace of the monotheistic emphasis that lies at the heart of its Western counterpart.

One of the things the Western tradition, at least in its mainstream, orthodox manifestations, has always rejected is the idea of *hopelessness*. To name only one obvious example, the extreme pessimism of the biblical book of Ecclesiastes, which contains as piercing a statement of existential despair as can be found anywhere in world literature, stands in vivid contrast to the progressive historical hope of the Jews for a post-mortem resurrection to eternal life instead of a gloomy eternity spent in sheol as predicted in Ecclesiastes. Even within Ecclesiastes itself, one may find expressed a considerable number of conventionally pious and hopeful ideas which many scholars take to be later interpolations intended to mitigate the book's message of despair. It is as if Jewish thought is constitutionally unable to rest with the idea of real, utter hopelessness. Additional examples of this attitude at work in Western religion are easy to come by. We may think of the Jewish hope for a messiah, and the way the Christian tradition has preached that this hope was fulfilled in the person of Jesus of Nazareth. Christianity itself is founded upon an attitude of hope for salvation and immortality based upon Jesus' crucifixion and resurrection. Generally speaking, in the eyes of these paired religious traditions and in Western religion as a whole, an attitude of hopelessness is something to be avoided, resisted, remedied, or otherwise denied.

This contrasts sharply with the explicit approach of some of the Eastern spiritual traditions which actually *embrace* hopelessness, and it is here that we may begin to explore the effectiveness of Eastern religious thought in offering a satisfying spiritual reading of the Living Dead films. One thinks first and foremost of Buddhism in this regard, and of the Buddha's first "noble truth," which teaches that "all life is suffering" or, interpreted differently, "all life is impermanence." To the Buddhist, the idea of "impermanence" refers to the realization that everything in life is fleeting, that there is no firm ground upon which to base one's sense of security, meaning, or identity. The entire phenomenal world, which for the Buddhist includes his or her own physical body and psychological makeup, is constantly shifting, changing, evolving. There is no enduring "essence" to any of it. This truth is the foundation and starting point of Buddhist practice, which takes the form of a rigorous repertoire of psychophysical exercises designed to increase one's experiential realization of this and the other noble truths.

So in a very real sense, the starting point of Buddhist practice is a piercing realization of the fact of existential *hopelessness*. Pema Chödrön, the renowned contemporary Buddhist nun and teacher, has written with clarity about the meaning and value of impermanence and the hopelessness is engenders. "Death and hopelessness," she writes, "provide proper motivation—proper motivation for living an insightful, compassionate life." She says the "experience of complete hopelessness, of completely giving up hope" is

> an important point. This is the beginning of the beginning. Without giving up hope—that there's somewhere better to be, that there's someone better to be—we will never relax with where we are or who we

> are. . . . When we talk about hopelessness and death, we're talking about facing the facts. No escapism. . . . If we totally experience hopelessness, giving up all hope of alternatives to the present moment, we can have a joyful relationship with our lives, an honest, direct relationship, one that no longer ignores the reality of impermanence and death.(65)

Obviously, this contrasts sharply with the Western attitude described above. Chödrön draws a connection between hope and theism on the one hand and hopelessness and nontheism on the other. Theism, she says, is too often based upon a wish for a cosmic "babysitter," someone or something that one can latch onto with an attitude of hopefulness. From the nontheistic perspective, abandoning hope is an act of affirmation, since it liberates one to deal with reality as it is instead of wasting one's energy pining after sugar-coated illusions. Chödrön also points out that, thanks to the Buddha's articulation of the first noble truth, suffering can be separated from guilt. "The first noble truth of the Buddha," she writes, "is that when we feel suffering, it doesn't mean that something is wrong. What a relief. Finally somebody told the truth. Suffering is part of life, and we don't have to feel it's happening because we personally made the wrong move." We recall that according to John in *Day of the Dead,* the characters in the Living Dead films suffer because of their own actions. The zombie plague is or may be a punishment from God. But he was speaking from a set of theistic assumptions that we have reason to regard as dubious in the world of these films. If his interpretation is fundamentally erroneous, then perhaps there is another way of interpreting suffering that has nothing to do with moral culpability and everything to do with the hopelessness inherent in the truth of impermanence.

The decision to turn to Buddhism looks all the more promising when we look into the classic Buddhist tradition and find much interesting material dealing with death and decay, which—as if it needs to be reiterated—are topics of central importance in the Living Dead films as well. Consider, for example, the Theravada text titled *The Book of Protection,* "the most widely known Pali book in Sri Lanka."[66] In this text, which purports to be an anthology of teachings by the Buddha himself, in the section titled *Girimananda Sutta,* the Buddha is said to have been approached by Ananda and asked to visit Girimananda, who was gravely ill from a disease. The Buddha thereupon gave Ananda a list of "ten contemplations" to recite to Girimananda, saying, "Should you, Ananda, visit the monk Girimananda and recite to him the ten contemplations, then that monk Girimananda having heard them, will be immediately cured of his disease."

These ten contemplations center almost entirely around the idea of impermanence, both physical and spiritual, and aim to engender an attitude of detachment in those who practice them, "detachment" being traditionally understood as an attitude of utter openness to the present moment, whatever may arise in it. One who has cultivated this attitude neither clings to nor rejects anything, for such a person has realized deeply the truth of impermanence, and in so doing has transcended the former sense of being bound or trapped by life in the body and the phenomenal realm. What is notable in the context of our current study is the explicit physicality, one might even say the *goriness,* of two of the contemplations the Buddha gives to Girimananda. The third one, titled "contemplation of foulness," is explained by the Buddha as follows:

> And what, Ananda, is contemplation of foulness? Herein, Ananda, a monk contemplates this body upwards from the soles of the feet, downwards from the top of the hair, enclosed in skin, as being full of many impurities. In this body there are head-hairs, body-hairs, nails, teeth, skin, flesh, sinews, bones, marrow, kidneys, heart, liver, pleura, spleen, lungs, intestines, intestinal tract, stomach, feces, bile, phlegm, pus, blood, sweat, fat, tears, grease, saliva, nasal mucous, synovium (oil lubricating the joints), and urine. Thus he dwells contemplating foulness in this body. This, Ananda, is called contemplation of foulness. [67]

The point of this exercise, as mentioned above, is to achieve an attitude of detachment. By directing attention specifically to the "foulness" of the body, to the very fact of its organic sliminess—to Roszak's "things amoeboid or fungoid that stick and cling, that creep and seep and grow . . . things that have the feel or spit or shit, snot or piss, sweat or pus or blood"—the aspirant learns not to identify him or herself with the body, not to be bound by a sense of loathing at its seeming horridness.

Similarly, the fourth contemplation, called "contemplation of disadvantage (or danger)," focuses upon the various diseases to which the body is susceptible:

> What, Ananda, is contemplation of disadvantage (danger)? Herein, Ananda, a monk having gone to the forest, or to the foot of a tree, or to a lonely place, contemplates thus: "Many are the sufferings, many are the disadvantages (dangers) of this body since diverse diseases are engendered in this body, such as the following: Eye-disease, ear-disease, nose-disease, tongue-disease, body-disease, headache, mumps, mouth-disease, tooth-ache, cough, asthma, catarrh, heart-burn, fever, stomach ailment, fainting, dysentery, swelling, gripes, leprosy, boils. . . ."(68)

The list goes on for quite awhile longer, naming a plethora of different diseases and illnesses, and as with the contemplation of foulness, one can see, especially in context with the tenor of the other eight contemplations (e.g., contemplation of impermanence, contemplation of *anatta* [no-soul], contemplation of detachment, contemplation of distaste for the whole world), that the point of the whole is to teach an attitude of detachment or aloofness, an attitude of not feeling imprisoned by or dependent upon either the body or the rest of the physical world. As the story goes, the treatment worked for Girimananda: "Thereupon the Venerable Ananda, having learned these ten contemplations from the Blessed One, visited the Venerable Girimananda, and recited to him the ten contemplations. When the Venerable Girimananda had heard them, his affliction was immediately cured. He recovered from that affliction, and thus disappeared the affliction of the Venerable Girimananda."

Lest the uninformed reader think that this story is only a quaint part of an obscure (to most Westerners) scripture, it is important to point out that the attitude expressed therein and the recommended list of contemplations has a real-life counterpart in actual Buddhist practice. Buddhism as a whole teaches of forty traditional "meditation themes," ten of which are grouped together under the category heading of "foul" or "loathsome" objects. *All of these ten objects are human corpses in various states of injury and decay.* They include the bloated corpse, the livid corpse, the festering corpse, the corpse cut open, the gnawed corpse, the scattered corpse, the hacked corpse, the bloody corpse, the worm-ridden corpse, and the skeleton. For centuries many Buddhists have engaged in the practice of meditating upon actual corpses in order to achieve a sense of disidentification from the impermanency of the body, and Buddhist literature is rife with descriptions of the meditative struggles of various advanced masters as they have deliberately contemplated or imagined corpses in various of the above-named ten states, and have succeeded in conquering their delusional attachment to the body as the linchpin of their sense of selfhood.

The point of dwelling upon all of this is, as indicated above, to demonstrate that a sense of utter, inescapable despair in the face of the combined spiritual-horrific and organic-horrific messages of the Living Dead trilogy is not the only possible reaction. It is possible—not necessary, but possible—to take an entirely different approach, one based on a Buddhist agnostic-contemplative outlook instead of a biblical monotheistic one, and to use, to *employ*, these films as contemplative tools similar to those used by Buddhists in their corpse meditations. For as we have seen, every one of the ten types of corpses described in Buddhism's list of "loathsome things" is present in the Living Dead films. And although the same could be said of many other films of the zombie subgenre, which is notorious for its over-the-top gore, Romero's trilogy holds the distinction of presenting a powerful spiritual message, as indicated by John in the final film. Just as the Buddha's recommended list of contemplations combines meditations on the foulness and vulnerability of the body with meditations on the impermanency of the human self, so do the films of Romero's Living Dead trilogy combine extreme body horror with extreme spiritual horror, such that, as we have seen, the two are inextricable. The violent abuse and deconstruction of the body in these films also heralds the violent abuse and deconstruction of the human self, and this self is shown via the trilogy's spiritual emphasis to be utterly without ground or hope in any possible transcendent spiritual realm. This two-pronged nature of the trilogy's thematic impact, one prong consisting of or emerging from the trilogy's graphic gore, the other from its spiritual focus, thus results in a situation where the choice to view these films in contemplative terms, that is, to direct one's attention deliberately to the graphic violence with the intention of allowing the depiction of corpse horror to loosen one's identification from the body, seems entirely warranted.

The results of such an exercise will surely be limited and will vary according to the will, intentions, and concentrative power of each individual viewer. But in general, if one wonders what the result of such a contemplative exercise might be, one might look for answers in the spiritual literature that makes mention of the contemplation of death and corpses. In the modern era there is, for instance, the story told by Danish-born writer and Zen Buddhist Janwillem van de Wetering at the end of his book *A Glimpse of Nothingness: Experiences in an American Zen Community*:

> A Chinese allegory tells how a monk sets off on a long pilgrimage to find the Buddha. He spends years and years on his quest and finally he comes to the country where the Buddha lives.
>
> He crosses a river, it is a wide river, and he looks about him while the boatman rows him across.
>
> There is a corpse floating on the water and it is coming closer.
>
> The monk looks. The corpse is so close he can touch it. He recognizes the corpse, it is his own.
>
> The monk loses all self-control and wails.
>
> There he floats, dead.
>
> Nothing remains.

> Anything he has ever been, ever learned, ever owned, floats past him, still and without life, moved by the slow current of the wide river.
>
> It is the first moment of his liberation.[69]

Even more recently, and perhaps in partial explanation of the story told by van de Wetering, there are the words of best-selling author and spiritual teacher Eckhart Tolle, who has written at some length about the power and value of death, and about the value of contemplating one's own death as a spiritual exercise. "One of the most powerful spiritual exercises," he writes,

> is to meditate deeply on the mortality of physical forms, including your own. This is called: die before you die. Go into it deeply. Your physical form is dissolving, is no more. Then a moment comes when all mind-forms or thoughts also die. Yet *you* are still there—the divine presence that you are. Radiant, fully awake. Nothing that was real ever died, only names, forms, illusions.[70]

Both Tolle, who claims to represent no specific tradition but whose teachings often have the flavor of Vedantic Hinduism and Christian mysticism, and van de Wetering, along with the entire tradition of Buddhism in general, are getting at a similar, if not the same, point: neither the physical reality of the body nor the psychological ego associated with it represent one's truest, deepest identity. Contemplating death, especially one's own, helps to verify and reinforce this fact.

When it comes to the films we have been examining, we may say that to view them in this way, as tools for aiding in this contemplation of physical and psychological mortality, is to experience them exactly as we have described them in this paper, with all their hopelessness, with all their gore and violence, all the horror of abjection attendant upon the sight of animated corpses, still active with full, emotionally penetrating effect, and yet to experience a veritably alchemical transmutation of the horror and hopelessness into something else, something that may approach a genuine epiphany about the nature and identity of one's true self.

Viewing the many acts of savagery and cannibalism on the screen, which, as we have argued, impacts the viewer emotionally and psychologically with a message about the vulnerability, instability, and ultimate fragility of the human subject, and which might well lead the viewer to a Gnostic loathing of the flesh while simultaneously denying him the possibility of salvation in some transcendent world of pure spirit, we now see that, when understood from a "higher" or "deeper" perspective, the self that can be injured, deconstructed, or destroyed through such acts is not one's true self at all. Only the ego, which is inextricably linked to the physical body, has been affected by such events.

In fact, our reading of the films, our exploration of them with the intent to elicit, understand, and experience to the greatest possible extent the body horror and spiritual horror they engender, has been nothing other than an intellectualized instance of this very contemplation, since it is the ego in its intellectual and emotional obsessiveness that has engaged in the reading and experienced the horror. Coming away from the reading, we realize that we have *benefited* from the experience, since we have come to recognize more clearly the difference between the ephemeral, illusory ego that commonly masquerades as our true self and the enduring empty center of awareness that always precedes and lies behind the extensional existence of the ego and the body. To quote Tolle a final time, "Only the ego dies. . . . The end of illusion—that's all that death is. It is painful only as long as you cling to illusion."(71)

NOTES

1. Gregory Waller, "Introduction to *American Horrors* (extract)," in Ken Gelder, ed., *The Horror Reader* (London and New York: Routledge, 2000), p. 258.
2. J. Hoberman and Jonathan Rosenbaum, *Midnight Movies* (New York: Harper & Row, 1983), 125.
3. Rumsey Taylor, review of *Dawn of the Dead* at *24 Frames Per Second*, http://www.24framespersecond.com/reactions/films_d/dawndead.html (accessed November 16, 2002).
4. Robin Wood, "What Lies Beneath?" *Senses of Cinema*, 2001, http://www.sensesofcinema.com/contents/01/15/horror_beneath.html (accessed November 16, 2002).

5. Rev. Dr. Richard Erhardt, "Vampires and Other Plagues," *South Nassau Unitarian Universalist Congregation* (10/29/00), http://members.aol.com/snuuc/snuuc/Sermons/vampire_and_other_plagues.htm (accessed November 16, 2002).
6. It would, however, be tempting to do so. "Romero and his backers," write Hoberman and Rosenbaum, "have often remarked that [*Night of the Living Dead*]'s social implications weren't consciously sought after, but were discovered only by later critics" (op. cit., 124). Journalist and film critic Tom Mes remarks that "*Night* has been analyzed to the point of dissection by film critics, resulting in the 'discovery' of the most ridiculous and far-fetched subtexts. People have read meaning into the film's use of black and white, the grainy look of the film stock (an accident because the lab had to switch to cheaper stock), the use of effects and the anonymous masses of the zombies." The real reasons for so many of the movie's "brilliant innovations," says Mes, were simply budget constraints. In the case of casting Duane Jones, a black actor, in the lead role of Ben (on which also see Hoberman and Rosenbaum), the decision rested on the fact that Jones was simply the best actor the producers could get with their budget. In other words, race had nothing to do with it (Tom Mes, "THE END IS NIGH! (And it starts in Pittsburgh): George Romero's Living Dead trilogy," *Project A: Cultfilm and Lifestyle e-zine*, http://www.projecta.net/george1.htm, accessed November 16, 2002). Even when the films' social commentary became overt and intentional, as in *Dawn of the Dead*, some critics insisted on offering patently far-fetched interpretations, as when Robin Wood read homosexual implications into the relationship between two male characters and claimed the "true nature of the relationship can be tacitly acknowledged only after Roger's death, in the symbolic orgasm of the spurting of a champagne bottle over his grave" (Robin Wood, *Hollywood from Vietnam to Reagan*, New York: Columbia University Press, 1986, 120).
7. Jonathan Lake Crane, *Terror and Everyday Life: Singular Moments in the History of the Horror Film* (Thousand Oaks, CA: Sage Publications, 1994), 1.
8. Jack Sargeant, "The Baying of Pigs: Reflections on the New American Horror Movie," *Senses of Cinema* 15 (July-August 2001), http://www.sensesofcinema.com/contents/01/15/biff_nightmare.html (accessed December 1, 2002).
9. Cynthia A. Freeland, *The Naked and the Undead: Evil and the Appeal of Horror*, Thinking Through Cinema series (Boulder: Westview Press, 2000), 242.
10. Anne Jerslev, "The Horror Film, the Body, and the Youth Audience," *Young: Nordic Journal of Youth Research* 2:3 (1994), http://www.alli.fi/nyri/young/1994-3/artikkelJerslev3-94.htm (accessed November 16, 2002).
11. Theodore Roszak, *Where the Wasteland Ends: Politics and Transcendence*

in Postindustrial Society (Berkeley: Celestial Arts, 1989), 96.

12. *Ibid.*, 93.
13. Philip Brophy, "Horrality—The Textuality of Contemporary Horror Films," in *The Horror Reader*, 280.
14. Sargeant, op. cit.
15. Crane, 30.
16. Roszak, 96.
17. Jerslev, op. cit.
18. Julia Kristeva, *Powers of Horror: An Essay on Abjection*, trans. Leon S. Roudiez (New York: Columbia University Press, 1982), 4.
19. Barbara Creed, "Kristeva, Femininity, and Abjection," in *The Horror Reader*, 66.
20. Jerslev, op. cit.
21. S. S. Prawer, *Caligari's Children: The Film as Tale of Terror* (Oxford: Oxford University Press, 1980), 75.
22. Mikita Brottman, "Supernatural Cannibals," *Creation Books* (2001), http://www.creationbooks.com/ text-meat.html (accessed November 23, 2002). Excerpt from Mikita Brottman, *Meat is Murder: Cannibal Films and Culture*, new edition (London: Creation Books, 2001).
23. Sargeant, op. cit.
24. Robert Hood, "Nights of the Celluloid Dead: A History of the Zombie Film," *Tabula Rasa*, http://www.tabula-rasa.info/Horror/ZombieFilms1.html (accessed November 12, 2002). First published in *Bloodsongs* #4, 1995.
25. Rose Wood, *Zombie: The Living Dead* (New York: Bounty Books, 1986), 98.
26. Prawer., 69.
27. *Ibid.*, p. 68.
28. Tom Mes, op. cit.
29. "Zombie Symbolism," *Monstrous*, http://death.monstrous.com/zombie_symbolism.htm (accessed November 16, 2002).
30. R. H. W. Dillard, *Horror Films* (New York: Monarch Press, 1976), 57, 58.
31. Bryan Stone, "The Sanctification of Fear: Images of the Religious in Horror Films," *Journal of Religion and Film* 5:2 (October 2001), http://www.unomaha.edu/~wwwjrf/sanctifi.htm (accessed November 9, 2002).
32. Dillard, 57.
33. Walter Kendrick, *The Thrill of Fear: 250 Years of Scary Entertainment* (New York: Grove Weidenfeld, 1991), 250.
34. Hood, op. cit.
35. Brottman, op. cit.
36. Roland Barthes, "Toward as Psychosociology of Contemporary Food Consumption," in Carole Counihan and Peny Van Esterik, eds., *Food and Culture: A Reader* (New York and London: Routledge, 1997), 21, 23.
37. Anna Meigs, "Food as a Cultural Construction," in Carole Counihan and

Penny Van Esterik, eds., *Food and Culture: A Reader* (New York and London: Routledge, 1997), 104-105.

38. Jerslev, op. cit.
39. Anne Marie Olesen, "Cannibalism and the Serial Killer as Metaphors for Transgression," *p.o.v.: A Danish Journal of Film Studies* 4 (December 1997), http://imv.au.dk/publikationer/pov/Issue_04/section_2/artc2A.html (accessed November 16, 2002).
40. Oleson, op. cit.
41. Gregory A. Waller, *The Living and the Undead* (Urbana and Chicago: University of Illinois Press, 1986), 280.
42. Ibid., 276.
43. Jerslev, op. cit.
44. Dillard, 112.
45. Freeland, 242.
46. Jerslev, op. cit.
47. *Ibid.*
48. The fact that it has been common in the West both to define the self according to the image of the body, as Jerslev contends, and also to be horrified by the fact of existing as a body at all, as Roszak has argued, merely highlights the ambiguous relationship between body and self in Western consciousness.
49. *Ibid.*
50. Marina Warner, "The Devil Inside," *The Guardian* (Saturday, November 2, 2002), http://books.guardian.co.uk/reviews/politicsphilosophyandsociety/0,6121,824095,00.html (accessed November 16, 2002).
51. Brophy, op. cit.
52. Crane, 12.
53. Waller, *The Living and the Undead*, 283.
54. Creed, 67.
55. Waller, *The Living and the Undead*, 276.
56. See 2 Peter 3:1-13, esp. verse 11: "But the day of the Lord will come like a thief. The heavens will disappear with a roar; the elements will be destroyed by fire, and the earth and everything in it will be laid bare." See also Acts 2:14-21, esp. vv. 17-21, which quote the Hebrew prophet Joel's prophecy about the apocalyptic "Day of the Lord" being preceded by various dramatic and fearsome celestial signs.
57. Hood, op. cit.
58. Nonstandard grammatical items in John's speech are due to the fact that he is Jamaican and speaks a subtle sort of pidgin English.
59. Waller, *The Living and the Undead*, 283-284, 290.
60. Incidentally, John first displays this attitude early on, in fact within the first ten minutes of the film, long before he gives his apocalyptic speech. As he and Sarah walk away from the helicopter after the opening scene's scouting expedition, he tells her that he thinks the ongoing project to study

the zombies is "bullshit" and "crazy." She asks him if he has a better idea, and he responds by telling her his plan to fly away to an island "and spend what time we got left soaking up some sunshine." She fixes him with a steely gaze and mutters with incredulous anger, "You could do that, couldn't you? Even with all this going on, you could do that without a second thought." To which he replies, "Shit, I could do that even if all this *wasn't* going on."

61. Hood, op. cit.
62. Sargeant, op. cit.
63. Roszak, 449.
64. Charles Derry, *Dark Dreams,* quoted in Dillard, 51.
65. Pema Chödrön, *When Things Fall Apart: Heart Advice for Difficult Times* (audiobook), Shambala Publications (1997).
66. *The Book of Protection,* trans. Piyadassi Thera, *Access to Insight: Readings in Theravada Buddhism* (translation copyright 1999), http://www.accesstoinsight.org/lib/bps/misc/protection.html (accessed November 4, 2003).
67. *Ibid.*
68. *Ibid.*
69. Janwillem van de Wetering, *A Glimpse of Nothingness: Experiences in an American Zen Community* (New York: Ballantine Books, 1988 [1974]), 180.
70. Eckhart Tolle, *The Power of Now: A Guide to Spiritual Enlightenment* (Vancouver, British Columbia: Namaste Publishing, Inc., 1997), 165.
71. *Ibid.*, 188, 121

WORKS CITED

Barthes, Roland. "Toward as Psychosociology of Contemporary Food Consumption." In *Food and Culture: A Reader,* ed. Carole Counihan and Penny Van Esterik, 20-27. New York and London: Routledge, 1997.

The Book of Protection. Trans. Piyadassi Thera. *Access to Insight: Readings in Theravada Buddhism.* Translation copyright 1999. http://www.accesstoinsight.org/lib/bps/misc/protection.html (accessed November 4, 2003).

Brophy, Philip. "Horrality—The Textuality of Contemporary Horror Films." In *The Horror Reader,* ed. Ken Gelder, 276-284. London and New York: Routledge, 2000.

Brottman, Mikita. "Supernatural Cannibals," *Creation Books.*

2001. http://www.creationbooks.com/text-meat.html (accessed November 23, 2002). Excerpt from Mikita Brottman, *Meat is Murder: Cannibal Films and Culture*, new edition. London: Creation Books, 2001.

Chödrön, Pema. *When Things Fall Apart: Heart Advice for Difficult Times* (audiobook). Shambala Publications, 1997.

Crane, Jonathan Lake. *Terror and Everyday Life: Singular Moments in the History of the Horror Film*. Thousand Oaks, CA: Sage Publications, 1994.

Creed, Barbara. "Kristeva, Femininity, and Abjection." In *The Horror Reader*, ed. Ken Gelder, 64-70. London and New York: Routledge, 2000.

Dillard, R. H. W. *Horror Films*. New York: Monarch Press, 1976.

Erhardt, Rev. Dr. Richard. "Vampires and Other Plagues." *South Nassau Unitarian Universalist Congregation*. October 29, 2000. http://members.aol.com/snuuc/snuuc/Sermons/vampire_and_other_plagues.htm (accessed November 16, 2002).

Freeland, Cynthia A. *The Naked and the Undead: Evil and the Appeal of Horror*. Thinking Through Cinema series. Boulder: Westview Press, 2000.

Hoberman, J. and Jonathan Rosenbaum. *Midnight Movies*. New York: Harper & Row, 1983.

Hood, Robert. "Nights of the Celluloid Dead: A History of the Zombie Film." *Tabula Rasa*. http://www.tabula-rasa.info/Horror/ZombieFilms1.html (accessed November 12, 2002). First published in *Bloodsongs* #4, 1995.

Jerslev, Anne. "The Horror Film, the Body, and the Youth Audience." *Young: Nordic Journal of Youth Research* 2:3 (1994). http://www.alli.fi/nyri/young/1994-3/

artikkelJerslev3-94.htm (accessed November 16, 2002).

Kendrick, Walter. *The Thrill of Fear: 250 Years of Scary Entertainment*. New York: Grove Weidenfeld, 1991.

Kristeva, Julia. *Powers of Horror: An Essay on Abjection*. Trans. Leon S. Roudiez. New York: Columbia UP, 1982.

Meigs, Anna. "Food as a Cultural Construction." In *Food and Culture: A Reader*, ed. Carole Counihan and Penny Van Esterik, 95-106. New York and London: Routledge, 1997.

Mes, Tom. "THE END IS NIGH! (And it starts in Pittsburgh): George Romero's Living Dead trilogy." *Project A: Cultfilm and Lifestyle e-zine*. http://www.projecta.net/ george1.htm (accessed November 16, 2002).

Olesen, Anne Marie. "Cannibalism and the Serial Killer as Metaphors for Transgression." *p.o.v.: A Danish Journal of Film Studies* 4 (December 1997). http://imv.au.dk/ publikationer/pov/Issue_04/section_2/artc2A.html (accessed March 29, 2005).

Prawer, S. S. *Caligari's Children: The Film as Tale of Terror*. Oxford: Oxford UP, 1980.

Roszak, Theodore. *Where the Wasteland Ends: Politics and Transcendence in Postindustrial Society*. Berkeley: Celestial Arts, 1989 (1972).

Sargeant, Jack. "The Baying of Pigs: Reflections on the New American Horror Movie." *Senses of Cinema* 15 (July-August 2001). http://www.sensesofcinema.com/contents/festivals/ 01/15/biff_nightmare.html (accessed March 29, 2005).

Stone, Bryan. "The Sanctification of Fear: Images of the Religious in Horror Films." *Journal of Religion and Film* 5:2 (October 2001). http://www.unomaha.edu/~wwwjrf/sanctifi.htm (accessed March 29, 2005).

Taylor, Rumsey. "Dawn of the Dead" (review). *24 Frames Per Second.* http://www.24framespersecond.com/reactions/films_d/dawndead.html (accessed November 16, 2002.).

Tolle, Eckhart. *The Power of Now: A Guide to Spiritual Enlightenment.* Vancouver, British Columbia: Namaste Publishing, Inc., 1997.

van de Wetering, Janwillem. *The Empty Mirror: Experiences in a Japanese Zen Monastery.* New York: Ballantine Books, 1988 (1974).

Waller, Gregory. "Introduction to *American Horrors* (extract)." In *The Horror Reader,* ed. Ken Gelder, 256-264. London and New York: Routledge, 2000.

Waller, Gregory A. *The Living and the Undead.* Urbana and Chicago: University of Illinois Press, 1986.

Warner, Marina. "The Devil Inside." *The Guardian,* Saturday, November 2, 2002. http://books.guardian.co.uk/reviewspoliticsphilosophyandsociety/0,6121,824095,00.html (accessed November 16, 2002).

Wood, Robin. *Hollywood from Vietnam to Reagan.* New York: Columbia UP, 1986.

Wood, Robin. "What Lies Beneath?" *Senses of Cinema* 15 (July-August 2001). http://www.sensesofcinema.com/contents/01/15/horror_beneath.html (accessed March 29, 2005).

Wood, Rose. *Zombie: The Living Dead.* New York: Bounty Books, 1986.

"Zombie Symbolism." *Monstrous.* http://death.monstrous.com/zombie_symbolism.htm (accessed November 16, 2002).

WORKS CONSULTED

Bourassa, Eric. "The End is Near!!! The Non-Regenerative Apocalyptic Horror Film." *HorrorTheory*. http://www.horrortheory.com/articles/bourassa_1.html (accessed December 1, 2002).

Grant, Barry Keith, ed. *Planks of Reason: Essays on the Horror Film*. Metuchen, N.J. and London: The Scarecrow Press, 1984.

Grant, Barry K. "Prolegomena to a Contextualistic Genre Criticism." http://www.sunyit.edu/~harrell/Pepper/pep_grant.htm (accessed November 16, 2002).

Humphrey, Clark. "Food for Thought on Cannibal Movies: Bite Me." 2001. http://www.miscmedia.com/cannibal_films.html (accessed November 16, 2002). Originally published in *The Stranger* (January 31, 1996).

Huss, Roy and T.J. Ross, eds. *Focus on the Horror Film*. Englewood Cliffs, N.J.: Prentice-Hall, 1972.

Jonas, Hans. *The Gnostic Religion: The message of the alien God and the beginnings of Christianity*. 2nd ed. Boston: Beacon Press, 1991 (1958).

Lavery, Dr. David. "The Horror Film and the Horror of Film." http://www.mtsu.edu/~dlavery/Writing/The%20Horror%20Film%20and%20the%20Horror%20of%20Film.htm (accessed November 16, 2002). Originally published in *Film Criticism* 7 (1983), 47-55.

Merritt, Greg. *Celluloid Mavericks: The History of American Independent Film*. New York: Thunder's Mouth Press, 2000.

Sanday, Peggy Reeves. *Divine Hunger: Cannibalism as a cultural system*. Cambridge: Cambridge University Press, 1986.

GODS AND MONSTERS, WORMS AND FIRE:

A HORRIFIC READING OF ISAIAH

Abstract: The Book of Isaiah, while ostensibly a religious text that presents an uplifting message of spiritual comfort, contains many passages of a deeply disturbing nature. The content and placement of these passages, which are located primarily in chapters 24 and 34, and in chapter 66, verse 24 (the final verse of the book), indicate that the book as a whole may be read in a horrific light. This paper analyzes Isaiah according to a tripartite scheme proposed by Roger C. Schlobin for determining whether a given text should be classified as a horror story. It also dwells upon the significance of Isaiah's final verse in achieving an effect of anticlosure that leaves the reader in an unsettled state.

INTRODUCTION:
TROUBLING QUESTIONS AND TAXONOMIC SCHEMES

Most educated people are familiar with the common moral and aesthetic problems that confront modern readers of certain Old Testament texts. *The NIV Study Bible,* a modern English translation with accompanying study notes that is widely used among contemporary evangelicals, devotes space in its introduction to the book of Joshua to point out one of these common problems: "Many readers of Joshua (and other OT books) are deeply troubled by the role that warfare plays in this account of God's dealings with his people." The introduction goes on to justify the pervasive practice of war and conquest by God's people in the book of Joshua (and, by implication, in the rest of the Old Testament) by framing it as "the story of how God, to whom the whole world belongs, at one stage in the history of redemption reconquered a portion of the earth from the powers of this world that had claimed it for themselves, defending their claims by force of arms and reliance on their false gods."(1)

That the editors of such a prominent, mainstream publication should feel it necessary to devote space to justifying the morality of the Old Testament is witness to the fact that much of what appears in this ancient library of texts seems bizarre and brutal to a host of modern readers. I, for one, feel that Joshua is hardly the only Old Testament book that warrants such a walking-on-eggshells approach. Many other books call for equal treatment, and not only because they, like Joshua, feature scenes of slaughter and cruelty performed at the behest of and sometimes directly by the hand of the biblical God, but also because of the outright horror, in a cosmic supernatural sense, that they generate.

Isaiah ranks among those other books that the authors and editors of *The NIV Study Bible* might have done well to approach with care. As a reader with a particular personal interest in the horror genre, I am fascinated by the fact that much of what appears in Isaiah might have been lifted right out of a horror story. Layered in with the familiar passages about the suffering servant and the comfort that Yahweh offers his people are disturbing scenes of bloodshed and mayhem, and even wholesale cosmic destruction, that clash violently with this softer stuff. Add to these the fact that the closing verse of the book—chapter 66, verse 24—rounds things out on an explicit note of graphic horror, and you have a situation in which an all-out horrific reading of seems warranted.

In order to present such a reading, I shall make use of a taxonomic tool formulated by Roger C. Schlobin and presented in his paper "Prototypic Horror: The Genre of the Book of Job." Schlobin offers a three-part scheme for judging whether or not a given text should be understood as a horror story, and applies this scheme to the book of Job in an effort to answer the longstanding question of the book's proper genre. In what follows I shall demonstrate that when the same scheme is applied to Isaiah, the book easily meets all of Schlobin's stated requirements. My evidence, in addition to 66:24, will include passages from chapters 24 and 34 in which Yahweh reduces the created world to a state of primeval chaos, and from chapter 40, which describes Yahweh's absolute aloofness and transcendence in forceful detail. I will argue that 66:24, coming as it does on the heels of these other passages, cements the validity of reading Isaiah as a horror story. Or rather, I will argue that it cements the *possibility* of such a reading (a distinction I will return to in my concluding thoughts).

On a methodological note, I should pause here to specify that my approach in this paper will be explicitly reader-oriented. I shall make unabashed leaps of the imagination, all of them founded upon the personal base of knowledge and set of interests that define me as a culturally and historically situated reader. Of course, such leaps may seem unwarranted to more traditional-minded readers of the historical-critical or social-scientific schools of thought. My entire paper, I suspect, may seem to such readers like nothing more (and, I hope, nothing less) than a flight of fancy. In my defense I will say only that I identify mightily with the following words of Edgar W. Conrad, which I feel comfortable in appropriating as my own:

> My reading, like every reading of every text, will produce meaning only because of my active participation in creating meaning in the reading process. Every reading is of necessity a reading *into*, or eisegesis. Indeed, the worst kind of eisegesis may be readings in which interpreters remain unaware of their involvement because they think they are reading meaning *out of* the text.(2)

In what follows I will be concerned, like Conrad, "with the text's aesthetic momentum, not its historical development."(3) And like Kathryn Darr, in contrast to Conrad's self-described mingling of objective methods with reader-oriented methods, I will take the further step of "remember[ing] that readers are required to actualize that potential aesthetic momentum."(4) This means that I will largely pass over the question of authorial intent, for I will be relying upon the fact, as stated by Darr, that "because readers themselves play a role in actualizing texts . . . we must leave open the possibility that they discern relationships between texts not, consciously or unconsciously, in the redactors' thoughts."(5)

To begin with, let us turn to Schlobin's identification of the "three, critical elements of horror": "(1) its distortion of cosmology . . . (2) its dark inversion of signs, symbols, processes, and expectations that cause this aberrant world; and (3) its monster-victim relationship with its archetypal devastation of individual will."[6] Since he gives no instructions that these criteria must be considered in this specific order, I will rearrange them to suit my purpose, and will consider the third element second and the second one last. That said, it is to the first of these elements—the distortion of cosmology—that I now turn.

I. DISTORTED COSMOLOGY IN ISAIAH: THE RETURN TO CHAOS

"In all of horror's refractions," writes Schlobin, "the aberrant world or distorted cosmology is one of its required characteristics." This world "must initially begin as a normal one" and then "crumble to chaos," even as it holds out "the futile hopes of success, triumph, and/or escape."[7] The Book of Job conforms to this criterion, he says, through its presentation of Job's initial state of prosperity and divine favor, followed by his period of great suffering during which he cries for justice, concluded by the revelation to him of Yahweh's transcendent unknowability.

This same element of distorted cosmology is found in Isaiah in the passages describing Yahweh's wrathful reduction of the world to a state of primordial chaos. Although a few other passages scattered throughout the book also make use of this motif, the bulk of them are concentrated in chapters 24 and 34, which, as we might do well to note, occupy places of considerable significance in the text. Chapter 24 is the first chapter of what has often been termed the "Isaiah Apocalypse," which consists of chapters 24-27. In the words of Brevard Childs, "Few sections within the book of Isaiah have called forth such a wide measure of scholarly disagreement on their analysis and interpretation as have these four chapters."[8] He calls attention to the importance of this section for the book as a whole when he claims it portrays "God's final purpose . . . by means of a reuse of the entire corpus of Isaianic material."[9] Jensen asserts a similar point when he writes that the section "gives a unified conception of how God's work in history will finally reach its term," and maintains that "its position after the collection of oracles against the nations (chaps. 13-23) is neither haphazard nor purposeless" since "It provides a framework within which to understand those other oracles."[10] Chapter 34, for its part, when taken in tandem with its companion chapter 35, has been called the "Little Apocalypse," and, according to Childs, supports a "holistic reading [of the book] by setting up a resonance with major themes taken from both before and after these chapters," and "function[s] redactionally as a diptych to form an editorial bridge combining the first part of Isaiah with the second."(11) With greater brevity, Peter D. Miscall says chapters 34 and 35 "stand in the physical center of the book and can perhaps tell us something about the whole book."(12) In terms of my own purpose here, the point of noting all this is simply to highlight the fact that these two sections of Isaiah occupy positions of major importance in Isaiah's overall scheme, and thus the implications for the rest of the book will be profound if they can be read horrifically.

Beginning with chapter 24, we see that the first verse states, "Now the LORD is about to lay waste the earth and make it desolate, and he will twist its surface and scatter its inhabitants." Commenting on this verse, John H. Hayes and Stuart A. Irvine aver that "Isaiah's proclamation that Yahweh is now moving to refashion and reorder the world opens with what appears as almost a thesis sentence."(13) And what a terrifying thesis sentence it is! The chapter that follows goes on to speak of the earth being "utterly laid waste and utterly despoiled" (v. 3). Early on the text makes reference to "the city of chaos" being "broken down, every house is shut up so that no one can enter" (v. 10). "City of chaos," as Hayes and Irvine point out, refers to the Assyrian citadel, and may be literally rendered as "*tohu*-town." The "name fits the imagery being employed by Isaiah," they say, "recalling as it does the imagery reflected in Genesis 1:2, in which the earth is *tohu* [formless, chaotic] before God's creation. The destruction of the citadel is thus viewed by Isaiah as part of the reversion to disorder and chaos out of which new order can arise."(14)

Other images of primordial chaos are found in v. 18, which describes "the windows of heaven" being opened and "the foundations of the earth" trembling. Hayes and Irvine note that through the use of these images, Isaiah demonstrates "the universality of Yahweh's actions. . . . As at the time of the flood, the earth is undergoing radical change."(15) Nor is the imagery itself the whole of the matter, for as Joseph Jensen incisively points out, the image of the "windows of heaven" carries with it an entire world view:

> The opening of the windows of heaven alludes not only to P's account of the great flood [that is, the account coming from the Priestly source of Genesis, as distinct from the portions coming from the (E)lohist and (J)ahwist sources] (see Gen 7:11; 8:2) but also to the cosmology behind it. In Gen 1:6-7 God separated the waters above from the waters below, thus marking off from the primal chaos what he was about to organize into earth and sea and sky; to allow the waters above to pour in again is a way of returning all to the original chaos. The author [of Isaiah] is invoking images to convey something of the cosmic nature of the calamity; so also the earthquake imagery which follows [in vv. 18c-20] points to something beyond a merely natural disaster.(16)

Such a sweeping, cosmic interpretation seems quite appropriate for the content of the first chapter of the "Isaiah Apocalypse." John B. Geyer, paraphrasing a point made by R. Murray in *The Cosmic Covenant*, emphasizes that although the imagery of Isaiah 24 may seem, on one level, to refer to the destruction of the land by enemy forces of a decidedly human, non-supernatural nature, they actually depict "the undoing of nature and its order."(17) And, as Harry Bultema points out in his commentary on this chapter, for the human inhabitants of the earth who experience these things, "the horror will be unspeakably great."(18)

Moving ahead ten chapters, we see that once again Isaiah chooses to focus loving attention upon horrific depictions of Yahweh's wrath. Chapter 34 depicts Yahweh as "enraged against all the nations, and furious against all their hoards; he has doomed them, has given them over for slaughter" (v. 2). Images of staggering violence populate the chapter, as in, for example, verse 3: "The slain shall be cast out, and the stench of their corpses shall rise; the mountains shall flow with their blood." Yahweh's sword is said to have "drunk its fill in the heavens," and "will descend upon Edom, upon the people I have doomed to judgment. . . . For the LORD has a great sacrifice in Bozrah, a great slaughter in the land of Edom" (vv. 5, 6c). A. S. Herbert describes the language of the chapter as "violent and terrifying," and says that as with chapter 24, the destruction being depicted has universal connotations:

> The specific mention of Edom (verse 6) must be understood in relation to the cruel advantage taken by the Edomites of the Babylonian invasion of Judah in 598 -587 B.C., referred to in Lam. 4:21-2 ; Ps.137:7. But in this chapter Edom has become a symbolic name for all the enemies of the people of God, as it does in Obadiah. The prophet sees the whole universe as involved in the divine judgment; it is a return to primeval chaos.[(19)]

Philip D. Stern agrees. "[I]n Isaiah 34, a breakdown of order and the reestablishment of primordial-type chaos are being described."[(20)] In fact, according to Stern, "Images of chaos appear in this chapter far more than anywhere else in the Bible,"[(21)] He appears especially impressed with the description in verses 11-15 of the land being given over to wild animals, "goat-demons," and the demoness Lilith, calling the passage "an ingenious evocation of chaos-imageries."[(22)] The import of all these chaos images is reinforced, he says, by the fact that the opening verse of the chapter, "an appeal to all the earth and its fullness to give heed, makes the point that the message to follow is one of cosmic dimensions."[(23)]

Having established that chapters 24 and 34 do indeed portray scenes of cosmic destruction and the reduction of the created order to primordial chaos, let us pause here to recall that our purpose is to establish that the chapters fulfill Schlobin's requirement that a horror story must display evidence of a distorted cosmology. In elaborating the meaning of this requirement, Schlobin quotes from H. P. Lovecraft's influential essay *Supernatural Horror in Literature*, and since Lovecraft's words sharpen my argument considerably by narrowing the type of horror we are seeking to establish, I shall quote them in full (in contrast to Schlobin's fragmentary presentation of them). According to Lovecraft, for a given story to be classified as a true tale of supernatural horror,

> A certain atmosphere of breathless and unexplainable dread of outer, unknown forces must be present; and there must be a hint, expressed with a seriousness and portentousness becoming its subject, of that most terrible conception of the human brain—a malign and particular suspension or defeat of those fixed laws of Nature which are our only safeguard against the assaults of chaos and the daemons of unplumbed space.(24)

A glimpse into an internal debate among horror theorists may help to clarify still further the type of horror in question. Certain genre scholars have maintained that Lovecraft's description of the necessary atmosphere of supernatural horror applies not to the genre as a whole but more specifically to the subgenre of "cosmic fear," a.k.a. "the weird tale." Noel Carroll, for example, argues in *The Philosophy of Horror* that cosmic fear

> may be relevant to explaining why some works of horror attract their audiences (though, I suspect, not as many works as Lovecraft has in mind); but it is not fundamental enough to explain the attractiveness of horror across the board. This point may be obscured while reading Lovecraft since, given his putative classificatory scheme of things, the genre is identified in terms of cosmic fear; but once we see that Lovecraft's classificatory scheme really represents a covert preference for one sort of (possibly) especially commendatory, horrific effect, we note that cosmic fear is a special source of interest, occurring only in some works of horror, and that it is not pervasive enough to account for generic fascination with the genre.(25)

Regardless of whether Lovecraft or his critics are correct in this matter, the very point of disagreement brings out more clearly the type of horror referenced by the term "distorted cosmology." What we are looking for in Isaiah is a situation in which the cosmos is assaulted from without by an unknown and unknowable force. The horror of cosmological distortion is the horror of knowing that the laws of nature are subject to violation, that creation might one day split open like an eggshell and reveal those "daemons of unplumbed space"—that is, the monsters of chaos. It is the horror of cosmic fear, of realizing that the limited human view of the cosmos is hopelessly myopic, because there are forces out there that may well break through into our cozy world and destroy us, or at the very least shatter our sense of metaphysical security. Schlobin does not specify the way in which this threat must present itself. In the Book of Job, Yahweh threatens Job's comfortable cosmology by overturning Job's cherished belief in a cosmic moral order in which righteousness will always be rewarded.[26] In Isaiah, Yahweh literally undoes the created world in an orgy of bloody violence. In both instances, he functions as exactly the type of threat Lovecraft describes.

But this means that in Isaiah, Yahweh plays the part of Lovecraft's "daemons of unplumbed space." In other words, Yahweh, in a very important way, functions as a chaos monster. And this leads us to our next point.

II. YAHWEH, KING OF THE MONSTERS

According to Schlobin, a second crucial factor in any horror story is

> its monster-victim relationship with its archetypal devastation of individual will. . . . In general, horror's creatures are blatantly oblivious to any human sense of order, ethics, or morality. They are so evil that good is either unknown to them or has no impact on them. . . . Their natures are incomprehensible to the epistemologies of their victims . . . and monsters are completely capable of disintegrating their victims' bodies and souls.[27]

In the story of Job, as read by Schlobin, Yahweh is revealed as precisely this sort of monster by his incomprehensible maltreatment of Job: "Job is helpless before the irrational forces and punishments forced upon him. Yahweh is a divine solipsist who has no expectation of losing the wager or suffering any consequences."(28)

Yahweh's monstrous role in Isaiah is seen, as stated above, in the fact of his assuming the role of a chaos monster. The idea of chaos monsters who threaten the created order is of course an old one. Eliade is only the most famous of many scholars who have written of the motif's prevalence among, and meaning for, virtually all traditional religious societies. "Since 'our world' is a cosmos," Eliade wrote,

> any attack from without threatens to turn it into chaos. . . . [T]he enemies who attack it are assimilated to the enemies of the gods, the demons, and especially the archdemon, the primordial dragon conquered by the gods at the beginning of time. An attack on "our world" is equivalent to an act of revenge by the mythical dragon, who rebels against the work of the gods, the cosmos, and struggles to annihilate it.(29)

The Old Testament is rife with instances of this motif in action. From the veiled references to the Babylonian chaos dragon *Tiamat* in the Hebrew cognate *tehom*, "the deep," found in Genesis 1:2 and elsewhere (such as Isaiah 24:10, already noted), to such direct references as—significantly—Isaiah's mention of Yahweh's victorious encounters with the chaos dragons Leviathan (27:1) and Rahab (51:9), Old Testament theology displays abundant evidence of being rooted in chaos mythology. "In the Hebrew Bible," writes David Penchansky, "great sea creatures and land giants lay [sic] waiting in the chaos just outside the imposed order of God's creation." But, as Penchansky also notes, "Sometimes . . . the divine figure itself functions as a monster."(30)

Timothy Beal has written at length about this duality in the Hebrew conception of the deity. He points out that while in some cases, as with the above-named battles between Yahweh and Leviathan and Rahab, the biblical God's relationship with primordial chaos monsters is adversarial and results in battles whose ultimate purpose is cosmogonic, at other times God actually allies himself with the chaos monsters, or even becomes one himself. An example is found in Isaiah 8, where

> Assyria is imagined as God's monstrous means of pronouncing judgment on Judah. . . . Here the king of Assyria . . . is personified as the flood waters of the great river Euphrates, which is associated with primordial chaos waters. Isaiah's audacious and horrifying claim is that God is raising up these mighty and massive flood waters against Judah. God is taking sides with the monstrous enemy against Judah.(31)

While Beal's recognition that God in this passage has allied himself with the forces of chaos against Judah is indeed full of import, I cannot help but feel that he (Beal) missed an opportunity when he failed to acknowledge that in chapters 24 and 34 of this same book, Yahweh takes an even more direct role as an agent of chaos, in that he accomplishes what he has prevented the classical chaos dragons themselves from doing: He destroys the creation from top to bottom, making it all like the "city of chaos" described in 24:10. Douglas A. Knight has pointed out that "The Hebrew myths dealing with the birth of the cosmos envision no struggle between the creator and any other beings or substances." Even though, as noted above, the ancient Babylonian chaos dragon Tiamat appears in veiled form in the Old Testament, and even though Leviathan and others are mentioned in various places, these "mythic figures offer no resistance whatsoever to YHWH, not even as a narrative foil."(32) In the reading of Isaiah that I am proposing, Yahweh, without any force to oppose him, becomes the very type of chaos monster that he has defeated. He slew Rahab and cut her into pieces, presumably as part of his original cosmogonic act. He is prophesied to kill Leviathan, "the fleeing serpent . . . the twisting serpent . . . the dragon that is in the sea," on "that day," i.e. the Day of Yahweh, when he will punish all evildoers and bring about the consummation of the creation (27:1). But it appears that the whole meaning of these acts has been merely to clear the way for Yahweh to bring about an even worse cosmic destruction than what these sinister serpents could have accomplished. Yahweh has saved the world from the archetypal chaos monsters only to *become* a chaos monster who, in his unopposed power, outdoes the others at their own horrific game.

Obviously, I am, as promised in my introduction, engaging in a deliberately creative reading at this point. I am picking certain signals, certain indicators in the text, and running with them. But aside from my own half-playful (and half-serious) desire to see how much horror I can wring from Isaiah, there is also the manifest fact that the biblical God is often portrayed as a source of horror as much as he is a source of comfort and blessing. One interesting speculation about this demonic or horrific aspect of the deity focuses on the fact that in a monotheistic world view, all aspects of divinity must necessarily be channeled into a single entity. "Since the divine sphere is held to be the cause of all that is inexplicable in the human sphere," writes Knight,

> these go to the account of the gods. In polytheistic religions demons or malicious gods are typically held responsible for the bizarre differences. Yahwism, however, could not tolerate any divine or semi-divine rivals to God. . . . Presumably the demonic element became 'absorbed' into the developing conception of YHWH, associated with his numinous character, and identified frequently with his theophanic appearances, not the least in the image of the divine warrior.[33]

Such an understanding goes a long way toward explaining the world's terror at God's self-manifestation as described in Isaiah and elsewhere. For instance, in Isaiah 2:10 the reader is warned to "Enter into the rock, and hide in the dust, from the terror of the LORD, and from the glory of his majesty." Jensen points out that "the primary source of the terror" is in fact "the glory of his majesty" itself.[34] One is reminded of Rudolf Otto's famous thesis about the origin of religious awe in "daemonic dread." Otto claimed that the first stirrings of mature religious awe were presaged in "the feeling of 'something uncanny', 'eerie', or 'weird'."[35] Although he believed this level of religious apprehension was crude and rightly superseded by higher forms, he maintained that

> Even when the worship of 'daemons' has long since reached the higher level of worship of 'gods', these gods still retain as *numina* something of the 'ghost' in the impress they make on the feelings of the worshipper, viz. the peculiar quality of the 'uncanny' and 'aweful', which survives with the quality of exaltedness and sublimity or is symbolized by means of it. And this element, softened though it is, does not disappear even on the highest level of all, where the worship of God is at its purest.(36)

In light of these thoughts, it is hardly inconsequential that Otto, in talking of the biblical God specifically, wrote,

> Specially noticeable is the *'ēmāh* of Yahweh ('fear of God'), which Yahweh can pour forth, dispatching almost like a daemon, and which seizes upon a man with paralyzing effect. . . . Here we have a terror fraught with an inward shuddering such as not even the most menacing and overpowering created thing can instill. It has something spectral about it.(37)

This persistence of the original element of creeping dread in the more exalted forms of religious awe—including the theology of ancient Israel—leaves us in a position where we have only a short imaginative leap to make from the theologically orthodox position, which maintains that Yahweh appears as a horror only because his absolute holiness reveals the nature of a sinful world to itself, to the burgeoning suspicion that Yahweh, in his very nature, may be horrific, may in fact be a monster.

This leads us to the final issue to be considered in this regard, an issue that Schlobin hits upon when he claims that in horror stories, the monsters' "natures are incomprehensible to the epistemologies of their victims." Isaiah chapter 40—the first chapter of Second Isaiah, the beginning of what *The NIV Study Bible* designates (with unintentional irony, in my view) "The Book of Comfort"—speaks famously of Yahweh's absolute transcendence and incomprehensibility. In words that echo Yahweh's divine self-concealment at the end of Job[38], verses 12-14 ask rhetorically,

> Who has measured the waters in the hollow of his hand, and marked off the heavens with a span, enclosed the dust of the earth in a measure, and weighted the mountains in scales and the hills in a balance? Who has directed the spirit of the LORD, or as his counselor has instructed him? Whom did he consult in his enlightenment, and who taught him the path of justice?

The answer, of course, is *nobody*. Nobody helped Yahweh create the universe. Nobody can know as much of creation's mysteries as he does. Yahweh transcends everything we puny mortals can possibly understand or accomplish. He alone is supreme in power and knowledge

Verses 15-24 present a creedal statement that emphasizes Yahweh's supreme superiority and authority over all the earth's rulers and inhabitants: the nations are nothing before him (vv. 15-17); nothing is comparable to him (18-20); he "sits above the circle of the earth, and its inhabitants are like grasshoppers," and he can do whatever he wants with earthly rulers (21-24). He is absolute, unapproachable, unknowable, unsearchable, supreme.

This leads inevitably to a rather cold conclusion about his character as portrayed in Isaiah. The book focuses intensely upon the issue of Yahweh's *holiness*. "Yahweh's holiness," writes Jensen, "is the quality that comes most to the fore in Isaiah's teaching."[39] John N. Oswalt concurs when he points out that "Isaiah's favorite appellation for God is 'the Holy One of Israel.'"[40] But as Jensen notes, "God's holiness . . . implies power even more than it implies moral goodness."[41]

Herbert elaborates: "The word 'holy' is primarily not an ethical term, but one indicating the otherness, the incalculable power, of God, his inaccessibility. He is 'the great stranger in the human world'. . . . *Holy* expressed the mysterious, incalculable, unapproachable quality of the divine in contrast to the human."[42]

Oswalt points out that this aspect of Yahweh's nature is the one most emphasized in Isaiah's famous call narrative: "Above everything else the realization which struck the prophet in his call experience (ch. 6) was the realization of the terrifying 'otherness' of god. He was not merely superhuman, as were the pagan gods, nor was he a great 'grandfather in the sky.' He was of a completely different order from his creatures."(43) This again calls to mind the words of Otto, who described the holy or numinous in terms of its awe-fullness, its overpoweringness, and of the sense one derives from it of being "a creature, submerged and overwhelmed by its own nothingness in contrast to that which is supreme above all creatures."(44)

If the above descriptions correctly express the way Yahweh is portrayed in Isaiah, and if Otto's words are an accurate description of the way humans are meant to feel and react toward Yahweh—and a rereading of chapter 40 indicates to me that the answer is affirmative on both counts—then the book most certainly meets Schlobin's requirement that the monsters in horror stories must be incomprehensible to their victims.(45)

The issue of incomprehensibility also factors into the final criterion of Schlobin's scheme that I will apply to Isaiah. Schlobin said that in the world of horror, signs, symbols, processes, and expectations will be inverted. Because of this, the victims will not be able to understand the meaning of what has happened to them. This describes all too well the state of those people whom Yahweh chooses to destroy in the book of Isaiah.

III. Cosmic Inversion and Closure in Corpses

Horror, says Schlobin, "generally . . . substitute[s] new meanings for signs. Rather than stripping significance from signs, horror fills them with inverted and deadly meanings, repugnant to the victims and attractive to the monsters (or to those who relish horror's punishment of its victims)."(46) In the book of Job, this can be seen in the inefficacy of Job's righteousness in protecting him from divine punishment.(47) "The most obvious" inversion, Schlobin says, "is the inversion of Job's relationship with Yahweh, which changes from covenant to betrayal." Job's very righteousness, and also the presence and words of his well-intentioned friends, then go from being sources of meaning and comfort to reminders of the horrific distortion that has been revealed to him at the heart of things.[(48)]

In Isaiah, this horrific inversion of signs can be clearly seen, first, in the way the cosmic destruction of chapters 24 and 34 is framed in positive terms. The reader will surely be aware, as mentioned several paragraphs ago, that in the overall scheme of the text, these catastrophes are meant to be seen in a positive light. As Hayes and Irvine noted, cosmic destruction in Isaiah is a "reversion to disorder and chaos *out of which new order can arise.*"[(49)] Yahweh undertakes these acts as part of his plan to sweep the evil out of the world and create a new world, "new heavens and a new earth," in which "the former things shall not be remembered or come to mind" (65:17). There will be no more suffering or weeping, everyone will live to a ripe old age (as in the pre-flood era), and there will be such a total absence of strife and contention that "The wolf and the lamb shall feed together, the lion shall eat straw like the ox" (65:25), an image recalling the conditions that existed in Eden. These are the intended theological complements of the scenes of bloody cosmic destruction that I have given such lengthy attention. There can be no doubt that in light of this glorious outcome, the reader is being encouraged to view the withering of the earth, "Terror, and the pit, and the snare" (24:17), stinking corpses and mountains stained with blood, wild animals and demons, and all the rest of the shocking and violent images of chapters 24 and 34, in an ultimately positive light. After all, these are the necessary precursors to the beautiful new creation! Such a reframing of what would intuitively seem to be horrific imagery into categories of desirability constitutes a radical inversion of the normal meanings attached to such signs, and thus shows that Isaiah, in this respect, meets Schlobin's criterion.

But I am getting ahead of myself. For of course the reader is meant to be *horrified* by chapters 24 and 34. He is meant to view these things as horrific examples of what will happen to him if he is not found righteous by the Holy One of Israel. It requires the recognition of yet another element of Isaiah's text for my interpretation to be justified, for thus far nothing I have pointed out has indicated that Isaiah *ought* to be read in a horrific light. I have merely managed to prove that it *can* be read this way.

This final element is found in the final verse of the book, chapter 66, verse 24, which rounds the book off on a note of horror that resounds all the way back to the first chapter. The final verse comes at the tail end of a long description of those new heavens and new earth, and of the requirements of worship in the new order of things. Of these requirements, the final one is this: "And they shall go out and look at the dead bodies of the people who have rebelled against me [Yahweh]; for their worm shall not die, their fire shall not be quenched, and they shall be an abhorrence to all flesh" (66:24). In other words, the ultimate act of worship in the new creation will be to gaze upon the corpses of Yahweh's slain enemies (who, according to verse 16, will be numerous). "Concluding the magisterial Book of Isaiah," writes P. D. Hanson, "with its celebration of the Holy God whose infinite love reaches out for lost mortals is a verse that holds up as an eternal memorial the worm-invested, smoldering bodies of those who have rebelled against their creator."[50]

The interpretive problems posed by such a concluding verse are obvious. Miscall points out that "most commentators are troubled by the harshness of the judgments expressed in vv. 15-17 and 24 and by the sharp contrast with the positive tones of the other verses."[51] Conrad describes the verse as "jolting." "As a contemporary reader," he writes, "I do not know what to do with this verse. I want to delete it as well as others of its kind."[52]

This reaction is not confined to contemporary readers alone. "Modern readers are not the first to flinch at the sight," says Hanson. In fact, ancient readers even tried to get around the problem by disobeying the text as it came to them: "According to the Masoretic notation," Hanson says, "verse 24 is to be repeated by the repetition of verse 23 in the synagogue."[53] Childs says critical scholars "are virtually unanimous that v. 24 is a later and unfortunate addition, which is then described as an apocalyptic portrayal of Gehenna," and says the ancient injunction to repeat verse 23 was motivated by the desire "to end the book on a note of promise."[54] But as Miscall points out, the problem may not be so easily solved, and in fact might be compounded by this proposed solution, since "Repeating v. 23 . . . can have the effect of emphasizing v. 24 by framing it in a chiastic structure."[55]

What all this discomfort amounts to is the recognition that we *want* Isaiah to end on that note of promise. Given the exalted message the book as a unified entity tries to put forth, we want it to end with more of those comforting words about the joy and happiness and utter absence of suffering in the new creation. We do not want to be reminded of Yahweh's wrath, which seems—let us admit it—disturbingly capricious. The picture of those eternally abused corpses in 66:24 bears much of the flavor of what Otto referred to when he said Yahweh's wrath often seems to have

> no concern whatever with moral qualities. There is something very baffling in the way in which is 'is kindled' and manifested. It is, as has been well said, 'like a hidden force of nature', like stored-up electricity, discharging itself upon anyone who comes too near. It is 'incalculable' and 'arbitrary'.[56]

Perhaps not tangentially, we might note that if by chance the reader is wondering at this point in my argument what has become of the theology of the covenant—the theology which holds that Yahweh pours out his wrath not arbitrarily, but in response to human evils, and in accord with principles that he has laid down clearly in advance—it merely takes a slight shift in perspective to recognize that the covenant itself is arbitrary. Yahweh is under no obligation to conform to human standards of morality and justice, and as we saw in the preceding section, we may not be able to look to his self-nature as a guarantor of his justice and lovingkindness. Indeed, the famous imagery of the potter and the clay, in which Yahweh is compared to a potter who can do whatever he wants with his "clay" (i.e. humans)—not excluding turning them against himself through no fault of their own, and thus making them subject to his punishment—while it may be best known to many Christian readers from its presentation in Paul's letter to the Romans (cf. Romans 9:14-21), actually has its origin in Isaiah, where it appears not once but twice.[57] Paul's commentary on the matter, wherein he attempts to mount a smooth dismissal of the subject, is most instructive, and reminds us yet again of Job, and of Schlobin's contention that Job suffers under the nightmarish torments of a monstrous God: "You will say to me then, 'Why then does he still find fault? For who can resist his will?" But who indeed are you, a human being, to argue with God?" (Romans 9:19-20a)

To return to our main subject: Schlobin said tales of horror strip from signs their accustomed meanings and substitute new and "deadly" meanings that are repugnant to the victims but attractive to the monsters. In the final verse of Isaiah, we see this principle at work in the form of human corpses being gnawed by worms and scorched by flames, and being presented to the viewers, and to the reader, as things attractive and desirable. It is a holy duty to watch these corpses being desecrated, no matter how repugnant the thought may be, let alone the sight.

We should note that the idea of exposing enemy corpses hardly begins with Isaiah 66:24. The practice was well-established in the ancient world, where remaining unburied after death "was the worst that could befall someone. . . . Exposing the corpse represented a final humiliation and a desecration, for most ancient peoples believed that proper, timely burial affected the quality of the afterlife."(58) The final verse of Isaiah thus employs a known motif in its depiction of the fate of Yahweh's enemies. But the motif may have been especially detestable to the Israelites, who took the necessity and propriety of corpse burial so seriously that their "law required even the body of an impaled criminal to be removed and buried at sunset rather than left to be devoured by birds and other animals."(59)

Furthermore—and here we hit upon the heart of the horror contained in Isaiah's final verse—the depiction of the peculiar state of the desecrated corpses in the new creation makes for a particularly potent inversion of signs, for one can see within the nature of the corpses' punishment a previously unsuspected aspect of Yahweh's hidden nature. The two punishments specific to the corpses in 66:24 are worms and fire. The worms we may take as a standard symbol of putrefaction, and also, perhaps as an invocation of the "wormlike" connotations of the ancient chaos serpents; Yahweh has given the corpses over to a figurative eternal assault by the likes of Leviathan, etc.

But what of the fire? What is its function? Where does it come from? Why does it continue to scorch eternally? The Hebrew word for "fire" in this verse is *'esh*. While the same word is used to refer simply to normal, physical fire, it is also used throughout the Old Testament to refer to the supernatural fire accompanying a theophany, and also, figuratively, to God's anger.(60) The fire that burns the corpses of Yahweh's slain enemies in the final verse of Isaiah is the same fire that is explicitly identified with him in Deuteronomy 4:24, which says, "For the LORD your God is a devouring fire." It is what the Israelites saw when Moses spent forty days and nights with Yahweh on Mount Sinai, and "the appearance of the LORD was like a devouring fire on the top of the mountain" (Exodus 24:17). It is the fire Yahweh rained down on Sodom and Gomorrah (Genesis 19:24). It is the fire the Israelites associated with Yahweh after they received the Ten Commandments and said, "For this great fire will consume us; if we hear the voice of the LORD our God any longer, we shall die. For who is there of all flesh that has heard the voice of the living God speaking out of fire, as we have, and has remained alive?" (Deuteronomy 5:25-26)

It is also the fire that appears in one of the most famous theophanies in the Bible: "Then the angel of the LORD appeared to [Moses] in a flame of fire out of a bush; he looked, and the bush was blazing, yet it was not consumed" (Exodus 3:2). When we consider this in light of the other instances of *'esh* mentioned above, and when we consider also the parallel between the bush that burns but is not consumed, and the corpses in the new creation whose "fire shall not be quenched," the answer to the riddle of the fire starts to become clear. The corpses in Isaiah 66:24 have become theophanies on the order of the burning bush in Exodus. Like the bush, they burn without being consumed, and the fire, *'esh*, that burns them, is the essence or manifestation of Yahweh himself. If we may be permitted to take a final leap of the imagination, the entire book of Isaiah has been a "setup" that Yahweh has employed to get us to the point where we can see him exercising his true purpose: He has redeemed a select group of people from out of the mass of doomed humanity, for the ultimate purpose of forcing them to witness his awful flaming essence eternally scorching and corrupting the corpses of those who opposed him. His motives, as we have seen, are inscrutable, and his power is inescapable. Thus, the best indication we have of his true nature and intentions comes from what we see him actually do. And what we see is appalling at every level. "Isaiah's whole vision," writes Miscall, "ends with a scene of perdition: undying worms, perpetual fire and finally 'a horror for all flesh'."[61]

The conclusion is clear. There is no escape. Yahweh is a chaos monster, a demon from beyond space, and the Book of Isaiah is the story of his breaking into the ordered world of life and light for the purpose of staging a show full of suffering and sickening violence, all for his own unfathomable reasons.

SOME CONCLUDING THOUGHTS ON CLOSURE, ANTICLOSURE, AND COGNITIVE DISSONANCE

I said above that the note of horror at the end of Isaiah "resounds all the way back to the first chapter." This is so not only because of the intensity of the verse's imagery and message. Nor is it only because of the fact that several elements found in chapter 66, including the fire in the final verse, are also found in chapter 1 [62], which has long been recognized as a kind of "table of contents" that must have been added in one of the final redactions of the book. A large measure of 66:24's power arises from the simple fact that it comes at the end. We have already seen that readers both ancient and modern have struggled with this ostensibly odd placement of such a difficult verse. Now the time has come to consider this more closely.

What galls all of us who try to find a way to assimilate 66:24 into our interpretive grids is the inescapable working of the literary element known as *closure*. Closure, according to Holman and Harmon's *A Handbook to Literature*, is "The principle that structured things do not just stop, they come to an end with a sense of conclusion, completeness, wholeness, integrity, finality, and termination."[63] David Heller, a literary theorist and student of the horror genre, says closure is "One of the features of a literary work that makes it seem whole. . . . At some point at or shortly after the end of the text, we expect to see all the prominent features of the work forming a harmony that can recede in memory as we turn to other objects in the world." In essence, Heller says the achievement of closure gives a literary work a sense of being "rounded off," of having reached a conclusion that emerges organically from what has led up to it.[(64)]

The question before us is, does the final verse of Isaiah achieve closure? Does it sum up everything that has come before it and provide us with a stopping point that seems organically related to what led up to it? Although, as noted, the verse refers to an image that first appears at the end of the first chapter, its obvious shock value and the trouble it has caused readers down through the centuries would seem to indicate that it does not, in fact, achieve closure in the traditional sense. It is too radically removed from the tenor of some of the other things—the more comforting and uplifting things—that appear in the book, for it to achieve closure as Heller has described it. Ronald E. Clements has even written an entire article, titled "Isaiah: A Book without an Ending?" based upon this very recognition. "When we read [66:24]," he writes, "we are not at all surprised that neither ancient readers nor modern scholars have been happy to regard this brief verse as the appropriate closure to the book. It is not at all typical of its overall message."[(65)] Closure, he says, is a "significant feature of a narrative ending. . . . Certainly it is this that we should look for in a collection of prophecies in which a 'final' prophecy, even if it does not actually occur at the end of a book, indicates a sense of fulfillment and completion."[(66)] He identifies the true—by which he means the thematically appropriate—close of the book as coming at the end of chapter 60, or possibly 61 or 62.[(67)]

So, the Isaian text in its received form definitely does not achieve closure in the traditional narrative or literary sense. But according to Holman and Harmon and Clements, it *should* achieve some sort of closure, since it is definitely a structured work and thus calls for "a sense of fulfillment and completion." Clements uses this as an excuse to find closure elsewhere, and to characterize the text in its received form as literarily defective. In contrast to this, I want to dwell upon the text as it stands, and to ask a new, slightly modified question: What exactly is the lasting, lingering effect of the close of the book as it has come down to us? With 66:24 screaming at us to be understood in some fashion, what is the subjective impact or meaning—or as Darr would call it, the "synchronic impact"—of closing upon such a note of horror?

Again, Heller—drawing heavily on the seminal work of philosopher Tzvetan Todorov in *The Fantastic: A Structural Approach to Literary Genre*—comes to our aid by offering the following thoughts on *anti*closure, which he sees as characterizing a particular type of terror tale, the *terror fantasy*:

> Like all literary texts, a terror fantasy invites the reader to use the signals of the text to construct an implied reader and to establish thereby an aesthetic relation to the text. Unlike most literary works, a terror fantasy offers at least two simultaneously valid but opposed readings, each of which illuminates the strengths of the other and betrays its own weaknesses. This splitting of the role of implied reader precludes the ending of that role. As a result, the terror fantasy produces anticlosure; it pointedly refuses to end.
>
> Anticlosure is not merely a failure to resolve thematic complications, nor is it a thematic assertion of the openness of reality. It is not at all like the story with its last page removed nor the "slice of life" in which it is presumed that life goes on after the arbitrary ending of the history. Anticlosure results from a tale's turning back on itself to form a closed loop. It is not the text that fails to end, but the reading, the activity of concretizing the work. This activity cannot stop because each of its possible resting places is disturbed by the presence of another.
>
> In these tales, then, the role of implied reader becomes a snare. And the trap by itself produces anxiety.[(68)]

I have quoted Heller at such length regarding anticlosure because his words are so pertinent to my own personal situation as a reader of Isaiah, and of many other biblical texts. Heller says anticlosure occurs when a text holds out two equally valid but opposed readings that mutually illuminate each other. The reader finds himself torn between these readings, unable to settle on either one, and ultimately this unresolved tension keeps him in a state of permanent terror and prevents him from ever reaching a satisfactory state of mind regarding the work. I have experienced this repeatedly over time with virtually every biblical text I have read. Isaiah is only one of the most pointed, owing to its overt intimations of horror.

Perhaps it is highly inappropriate to end an academic exploration like this one on a pointedly personal note, but since everything I have said in this paper stems from my personal motivations in tackling such a subject, I will go ahead and take the risk. I have been torn between reading biblical texts in a conventionally pious way and an imaginatively horrific way for many years now.[(69)] The intimations of a darker interpretation lurking beneath the more common one(s) have come to me almost involuntarily as I have studied the Bible in increasing depth over time and seen the various ways in which darkness might enter in through the cracks, as it were, and pervade everything with an underlying mood of shadow. The reading of Isaiah I have been pursuing here is only one example of this type of thinking—and, I fear, not an entirely successful one. I have had to focus at length upon isolated sections of the text and ignore others altogether in order to prove my point. I have indeed demonstrated that Isaiah meets Schlobin's three requirements for a horror story, but had I chosen other passages, I would have found my horrific interpretation challenged at many steps.

But then again, and hopefully not in marked conflict with my self-avowed reader-oriented approach, I do believe many of the elements of horror that I have noted in Isaiah are there for the reading, and are not merely the result of willful eisegesis. The fact that readers have struggled for centuries to figure out how to handle 66:24 is sufficient evidence to assure me that I am not alone on an island of imaginative thinking.

This dithering back and forth is, I believe, evidence that Isaiah indeed presents us with an instance of anticlosure as described by Heller. The questions posed by my horrific reading and the recognition of its largely arbitrary nature are insoluble. Should Yahweh be viewed as a majestic, holy, compassionate God or as a secret trickster, a chaos monster in disguise, who engineers everything in order to arrive at a point where he can enjoy the horrified gaze of his chosen ones as they watch him commit an eternal, meaningless act of vindictiveness? Should the cosmic destructions of chapters 24 and 34 be viewed as the just rewards of a world that has rejected the transcendent source of goodness and light, or should they be viewed as assaults by a monstrous alien force that in its very nature rightly induces horror more than love and reverence? The more I consider these issues, the more I find I am unable to decide which is the more purely imaginative—which is to say, *fictional*—interpretation, and thus I find I am stuck in a state of anticlosure that will not let me rest. Appropriately enough, this effect of my reading harks back to my explicitly subjective methodological approach to Isaiah, since, as Edgar V. McKnight has pointed out, "Reader-oriented theories not only emphasize the reader's role in the process of achieving meaning but also see the result of reading in terms of an effect upon the reader."(70)

It is perhaps tangential but not totally insignificant that Lovecraft, whose quotation from *Supernatural Horror in Literature* helped to define the specific type of horror we were seeking in Isaiah, harbored a similar disparity in his own temperament. We have already seen that he deemed the breaking or suspension of natural laws the "most terrible conception of the human brain." Yet in another context, when discussing his motivations and methods as an author of horror fiction, he wrote,

> I choose weird stories because they suit my inclination best—one of my strongest and most persistent wishes being to achieve, momentarily, the illusion of some strange suspension or violation of the galling limitations of time, space, and natural law which forever imprison us and frustrate our curiosity about the infinite cosmic spaces beyond the radius of our sight and analysis."(71)

Here and elsewhere, Lovecraft was a bundle of contradictions, and we may view it as appropriate that the man whose words about those "daemons from unplumbed space" have guided us on a large part of our journey through Isaiah could not even agree with himself, as we cannot agree with ourselves, on the question of whether the assaults of those extracosmic demons on the brittle shell of the created universe—assaults which are as existentially real as anything we encounter in empirical reality—should be received joyously, as opportunities for ultimate liberation, or with abject horror, as confirmations of our most awful metaphysical and ontological fears.

NOTES

1. Kenneth Barker, general editor, *The NIV Study Bible* (Grand Rapids: Zondervan, 1985), 290.
2. Edgar W. Conrad, *Reading Isaiah*, Overtures in Biblical Theology (Minneapolis: Fortress Press, 1991), 29, author's emphases.
3. Ibid.
4. Katheryn Pfisterer Darr, *Isaiah's Vision and the Family of God*, Literary Currents in Biblical Interpretation (Louisville, KY: Westminster John Knox Press, 1994), 20.
5. Darr, 22.
6. Roger C. Schlobin, "Protoypic Horror: The Genre of the Book of Job," *Semeia* 60 (1992): 24.
7. Ibid.
8. Brevard S. Childs, *Isaiah* (Louisville: Westminster John Knox Press, 2001), 171.
9. Ibid., 174.
10. Joseph Jensen, O.S.B., *Isaiah 1-39*, Old Testament Message, no. 8 (Wilmington, DE: Michael Glazier, 1984), 192.
11. Childs., 200, 253.
12. Peter D. Miscall, *Isaiah 34-35: A Nightmare/A Dream*, JSOT Supplement Series, no. 281 (Sheffield, England: Sheffield Academic Press, 1999), 18.
13. John H. Hayes and Stuart A. Irvine, *Isaiah, the Eighth-century Prophet: His Times and Preaching* (Nashville: Abingdon, 1987), 300.
14. Ibid., 301.
15. Ibid., 304.
16. Jensen, 196.
17. John B. Geyer, "Desolation and Cosmos," *Vetus Testamentum* 49:1 (1999): 49.
18. Harry Bultema, *Commentary on Isaiah* (Grand Rapids: Kregel Publications, 1981), 236.
19. A.S. Herbert, *Isaiah 1-39*, The Cambridge Bible Commentary series (Cambridge: Cambridge University Press, 1973), 193.
20. Philip D. Stern, "Isaiah 34, Chaos, and the Ban," in *Ki Baruch Hu: Ancient*

Near Eastern, Biblical, and Judaic Studies in Honor of Baruch A. Levine, ed. Robert Chazan, William W. Hallo, and Lawrence H. Schiffman (Winona Lake, Indiana: Eisenbrauns, 1999): 389.

21. Ibid., 387.
22. Ibid., 399. The same, or a similar, motif appears in the Song of the Vineyard in chapter 5, verses 5-6, where the prophet speaks of punishing the unruly vineyard by "remov[ing] its hedge, and it shall be devoured; I will break down its wall, and it shall be trampled down. I will make it a waste; it shall not be pruned or hoed, and it shall be overgrown with briers and thorns; I will also command the clouds that they rain no rain upon it." Commenting on this passage, Victor Matthews writes that the "only solution" to the problem of the wicked vine that produces the wrong sort of grapes "is the complete destruction of the vine and a return to the 'chaos' that existed prior to the establishment of the vineyard (compare the flood epic of Genesis 6-9)." In an observation that recalls the overrunning of the land by wild animals mentioned in chapter 34, Matthews says of the vineyard, "With the terraces destroyed, the soil will erode away and what remains will only nurture thorns and weeds. Wild animals will prowl through this once civilized place and the withholding of the rains is the final insult that can be applied to an unclean place. It spells disaster for all." See Matthews, "Treading the Winepress: Actual and Metaphorical Viticulture in the Ancient Near East," *Semeia* 86 (1999): 28.
23. Stern, 388.
24. H. P. Lovecraft, *Supernatural Horror in Literature*, in *Dagon and Other Macabre Tales*, ed. August Derleth and S.T. Joshi (Sauk City, WI: Arkham House Publishers, 1987), 368.
25. Noel Carroll, *The Philosophy of Horror* (New York and London: Routledge, 1990), 165.
26. See, for example, Job's lament in Job 21, where he expresses extreme horror at the inverted morality he sees at work in the world: "When I think of it I am dismayed, and shuddering seizes my flesh. Why do the wicked live on, reach old age, and grow mighty in power? Their children are established in their presence, and their offspring before their eyes. Their houses are safe from fear, and no rod of God is upon them" (vv. 6-9).
27. Schlobin., 24, 30.
28. Ibid., 31.
29. Mircea Eliade, *The Sacred and the Profane: The Nature of Religion*, trans. Willard R. Trask (San Diego: Harcourt, 1987), 47-48.
30. David Penchansky, "God the Monster: Fantasy in the Garden of Eden," in *The Monstrous and the Unspeakable: The Bible as Fantastic Literature*, ed. George Aichele & Tina Pippin, Playing with Texts, no. 1 (Sheffield, England: Sheffield Academic Press, 1997), 43.
31. Timothy Beal, *Religion and Its Monsters* (New York: Routledge, 2002), 32.
32. Douglas A. Knight, "Cosmogony and Order in the Hebrew Tradition," in *Cosmogony and Ethical Order: New Studies in Comparative Ethics*, ed. Robin

W. Lovin and Frank E. Reynolds (Chicago: University of Chicago Press, 1985), 142.

33. Ibid, 146.
34. Jensen, 62.
35. Rudolf Otto, *The Idea of the Holy,* trans. John W. Harvey (New York: Oxford University Press, 1958), 14.
36. Ibid., 17.
37. Ibid., 13-14.
38. See, for example, Job 38:4-7: "Where were you when I laid the foundation of the earth? Tell me, if you have understanding. Who determined its measurements—surely you know! Or who stretched the line upon it? On what were its bases sunk, or who laid its cornerstone when the morning stars sang together and all the heavenly beings shouted for joy?"
39. Jensen, 33.
40. John N. Oswalt, *The Book of Isaiah: Chapters 1-39,* The New International Commentary on the Old Testament (Grand Rapids, MI: William B. Eerdmans Publishing Company, 1986), 33.
41. Jensen., 21.
42. Herbert, 15, 59.
43. Oswalt, 33. I should point out that Oswalt, who is a conservative, evangelical scholar, disagrees with the point I am making here about Yahweh's holiness in Isaiah meaning primarily ontological separation and power. "It was not merely God's ontological otherness which captured Isaiah's thinking," Oswalt writes. "In fact, the primary characteristic that set this God apart from humanity, made him holy, was his moral and ethical perfection."
44. Otto, 10.
45. For intertextual support for the idea of Yahweh's incomprehensibility, we might look to the opening chapters of Ezekiel, which constitute the prophet's call narrative, and which famously describe a theophanic vision of Yahweh and his attendants that inspires equal measures of stunned awe and giddy terror. See, e.g., the four-faced, four-winged creatures described in Ezekiel 1:5-14, and the four wheels within wheels, rimmed with eyes, in vv. 15-21, and then in vv. 26-28, the awesome vision of "the likeness of the glory of the LORD": "There was something like a throne, in appearance like sapphire; and seated above the likeness of a throne was something that seemed like a human form. Upward from what appeared like the loins I saw something like gleaming amber, something that looked like fire enclosed all around; and downward from what looked like the loins I saw something that looked like fire, and there was a splendor all around. Like the bow in a cloud on a rainy day, such was the appearance of the splendor all around. This was the appearance of the likeness of the glory of the LORD."
46. Schlobin, 27.
47. See, for example, Job 16:16-17: "My face is red with weeping, and deep darkness is on my eyelids, though there is no violence in my hands, and my

prayer is pure." To the possible observation/criticism that Job is technically not a victim of divine punishment, but simply of Yahweh's permissiveness in allowing Satan to attack Job, I would point out that Satan was merely fulfilling the task Yahweh had ordained for him, which was to test the mettle of creation, and that this makes Yahweh all the more monstrous in the story. For a detailed investigation of Yahweh's status as a monster in the Book of Job, I refer the reader, of course, to Schlobin's article.

48. Schlobin, 28-29.
49. Hayes and Irvine, 301, my emphasis.
50. Quoted in Miscall, 126, note 11.
51. Ibid, 126.
52. Conrad, 162.
53. Miscall, 126, note 11.
54. Childs, 542.
55. Miscall, 126, note 11.
56. Otto, 18.
57. See Isaiah 29:16 and 45:9.
58. John H. Walton, Victor H. Matthews, and Mark W. Chavalas, *The IVP Bible Background Commentary: Old Testament* (Downers Grove, IL: InterVarsity Press, 2000), 373.
59. Ibid., 373. For instances of this motif being used in the Hebrew scriptures other than Isaiah, see, for example, 1 Samuel 31:8-13, in which the Philistines behead Saul's corpse and hang it on a wall, only to have it stolen by the inhabitants of Jabesh-gilead, who burn it and bury the bones. See also 2 Samuel 21:4-14, in which David halts a three-year famine by handing over seven of Saul's descendants to the Gibeonites, whom Saul had nearly wiped out. The Gibeonites impale these seven men "before the Lord" and leave their bodies exposed. Rizpah, the mother of two of them, protects the bodies from being defiled by birds and wild animals "until rain [falls] on them from the heavens" (i.e. until the drought, the cause of the famine, breaks). David hears of it and brings Saul and Jonathan's bones back from the people of Jabeth-gilead to be properly buried in the rightful tomb. He also gathers up the remains of the seven who had been impaled. "After that, God heeded the supplications for the land" (v. 14).
60. See the Hebrew linguistic resources available at http://www.blueletterbible.org.
61. Miscall, 136.
62. Cf. chapter 1, verse 31: "The strong shall become like tinder, and their work like a spark; they and their work shall burn together, with no one to quench them."
63. C. Hugh Holman and William Harmon, *A Handbook to Literature*, Sixth Edition (New York: Macmillan, 1992), 91.
64. David Heller, *The Delights of Terror: An Aesthetics of the Tale of Terror* (Urbana and Chicago: University of Illinois Press, 1987), chapter one. Internet edition published 2002. <http://www.public.coe.edu/~theller/

essays/delights/dt1.html>. Site accessed February 25, 2003.

65. Ronald E. Clements, "Isaiah: A Book without an Ending?" *Journal for the Study of the Old Testament* 97 (2002), 109.
66. Ibid., 114-115.
67. Ibid., 109.
68. Heller., chapter ten.
69. Another obvious possibility—the noncommittal scholarly approach, based simply on secular interest—is not an option for me, since I am not able (or willing) to pay attention to a text at all unless it engages my emotions, interests, and energies on a deeply personal level.
70. Edgar V. McKnight, "Reader-Response Criticism," *To Each Its Own Meaning: An Introduction to Biblical Criticisms and Their Application*, eds. Steven L. McKenzie and Stephen R. Haynes (Louisville, KY: Westminster/John Knox Press, 1993), 203.
71. H. P. Lovecraft, "Notes on the Writing of Weird Fiction," in *Miscellaneous Writings*, ed. S.T. Joshi (Sauk City, WI: Arkham House Publishers, 1995), 113.

BIBLIOGRAPHY

Barker, Kenneth, general ed. *The NIV Study Bible*. Grand Rapids: Zondervan, 1985.

Beal, Timothy. *Religion and Its Monsters*. New York: Routledge, 2002.

Bultema, Harry. *Commentary on Isaiah*. Grand Rapids: Kregel Publications, 1981.

Carroll, Noel. *The Philosophy of Horror*. New York and London: Routledge, 1990.

Childs, Brevard S. *Isaiah*. Louisville: Westminster John Knox Press, 2001.

Clements, Ronald E. "Isaiah: A Book without an Ending?" *JSOT* 97 (2002): 109-126.

Conrad, Edgar W. *Reading Isaiah*. Overtures in Biblical Theology. Minneapolis: Fortress Press, 1991.

Darr, Katheryn Pfisterer. *Isaiah's Vision and the Family of God.* Literary Currents in Biblical Interpretation. Louisville, KY: Westminster John Knox Press, 1994.

Eliade, Mircea. *The Sacred and the Profane: The Nature of Religion.* Trans. Willard R. Trask. San Diego: Harcourt, 1987 (1957).

Geyer, John B. "Desolation and Cosmos." *Vetus Testamentum* 49:1 (1999): 49-64.

Hayes, John H. and Stuart A. Irvine. *Isaiah, the Eighth-century Prophet: His Times and Preaching.* Nashville: Abingdon, 1987.

Heller, David. *The Delights of Terror: An Aesthetics of the Tale of Terror.* Urbana and Chicago: University of Illinois Press, 1987. Internet edition published 2002. <http://www.public.coe.edu/~theller/essays/delights/dt1.html>. Site accessed February 25, 2003

Herbert, A. S. *Isaiah 1-39.* The Cambridge Bible Commentary Series. Cambridge: Cambridge University Press, 1973.

Holman, C. Hugh and William Harmon. *A Handbook to Literature.* 6th ed. New York: Macmillan, 1992.

Jensen, Joseph, O. S. B. *Isaiah 1-39.* Old Testament Message, no. 8. Wilmington, DE: Michael Glazier, 1984.

Knight, Douglas A. "Cosmogony and Order in the Hebrew Tradition." In *Cosmogony and Ethical Order: New Studies in Comparative Ethics,* ed. Robin W. Lovin and Frank E. Reynolds, 133-157. Chicago: University of Chicago Press, 1985.

Lovecraft, H. P. "Notes on the Writing of Weird Fiction." In *Miscellaneous Writings,* ed. S. T. Joshi, 113-116. Sauk City, WI: Arkham House Publishers, 1995.

———. *Supernatural Horror in Literature*. In *Dagon and Other Macabre Tales*, ed. August Derleth and S. T. Joshi, 365-436. Sauk City, WI: Arkham House Publishers, 1987 (1965).

Matthews, Victor. "Treading the Winepress: Actual and Metaphorical Viticulture in the Ancient Near East." *Semeia* 86 (1999): 19-32.

McKnight, Edgar V. "Reader-Response Criticism." In *To Each Its Own Meaning: An Introduction to Biblical Criticisms and Their Application*, ed. Steven L. McKenzie and Stephen R. Haynes, 197-219. Louisville, KY: Westminster/John Knox Press, 1993

Miscall, Peter D. *Isaiah 34-35: A Nightmare/A Dream*. JSOT Supplement Series, no. 281. Sheffield, England: Sheffield Academic Press, 1999.

Oswalt, John N. *The Book of Isaiah: Chapters 1-39*. The New International Commentary on the Old Testament. Grand Rapids, MI: William B. Eerdmans Publishing Company, 1986.

Otto, Rudolf. *The Idea of the Holy*. Trans. John W. Harvey. New York: Oxford University Press, 1958.

Penchansky, David. "God the Monster: Fantasy in the Garden of Eden." In *The Monstrous and the Unspeakable: The Bible as Fantastic Literature*, ed. George Aichele & Tina Pippin, 40-58. Playing with Texts, no. 1. Sheffield, England: Sheffield Academic Press, 1997.

Schlobin, Roger C. "Protoypic Horror: The Genre of the Book of Job." *Semeia* 60 (1992): 23-38.

Stern, Philip D. "Isaiah 34, Chaos, and the Ban." In *Ki Baruch Hu: Ancient Near Eastern, Biblical, and Judaic Studies in Honor of Baruch A. Levine*, ed. Robert Chazan, William W. Hallo, and Lawrence H. Schiffman, 387-400. Winona Lake, Indiana:

Eisenbrauns, 1999.

Walton, John H., Victor H. Matthews, and Mark W. Chavalas. *The IVP Bible Background Commentary: Old Testament.* Downers Grove, IL: InterVarsity Press, 2000.

Also by Mythos Books LLC

www.ingramcontent.com/pod-product-compliance
Lightning Source LLC
Chambersburg PA
CBHW030808310726
48980CB00006B/420/J

* 9 7 8 0 9 7 2 8 5 4 5 6 6 *